They were the remnant of a Fleet, against a widespread power which had inexhaustible lives, and supply, and worlds, and they did not.

After so long a struggle . . . the last of the Fleet, the last of Company power. She had watched it go; had fought to hold the two together, Earth and Union, humanity's past—and future. It was supreme irony that Union had become the pro-space side of this war and the founding Company fought against; irony that they who most believed in the Beyond ended up fighting against what it was becoming, to die for a Company which had stopped caring.

There had been a time when the dream of the old exploration ships had drawn her into this, a dream long revised to the realities the Company captain's emblem had come to mean. Long ago she had realized there was no winning.

*The Fleet went it alone, without merchanter or stationer support, as they had gone it alone for years before this.*

DAW TITLES BY C.J. CHERRYH

THE ALLIANCE-UNION UNIVERSE

*The Company Wars*
DOWNBELOW STATION

*The Era of Rapprochement*
SERPENT'S REACH
FORTY THOUSAND IN GEHENNA
MERCHANTER'S LUCK

*The Chanur Novels*
THE PRIDE OF CHANUR
CHANUR'S VENTURE
THE KIF STRIKE BACK
CHANUR'S HOMECOMING
CHANUR'S LEGACY

*The Mri Wars*
THE FADED SUN: KESRITH
THE FADED SUN: SHON'JIR
THE FADED SUN: KUTATH

*Merovingen Nights (Mri Wars period)*
ANGEL WITH THE SWORD

*The Age of Exploration*
CUCKOO'S EGG
VOYAGER IN NIGHT
PORT ETERNITY

*The Hanan Rebellion*
BROTHERS OF EARTH
HUNTER OF WORLDS

THE MORGAINE CYCLE
GATE OF IVREL
WELL OF SHIUAN
FIRES OF AZEROTH
EXILE'S GATE

THE EALDWOOD FANTASY NOVELS
THE DREAMSTONE
THE TREE OF SWORDS AND JEWELS

OTHER CHERRYH NOVELS
PORT ETERNITY
HESTIA
WAVE WITHOUT A SHORE

THE FOREIGNER UNIVERSE
FOREIGNER
INVADER
INHERITOR

# DOWNBELOW STATION

C.J. CHERRYH

DAW BOOKS, INC.
DONALD A. WOLLHEIM, FOUNDER
375 Hudson Street, New York, NY 10014
ELIZABETH R. WOLLHEIM
SHEILA E. GILBERT
PUBLISHERS

Cover art by David B. Mattingly.
Cross sections by C. J. Cherryh.
DAW Book Collectors No. 420.



First Printing, February 1981

11 12 13 14

DAW TRADEMARK REGISTERED
U.S. PAT. OFF. AND FOREIGN COUNTRIES
—MARCA REGISTRADA
HECHO EN U.S.A.

PRINTED IN THE U.S.A.

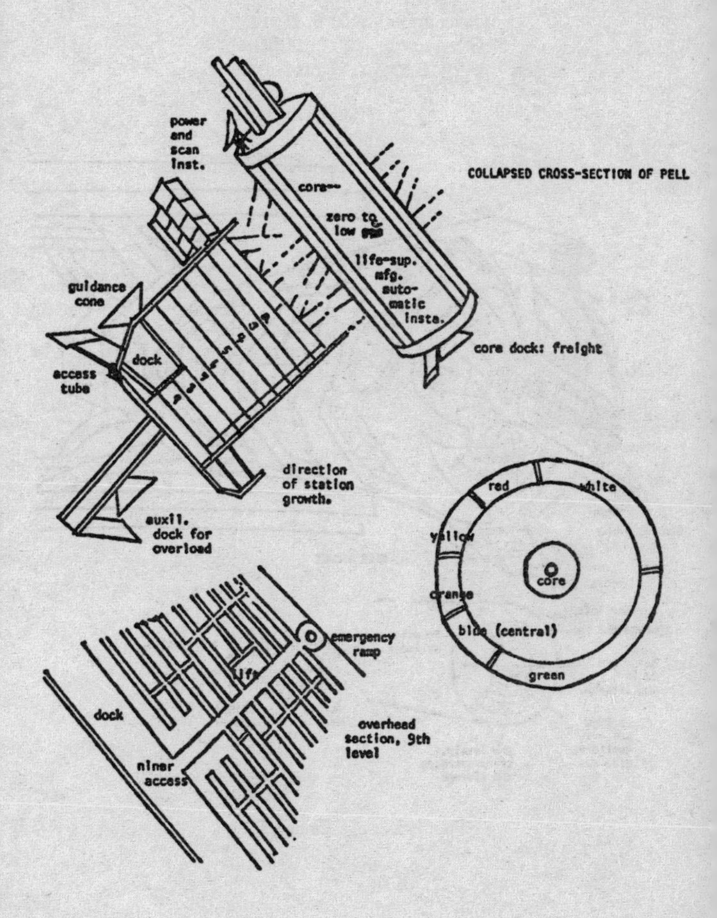
COLLAPSED CROSS-SECTION OF PELL
power and scan inst.
core
zero to low g
life-sup. mfg. automatic insta.
guidance cone
dock
access tube
core dock: freight
direction of station growth.
auxil. dock for overload
red
white
yellow
core
orange
blue (central)
green
emergency ramp
lift
dock
overhead section, 9th level
miner access

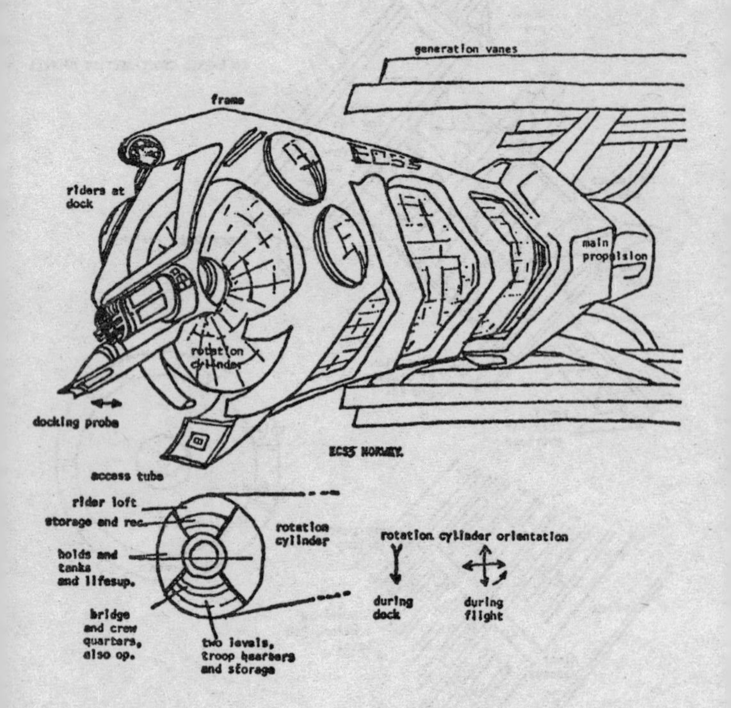
generation vanes
frame
riders at dock
main propulsion
rotation cylinder
docking probe
ECSS NORWAY
access tube
rider loft
storage and rec.
rotation cylinder
holds and tanks and lifesup.
bridge and crew quarters, also op.
two levels, troop quarters and storage
rotation cylinder orientation
during dock
during flight

# BOOK ONE

# 1

## Earth and Outward: 2005–2352

The stars, like all man's other ventures, were an obvious impracticality, as rash and improbable an ambition as the first venture of man onto Earth's own great oceans, or into the air, or into space. Sol Station had existed profitably for some years; there were the beginnings of mines, the manufacturies, the power installations in space which were beginning to pay. Earth took them for granted as quickly as it did all its other comforts. Missions from the station explored the system, a program far from public understanding, but it met no strong opposition, since it did not disturb the comfort of Earth.

So quietly, very matter of factly, that first probe went out to the two nearest stars, unmanned, to gather data and return, a task in itself of considerable complexity. The launch from station drew some public interest, but years was a long time to wait for a result, and it passed out of media interest as quickly as it did out of the solar system. It drew a great deal more attention on its return, nostalgia on the part of those who recalled its launch more than a decade before, curiosity on the part of the young who had known little of its beginning and wondered what it was all about. It was a scientific success, bringing back data enough to keep the analysts busy for years . . . but there was no glib, slick way to explain the full meaning of its observations in layman's terms. In public relations the mission was a failure; the public, seeking to understand on their own terms, looked for material benefit, treasure, riches, dramatic findings.

What the probe had found was a star with reasonable possibilities for encouraging life; a belt of debris, including particles, planetoids, irregular chunks somewhat under planet size with interesting implications for systemic formation, and a planetary companion with its own system of debris and moons . . . a planet desolate, baked, forbidding. It was no Eden, no second Earth, no better than what existed in the sun's own system, and it was a far journey to have gone to find that out. The press grappled with questions it could not easily grasp itself, sought after something to give the viewers, lost interest quickly. If anything, there were questions raised about cost, vague and desperate comparisons offered to Columbus, and the press hared off quickly onto a political crisis in the Mediterranean, much more comprehensible and far bloodier.

The scientific establishment on Sol Station breathed a sigh of relief and with equal quiet caution invested a portion of its budget in a modest manned expedition, to voyage in what amounted to a traveling miniature of Sol Station itself, and to stay a time making observations in orbit about that world.

And very quietly, to further imitate Sol Station, to test manufacturing techniques which had built Earth's great second satellite . . . in stranger conditions. Sol Corporation supplied a generous grant, having a certain curiosity, a certain understanding of stations and what profits could be looked for from their development.

That was the beginning.

The same principles which had made Sol Station practical made the first star-station viable. It needed a bare minimum of supply in biostuffs from Earth . . . mostly luxuries to make life more pleasant for the increasing number of techs and scientists and families stationed there. It mined; and as its own needs diminished, would send back the surplus of its ores . . . so the first link in the chain was made. No need, no need at all, that first colony had proven, that a star have a world friendly to humans, no need even for a moderate sun-type star . . . just the solar wind and the usual accompanying debris of metals and rock and ice. One station built, a station module could be hauled to the next star, whatever it was. Scientific bases, manufacture: bases from which the next hopeful star could be reached; and the next and the next and the next. Earth's outward exploration developed in one narrow vector, one little fan which grew at its broader end.

Sol Corporation, swollen beyond its original purpose

and holding more stations than Sol itself, became what the star-stationers called it: the Earth Company. It wielded power . . . certainly over the stations which it directed long-distance, years removed in space; and power on Earth too, where its increasing supply of ores, medical items, and its possession of several patents were enormously profitable. Slow as the system was in starting, the steady arrival of goods and new ideas, however long ago launched, was profit for the Company and consequent power on Earth. The Company sent merchant carriers in greater and greater numbers: that was all it needed to do now. The crews which manned those ships on the long flights grew into an inward-turned and unique way of life, demanding nothing but improvement of equipment which they had come to think of as their own; station in turn supported station, each shifting Earth's goods a step further on to its nearest neighbor, and the whole circular exchange ending up back on Sol Station where the bulk of it was drained off in high rates charged for biostuffs and such goods as only Earth produced.

Those were the great good days for those who sold this wealth: fortunes rose and fell; governments did; corporations took on more and more power, and the Earth Company in its many guises reaped immense profits and moved the affairs of nations. It was an age of restlessness. Newly industrialized populations and the discontents of every nation set out on that long, long track in search of jobs, wealth, private dreams of freedom, the old lure of the New World, human patterns recapitulated across a new and wider ocean, to stranger lands.

Sol Station became a stepping-off place, no longer exotic, but safe and known. The Earth Company flourished, drinking in the wealth of the star-stations, another comfort which those who received it began to take for granted.

And the star-stations clung to the memory of that lively, diverse world which had sent them, Mother Earth in a new and emotion-fraught connotation, she who sent out precious stuffs to comfort them; comforts which in a desert universe reminded them there was at least one living mote. The Earth Company ships were the lifeline . . . and the Earth Company probes were the romance of their existence, the light, swift exploration ships which let them grow more selective about next steps. It was the age of the Great Circle, no circle at all, but the course which the Earth Company freighters ran in constant travel, the beginning and end of which was Mother Earth.

Star after star after star . . . nine of them—until Pell, which proved to have a livable world, and life.

That was the thing which cancelled all bets, upset the balance, forever.

Pell's Star, and Pell's World, named for a probe captain who had located it—finding not alone a world, but indigenes, natives.

It took a long time for word to travel the Great Circle back to Earth; less for word of the find to get to the nearer star-stations . . . and more than scientists came flocking to Pell's World. Local station companies who knew the economics of the matter came rushing to the star, not to be left behind; population came, and two of the stations orbiting less interesting stars nearby were dangerously depleted, ultimately to collapse altogether. In the burst of growth and the upheaval of building a station at Pell, ambitious people were already casting eyes toward two farther stars, beyond Pell calculating with cold foresight, for Pell was itself a source of Earthlike goods, luxuries—a potential disturbance in the directions of trade and supply.

For Earth, as word rode in with arriving freighters . . . a frantic haste to ignore Pell. Alien life. It sent shock waves through the Company, touched off moral debates and policy debates in spite of the fact that the news was almost two decades old—as if they could set hand now to whatever decisions were being made out there in the Beyond. It was all out of control. Other life. It disrupted man's dearly held ideas of cosmic reality. It raised philosophical and religious questions, presented realities some committed suicide rather than face. Cults sprang up. But, other arriving ships reported, the aliens of Pell's World were not outstandingly intelligent, nor violent, built nothing, and looked more like lower primates than not, brown-furred and naked and with large, bewildered eyes.

Ah, earthbound man sighed. The human-centered, Earth-centered universe in which Earth had always believed had been shaken, but quickly righted itself. The isolationists who opposed the Company gathered influence and numbers in reaction to the scare—and to a sudden and marked drop in trade.

The Company was in chaos. It took *long* to send instructions, and Pell grew, out of the Company's control. New stations unauthorized by the Earth Company sprang into existence at farther stars, stations called Mariner and Viking; and they spawned Russell's and Esperance. By the time Company instructions arrived down the line, bidding now-stripped nearer stations take this and that action to stabilize trade, the orders were patent nonsense.

In fact, a new pattern of trade had already developed. Pell had the necessary biostuffs. It was closer to most of the star-stations; and star-station companies which had once seen Earth as beloved Mother now saw new opportunities, and seized them. Still other stations formed. The Great Circle was broken. Some Earth Company ships kited off to trade with the New Beyond, and there was no way to stop them. Trade continued, never what it had been. The value of Earth's goods fell, and consequently it cost Earth more and more to obtain the one-time bounty of the colonies.

A second shock struck. Another world lay Beyond, discovered by an enterprising merchanter . . . Cyteen. Further stations developed—Fargone and Paradise and Wyatt's, and the Great Circle stretched farther still.

The Earth Company took a new decision: a payback program, a tax of goods, which would make up recent losses. They argued to the stations of the Community of Man, the Moral Debt, and the burden of gratitude.

Some stations and merchanters paid the tax. Some refused it, particularly those stations beyond Pell, and Cyteen. The Company, they maintained, had had no part in their development and had no claim on them. There was a system of papers and visas instituted, and inspections called for, bitterly resented by the merchants, who viewed their ships as their own.

More, the probes were pulled back, tacit statement that the Company was putting an official damper on further growth of the Beyond. They were *armed,* the swift exploration ships, as they had always been, venturing as they did into the unknown; but now they were used in a new way, to visit stations and pull them into line. That was bitterest of all, that the crews of the probe ships, who had been the heroes of the Beyond, became the Company enforcers.

Merchanters armed in retaliation, freighters never built for combat, incapable of tight turns. But there were skirmishes between the converted probe ships and rebel merchanters, although most merchanters declared their reluctant consent to the tax. The rebels retreated to the outermost colonies, least convenient for enforcement.

It became war without anyone calling it war . . . armed Company probes against the rebel merchanters, who served the farther stars, a circumstance possible because there was Cyteen, and even Pell was not indispensable.

So the line was drawn. The Great Circle resumed, exclusive of the stars beyond Fargone, but never so profitable as it had been. Trade continued across the line after strange fashion, for tax-paying merchanters could go where they would, and rebel merchanters could not, but stamps could be faked, and were. The war was leisurely, a matter of shots fired when a rebel was clearly available as a target. The Company ships could not resurrect the stations immediately Earthward of Pell; they were no longer viable. The populations drifted to Pell and Russell's and Mariner and Viking, and to Fargone and farther still.

Ships were built, as stations had been, in the Beyond. The technology was there, and merchanters proliferated. Then *jump* arrived—a theory originated in the New Beyond, at Cyteen, quickly seized upon by shipbuilders at Mariner on the Company side of the line.

And that was the third great blow to Earth. The old lightbound way of figuring was obsolete. Jump freighters skipped along in short transits into the between; but the time it took from star to star went from years to periods of months and days. Technology improved. Trade became a new kind of game and strategy in the long war changed . . . stations knit closer together.

Suddenly, out of this, there was an organization among the rebels farthest Beyond. It started as a coalition of Fargone and its mines; it swept to Cyteen, gathered to itself Paradise and Wyatt's, and reached for other stars and the merchanters who served them. There were rumors . . . of vast population increases going on for years unreported, technology once suggested on the Company side of the line, when the need was for men, for human lives to fill up the vast dark nothingness, to work and to build. Cyteen had been doing it. This organization, this *Union,* as it called itself, bred and multiplied geometrically, using installations already in operation, birth-labs. Union *grew.* It had, in the course of two decades, increased enormously in territory and in population density, it offered a single, unswerving ideology of growth and colonization, a focused direction to what had been a disorganized rebellion. It silenced dissent, mobilized, organized, pushed hard at the Company.

And in final, outraged public demand for results in the deteriorating situation, the Earth Company back on Sol Station gave up the tax, diverted that fund to the building of a great Fleet, all jumpships, engines of destruction, *Europe* and *America* and all their deadly kindred.

So was Union building, developing specialized warships, changing style as it changed technology. Rebel captains who had fought long years for their own reasons were charged with softness at the first excuse; ships were put into the hands of commanders with the right ideology, with more ruthlessness.

Company successes grew harder. The great Fleet, outnumbered and with an immense territory to cover, did not bring an end to the war in a year or in five years. And Earth grew vexed with what had become an inglorious, exasperating conflict. *Cut all the starships,* the cry was now in the financing corporations. *Pull back our ships and let the bastards starve.*

It was of course the Company Fleet which starved; Union did not, but Earth seemed incapable of understanding that, that it was no longer a question of fragile colonies in rebellion but of a forming power, well-fed, well-armed. The same myopic policies, the same tug-of-war between isolationists and Company which had alienated the colonies in the first place drew harder and harder lines as trade diminished; they lost the war not in the Beyond, but in the senate chambers and the boardrooms on Earth and Sol Station, going for mining within Earth's own system, which was profitable, and devil take the exploratory missions in any direction at all, which were not.

No matter that they had jump now and that the stars were near. Their minds were geared to the old problems and to their own problems and their own politics. Earth banned further emigration, seeing the flight of its best minds. It weltered in economic chaos, and the drain of Earth's natural resources by the stations was an easy focus of discontent. *No more war,* they said; peace suddenly became good politics. The Company Fleet, deprived of funds in a war in which it was engaged on a wide front, obtained supplies where and as it could.

At the end, they were patchwork, fifteen carriers out of the once proud fifty, cobbled together at the stations still open to them. Mazian's Fleet, they called it, in the tradition of the Beyond, where ships were so few at first that enemies knew each other by name and reputation . . . a recognition less common now, but some names were known. Conrad Mazian of *Europe* was a name Union knew to its regret; and Tom Edger of *Australia* was another; and Mika Kreshov of *Atlantic,* and Signy Mallory of *Norway;* and all the rest of the Company captains, down to those of the rider-ships. They still served Earth and the Company, with less and less love of either. None of this generation was Earthborn; they received few replacements, none from Earth, none from the stations in their territory either, for the stations feared obsessively for their neutrality in the war. Merchanters were their source of skilled crew and of troops, most of them unwilling.

The Beyond had once begun with the stars nearest Earth; and now it started with Pell, for the oldest stations were all shut down as Earthward trade phased out and the pre-jump style of trade passed forever. The Hinder Stars were all but forgotten, unvisited.

There were worlds beyond Pell, beyond Cyteen, and Union had them all now, real worlds, of the far-between stars which jump could reach; where Union used the birth labs still to expand populations, giving them workers and soldiers. Union wanted all the Beyond, to direct what would be the course of the future of man. Union had the Beyond, all but the thin arc of stations which Mazian's Fleet still thanklessly held for Earth and the Company, because they had once been set to do that, because they saw nothing they could do but that. At their backs was only Pell . . . and the mothballed stations of the Hinder Stars. Remoter still, isolate . . . sat Earth, locked in its inner contemplations and its complex, fragmented politics.

No trade of substance came out of Sol now, or to it. In the insanity which was the War, free merchanters plied Unionside and Company Stars alike, crossed the battle lines at will, although Union discouraged that traffic by subtle harassments, seeking to cut Company supply.

Union expanded and the Company Fleet just held on, worldless but for Pell which fed them, and Earth which ignored them. On Unionside, stations were no longer built on the old scale. They were mere depots for worlds now, and probes sought still further stars. They were generations which had never seen Earth . . . humans to whom *Europe* and *Atlantic* were creatures of metal and terror, generations whose way of life was stars, infinities, unlimited growth, and time which looked to forever. Earth did not understand them.

But neither did the stations which remained with the Company or the free merchanters who carried on that strange crosslines trade.

# 2

## i
## In Approach to Pell: 5/2/52

The convoy winked in, the carrier *Norway* first, and then the ten freighters—more, as *Norway* loosed her four riders and the protective formation spread itself wide in its approach to Pell's Star.

Here was refuge, one secure place the war had never yet reached, but it was the lapping of the tide. The worlds of the far Beyond were winning, and certainties were changing, on both sides of the line.

On the bridge of the *ECS 5,* the jump-carrier *Norway,* there was rapid activity, the four auxiliary command boards monitoring the riders, the long aisle of com operations and that of scan and that of their own command. *Norway* was in constant com link with the ten freighters, and the reports passed back and forth on those channels were terse, ships' operations only. *Norway* was too busy for human disasters.

No ambushes. The station at Pell's World received signal and gave reluctant welcome. Relief whispered from post to post of the carrier, private, not carried on intership com. Signy Mallory, *Norway*'s captain, relaxed muscles she had not known were tense and ordered armscomp downgraded to standby.

She held command over this flock, third captain in seniority of the fifteen of Mazian's Fleet. She was forty-nine. The Beyonder Rebellion was far older than that; and she had been freighter pilot, rider captain, the whole gamut, all in the Earth Company's service. Her face was still young. Her hair was silver gray. The rejuv treatments which caused the gray kept the rest of her at somewhere near biological thirty-six; and considering what she shepherded in and what it portended, she felt aged beyond the forty-nine.

She leaned back in her cushion which looked over the upcurving, narrow aisles of the bridge, punched in on her arm console to check operations, stared out over the active stations and the screens which showed what vid picked up and what scan had. Safe. She lived by never quite believing such estimations.

And by adapting. They all did, all of them who fought this war. *Norway* was like her crew, varied salvage: of *Brazil* and *Italia* and *Wasp* and jinxed *Miriam B,* parts of her dating all the way back to the days of the freighter war. They took what they could, gave up as little as possible . . . as from the refugee ships she guided, under her protection. There had been in decades before, a time of chivalry in the war, of quixotic gestures, of enemy rescuing enemy and parting under truce. They were human and the Deep was wide, and they all had known it. No more. From among these civilians, neutrals, she had extracted the useful ones for herself, a handful who might adapt. There would be protests at Pell. It would do them no good. No protests would, on this or other matters. The war had taken another turn, and they were out of painless choices.

They moved slowly, at the crawl which was the best the freighters could manage in realspace, distance *Norway* or the riders, unemcumbered, could cross pushing light.

They had come in dangerously close to the mass of Pell's Star, out of plane with the system, risking jump accident and collisions. It was the only way these freighters could make haste . . . and lives rode on making time.

"Receiving approach instructions from Pell," com told her.

"Graff," she said to her lieutenant, "take her in." And punching in another channel: "Di, put all troops on standby, full arms and gear." She switched back to com: "Advise Pell it had better evacuate a section and seal it. Tell the convoy if anyone breaks formation during approach we'll blow them. Make them believe it."

"Got it," com senior said; and in due time: "Stationmaster's on in person."

The stationmaster protested. She had expected so.

"You do it," she told him—Angelo Konstantin, of *the* Konstantins of Pell. "You clear that section or we do. You start now, strip out everything of value or hazard, down to the walls; and you put those doors on lock and weld the access panels shut. You don't know what we're bringing you. And if you delay us, I may have a shipload dead: *Hansford*'s life support is going. You do it, Mr. Konstantin, or I send the troops in. And you don't do it right, Mr. Konstantin, and you have refugees scattered like vermin all over your station, with no ID's and ugly-desperate. Forgive my bluntness. I have people dying in their own filth. We number seven thousand frightened civs on these ships, what left Mariner and Russell's Star. They're out of choices and out of time. You're not going to tell me no, sir."

There was a pause, distance, and more than enough delay for distance. "We've sounded the evacuation for sections of yellow and orange dock, Captain Mallory. Medical services will be available, all that we can spare. Emergency crews are moving. We copy regarding sealing of the affected areas. Security plans will be set in motion at once. We hope that your concern is as great for our citizens. This station will not permit the military to interfere in our internal-security operations or to jeopardize our neutrality, but assistance under our command will be appreciated. Over."

Signy relaxed slowly, wiped sweat from her face, drew an easier breath. "Assistance will be given, sir. Estimated docking . . . four hours, if I delay this convoy all I can. I can give you that much time to get ready. Has news about

Mariner gotten to you yet? It was blown, sir, sabotage. Over."

"We copy four hours. We appreciate the measures you urge us to take and we are taking them in earnest. We are distressed to hear about the Mariner disaster. Request detailed briefing. Further advise you we have a Company team here at the moment. It's highly distressed at these proceedings."

She breathed an obscenity into the com.

". . . and they're demanding to have all of you turned down for some other station. My staff is attempting to explain to them the condition of the ships and the hazard to life aboard them, but they're putting pressure on us. They consider Pell's neutrality threatened. Kindly appreciate that in your approach and bear in mind that the Company agents have requested contact with you in person. Over."

She repeated the obscenity, expelled a breath. The Fleet avoided such meetings when possible, rare as they were in the last decade. "Tell them I'll be busy. Keep them off the docks and out of our area. Do they need pictures of starving colonists to take back with them? Bad press, Mr. Konstantin. Keep them out of our way. Over."

"They're armed with government papers. Security Council. *That* kind of Company team. They have rank to use and they're demanding transport deeper Beyond. Over."

She chose a second obscenity and swallowed it. "Thank you, Mr. Konstantin. I'll capsule you my recommendations on procedures with the refugees; they've been worked out in detail. You can, of course, ignore them, but I'd advise against it. We can't even guarantee you that what we're disembarking on Pell isn't armed. We can't get among them to find out. Armed troops can't get in there, you understand? That's what we're giving you. I'd advise you keep the Company boys out of our docking area entirely before we have hostages to deal with. Copy? End transmission."

"We copy. Thank you, captain. End transmission."

She slumped in place, glared at the screens and shot an order to com to capsule the instructions to station command.

Company men. And refugees from lost stations. Information kept coming steadily from stricken *Hansford,* with a calm on the part of its crew she admired. Strictly procedures. They were dying over there. Crew was sealed into command and armed, refusing to abandon ship, refusing to let a rider take *Hansford* in tow. It was their ship. They stayed by it and did what they could for those aboard, by remote. They had no thanks from the passengers, who were tearing the ship apart—or had been doing so, until the air fouled and the systems began to break down.

Four hours.

## ii

*Norway.* Russell's had met disaster, and Mariner. Rumor ran through the station corridors, aboil with the confusion and anger of residents and companies that had been turned out with all their property. Volunteers and native workers aided in the evacuation; dock crews used the loading machinery to move personal belongings out of the area selected for quarantine, tagging items and trying not to confuse them or allow pilferage. Com echoed with announcements.

"Residents of yellow one through one nineteen are asked to send a representative to the emergency housing desk. There is a lost child at the aid station, May Terner. Will a relative please come at once to the aid station? . . . Latest estimates from station central indicate housing available in guest residency, one thousand units. All nonresidents are being removed in favor of permanent station residents, priority to be determined by lottery. Apartments available by condensation of occupied units: ninety-two. Compartments available for emergency conversion to residential space, two thousand, including public meeting areas and some mainday/alterday rotation of occupancy. The station council urges any person with personal arrangements possible through lodging with relatives or friends to secure same and to key this information to comp at the earliest possible; housing on private initiative will be compensated to the home resident at a rate equivalent to per capita expense for other housing. We are five hundred units deficient and this will require barracks-style housing for on-station residency, or transfer on a temporary basis for Downbelow residency, unless this deficiency can be made up by volunteering of housing or willingness of individuals to share assigned living space. Plans are to be considered immediately for residential use of section blue, which should free five hundred units within the next one hundred eighty days . . .

Thank you . . . Will a security team please report to eight yellow? . . ."

It was a nightmare. Damon Konstantin stared at the flow of printout and intermittently paced the matted floors of dock command blue sector, above the area of the docks where techs tried to cope with the logistics of evacuation. Two hours left. He could see from the series of windows the chaos all along the docks where personal belongings had been piled under police guard. Everyone and every installation in yellow and orange sectors' ninth through fifth levels had been displaced: dockside shops, homes, four thousand people crowded elsewhere. The influx spilled past blue, around the rim to green and white, the big main-residence sectors. Crowds milled about, bewildered and distraught. They understood the need: they moved—everyone on station was subject to such transfers of residence, for repairs, for reorganizations . . . but never on this kind of notice and never on this scale, and never without knowing where they were to be assigned. Plans were cancelled, four thousand lives upset. Merchanters of the two score freighters which happened to be in dock had been rudely ousted from sleepover accommodations and security did not want them on the docks or near the ships. His wife, Elene, was down there in a knot of them, a slim figure in pale green. Liaison with the merchanters . . . that was Elene's job, and he was at her office fretting about it. He nervously watched the manner of the merchanters, which was angry, and meditated sending station police down there for Elene's protection; but Elene seemed to be matching them shout for shout, all lost in the soundproofing and the general buzz of voices and machine noise which faintly penetrated the elevated command post. Suddenly there were shrugs, and hands offered all round, as if there had been no quarrel at all. Some matter was either settled or postponed, and Elene walked away and the merchanters strode off through the dispossessed crowds, though with shakes of their heads and no happiness evident. Elene had disappeared beneath the slanted windows . . . to the lift, to come up here, Damon hoped. Off in green section his own office was dealing with an angry-resident protest; and there was the Company delegation fretting in station central making demands of its own on his father.

"Will a medical team please report to section eight

yellow?" com asked silkily. Someone was in trouble, off in the evacuated sections.

The lift doors opened into the command center. Elene joined him, her face still flushed from argument.

"Central's gone stark mad," she said. "The merchanters were moved out of hospice and told they had to lodge on their ships; and now they've got station police between them and their ships. They're wanting to cast off from station. They don't want their ships mobbed in some sudden evacuation. Read it that they'd just as soon be out of Pell's vicinity entirely at the moment. Mallory's been known to recruit merchanters at gunpoint."

"What did you tell them?"

"To stand fast and figure there are going to be some contracts handed out for supplies to take care of this influx; but they won't go to any ship that bolts the dock, or that tangles with our police. And that has the lid on them, at least for a while."

Elene was afraid. It was clear behind the brittle, busy calm. They were all afraid. He slipped his arm about her; hers fitted his waist and she leaned there, saying nothing. Merchanter, Elene Quen, off the freighter *Estelle,* which had gone its way to Russell's, and to Mariner. She had missed that run for him, to consider tying herself to a station for good, for his sake; and now she ended up trying to reason with angry crews who were probably right and sensible in her eyes, with the military in their laps. He viewed matters in a cold, quiet panic, stationer's fashion. Things which went wrong onstation went wrong sitting still, by quadrants and by sections, and there was a certain fatalism bred of it: if one was in a safe zone, one stayed there; if one had a job which could help, one did it; and if it was one's own area in trouble, one still sat fixed—it was the only heroism possible. A station could not shoot, could not run, could only suffer damage and repair it if there was time. Merchanters had other philosophies and different reflexes in time of trouble.

"It's all right," he said, tightening his arm briefly. He felt her answering pressure. "It's not coming here. They're just putting civilians far behind the lines. They'll stay here till the crisis is over and then go back. If not, we've had big influxes before, when they shut down the last of the

Hinder Stars. We added sections. We'll do it again. We just get larger."

Elene said nothing. There were dire rumors drifting through com and down the corridors regarding the extent of the disaster at Mariner, and *Estelle* was not one of the incoming freighters. They knew that now for certain. She had hoped, when they had gotten the first news of the arrival; and feared, because there was damage reported on those ships out there, moving at freighters' slow pace, jammed with passengers they were never designed to handle, in the series of small jumps a freighter's limited range made necessary. It added up to days and days in real-space as far as they had come in, and living hell on those vessels. There was some rumor they had not had sufficient drugs to get them through jump, that some had made it without. He tried to imagine it—reckoned Elene's worry. *Estelle*'s absence from that convoy was good news and bad. Likely she had shied off her declared course, catching wind of trouble, and gone elsewhere in a hurry . . . still cause for anxiety, with the war heating up out on the edge. A station . . . gone, blown. Russell's, evacuating personnel. The safe edge was suddenly much too close, much too fast.

"It's likely," he said, wishing that he could save the news for another day, but she had to know, "that we'll be moved to blue, into maybe cramped quarters. The clean-clearance personnel are the ones that can be transferred to that section. We'll have to be among the ones to go."

She shrugged. "That's all right. It's arranged?"

"It will be."

A second time she shrugged; they lost their home and she shrugged, staring at the windows onto the docks below, and the crowds, and the merchanter ships.

"It's not coming here," he insisted, trying to believe it, for Pell was his home, in a way no merchanter was likely to understand. Konstantins had built this place, from the days of its beginning. "Whatever the Company losses—not Pell."

And a moment later, moved by conscience if not by courage: "I've got to get over there, onto the quarantine docks."

## iii

*Norway* eased in ahead of the others, with the hubbed, unsightly torus of Pell a gleaming sprawl in her vid screens. The riders were fanned out, fending off the freighters for the moment. The merchanter crews in command of those refugee ships wisely held the line, giving her no trouble. The pale crescent of Pell's World . . . Downbelow, in Pell's matter-of-fact nomenclature . . . hung beyond the station, swirled with storms. They matched up with Pell Station's signal, drawing even with the flashing lights on the area designated for their docking. The cone which would receive their nose probe glowed blue with the come-aheads. SECTION ORANGE, the distorted letters read on vid, beside a tangle of solar vanes and panels. Signy punched in scan, saw things where they ought to be on Pell's borrowed image. Constant chatter flowed from Pell central and the ship channels, keeping a dozen techs busy at com.

They entered final approach, lost gee gently as *Norway*'s rotating inner cylinder, slung gutwise in its frame, slowed and locked to docking position, all personnel decks on the station's up and down. They felt other stresses magnified for a time, a series of reorientations. The cone loomed, easy dock, and they met the grapple, a dragging confirmation of the last slam of gee—opened accesses for Pell's dock crews, stable now, and solidly part of Pell's rotation.

"I'm getting an all-quiet on dockside," Graff said. "The stationmaster's police are all over the place."

"Message," com said. "Pell stationmaster to *Norway:* request military cooperation with desks set up to facilitate processing as per your instructions. All procedures are as you requested, with the stationmaster's compliments, captain."

"Reply: *Hansford* coming in immediately with crisis in lifesupport and possible riot conditions. Stay back of our lines. Endit.—Graff, take over operations. Di, get me those troops out on that dock doubletime."

She left matters there, rose and strode back through the narrow bowed aisles of the bridge to the small compartment which served her as office and oftentimes sleeping quarters. She opened the locker there and slipped on a jacket, slipped a pistol into her pocket. It was not a uniform. No one in the Fleet, perhaps, possessed a full-regulation uniform. Supply had been that bad, that long. Her captain's circle on her collar was her only distinction from a merchanter. The troops were no better uniformed, but armored: *that,* they kept in condition, at all costs. She hastened down via the lift into the lower corridor, proceeding amid the rush of troops Di Janz had ordered to the dock, combat-rigged, through the access tube and out into the chill wide spaces.

The whole dock was theirs, vast, upward-curving perspective, section arches curtained by ceiling as the station rim curve swept leftward toward gradual horizon; on the right a section seal was in use, stopping the eye there. The place was vacant of all but the dock crews and their gantries; and station security and the processing desks, and those were well back of *Norway*'s area. There were no native workers, not here, not in this situation. Debris lay scattered across the wide dock, papers, bits of clothing, evidencing a hasty withdrawal. The dockside shops and offices were empty; the niner corridor midway of the dock showed likewise vacant and littered. Di Janz's deep bellow echoed in the metal girders overhead as he ordered troops deployed about the area where *Hansford* was coming in.

Pell dockers moved up. Signy watched and gnawed her lip nervously, glanced aside as a civ came up to her, youngish, darkly aquiline, bearing a tablet and looking like business in his neat blue suit. The plug she had in one ear kept advising her of *Hansford*'s status, a constant clamor of bad news. "What are *you*?" she asked.

"Damon Konstantin, captain, from Legal Affairs."

She spared a second look. A Konstantin. He could be that. Angelo had had two boys before his wife's accident. "Legal Affairs," she said with distaste.

"I'm here if you need anything . . . or if they do. I've got a com link with central."

There was a crash. *Hansford* made a bad dock, grated down the guidance cone and shuddered into place.

"Get her hooked up and get out!" Di roared at the dock crews: no com for him.

Graff was ordering matters from *Norway*'s command. *Hansford*'s crew would stay sealed on their bridge, working debarcation by remote. "Tell them walk out," she heard relayed from Graff. "Any rush at troops will be met with fire."

The hookups were complete. The ramp went into place.

*"Move!"* Di bellowed. Dockers pelted behind the lines of troops; rifles were levelled. The hatch opened, a crash up the access tube.

A stench rolled out onto the chill of the dock. Inner hatches opened and a living wave surged out, trampling each other, falling. They screamed and shouted and rushed out like madmen, staggered as a burst of fire went over their heads.

"Hold it!" Di shouted. "Sit down where you are and put your hands on your heads."

Some were sitting down already, out of weakness; others sank down and complied. A few seemed too dazed to understand, but came no farther. The wave had stopped. At Signy's elbow Damon Konstantin breathed a curse and shook his head. No word of laws from him; sweat stood visibly on his skin. His station stared riot in the face . . . collapse of systems, *Hansford*'s death ten thousandfold. There were a hundred, maybe a hundred fifty living, crouched on the dock by the umbilical gantry. The ship's stench spread. A pump labored, flushing air through *Hansford*'s systems under pressure. There were a thousand on that ship.

"We're going to have to go in there," Signy muttered, sick at the prospect. Di was moving the others one at a time, passing them under guns into a curtained area where they were to be stripped, searched, scrubbed, passed on to the desks or to the medics. Baggage there was none, not with this group, nor papers worth anything.

"Need a security team suited up for a contamination area," she told young Konstantin. "And stretchers. Get us a disposal area prepared. We're going to vent the dead; it's all we can do. Have them ID'ed as best you can, fingerprints, photos, whatever. Every corpse passed out of here unidentified is future trouble for your security."

Konstantin looked ill. That was well enough. So did some of her troops. She tried to ignore her own stomach.

A few more survivors had made their way to the opening of the access, very weak, almost unable to get down the ramp. A handful, a scant handful.

*Lila* was coming in, her approach begun in her crew's panic, defying instructions and riders' threats. She heard Graff's voice reporting it, activated her own mike. "Stall them off. Clip a vane off them if you have to. We've got our hands full. Get me a suit out here."

They found seventy-eight more living, lying among the decomposing dead. The rest was cleanup, and no more threat. Signy passed decontamination, stripped off the suit, sat down on the bare dock and fought a heaving stomach. A civ aid worker chose a bad time to offer her a sandwich. She pushed it away, took the local herbal coffee and caught her breath in the last of the processing of *Hansford*'s living. The place stank now of antiseptic fogging.

A carpet of bodies in the corridors, blood, dead. *Hansford*'s emergency seals had gone into place during a fire. Some of the dead had been cut in two. Some of the living had broken bones from being trampled in the panic. Urine. Vomit. Blood. Decay. They had had closed systems, had not had to breathe it. The *Hansford* survivors had had nothing at the last but the emergency oxygen, and that had possibly been a cause of murder. Most of the living had been sealed into areas where the air had held out less fouled than the badly ventilated storage holds where most of the refugees had been crammed.

"Message from the stationmaster," com said into her ear, "requesting the captain's presence in station offices at the earliest."

"No," she sent back shortly. They were bringing *Hansford*'s dead out; there was some manner of religious service, assembly-line fashion, some amenity for the dead before venting them. Caught in Downbelow's gravity well, they would drift in that direction, eventually. She wondered vaguely whether bodies burned in falling: likely, she thought. She had not much to do with worlds. She was not sure whether anyone had ever cared to find out.

*Lila*'s folk were exiting in better order. They pushed and shoved at the first, but they stopped it when they saw the armed troops facing them. Konstantin intervened with useful service over the portable loudspeaker, talking to the terrified civs in stationers' terms and throwing stationers' logic in their faces, the threat of damage to fragile balances, the kind of drill and horror story they must have heard all their confined lives. Signy put herself on her feet again during the performance, still holding the coffee cup, watched with a calmer stomach as the procedures she had outlined began to function smoothly, those with papers to one area and those without to another, for photographing and ID by statement. The handsome lad from Legal Affairs proved to have other uses, a voice of ringing authority when it regarded disputed paper or confused station staff.

"*Griffin*'s moving up on docking," Graff's voice advised her. "Station advises us they're wanting back five hundred units of confiscated housing based on *Hansford*'s casualties."

"Negative," she said flatly. "My respects to station command, but out of the question. What's the status on *Griffin*?"

"Panicky. We've warned them."

"How many others are coming apart?"

"It's tense everywhere. Don't trust it. They could bolt, any one of them. *Maureen* was one dead, coronary, another ill. I'm routing her in next. Stationmaster asks whether you'll be available for conference in an hour. I pick up that the Company boys are making demands to get into this area."

"Keep stalling." She finished the coffee, walked along the lines in front of *Griffin*'s dock, the whole operation moving down a berth, for there was nothing left at *Hansford*'s berth worth guarding. There was quiet from the processed refugees. They had the matter of locating their lodgings to occupy them, and the station's secure environment to comfort them. A suited crew stood by to move *Hansford* out; they had only four berths at this dock. Signy measured with her eye the space the station had allotted them, five levels of two sections and the two docks. Crowded, but they would manage for a while. Barracks could solve some of it . . . temporarily. Things would get tighter. No luxuries, that was certain.

They were not the only refugees adrift; they were simply the first. And upon that knowledge she kept her mouth shut.

It was *Dinah* that broke the peace; a man caught with weapons in scan, a friend who turned ugly on his arrest: two dead, then, and sobbing, hysterical passengers afterward. Signy watched it, simply tired, shook her head and ordered the bodies vented with the rest, while Konstantin approached her with angry arguments. "Martial law," she said, ending all discussion and walk away.

*Sita, Pearl, Little Bear, Winifred.* They came in with agonizing slowness, unloaded refugees and property, and the processing inches its way along.

Signy left the dock then, went back aboard *Norway* and took a bath. She scrubbed three times all over before she began to feel that the smell and the sights had left her.

Station had entered alterday; complaints and demands had fallen silent at least for a few hours.

Or if there were any, *Norway*'s alterday command fended them off her.

There was comfort for the night, company of sorts, a leave-taking. He was another item of salvage from Russell's and Mariner . . . not for transport on the other ships. They would have torn him apart. He knew this, and appreciated matters. He had no taste for the crew either, and understood his situation.

"You're getting off here," she told him, staring at him, who lay beside her. The name did not matter. It confused itself in her memory with others, and sometimes she called him by the wrong one, late, when she was half asleep. He showed no emotion at that statement, only blinked, indication that he had absorbed the fact. The face intrigued her: innocence, perhaps. Contrasts intrigued her. Beauty did. "You're lucky," she said. He reacted to that the same way, as he reacted to most things. He simply stared, vacant and beautiful; they had played with his mind on Russell's. There was a sordidness in her sometimes, a need to deal wounds . . . limited murder, to blot out the greater ones. To deal little terrors, to forget the horror outside. She had sometime nights with Graff, with Di, with whoever took her fancy. She never showed this face to those she valued, to friends, to crew. Only sometimes there were voyages like this one, when her mood was black. It was a common disease, in the Fleet, in the sealed worlds of ships without discharge, among those in absolute power. "Do you care?" she asked; he did not, and that was, perhaps, his survival.

*Norway* remained, her troops visibly on duty on the dockside, the last ship berthed in quarantine. On the dock, the lights were still at bright noon, over lines which moved only slowly, under the presence of the guns.

# 3

## i
## Pell: 5/2a*/52

Too many sights, too much of such things. Damon Konstantin took a cup of coffee from one of the aid workers who passed the desk and leaned on his arm, stared out across the docks and tried to rub the ache from his eyes. The coffee tasted of disinfectant, as everything here smelled of it, as it was in their pores, their noses, everywhere. The troops stayed on guard, keeping this little area of the dock safe. Someone had been knifed in Barracks A. No one could explain the weapon. They thought that it had come from the kitchen of one of the abandoned restaurants on dockside, a piece of cutlery unthinkingly left behind, by someone who had never realized the situation. He found himself exhausted beyond sense. He had no answers; station police could not find the offender in the lines of refugees which still wended their way out there across the docks, inching along to housing desks.

A touch descended on his shoulder. He turned an aching neck, blinked up at his brother. Emilio settled in the vacant chair next to him, hand still on his shoulder. Elder brother. Emilio was in alterday central command. It *was* alterday now, Damon realized muzzily. The wake-sleep worlds in which they two seldom met on duty had gotten lapped in the confusion.

"Go home," Emilio said gently. "My turn, if one of us has to be here. I promised Elene I'd send you home. She sounded upset."

"All right," he agreed, but he failed to move, lacking the volition or the energy. Emilio's hand tightened, fell away.

*Alterday

"I saw the monitors," Emilio said. "I know what we've got here."

Damon tightened his lips against a sudden rush of nausea, staring straight before him, not at refugees, but at infinity, at the future, at the undoing of what had always been stable and certain. Pell. *Theirs,* his and Elene's, his and Emilio's. The Fleet took license on itself to do this to them and there was nothing they could do to stop it, because the refugees were poured in too suddenly, and they had no alternatives ready. "I've seen people shot down," he said. "I didn't do anything. I couldn't. Couldn't fight the military. Dissent . . . would have caused a riot. It would have taken all of us under. But they shot people for breaking a line."

"Damon, get out of here. It's my concern now. We'll work something out."

"We haven't any recourse. Only the Company agents; and we don't need them involved. Don't let them into this."

"We'll handle it," Emilio said. "There are limits; even the Fleet understands them. They can't jeopardize Pell and survive. Whatever else they do, they won't risk us."

"They have," Damon said, focused his eyes on the lines across the docks, turned a glance then on his brother, on a face the image of his own plus five years. "We've gotten something I'm not sure we can ever digest."

"So when they shut down the Hinder Stars. We managed."

"Two stations . . . six thousand people reach us out of what, fifty, sixty thousand?"

"In Union hands, I'd surmise," Emilio muttered. "Or dead with Mariner; no knowing what casualties there. Or maybe some got out in other freighters, went elsewhere." He leaned back in the chair, his face settled into morose lines. "Father's probably asleep. Mother too, I hope. I stopped by the apartment before I came. Father says it was crazy for you to come here; I said I was crazy too and I could probably clean up what you didn't get to. He didn't say anything. But he's worried—Get on back to Elene. She's been working the other side of this chaos, passing papers on the refugee merchanters. She's been asking questions of her own. Damon, I think you ought to get home.

*"Estelle."* Apprehension hit through to him. "She's hunting rumors."

"She went home. She was tired or upset; I don't know. She just said she wanted you to get home when you could."

"Something's come in." He pushed himself to his feet, gathered up his papers, realized what he was doing, pushed them at Emilio and left in haste, past the guard-point, into the chaos of the dock on the other side of the passage which divided man station from quarantine. Native labor scurried out of his way, furred, skulking forms more alien by reason of the breather-masks they wore outside their maintenance tunnels; they were moving equipage and cargo and belongings in frantic haste . . . shrieked and shouted among themselves in insane counterpoint to the commands of human overseers.

He took the lift over to green, walked the corridor into their own residence area, and even this was littered with displaced belongings in boxes, a security guard dozing at his post among them. They were all overshift, particularly security. Damon passed him, turned a face to a belated and embarrassed challenge, walked to the door of the apartment.

He keyed it open, saw with relief the lights on, heard the familiar rattle of plastic in the kitchen.

"Elaine?" He walked in. She was watching the oven, her back to him. She did not turn. He stopped, sensing disaster, another world amiss.

The timer went off. She removed the plate from the oven, set it on the counter, turned, managed composure to look at him. He waited, hurting for her, and after a moment came and took her in his arms. She gave a short sigh. "They're gone," she said. And a moment later another short gasp and a release. "Blown with Mariner. *Estelle*'s gone, with everyone aboard. No possible survivors. *Sita* saw her go; they couldn't get undocked . . . all those people trying to get aboard. Fire broke out. And that part of the station went, that's all. Exploded, blew the nose shell off."

Fifty-six aboard. Father, mother, cousins, remoter relatives. A world unto itself, *Estelle*. He had his own, however damaged. He had a family. Hers was dead.

She said nothing more, no word of grief for her loss or

of relief to have been spared, to have stayed behind from the voyage. She gave a few more convulsive breaths, hugged him, turned, dry-eyed, to put a second dinner in the microwave.

She sat down, ate, went through all the normal motions. He forced his own meal down, still with a disinfectant taint in his mouth, reckoning it clung all about him. He succeeded finally in catching her eyes looking at him. They were as stark as those of the refugees. He found nothing to say. He got up, walked around the table and hugged her from behind.

Her hands covered his. "I'm all right."

"I wish you'd called me."

She let go his hands and stood up, touched his arm, a weary gesture. Looked at him suddenly, directly, with that same dark tiredness. "There's one of us left," she said. He blinked, perplexed, realized then that she meant the Quens. *Estelle*'s folk. Merchanters owned names as stationers had a home. She was Quen; that meant something he knew he did not understand, in the months they had been together. Revenge was a merchanter commodity; he knew that . . . among folk where name alone was a property and reputation went with it.

"I want a child," she said.

He stared at her, struck with the darkness in her eyes. He loved her. She had walked into his life off a merchanter ship and decided to try station life, though she still spoke of *her* ship. Four months. For the first time in their being together he had no desire for her, not with that look and *Estelle*'s death and her reasons for revenge. He said nothing. They had agreed there would be no children until she knew for certain whether she could bear to stay. What she offered him might be that agreement. It might be something else. It was not the time to talk about it, not now, with insanity all about them. He simply gathered her against him, walked with her to the bedroom, held her through the long dark hours. She made no demands and he asked no questions.

## ii

"No," the man at the operations desk said, without looking this time at the printout; and then with a weary impulse toward humanity: "Wait. I'll do another search. Maybe it wasn't posted with that spelling."

Vasilly Kressich waited, sick with terror, as despair hung all about this last, forlorn gathering of refugees which refused to leave the desks on dockside: families and parts of families, who hunted relatives, who waited on word. There were twenty-seven of them on the benches near the desk, counting children; he had counted. They had gone from station mainday into alterday, and another shift of operators at the desk which was station's one extension of humanity toward them, and there was nothing more coming out of comp but what had been there before.

He waited. The operator keyed through time after time. There was nothing; he knew that there was nothing, by the look the man turned toward him. Of a sudden he was sorry for the operator too, who had to sit out here obtaining nothing, knowing there was no hope, surrounded by grieving relatives, with armed guards stationed near the desk in case. Kressich sat down again, next to the family who had lost a son in the confusion.

It was the same tale for each. They had loaded in panic, the guards more concerned for getting themselves onto the ships than for keeping order and getting others on. It was their own fault; he could not deny that. The mob had hit the docks, men forcing their way aboard who had no passes allotted to those critical personnel meant for evacuation. The guards had fired in panic, unsure of attackers and legitimate passengers. Russell's Station had died in riot. Those in the process of loading had been hurried aboard the nearest ship at the last, doors had been sealed as soon as the counters reached capacity. Jen and Romy should have been aboard before him. He had stayed, trying to keep order at his assigned post. Most of the ships had gotten sealed in time. It was *Hansford* the mob had gotten wide open, *Hansford* where the drugs had run out, where the pressure of lives more than the systems could bear had broken everything down and a shock-crazed mob had run riot. *Griffin* had been bad enough; he had gotten aboard well before the wave the guards had had to cut down. And he had trusted that Jen and Romy had made it into *Lila.* The passenger list had said that they were on

*Lila,* at least what printout they had finally gotten in the confusion after launch.

But neither of them had gotten off at Pell; they had not come off the ship. No one of those critical enough to be taken to station hospital matched their descriptions. They could not be impressed by Mallory: Jen had no skills Mallory would need, and Romy—somewhere the records were wrong. He had believed the passenger list, had had to believe it, because there were too many of them that ship's com could pass direct messages. They had voyaged in silence. Jen and Romy had not gotten off *Lila.* Had never been there.

"They were wrong to throw them out in space," the woman nearest him moaned. "They didn't identify them. He's gone, he's gone, he must have been on the *Hansford.*"

Another man was at the desk again, attempting to check, insisting that Mallory's ID of impressed civilians was a lie; and the operator was patiently running another search, comparing descriptions, negative again.

"He was there," the man shouted at the operator. "He was on the list and he didn't get off, and he was there." The man was crying. Kressich sat numb.

On *Griffin,* they had read out the passenger list and asked for ID's. Few had had them. People had answered to names which could not possibly be theirs. Some answered to two, to get the rations, if they were not caught at it. He had been afraid then, with a deep and sickly fear; but a lot of people were on the wrong ships, and one of them had then realized the situation on *Hansford.* He had been sure they were aboard.

Unless they had gotten worried and gotten off to go look for him. Unless they had done something so miserably, horribly stupid, out of fear, for love.

Tears started down his face. It was not the likes of Jen and Romy who could have gotten onto *Hansford,* who could have forced their way among men armed with guns and knives and lengths of pipe. He did not reckon them among the dead of that ship. It was rather that they were still on Russell's Station, where Union ruled now. And he was here; and there was no way back.

He rose finally, and accepted it. He was the first to leave. He went to the quarters which were assigned him, the barracks for single men, who were many of them young, and probably many of them under false ID's, and not the techs and other personnel they were supposed to be. He found a cot unoccupied and gathered up the kit the supervisor provided each man. He bathed a second time . . . no bathing seemed enough . . . and walked back among the rows of sleeping, exhausted men, and lay down.

There was mindwipe for those prisoners who had been high enough to be valuable and opinionated. *Jen,* he thought, *O Jen,* and their son, if he were alive . . . to be reared by a shadow of Jen, who thought the approved thoughts and disputed nothing, liable to Adjustment because she had been his wife. It was not even certain that they would let her keep Romy. There were state nurseries, which turned out Union's soldiers and workers.

He thought of suicide. Some had chosen that rather than board the ships for some strange place, a station which was not theirs. That solution was not in his nature. He lay still and stared at the metal ceiling, in the near dark, and survived, which he had done so far, middle-aged and alone and utterty empty.

# 4

## Pell: 5/3/52

The tension set in at the beginning of mainday, the first numb stirrings-forth by the refugees to the emergency kitchens set up on the dock, the first tentative efforts of those with papers and those without to meet with station representatives at the desks and to establish rights of residency, the first awakening to the realities of quarantine.

"We should have pulled out last shift," Graff said, reviewing dawn's messages, "while it was all still quiet."

"Would now," Signy said, "but we can't risk Pell. If they can't hold it down, we have to. Call station council and tell them I'm ready to meet with them now. I'll go to them. It's safer than bringing them out on the docks."

"Take a shuttle round the rim," Graff suggested, his broad face set in habitual worry. "Don't risk your neck out there with less than a full squad. They're less controlled now. All it takes is something to set them off."

The proposal had merits. She considered how that timidity would look to Pell, shook her head. She went back to her quarters and put on what passed for dress uniform, the proper dark blue at least. When she went it was with Di Janz and a guard of six armored troopers, and they walked right across the dock to the quarantine checkpoint, a door and passage beside the huge intersection seals. No one tried to approach her, although there were some who looked as if they might want to try it, hesitating at the armed troops. She made the door unhindered and was passed through, up the ramp and to another guarded door, then down into the main part of the station.

After that it was as simple as taking a lift through the varied levels and into the administrative section, blue upper corridor. It was a sudden change of worlds, from the barren steel of the docks and the stripped quarantine area, into a hall tightly controlled by station security, into a glass-walled foyer with sound-deadening matting underfoot, where bizarre wooden sculptures met them with the aspect of a cluster of amazed citizenry. Art. Signy blinked and stared, bemused at this reminder of luxuries and civilizations. Forgotten things, rumored things. Leisure to make and create what had no function but itself, as man had done, but himself. She had lived her whole life insulated from such things, only knowing at a distance that civilization existed, and that rich stations maintained luxury at their secret hearts.

Only they were not human faces which stared out from curious squat globes, among wooden spires, but faces round-eyed and strange: Downbelow faces, patient work in wood. Humans would have used plastics or metal.

There were indeed more than humans here: that fact was evident in the neat braided matting, in the bright painting which marched in alien geometrics and overlays about the walls, more of the spires, more of the wooden globes with the faces and huge eyes all about them, faces repeated in the carved furniture and even in the doors, staring out from a gnarled and tiny detail, as if all those eyes were to remind humans that Downbelow was always with them.

It affected them all. Di swore softly before they walked up to the last doors and officious civs let them in, walked with them into the council hall.

Human faces stared at them this time, in six tiers of chairs on a side, an oval table in the pit between, their expressions and those of the alien carvings remarkably alike in that first impression.

The white-haired man at the end of the table stood up, made a gesture offering them the room into which they had already come. Angelo Konstantin. Others remained seated.

And beside the table were six chairs which were not part of the permanent arrangement; and six, male and female, who were not, by their style of dress, part of the station council or even of the Beyond.

Company men. Signy might have dismissed the troops to the outer chamber in courtesy to the council, rid herself of the threat of rifles and the remainder of force. She stood where she was, unresponsive to Konstantin smiles.

"This can be short," she said. "Your quarantine zone is set up and functioning. I'd advise you to guard it heavily. I'll warn you now that other freighters jumped without our clearance and made no part of our convoy. If you're wise, you'll follow the recommendations I made and board any incoming merchanter with security before letting it in near you. You've had a look at Russell's disaster here. I'll be pulling out in short order; it's your problem now."

There was a panicked muttering in the room. One of the Company men stood up. "You've behaved very highhandedly, Captain Mallory. Is that the custom out here?"

"The custom is, sir, that those who know a situation handle it and those who don't watch and learn, or get out of the way."

The Company man's thin face flushed visibly. "It seems we're constrained to bear with that kind of attitude . . . temporarily. We need transport up to whatever exists as a border. *Norway* is available."

She drew a sharp breath and drew herself up. "No, sir, you're not constrained, because *Norway* isn't available to civ passengers, and I'm not taking any on. As for the border, the *border* is wherever the fleet sits at the moment, and nobody but the ships involved knows where that is. There aren't borders. Hire a freighter."

There was dead silence in the hall.

"I dislike, captain, to use the word court-marital."

She laughed, a mere breath. "If you Company people want to tour the war, I'm tempted to take you in. Maybe you'd benefit by it. Maybe you could widen Mother Earth's sight; maybe we could get a few more ships."

"You're not in a position to make requisitions and we don't take them. We're not here to see only what it's determined we should see. We'll be looking at everything, captain, whether or not it suits you."

She set her hands on her hips and surveyed the lot of them. "Your name, sir."

"Segust Ayres, of the Security Council, second secretary."

"Second secretary. Well, we'll see what space we come up with. No baggage beyond a duffle. You understand that. No frills. You go where *Norway* goes. I don't take my orders from anyone but Mazian."

"Captain," another put forth, "your cooperation is earnestly requested.

"You have what I'll give and not a step further."

There was silence, a slow murmuring from the tiers. The man Ayres's face reddened further, his precise dignity that instinctively galled her now further and further ruffled. "You're an extension of the Company, captain, and you hold your commission from it. Have you forgotten that?"

"Third captain of the Fleet, Mr. Second Secretary, which is military and you're not. But if you intend to come, be ready within the hour."

"No, captain," Ayres declared firmly. "We'll take your suggestion about freighter transport. It got us here from Sol. They'll go where they're hired to go."

"Within reason, I don't doubt." Good. That problem was shed. She could reckon Mazian's consternation at *that* in the midst of them. She looked beyond Ayres, at Angelo Konstantin. "I've done my service here. I'm leaving. Any message will be relayed."

"Captain." Angelo Konstantin left the head of the table

and walked forward, offered his hand, an unusual courtesy and the stranger considering what she had done to them, leaving the refugees. She took the firm handclasp, met the man's anxious eyes. They knew each other, remotely; had met in years past. Six generations a Beyonder, Angelo Konstantin; like the young man who had come down to help on the dock, a seventh. The Konstantins had built Pell; were scientists and miners, builders and holders. With this man and the others she felt a manner of bond, for all their other differences. This kind of man the Fleet had for its charge, the best of them.

"Good luck," she wished them, and turned and left, taking Di and the troopers with her.

She returned the way she had come, through the beginning establishment of Q zone, and back into the familiar environs of *Norway,* among friends, where law was as she laid it down and things were as she knew. There were a few last details to work out, a few matters still to be arranged, a few last gifts to bestow on station; her own security's dredgings—reports, recommendations, a live body, and what salvaged reports came with it.

She put *Norway* on ready then, and the siren went and what military presence Pell had for its protection slipped free and left them.

She went to follow a sequence of courses which was in her head, and of which Graff knew, her second. It was not the only evacuation in progress; the Pan-Paris station was under Kreshov's management; Sung of *Pacific* had moved in on Esperance. By now other convoys were on their way toward Pell, and she had only set up the framework.

The push was coming. Other stations had died, beyond their reach, beyond any salvage. They moved what they could, making Union work for what they took. But in her private estimate they were themselves doomed, and the present maneuver was one from which most of them would not return. They were the remnant of a Fleet, against a widespread power which had inexhaustible lives, and supply, and worlds, and they did not.

After so long a struggle . . . her generation, the last of the Fleet, the last of Company power. She had watched it go; had fought to hold the two together, Earth and Union, humanity's past—and future. Still fought, with what she had, but no longer hoped. At times, she even thought of bolting the Fleet, of doing what a few ships had done and going over to Union. It was supreme irony that Union had become the pro-space side of this war and the founding Company fought against; irony that they who most believed in the Beyond ended up fighting against what it was becoming, to die for a Company which had stopped caring. She was bitter; she had long ago stopped being politic in any discussion of Company policies.

There had been a time, years ago, when she had looked differently on things, when she had looked as an outsider on the great ships and the power of them, and when the dream of the old exploration ships had drawn her into this, a dream long revised to the realities the Company captain's emblem had come to mean. Long ago she had realized there was no winning.

Perhaps, she thought, Angelo Konstantin knew the odds too. Maybe he had taken her meaning, answered it, behind the gesture of saying farewell—offered support in the face of Company pressure. For a moment it had seemed so. Maybe many of the stationers knew . . . but that was too much to expect of stationers.

She had three feints to make, which would take time; a small operation, and a jump afterward to a rendezvous with Mazian, on a certain date. If enough of their ships survived the initial operation. If Union responded as they hoped. It was madness.

The Fleet went it alone, without merchanter or stationer support, as they had gone it alone for years before this.

# 5

## Pell: 5/5/52

Angelo Konstantin looked up sharply from the desk covered with notes and emergencies which wanted immediate attention. "Union?" he asked in dismay.

"A prisoner of war," the security head told him, standing uncomfortably before the desk. "Part of the Russell's evacuation. Turned over to our security separate of the others. A pickup from a capsule, minor ship, armscomper, confined at Russell's. *Norway* carried him in . . . no turning *him* loose among the refugees. They'd kill him. Mallory added a note to his file: *He's your problem now.* Her words, sir."

Angelo opened the file, stared at a young face, a record of several pages of interrogation, Union ID, and a scrap of notepaper with Mallory's signature and a scrawl: *Young and scared.*

Joshua Halbraight Talley. Armscomper. Union fleet minor probe.

He had five hundred individuals and groups who had thought they were headed back to their original housing; warnings of further evacuations in the secret instructions Mallory had left, which was going to take at least most of orange and yellow sections, dislocating more offices; and six Company agents who thought they were headed beyond to inspect the war, with no merchanter who would agree to take Company scrip to take them aboard. He did not need problems from lower levels.

The boy's face haunted him. He turned back to that page, leafed again through the interrogation report, scanned it, remembered the security chief still standing there. "So what are you doing with him?"

"Holding him in detention. None of the other offices agrees what to do with him."

Pell had never had a prisoner of war. The war had never come here. Angelo thought it over and fretted the more for the situation. "Legal Affairs have a suggestion?"

"Suggested I get a decision here."

"We're not equipped for that kind of detention."

"No, sir," the security chief agreed. It was a hospital facility down there. The setup was for retraining. Adjustment . . . what rare times it had ever been needed.

"We can't treat him."

"Those cells aren't set up for long stays, sir. Maybe we could rig up something more comfortable."

"We've got people without lodgings as it is. How are we going to explain that?"

"We could set up something in detention itself. Take a panel out; at least get a bigger room."

"Postpone that." Angelo ran a hand through his sparse hair. "I'll consider policy on the case as soon as I get the emergency matters settled. Deal with him as best you can with what you have at hand. Ask the lower offices to apply some imagination to the case and send me the recommendations."

"Yes, sir." The security chief left. Angelo put the folder away for later use. A prisoner of that kind was not what they needed at the moment. What they did need was a means to secure housing and feed extra mouths and to cope with what was coming. They had trade goods which were suddenly going nowhere; those could be consumed on Pell and on Downbelow at the base, and out in the mines. But they needed others. They had economics to worry about, markets which had collapsed, the value of any currency in doubt as far as merchanters were concerned. From a star-spanning economy, Pell had to be turned to feed itself, to self-sufficiency; and perhaps—to face other changes.

It was not the single Union prisoner they had in hand, identified, who had him worried. It was the likely number of Unionists and sympathizers who would grow in quarantine, folk for whom any change was going to look better than what they had. There were only some of the refugees with papers, and many of those had been discovered not to match the prints and photos attached to them.

"We need some sort of liaison with the quarantine zone residents," he advised council at that afternoon's meeting. "We'll have to set up a government on the other side of the line, someone of their choosing, some manner of elections; and we'll have to deal with what results."

They accepted that, as they had accepted all else. It was the concerns of their own constituencies which had them distraught, the councillors from dislodged orange and yellow, from green and white which had gotten most of the influx of station residents. Red sector, untouched, abutting yellow from the other side, was anxious; the others were jealous. There was a deluge of complaints and protests and rumors of rumor. He made note of them.

There was debate. It finally came to the necessary conclusion that they had to relieve pressure on the station itself.

"We do not authorize further construction here," the man Ayres interposed, rising from his seat. Angelo simply stared at him, given heart to do so by Signy Mallory, who had called a bluff on the Company and made it good.

"I do," Angelo said. "I have the resources to do it, and I will."

There was a vote. It went the only sane way, with the Company observers sitting in silent anger, vetoing what was passed, which veto was simply ignored while plans proceeded.

The Company men left the meeting early. Security reported them later agitating on the docks, and trying to engage a freighter at inflated rates, with gold.

There was not a freighter moving, for anything except in-system hauling, ordinary runs to the mines. It did not surprise Angelo when he heard that. There was a cold wind blowing, and Pell felt it; everyone with instincts bred of the Beyond felt it.

Eventually perhaps the Company men did, at least two of them, for those two engaged a ship home, to Sol, the same which had brought them, a smallish and decrepit jump-freighter, the only merchanter with an EC designation which had docked at Pell in the better part of a decade, laden with Downbelow curios and delicacies for its return, as it had brought in goods from Earth, which sold high, for their curiosity. The four other Company representatives upped their offers, and boarded a freighter for an unguaranteed run on the freighter's own schedule, to call at Viking and wherever else the uncertain times left safe. They accepted Mallory's conditions from a merchanter captain, and paid for the privilege.

# 6

## i
## Downbelow main bases: 5/20/52

It was storm on Downbelow when the shuttle came down, and that was not uncommon, on a world of abundant cloud, when all the winter on the northern continent was wrapped in sea-spawned overcast, seldom cold enough to freeze, not warm enough for human comfort—never a clear sight of sun or stars for month on dreary month. The unloading of the passengers at the landing site was proceeding in a cold, pelting rain, a line of tired and angry people trudging over the hill from the shuttle, to be settled into various warehouse digs amid stacks of mats and musty sacks of *prosh* and *fikli.* "Move it over and stack it up," the supervisors shouted when the crowding became evident; and the noise was considerable, cursing voices, the beating of rain in the inflated domes, the inevitable thump of compressors. The tired stationers sulked and finally began to do as they were told . . . young, most of them, construction workers and a few techs, virtually without baggage and no few of them frightened at their first experience of weather. They were station-born, wheezing at a kilo or so extra weight from Downbelow's gravity, wincing at thunder and at lightning which chained across the roiling skies. No sleep for them until they could set up some manner of dormitory space; no rest for anyone, native or human, who labored to carry foodstuffs over the hill to lade the shuttle, or the crews trying to cope with the inevitable flooding in the domes.

Jon Lukas oversaw some of it, scowling, walked back to the main dome where the operations center was. He paced, listened to the rain, waited the better part of an hour, finally suited up again and masked to walk to the shuttle. "Good-bye, sir," the com operator offered rising from his desk.

Others stopped work, the few who were there. He shook hands, still frowning, and finally walked out the flimsy lock and up the wooden steps to the path, spattered again by the cold rain. His fiftyish overweight was unflattered by the bright yellow plastic. He had always been conscious of the indignity and hated it, hated walking in mud up to the ankles and feeling a chill which penetrated even the suit and the liner. Raingear and the necessary breathers turned all the humans at the base into yellow monsters, blurred in the downpour. Downers scurried about naked and enjoying it, the brown fur of their spindly limbs and lithe bodies dark with moisture and plastered to them, their faces, round-eyed and with mouths set in permanent o's of surprise, watched and chattered together in their own language, a babble in the rain and the constant bass of thunder. He walked the direct trail to the landing site, not that which led on the other leg of the triangle, past the storage domes and barracks domes. This one had no traffic. No meetings. No good-byes. He looked across to fields which were aswim; the gray-green brush and the ribbon trees on the hills about the base showed through curtains of rain, and the river was a broad, overflowed sheet on the farside bank, where a marsh tended to form, for all their attempts to drain it . . . disease among the native workers again, if any Downers had slipped in unvaccinated. It was no paradise, Downbelow base. He had no reluctance to leave it and the new staff and the Downers to each other. It was the manner of the recall which rankled.

"Sir."

At last, parting nuisance came splashing after him on the trail. Bennett Jacint. Jon half turned, kept walking, made the man work to overtake him in the mud and the downpour.

"The mill dike," Jacint gasped through the stops and hisses of the breather. "Need some human crews over there with heavy equipment and sandbags."

"Not my problem now," Jon said. "Get to it yourself. What are you good for? Put those coddled Downers to it. Take an extra crew of them. Or wait on the new supervisors, why don't you? You can explain it all to my nephew."

"Where are they?" Jacint asked. A skilled obstructionist, Bennett Jacint, always on the line with objections when it came to any measures for improvement. More than once Jacint had gone over his head to file a protest. One construction project he had outright gotten stopped, so that the road to the wells stayed a mired track. Jon smiled and pointed across the grounds, far across, back toward the warehouse domes.

"There's not time."

"That's your problem."

Bennett Jacint cursed him to his face and started to run it, then changed his mind and raced back again toward the mill. Jon laughed. Soaked stock in the mill. Good. Let the Konstantins solve it.

He came over the hill, started down to the shuttle, which loomed alien and silver in the trampled meadow, its cargo hatch lowered, Downers toiling to and fro and a few yellow-suited humans among them. His trail joined that on which the Downers moved, churned mud; he walked on the grassy margin, cursed when a Downer with a load swayed too near him, and had the satisfaction at least that they cleared his path. He walked into the landing circle, nodded curtly to a human supervisor and climbed the cargo ramp into the shadowed steel interior. He stripped the wet rainsuit there in the cold, keeping the mask on. He ordered a Downer gang boss to clean up the muddied area, and walked on through the hold to the lift, rode it topside, into a steel, clean corridor, and a small passenger compartment with padded seats.

Downers were in it, two laborers making the shift to station. They looked uncertain when they saw him, touched each other. He sealed the passenger area and made the air-shift, so that he could discard his breather and they had to put theirs on. He sat down opposite them, stared through them in the windowless compartment. The air stank of wet Downer, a smell he had lived with for three years, a smell with which all Pell lived, if one had a sensitive nose, but Downbelow base worst of all: with dusty grain and distilleries and packing plants and walls and mud and muck and the smoke of the mills, latrines that flooded out, sump pools that grew scum, forest molds that could ruin a breather and kill a man who was caught without a spare—all of this and managing half-witted Downer labor with their religious taboos and constant excuses. He was proud of his record, increased output, efficiency where there had been hands-folded complacency that Downers were Downers and could not comprehend schedules. They could, and did, and set records in production.

No thanks of it. Crisis hit the station and the Downbelow expansion which had limped along in and out of planning sessions for a decade was suddenly moving. Plants would get the additional facilities he had made possible, manned by workers whose supply and housing he had made possible, using Lukas Company funds and Lukas Company equipment.

Only a pair of Konstantins was sent down to supervise during that stage, without a thank you, Mr. Lukas, or a well done, Jon, thanks for leaving your own company offices and your own affairs, thanks for doing the job for three years. *Emilio Konstantin and Miliko Dee appointed Downbelow supervisors; please arrange affairs and shuttle up at the earliest.* His nephew Emilio. Young Emilio was going to run things during construction. Konstantins were always in at the last stage, always there when the credit was about to be handed out. They had democracy in the council, but it was dynasty in the station offices. Always Konstantins. Lukases had arrived at Pell as early, sunk as much into its building, an important company back in the Hinder Stars; but Konstantins had maneuvered and gathered power at every opportunity. Now again, his equipment, his preparation, and Konstantins in charge when it reached a stage when the public might notice. Emilio: his sister Alicia's son, and Angelo's. People could be manipulated, if the Konstantin name was all they were ever allowed to hear; and Angelo was past master at that tactic.

It would have been courtesy to have met his nephew and his wife when they came in, to have stayed a few days to trade information, or at the least to have informed them of his immediate departure on the shuttle which had brought them down. It would also have been courtesy on their part to have come at once to the domes for an official greeting, some acknowledgment of his authority at the base—but they had not. Not even a com-sent hello, uncle, when they landed. He was in no mood for empty courtesies now, to stand in the rain shaking hands and mouthing amenities with a nephew with whom he seldom spoke. He had opposed his sister's marriage; argued with her; it had not linked him *in* to the Konstantin family: with her attitude, it was rather a desertion. He and Alicia had not spoken since, save officially; not even that, in the last several years . . . her presence depressed him. And the boys looked like Angelo, as Angelo had been in his younger days; he avoided them, who probably hoped to get their hands on Lukas Company . . . at least a share of it, after him, as nearest kin. It was that hope, he was still persuaded, which had attracted Angelo to Alicia: Lukas Company was still the biggest independent on Pell. But he had maneuvered out of the trap, surprised them with an heir, not one to his taste, but a live body all the same. He had worked these years on Downbelow, reckoning at first it might be possible to expand Lukas Company down here, through construction. Angelo had seen it coming, had maneuvered the council to block that. Ecological concerns. Now came the final move.

He accepted the letter of his instruction to return, took it just as rudely as it was delivered, left without baggage or fanfare, like some offender ordered home in disgrace. Childish it might be, but it might also make a point with council . . . and if all the stock in the mill was soaked on the first day of the Konstantin administration here, so much the better. Let them feel shortages on station; let Angelo explain that to council. It would open a debate in which he would be present in council to participate, and ah, he wanted that.

He had deserved something more than this.

Engines finally activated, heralding lift. He got up, searched up a bottle and a glass from the locker. He received a query from the shuttle crew, declared he needed nothing. He settled in, belted, and the shuttle began lift. He poured himself a stiff drink, nerving himself for flight, which he always hated, drank, with the amber liquid quivering in the glass under the strain of his arm and the vibration of the ship. Across from him the Downers held each other and moaned.

## ii

## Pell Detention: red sector one: 5/20/52; 0900 hrs.

The prisoner sat still at the table with the three of them, stared at the guard supervisor in preference, his eyes seeming focused somewhere beyond. Damon laid the folder on the table again and studied the man, who was most of all trying not to look at him. Damon found himself intensely uncomfortable in this interview . . . different from the criminals he dealt with in Legal Affairs—this man, this face like an angel in a painting, this too-perfect humanity with blond hair and eyes that gazed through things. Beautiful, the word occurred to him. There were no flaws. The look was complete innocence. No thief, no brawler; but this man would kill . . . if such a man could kill . . . for politics. For duty, because he was Union and they were not. There was no hate involved. It was disturbing to hold the life or death of such a man in his hands. It gave *him* choices in turn, mirror-imaged choices—not for hate, but for duty, because he was not Union, and this man was.

*We're at war,* Damon thought miserably. *Because he's come here, the war has.*

An angel's face.

"No trouble to you, is he?" Damon asked the supervisor.

"No."

"I've heard he's a good midge player."

That got a flicker from both of them. There were illicit gamblings at the detention station, as in most slow posts during alterday. Damon offered a smile when the prisoner looked his way, the least shifting of the pale blue eyes . . . went sober again as the prisoner failed to react. "I'm Damon Konstantin, Mr. Talley, of the station legal office. You've given us no trouble and we appreciate that. We're not your enemies; we'd dock a Union fleet as readily as a Company ship—in principle; but you don't leave stations neutral any longer, not from what we hear, so our attitude has to change along with that. We just can't take chances having you loose. Repatriation . . . no. We're given other instructions. Our own security. You understand that."

No response.

"Your counsel's made the point that you're suffering in this close confinement and that the cells were never meant for long-term detention. That there are people walking loose in Q who are far more a threat to this station; that there's a vast difference between a saboteur and an armscomper in uniform who had the bad luck to be picked up by the wrong side. But having said all that, he still doesn't recommend your release except to Q. We have an arrangement worked out. We can fake an ID that would protect you, and still let us keep track of you over there. I don't like the idea, but it seems workable."

"What's Q?" Talley asked, a soft, anxious voice, appealing to the supervisor and to his own counsel, the older Jacoby, who sat at the end of the table. "What are you saying?"

"Quarantine. The sealed section of the station we've set apart for our own refugees."

Talley's eyes darted nervously from one to the other of them. "No. No. I don't want to be put with them. I never asked him to set this up. I didn't."

Damon frowned uncomfortably. "We've got another convoy coming in, Mr. Talley, another group of refugees. We have arrangements underway to mix you with them with faked papers. Get you out of here. It would still be a kind of confinement, but with wider walls, room to walk where you want, live life . . . as it's lived in Q. That's a good part of the station over there. Not regimented—open. No cells. Mr. Jacoby's right: you're no more dangerous than some over there. Less, because we'd always know who you are."

Talley cast another look at his counsel. Shook his head, pleading.

"You absolutely reject it?" Damon prodded him, vexed. All solutions and arrangements collapsed. "It's not prison, you understand."

"My face—is known there. Mallory said—"

He lapsed into silence. Damon stared at him, marked the fevered anxiety, the sweat which stood on Talley's face. "*What* did Mallory say?"

"That if I made trouble—she'd transfer me to one of the other ships. I think I know what you're doing: you think if there are Unionists with them they'd contact me if you put me over there in your quarantine. Is that it? But I wouldn't live that long. There are people who know me by sight. Station officials. Police. They're the kind who got places on those ships, aren't they? And they'd know me. I'll be dead in an hour if you do that. I heard what those ships were like."

"Mallory told you."

"Mallory told me."

"There are some, on the other hand," Damon said bitterly, "who'd balk at boarding one of Mazian's ships, stationers who'd swear an honest man's survival wasn't that likely. But I'd reckon you had a soft passage, didn't you? Enough to eat and no worries about the air? The old spacer-stationer quarrel: leave the stationers to suffocate and keep her own deck spotless. But *you* rated differently. You got special treatment."

"It wasn't all that pleasant, Mr. Konstantin."

"Not your choice either, was it?"

"No," the answer came hoarsely. Damon suddenly repented his baiting, nagged by suspicions, evil rumor of the Fleet. He was ashamed of the role in which he was cast. In which Pell was. War and prisoners of war. He wanted no part of it.

"You refuse the solution we offer," he said. "That's your privilege. No one will force you. We don't want to endanger your life, and that's what it would be if things are what you say. So what do you do? I suppose you go on playing midge with the guards. It's a very small confinement. Did they give you the tapes and player? You got that?"

"I would like—" The words came out like an upwelling of nausea. "I want to ask for Adjustment."

Jacoby looked down and shook his head. Damon sat still.

"If I were Adjusted I could get out of here," the prisoner said. "Eventually *do* something. It's my own request. A prisoner always has the option to have that, doesn't he?"

"Your side uses that on prisoners," Damon said. "We don't."

"I ask for it. You have me locked up like a criminal. If I'd killed someone, wouldn't I have a right to it? If I'd stolen or—"

"I think you ought to have some psychiatric testing if you keep insisting on it."

"Don't they test—when they process for Adjustment?"

Damon looked at Jacoby.

"He's been increasingly depressed," Jacoby said. "He's asked me over and over to lodge that request with station, and I haven't."

"We've never mandated Adjustment for a man who wasn't convicted of a crime."

"Have you ever," the prisoner asked, "*had* a man in here who wasn't?"

"Union uses it," the supervisor said in a low voice, "without blinking. Those cells are small, Mr. Konstantin."

"A man doesn't ask for a thing like that," Damon said.

"I ask," Talley insisted. "I ask you. I want out of here."

"It would solve the problem," Jacoby said.

"I want to know why he wants it."

*"I want out!"*

Damon froze. Talley caught his breath, leaning against the table, and recovered his composure a little short of tears. Adjustment was not a punitive procedure, was never intended to be. It had double benefits . . . altered behavior for the violent and a little wiping of the slate for the troubled. It was the latter, he suspected, meeting Talley's shadowed eyes. Suddenly he felt an overwhelming pity for the man, who was sane, who seemed very, very sane. The station was in crisis. Events crowded in on them in which individuals could become lost, shoved aside. Cells in detention were urgently needed for real criminals, out of Q, which they had in abundance. There were worse fates than Adjustment. Being locked in a viewless eight-by-ten room for life was one.

"Pull the commitment papers out of comp," he told the supervisor, and the supervisor passed the order via com. Jacoby fretted visibly, shuffling papers and not looking at any of them. "What I'm going to do," Damon said to Talley, feeling as if it were some shared bad dream, "is put the papers in your hands. And you can study all the printout of explanation that goes with them. If that's still what you want tomorrow, we'll accept them signed. I want you also to write us a release and request in your own words, stating that this was your idea and your choice, that you're not claustrophobic or suffering from any other disability—"

"I was an *armscomper,*" Talley interjected scornfully. It was not the largest station on a ship.

"—or condition which would cause you unusual duress. Don't you have kin, relatives, someone who would try to talk you out of this if they heard about it?"

The eyes reacted to that, ever so slightly.

"Do you have someone?" Damon asked, hoping he had

found a handhold, some reason to apply against this. "Who?"

"Dead," Talley said.

"If this request is in reaction to that—"

"A long time ago," Talley said, cutting that off. Nothing more.

An angel's face. Humanity without flaw. Birth labs? The thought came to him unbidden. It had always been abhorrent to him, Union's engineered soldiers. His own possible prejudice worried at him. "I haven't read your file in full," he admitted. "This has been handled at other levels. They thought they had this settled. It bounced back to me. You *had* family, Mr. Talley?"

"Yes," Talley said faintly, defiantly, making him ashamed of himself.

"Born where?"

"Cyteen." The same small, flat voice. "I've given you all that. I had parents. I was *born,* Mr. Konstantin. Is that really pertinent?"

"I'm sorry. I'm very sorry. I want you to understand this: it's not final. You can change your mind, right up to the moment the treatment begins. All you have to say is stop, I don't want this. But after it goes so far, you're not competent. You understand . . . you're no longer able. You've seen Adjusted men?"

"They recover."

"They do recover. I'll follow the case, Mr. Talley . . . Lt. Talley . . . so much as I can. You see to it," he said to the supervisor, "that any time he sends a message, at any stage of the process, it gets to me on an emergency basis, day or night. You see that the attendants understand that too, down to the orderlies. I don't think he'll abuse the privilege." He looked at Jacoby. "Are you satisfied about your client?"

"It's his right to do what he's doing. I'm not pleased with it. But I'll witness it. I'll agree it solves things . . . maybe for the best."

The comp printout arrived. Damon handed the papers to Jacoby for scrutiny. Jacoby marked the lines for signature and passed the folder to Talley. Talley folded it to him like something precious.

"Mr. Talley," Damon said, rising, and on impulse offered

his hand, against all the distaste he felt. The young armscomper rose and took it, and the look of gratitude in his suddenly brimming eyes cancelled all certainties. "Is it possible," Damon asked, "is it remotely possible that you have information you want wiped? That *that's* why you're doing this? I warn you it's more likely to come out in the process than not. And we're not interested in it, do you understand that? We have no military interests."

That was not it. He much doubted that it could be. This was no high officer, no one like himself, who knew comp signals, access codes, the sort of thing an enemy must not have. No one had discovered the like in this man . . . nothing of value, not here, not at Russell's.

"No," Talley said. "I don't know anything."

Damon hesitated, still nagged by conscience, the feeling that Talley's counsel, if no one else, ought to be protesting, doing something more vigorous, using all the delays of the law on Talley's behalf. But that got him prison; got him . . . no hope. They were bringing Q outlaws into detention, far more dangerous; men who might know him, if Talley was right. Adjustment saved him, got him out of there; gave him the chance for a job, for freedom, a life. There was no one sane who would carry out revenge on someone after a mindwipe. And the process was humane. It was always meant to be.

"Talley . . . have you complaint against Mallory or the personnel of *Norway*?"

"No."

"Your counsel is present. It would be put on record . . . if you wanted to make such a complaint."

"No."

So that trick would not work. No delaying it for investigation. Damon nodded, walked out of the room, feeling unclean. It was a manner of murder he was doing, an assistance in suicide.

They had an abundance of those too, over in Q.

### iii

### Pell: sector orange nine: 5/20/52; 1900 hrs.

Kressich winced at the crash of something down the hall, beyond the sealed door, tried not to show his terror. Something was burning, smoke reaching them through the ventilation system. That more frightened him, and the half hundred gathered with him in this section of hallway. Out on the docks the police and the rioters still fired at each other. The violence was subsiding. The few with him, the remainder of Russell's own security police, a handful of elite stationers and a scattering of young people and old . . . they had held the hallway against the gangs.

"We're afire," someone muttered, on the edge of hysteria.

"Old rags or something," he said; *shut it up,* he thought. They did not need panic. In a major fire, station central would blow a section to put it out . . . death for all of them. They were not valuable to Pell. Some of them were out there shooting at Pell police with guns they had gotten off dead policemen. It had started with the knowledge that there was another convoy coming in, more ships, more desperate people to crowd into the little they had; had started with the simple word that this was about to happen . . . and a demand for faster processing of papers; then raids on barracks and gangs confiscating papers from those who did have them.

*Burn all records,* the cry had gone out through quarantine, in the logic that, recordless, they would all be admitted. Those who would not yield up their papers were beaten and robbed of them; of anything else of value. Barracks were ransacked. Gangs of the ruffians who had forced *Griffin* and *Hansford* gained membership among the desperate, the young, the leaderless and the panicked.

There was quiet for a time outside. The fans had stopped; the air began to go foul. Among those who had seen the worst of the voyage, there was panic, quietly contained; a good number were crying.

Then the lights brightened and a cool draft came through the ducts. The door whipped open. Kressich got to his feet and looked into the faces of station police, and the barrels of leveled rifles. Some of his own band had knives, sections of pipe and furniture, whatever weapons they had improvised. He had nothing . . . held up frantic hands.

"No," he pleaded. No one moved, not the police, not his own. "Please. We weren't in it. We only defended this section from them. None . . . none of these people were involved. They were the victims."

The police leader, face haggard with wariness and soot and blood, motioned with his rifle toward the wall. "You have to line up," Kressich explained to his ill-assorted companions, who were not the sort to understand such procedures, except only the ex-police. "Drop whatever weapons you have." They lined up, even the old and the sick, and the two small children.

Kressich found himself shaking, while he was searched and after, left leaning against the corridor wall while the police muttered mysteriously among themselves. One seized him by the shoulder, faced him about. An officer with a slate walked from one to the other of them asking for ID's.

"They were stolen," Kressich said. "That's how it started. The gangs were stealing papers and burning them."

"We know that," the officer said. "Are you in charge? What's your name and origin?"

"Vassily Kressich, Russell's."

"Others of you know him?"

Several confirmed it. "He was a councillor on Russell's Station," said a young man. "I served there in security."

"Name."

The young man gave it. Nino Coledy. Kressich tried to recall him and could not. One by one the questions were repeated, cross-examination of identifications, mutual identifications, no more reliable than the word of those who gave them. A man with a camera came into the hallway and photographed them all standing against the wall. They stood in a chaos of com-chatter and discussion.

"You can go," the police leader said, and they began to file out; but when Kressich started to leave the officer caught his arm. "Vassily Kressich. I'll be giving your name to headquarters."

He was not sure whether that was good or bad; anything was a hope. Anything was better than what existed here in Q, with the station stalling and unable to place them or clear them out.

He walked out onto the dock itself, shaken by the sight of the wreckage that had been made here, with the dead still lying in their blood, piles of combustibles still smouldering, what furnishings and belongings had remained heaped up to burn. Station police were everywhere, armed with rifles, no light arms. He stayed on the docks, close to the police, afraid to go back into the corridors for fear of the terrorist gangs. It was impossible to hope the police had gotten them all. There were far too many.

Eventually the station set up an emergency dispensary for food and drink near the section line, for the water had been shut down during the emergency, the kitchens vandalized, everything turned to weapons. Com had been vandalized; there was no way to report damage; and no repair crews were likely to want to come into the area.

He sat on the bare dock and ate what they were given, in company with other small knots of refugees who had no more than he. People looked on each other in fear.

"We aren't getting out," he heard repeatedly. "They'll never clear us to leave now."

More than once he heard mutterings of a different sort, saw men he knew had been in the gangs of rioters, which had begun in his barracks, and no one reported them. No one dared. They were too many.

Unionizers were among them. He became sure that these were the agitators. Such men might have most to fear in a tight check of papers. The war had reached Pell. It was among them, and they were as stationers had always been, neutral and empty-handed, treading carefully among those who meant murder . . . only now it was not stationers against warships, metal shell against metal shell; the danger was shoulder to shoulder with them, perhaps the young man with the hoarded sandwich, the young woman who sat and stared with hateful eyes.

The convoy came in, without troops for escort. Dock crews under the protection of a small army of station police managed the unloading. Refugees were let through, processed as best could be with most of the housing wrecked, with the corridors become a jungle. The newcomers stood, baggage in hand, staring about them with terror in their eyes. They would be robbed by morning, Kressich reckoned, or worse. He heard people round him simply crying softly, despairing.

By morning there was yet another group of several hundred; and by now there was panic, for they were all hungry and thirsty and food arrived from main station very slowly.

A man settled on the deck near him: Nino Coledy.

"There's a dozen of us," Coledy said. "Could sort some of this out; been talking to some of the gang survivors. We don't give out names and they cooperate. We've got strong arms . . . could straighten this mess out, get people back into residences, so we can get some food and water in here."

"What, we?"

Coledy's face took on a grimace of earnestness. "You were a councillor. You stand up front; you do the talking. We keep you there. Get these people fed. Get ourselves a soft place here. Station needs that. We can benefit by it."

Kressich considered it. It could also get them shot. He was too old for this. They wanted a figurehead. A police gang wanted a respectable figurehead. He was also afraid to tell them no.

"You just do the talking out front," Coledy said.

"Yes," he agreed, and then, setting his jaw with more firmness than Coledy might have expected of a tired old man: "You start rounding up your men and I'll have a talk with the police."

He did so, approaching them gingerly. "There's been an election," he said. "I'm Vassily Kressich, councillor from red two, Russell's Station. Some of our own police are among the refugees. We're prepared to go into the corridors and establish order . . . without violence. We know faces. You don't. If you'll consult your own authorities and get it cleared, we can help."

They were not sure of that. There was hesitation even about calling in. Finally a police captain did so, and Kressich stood fretting. The captain nodded at last. "If it gets out of hand," the captain said, "we won't discriminate in firing. But we're not going to tolerate any killing on your part, councillor Kressich; it's not an open license."

"Have patience, sir," Kressich said, and walked away, mortally tired and frightened. Coledy was there, with several others, waiting for him by the niner corridor access. In a few moments there were more drifting to them, less savory than the first. He feared them. He feared not to have them. He cared for nothing now, except to live; and to be atop the force and not under it. He watched them go, using terror to move the innocent, gathering the dangerous into their own ranks. He knew what he had done. It terrified him. He kept silent, because he would be caught in the second riot, part of it, if it happened. *They* would see to that.

He assisted, used his dignity and his age and the fact that his face was known to some: shouted directions, began to have folk addressing him respectfully as councillor Kressich. He listened to their griefs and their fears and their angers until Coledy flung a guard about him to protect their precious figurehead.

Within the hour the docks were clear and the legitimized gangs were in control, and honest people deferred to him wherever he went.

# 7

## i
## Pell: 5/22/52

Jon Lukas settled into the council seat his son Vittorio had sat proxy for during the last three years, and sat scowling. Already he had been up against one in-family crisis: he had lost three rooms of his five-room lodging, literally sliced off by moving a partition, to accommodate two Jacoby cousins and their partners in alterday rotation, one of them with children who banged the wall and cried. His furnishings had been piled by workmen into what was left of his privacy . . . lately occupied by son Vittorio and his current affection. *That* had been a homecoming. He and Vittorio had reached a quick understanding: the woman walked out and Vittorio stayed, finding the possession of an apartment and an expense account more important, and far better than transfer to Downbelow base, which was actively seeking young volunteers. Physical labor, and on Downbelow's rainy surface, was not to Vittorio's taste. As figurehead up here he had been useful, voted as he was told, managed as he was told, had kept Lukas Company out of chaos, at least, having sense enough to solve minor problems on his own and to ask about the major ones. What he had done with the expense account was another matter. Jon had spent his time, after adjusting to station hours, down in company offices going over the books, reviewing personnel and those expense accounts.

Now there was some kind of alert on, ugly and urgent; he had come as other councillors had come, brought in by a message that a special meeting was called. His heart was still hammering from the exertion. He keyed in his desk unit and his mike, listening to the thin com chatter which occupied council at the moment, with a succession of ship scan images on the screens overhead. More trouble. He had heard it all the way up from the dockside offices. Something was coming in.

"What number do you have?" Angelo was asking, and getting no response from the other side.

"What is this?" Jon asked the woman next to him, a green sector delegate, Anna Morevy.

"More refugees coming in, and they're not saying anything. The carrier *Pacific*. Esperance Station: that's all we know. We're not getting any cooperation. But that's Sung out there. What do you expect?"

Other councillors were still arriving, the tiers filling rapidly. He slipped the personal audio into his ear, punched in the recorder, trying to get current of the situation. The convoy on scan had come in far too close for safety, above system plane. The voice of the council secretary whispered on, summarizing, offering visuals to his desk screen, none of it much more than what they had before them live.

A page worked through to the back row, leaned over his shoulder and handed him a handwritten note. *Welcome back,* he read, perplexed. *You are designated proxy to Emilio Konstantin's seat, number ten. Your immediate experience of Downbelow deemed valuable. A. Konstantin.*

His heart sped again, for a different reason. He gathered himself to his feet, laid down the earplug and turned off the channels, walked down the aisle under the view of all of them, to that vacant seat on the central council, the table amid the tiers, the seats which carried most influence. He reached that seat, settled into the fine leather and the carved wood, one of the Ten of Pell; and felt an irrepressible flush of triumph amid these events—justice done, finally, after decades. The great Konstantins had held him off and maneuvered him out of the Ten all his life, despite his strivings and his influence and his merits, and now he was here.

Not by any change of heart on Angelo's part, he was absolutely sure. It had to be voted. He had won some general vote here in council, the logical consequence of his long, tough service on Downbelow. His record had found appreciation in a council majority.

He met Angelo's eyes, down the table, Angelo holding the audio plug to his ear, looking at him still with no true welcome, no love, no happiness whatsoever. Angelo accepted his elevation because he must, that was clear. Jon smiled tightly, not with his eyes, as if it were an offer of support. Angelo returned it, and not with the eyes either.

"Put it through again," Angelo said to someone else, via com. "Keep sending. Get me contact direct to Sung."

The assembly was hushed, reports still coming in, chatter from central, the slow progress of approaching freighters; but *Pacific* was gathering speed, going into comp-projected haze on scan.

"Sung here," a voice reached them. "Salutations to Pell Station. Your own establishment can attend the details."

"What is the number you're giving us?" Angelo asked. "What number is on those ships, captain Sung?"

"Nine thousand."

A murmur of horror broke in the chamber.

"Silence!" Angelo said; it was obscuring com. "We copy, nine thousand. This will tax our facilities beyond safety. We request you meet us here in council, captain Sung. We have had refugees come in from Russell's on unescorted merchanters; we were constrained to accept them. For humanitarian reasons it is impossible to refuse such dockings. Request you inform Fleet command of this dangerous situation. We need military support, do you understand, sir? Request you come in for urgent consultation with us. We are willing to cooperate, but we are approaching a point of very difficult decision. We appeal for Fleet support. Repeat: will you come in, sir?"

There was a little silence from the other side. The council shifted in their seats, for approach alarms were flashing, screens flicking and clouding madly in their attempt to reckon with the carrier's accelerating approach.

"A last scheduled convoy," the reply came, "is coming in under Kreshov of *Atlantic* from Pan-Paris. Good luck, Pell Station."

The contact was abruptly broken. Scan flashed, the vast carrier still gathering speed more than anything should in a station's vicinity.

Jon had never seen Angelo angrier. The murmur in the council chamber deafened, and finally the microphone established relative silence again. *Pacific* shot to their zenith, disrupting the screens into breakup. When they cleared, it had passed on, to take an unauthorized course, leaving them its flotsam, the freighters moving in at their slow, inexorable pace toward dock. Somewhere there was a muted call for security to Q.

"Reserve forces," Angelo ordered one of the section chiefs over com. "Call up off-duty personnel—I don't care how many times they've had callup. Keep order in there if you have to shoot to do it. Central, scramble crews to the shuttles, herd those merchanters into the right docks. Throw a cordon of short-haulers in the way if that's what it takes."

And after a moment as the collision alarms died and there was only the steady remaining report of the freighters on their slow way toward station: "We have to get more space for Q." Angelo said, staring around him. "And with regret, we're going to have to take those two levels of red section . . . partition them in with Q—immediately." There was a sorrowful murmur from the tiers, and the screens flashed with an immediate registered objection from red-section delegates. It was perfunctory. There were no supporters on the screen to second their objection and bring it to vote. "Absolutely," Angelo continued, without even looking at it, "we can't dislodge any more residents, or lose those upper-level routings for the transport system. Can't. If we can't get support from the Fleet . . . we have to take other measures. And on a major scale, we have to start shifting population somewhere. Jon Lukas, with apologies for short notice, but we wish you could have made yesterday's meeting. That tabled proposal of yours . . . Our on-station construction can't handle security-risk workers. At one time you had plans in some detail for widening the base on Downbelow. What's the status of those?"

He blinked, suspicious and hopeful at once, frowned at the barb Angelo had to sling, even now. He gathered himself to his feet, which he did not need to do, but he wanted to see faces. "If I had received notification of the situation, I would have made every effort; as it was, I came with all possible haste. As for the proposal, by no means impossible: housing that number on Downbelow could be done in short order, with no difficulty . . . except for those housed there. The conditions . . . after three years, I can tell you . . . are primitive. Downer labor making pit housing, airtightened to a reasonable extent; enough compressors; and the simplest locally available materials for the bracing. Downer labor is always the most efficient down there; no inconvenience of breathers; but humans in great enough numbers can replace them—field work, manufacture, clearing land, digging their own dome shells. Just enough Pell staff to supervise and guard them. Confinement is no problem; particularly your more difficult cases would do well down there—you take those breathers away, and they're not going anywhere or doing anything you don't want."

"Mr. Lukas." Anton Eizel stood up, an old man, a friend of Angelo's and a stubborn do-gooder. "Mr. Lukas, I must misunderstand what I'm hearing. These are free citizens. We're not talking about establishing penal colonies. These are refugees. We're not turning Downbelow into a labor camp."

*"Tour Q!"* someone shouted from the tiers. "See what a wreck they've made out of those sections! We had homes there, beautiful homes. Vandalism and destruction. They're tearing up the place. They've attacked our security people with pipes and kitchen knives, and who knows if we got all the guns back after the riot?"

"There've been murders over there," someone else shouted. "Gangs of hoodlums."

"No," said a third, a strange voice in council. Heads turned to the thin man who had taken a seat, Jon saw, in the place he himself had vacated above. The person stood up, a nervous, sallow-faced individual. "My name is Vassily Kressich. I was invited to come out of Q. I was a councillor on Russell's Station. I represent Q. All that you say did happen, in a panic, but there's order now, and the hoodlums have been removed to your detention."

Jon drew a breath. "Welcome to councillor Kressich. But for the sake of Q itself, pressures should be relieved. Population should be transferred. The station has waited a decade on the Downbelow expansion, and now we have the manpower to begin it on a large scale. Those who work become part of the system. They build what they themselves live in. Does the gentleman from Q not agree?"

"We need our papers cleared. We refuse to be transferred anywhere without papers. This happened to us once, and look at our situation. Further transfers without clear paper can only add to our predicament, taking us further and further from any hope of establishing identity. The people I represent will not let it happen again."

"Is this a threat, Mr. Kressich?" Angelo asked.

The man looked close to collapse. "No," he said quickly. "No, sir. Only I—am speaking the opinion of the people I represent. Their desperation. They have to have their papers cleared. Anything else, any other solution is what the gentleman says—a labor camp for the benefit of Pell. Is that what you intend?"

"Mr. Kressich, Mr. Kressich," said Angelo. "Will everyone please settle themselves to take things in order. You'll be heard in your turn, Mr. Kressich. Jon Lukas, will you continue?"

"I'll have the precise figures as soon as I can have access to central comp. I need to be brought current with the keys. Every facility on Downbelow can be expanded, yes. I still have the detailed plans. I'll have a cost and labor analysis available within a matter of days."

Angelo nodded, looked at him, frowning. It could not be a pleasant moment for him.

"We're fighting for our survival." Angelo said. "Plainly, there's a point where we seriously have to worry about our life-support systems. Some of the load has to be moved. Nor can we allow the ratio of Pell citizens to refugees to become unbalanced. We have to be concerned about riot . . . there and here. Apologies, Mr. Kressich. These are the realities under which we live, not of our choosing, nor, I'm sure, of yours. We can't risk the station or the base on

Downbelow; or we find ourselves all on freighters bound for Earth, stripped of everything. That is the third choice."

"No," the murmur went around the room.

Jon sat down, silent, staring at Angelo, reckoning Pell's present fragile balance and odds as they existed. *You've lost already,* he thought of saying, of standing up in council and laying things out as they were. He did not. He sat with his mouth tightly closed. It was a matter of time. Peace . . . might afford a chance. But that was far from what was shaping out there with this influx of refugees from all these stations. They had all the Beyond flowing in two directions like a watershed, toward themselves and toward Union; and they were not equipped to handle it under Angelo's kind of rules.

Year upon year of Konstantin rule, Konstantin social theory, the vaunted "community of law" which disdained security and monitoring and now refused to use the clenched fist on Q, hoping that vocal appeals were going to win a mob over to order. He could bring that matter up too. He sat still.

There was a bad taste in his mouth, reckoning that what chaos Konstantin leniency had wrought on the station it would manage to wreak on Downbelow too. He foresaw no success for the plans he was asked for: Emilio Konstantin and his wife would be in charge of the work, two of a kind, who would let the Downers take their own time about schedules and protect their superstitions and let them do things their own leisurely, lackadaisical way, which ended with equipment damaged and construction delayed. And what that pair would do with what was over in Q offered worse prospects.

He sat still, estimating their chances, and drawing unhappy conclusions.

## ii

"It can't survive," he said to Vittorio that night, to his son Vittorio and to Dayin Jacoby, the only relative he favored. He leaned back in his chair and drank bitter Downer wine, in his apartment which was piled with the stacked expensive furniture which had been in the other, severed, rooms. "Pell's falling apart under us. Angelo's soft-handed policies are going to lose it for us, and maybe get our throats cut in riot into the bargain. It's going, you understand me? And do we sit and take what comes?"

Vittorio looked suddenly whey-faced as his habit was when talk turned serious. Dayin was of another sort. He sat grim and thoughtful.

"A contact," Jon said yet more plainly, "has to exist."

Dayin nodded. "In times like these, two doors might be a sensible necessity. And I'm sure doors exist all over this station . . . with the right keys."

"How compromised . . . do you reckon those doors are? And where? Your cousin's handled cases of some of our transients. You have any ideas?"

"Black market in rejuv drugs and others. That's in full flower here, don't you know? Konstantin himself gets it; you got it on Downbelow."

"It's legal."

"Of course it's legal; it's *necessary*. But how does it get here? Ultimately it comes from Unionside; merchanters deal; it comes through. Someone, somewhere, is into the pipeline . . . merchanters . . . maybe even station-side contacts."

"So how do we get one to get a contact back up the pipeline?"

"I can learn."

"I know one," Vittorio said, startling them both. He licked his lips, swallowed heavily. "Roseen."

"That whore of yours?"

"She knows the market. There's a security officer . . . high up. Clean paper all the way, but he's bought by the market. You want something unloaded or loaded, want a blind eye turned—he can arrange it."

Jon stared at his son, this product of a year's contract, his desperation to have an heir. It was not, after all, surprising that Vittorio knew such things. "Excellent," he said dryly. "You can tell me about it. Maybe we can trace something. Dayin, our holdings at Viking—we should look into them."

"You aren't serious."

"I'm very serious. I've engaged *Hansford*. Her crew is still in hospital. Her interior's a shambles, but she'll go. They need the money desperately. And you can find a crew . . . through those contacts of Vittorio's. Don't have to tell them everything, just sufficient to motivate them."

"Viking's the next likely trouble spot. The next certain trouble spot."

"A risk, isn't it? A lot of freighters have accidents with things as they are. Some vanish. I'll hear from Konstantin over it; but I'll have the out . . . an act of faith in Viking's future. A confirmation, a vote of confidence." He drank the wine with a twist of his mouth. "You'd better go fast, before some flood of refugees hits us from Viking itself. You make contact with the pipeline there, follow it as far as you can. What chance has Pell got now but with Union? The Company's no help. The Fleet's adding to our problem. We can't stand forever. Konstantin's policies are going to see riot here before all's done, and it's time for a changing of the guard. You'll make that clear to Union. You understand . . . they get an ally; we get . . . as much as we can get out of the association. That second door to jump through, at worst. If Pell holds, we just sit still, safe; it not, we're better off than others, aren't we?"

"And I'm the one risking my neck," Dayin said.

"So, would you rather be here when a riot finally breaks through those barriers? Or would you rather have a chance to make some personal gain with a grateful opposition . . . line your own pockets? I'm sure you will; and I'm sure you'll have deserved it."

"Generous," Dayin said sourly.

"Life here," Jon said, "isn't going to be any better. It could be very uncomfortable. It's a gamble. What isn't?"

Dayin nodded slowly. "I'll run down some prospects for a crew."

"Thought you would."

"You trust too much, Jon."

"Only this side of the family. Never Konstantins. Angelo should have left me there on Downbelow. He probably wishes he could have. But council voted otherwise; and maybe that was lucky for them. Maybe it was."

# 8

## Pell: 5/23/52

They offered a chair. They were always courteous, always called him *Mr. Talley* and never by his rank—civ habit; or maybe they made the point that here Unioners were still counted rebels and had no rank. Perhaps they hated him, but they were unfailingly gentle with him and unfailingly kind. It frightened him all the same, because he suspected it false.

They gave him more papers to fill out. A doctor sat down opposite him at the table and tried to explain the procedures in detail. "I don't want to hear that," he said. "I just want to sign the papers. I've had days of this. Isn't that enough?"

"Your tests weren't honestly taken," the doctor said. "You lied and gave false answers in the interview. Instruments indicated you were lying. Or under stress. I asked was there constraint on you and the instruments said you lied when you said there wasn't."

"Give me the pen."

"Is someone forcing you? Your answers are being recorded."

"No one's forcing me."

"This is also a lie, Mr. Talley."

"No." He tried and failed to keep his voice from shaking.

"We normally deal with criminals, who also tend to lie." The doctor held up the pen, out of easy reach. "Sometimes with the self-committed, very rarely. It's a form of suicide. You have a medical right to it, within certain legal restrictions; and so long as you've been counseled and understand what's involved. If you continue your therapy on schedule, you should begin to function again in about a month. Legal independence with six more. Full function—you understand that there may be permanent impairment to your ability to function socially; there could be other psychological or physical impairments. . . ."

He snatched the pen and signed the papers. The doctor took them and looked at them. Finally the doctor drew a paper from his pocket, pushed it across the table, a rumpled and much-folded scrap of paper.

He smoothed it out, saw a note with half a dozen signatures. *Your account in station comp has 50 credits. For anything you want on the side.* Six of the detention guards had signed it; the men and women he played cards with. Given out of their own pockets. Tears blurred his eyes.

"Want to change your mind?" the doctor asked.

He shook his head, folded the paper. "Can I keep it?"

"It will be kept along with your other effects. You'll get everything back on your release."

"It won't matter then, will it?"

"Not at that point," the doctor said, "Not for some time."

He handed the paper back.

"I'll get you a tranquilizer," the doctor said, and called for an attendant, who brought it in, a cup of blue liquid. He accepted it and drank it and felt no different for it.

The doctor pushed blank paper in front of him, and laid the pen down. "Write down your impressions of Pell. Will you do that?"

He began. He had had stranger requests in the days that they had tested him. He wrote a paragraph, how he had been questioned by the guards and finally how he felt he had been treated. The words began to grow sideways. He was not writing on the paper. He had run off the edge onto the table and couldn't find his way back. The letters wrapped around each other, tied in knots.

The doctor reached and lifted the pen from his hand, robbing him of purpose.

# 9

## i
## Pell: 5/28/52

Damon looked over the report on his desk. It was not the procedure he was used to, the martial law which existed in Q. It was rough and quick, and came across his desk with a trio of film cassettes and a stack of forms condemning five men to Adjustment.

He viewed the film, jaw clenched, the scenes of riot leaping across the large wall-screen, flinched at recorded murder. There was no question of the crime or the identification. There was, in the stack of cases which had flooded the LA office, no time for reconsiderations or niceties. They were dealing with a situation which could bring the whole station down, turn it all into the manner of thing that had come in with *Hansford.* Once life-support was threatened, once men were crazy enough to build bonfires on a station dock . . . or go for station police with kitchen knives . . .

He pulled the files in question, keyed up printout on the authorization. There was no fairness in it, for they were the five the security police had been able to pull across the line, five out of many more as guilty. But they were five who would not kill again, nor threaten the frail stability of a station containing many thousands of lives. *Total Adjustment,* he wrote, which meant personality restruct. Processing would turn up injustice if he had done one. Questioning would determine innocence if any existed at this point. He felt foul in doing what he did, and frightened. Martial law was far too sudden. His father had agonized the night long in making one such decision after a board had passed on it.

A copy went to the public defender's office. They would interview in person, lodge appeals if warranted.

That procedure too was curtailed under present circumstance. It could be done only by producing evidence of error; and evidence was in Q, unreachable. Injustices were possible. They were condemning on the word of police under attack and the viewing of film which did not show what had gone before. There were five hundred reports of theft and major crimes on his desk when before there had been a Q, they might have dealt with two or three such complaints a year. Comp was flooded with data requests. There had been days of work done on ID's and papers for Q, and all of that was scrapped. Papers had been stolen and destroyed to such an extent in Q that no paper could be trusted to be accurate. Most of the claims to paper were probably fraudulent, and loudest from the dishonest. Affidavits were worthless where threat ruled. People would swear to anything for safety. Even the ones who had come in good order were carrying paper they had no confirmation on: security confiscated cards and papers to save those from theft, and they were passing some few out where they were able to establish absolute ID and find a station-side sponsor for them—but it was slow, compared to the rate of influx; and main station had no place to put them when they did. It was madness. They tried with all their resources to eliminate red tape and hurry; and it just got worse.

"Tom," he keyed, a private note to Tom Ushant, in the defender's office, "if you get a gut feeling that something's wrong in any of these cases, appeal it back to me regardless of procedures. We're putting through too many condemnations too fast; mistakes are possible. I don't want to find one out after processing starts."

He had not expected reply. It came through. "Damon, look at the Talley file if you want something to disturb your sleep. Russell's used Adjustment."

"You mean he's *been* through it?"

"Not therapy. I mean they used it questioning him."

"I'll look at it." He keyed out, hunted the access number, pulled the file in comp display. Page after page of their own interrogation data flicked past on the screen, most of it uninformative: ship name and number, duties . . . an armscomper might know the board in front of him and what he shot at, but little more. Memories of home then . . . family killed in a Fleet raid on Cyteen system mines; a brother, killed in service—reason enough to carry grudges if a man wanted to. Reared by his mother's sister on Cyteen proper, a plantation of sorts . . . then a government school, deep-teaching for tech skills. Claimed no knowledge of higher politics, no resentments of the situation. The pages passed into actual transcript, uncondensed, disjointed ramblings . . . turned to excruciatingly personal things, the kind of intimate detail which surfaced in Adjustment, while a good deal of self was being laid bare, examined, sorted. Fear of abandonment, that deepest; fear of being a burden on his relatives, of deserving to be abandoned: he had a tangled kind of guilt about the loss of his family, had a pervading fear of it happening again, in any involvement with anyone. Loved the aunt. *Took care of me,* the thread of it ran at one point. *Held me sometimes. Held me . . . loved me.* He had not wanted to leave her home. But Union had its demands; he was supported by the state, and they took him, when he came of age. After that, it was state-run deep-teach, taped education, military training and no passes home. He had had letters from the aunt for a while; the uncle had never written. He believed the aunt was dead now, because the letters had stopped some years ago. *She would write,* he believed. *She loved me.* But there were deeper fears that she had not; that she had really wanted the state money; and there was guilt, that he had not come home; that he had deserved this parting too. He had written to the uncle and gotten no answer. That had hurt him, though he and the uncle had never loved each other. Attitudes, beliefs . . . another wound, a broken friendship; an immature love affair, another case in which letters stopped coming, and that wound involved itself with the old ones. A later attachment, to a companion in service . . . uncomfortably broken off. He tended to commit himself to a desperate extent. *Held me,* he repeated, pathetic and secret loneliness. And more things.

He began to find it. Terror of the dark. A vague, recurring nightmare: a white place. Interrogation. Drugs. Russell's had used drugs, against all Company policy, against all human rights—had wanted badly something Talley simply did not have. They had gotten him from Mariner zone—from *Mariner*—transferred to Russell's at the height of the panic. They had wanted information at that threatened station; had used Adjustment techniques in interrogation. Damon rested his mouth against his hand, watched the fragmentary record roll past, sick at his stomach. He felt ashamed at the discovery, naive. He had not questioned Russell's reports, had not investigated them himself; had had other things on his hands, and staff to take care of that matter; had not—he admitted it—wanted to deal with the case any more than he absolutely had to. Talley had never called him. Had conned him. Had held himself together, already unstrung from previous treatment, to con Pell into doing the only thing that might put an end to his mental hell. Talley had looked him straight in the eye and arranged his own suicide.

The record rambled on . . . from interrogation under drugs to chaotic evacuation, with stationer mobs on one side and the military threatening him on the other.

And what it had been, what had happened during that long voyage, a prisoner on one of Mazian's ships. . . .

*Norway* . . . and Mallory.

He killed the screen, sat staring at the stack of papers, the unfinished condemnations. After a time he set himself to work again, his fingers numb as he signed the authorizations.

Men and women had boarded at Russell's Star, folk who, like Talley, might have been sane before it all started. What had gotten off those ships, what existed over in Q . . . had been made, of folk no different than themselves.

He simply pushed the destruct on lives like Talley's, which were already gone. On men like himself, he thought, who had gone over civilized limits, in a place where civilization had stopped meaning anything.

Mazian's Fleet—even they, even the likes of Mallory—had surely started differently.

"I'm not going to challenge," Tom told him, over a lunch they both drank more than ate.

And after lunch he went to the small Adjustment facility over in red, and back into the treatment area. He saw Josh Talley. Talley did not see him, although perhaps it would not have mattered. Talley was resting at that hour, having eaten. The tray was still on the table, and he had eaten well. He sat on the bed with a curiously washed expression on his face, all the lines of strain erased.

## ii

Angelo looked up at the aide, took the report of the ship outbound and scanned the manifest, looked up. "Why *Hansford*?"

The aide shifted his weight, distressed. "Sir?"

"Two dozen ships idle and *Hansford* has a commission to launch? Unfitted? And with what crew?"

"I think crew was hired off the inactive list, sir."

Angelo leafed through the report. "Lukas Company. Viking-bound with a stripped ship and a dock-bound crew and Dayin Jacoby for a passenger? Get Jon Lukas on the com."

"Sir," the aide said, "the ship has already left dock."

"I can see the time. Get me Jon Lukas."

"Yes, sir."

The aide went out. In moments the screen on the desk went bright and Jon Lukas came on. Angelo took a deep breath, calmed himself, angled the report toward the pickup. "See that?"

"You have a question?"

"What's going on here?"

"We have holdings at Viking. Business to carry on. Shall we let our interest there sink into panic and disorder? They're due some reassurance."

"With *Hansford*?"

"We had an opportunity to engage a ship at below standard. Economics, Angelo."

"Is that all?"

"I'm not sure I take your meaning."

"She carried nothing like full cargo. What kind of commodity do you plan to pick up at Viking?"

"We carry as much as we can with *Hansford* in her present condition. She'll refit there, where facilities are less crowded. Refitting is the hire for which we got her use, if you must know. What she carries will pay the bill; she'll lade full on return, critical supplies. I'd think you'd be pleased. Dayin is aboard to supervise and to administer some business at our Viking office."

"You're not minded, are you, that this full lading include Lukas Company personnel . . . or others? You're not going to sell passage off Viking. You're not going to pull that office out."

"Ah. *That's* your concern."

"That has to be my concern when ships go out of here with no sufficient cargo to justify their moving, headed for a population we can't handle if it panics. I'm telling you, Jon, we can't take chances on some loose talk or some single company pulling its favored employees out and starting a panic on another station. You hear me?"

"I did discuss the matter with Dayin. I assure you our mission is supportive. Commerce has to continue, doesn't it, or we strangle. And before us, Viking. Stations they rely on have collapsed. Let Viking start running into shortages and they may be here in our laps with no invitation. We're taking them foodstuffs and chemicals; nothing Pell may run short of . . . and we have the only two usable holds on the ship fully loaded. Is every ship launched subject to this inquisition? I can provide you with the company books if you want to see them. I take this amiss. Whatever our private feelings, Angelo, I think Dayin deserves commendation for being willing to go out there under the circumstances. It doesn't deserve a fanfare—we asked for none—but we would have expected something other than accusations. Do you want the books, Angelo?"

"Hardly. Thank you, Jon, and my apologies. So long as Dayin and your ship's master appreciate the hazards. Every ship that launches is going to be scrutinized, yes. Nothing personal."

"Any questions you have, Angelo, so long as they're equally applied. Thank you."

"Thank you, Jon." Jon keyed out. Angelo did so, sat staring at the report, riffled through it, finally signed the authorization after the fact and dumped it into the Record tray; all the offices were running behind. Everyone. They were using too many man-hours and too much comp time on the Q processing.

"Sir." It was his secretary, Mills. "Your son, sir."

He keyed acceptance of a call, looked up in some surprise as the door opened instead and Damon walked in. "I brought the processing reports myself," Damon said. He sat down, leaned on the desk with both arms. Damon's eyes looked as tired as he himself felt, which was considerable. "I've processed five men into Adjustment this morning."

"Five men isn't a tragedy," Angelo said wearily. "I've got a lottery process set up for comp to pick who goes and stays on station. I've got another storm on Downbelow that's flooded the mill again, and they've just found the victims from the last washout. I've got ships pulling at the tether now that the panic's worn down, one that's just slipped, two more to go tomorrow. If rumor has it that Mazian's chosen Pell for a refuge, where does that leave the remaining stations? What when they panic and head here by the shipload? And how do we know that someone isn't out there right now, selling passage to more frightened people? Our life-support won't take much more." He gestured loosely toward a stack of documents. "We're going to militarize what freighters we can, by some pretty strong financial coercion."

"To fire on refugee ships?"

"If ships come in that we can't handle—yes. I'd like to talk to Elene sometime today; she'd be the one to make the initial approach to the merchanters. I can't muster sympathy for five rioters today. Forgive me."

His voice cracked. Damon reached across the desk, caught his wrist and pressed it, let it go again. "Emilio needs help down there?"

"He says not. The mill's a shambles. Mud everywhere."

"They find all of them dead?"

He nodded. "Last night. Bennett Jacint and Ty Brown; Wes Kyle yesterday noon . . . this long, to hunt the banks and the reeds. Emilio and Miliko say morale is all right, considering. The Downers are building dikes. More of them have been anxious for human trade; I've ordered more let into base and I've authorized some of the trained ones into maintenance up here: *their* life-support is in good shape, and it frees up some techs we can upgrade. I'm shuttling down every human volunteer who'll go, and that means even trained dock hands; they can handle construction equipment. Or they can learn. It's a new age. A tighter one." He pressed his lips together, sucked in a long breath. "Have you and Elene thought of Earth?"

"Sir?"

"You, your brother, Elene and Miliko—think about it, will you?"

"No," Damon said. "Pull out and run? You think that's what it's coming to?"

"Figure the odds, Damon. We didn't get help from Earth, just observers. They're figuring on cutting their losses, not sending us reinforcements or ships. No. We're just settling lower and lower. Mazian can't hold forever. The shipyards at Mariner . . . were vital. It's Viking soon; and whatever else Union reaches out to take. Union's cutting the Fleet off from supply; Earth already has. We're out of everything but room to run."

"The Hinder Stars—you know there's some talk about reopening one of those stations—"

"A dream. We'd never have the chance. If the Fleet goes . . . Union would make it a target, same as us, just as quickly. And selfishly, completely selfishly, I'd like to see my children out of here."

Damon's face was very white. "No. Absolutely no."

"Don't be noble. I'd rather your safety than your help. Konstantins won't fare well in years to come. It's mindwipe if they take us. You worry about your criminals; consider yourself and Elene. That's Union's solution . . . puppets in the offices; lab-born populations to fill up the world . . . they'll plow up Downbelow and build. Heaven help the Downers. I'd cooperate with them . . . so would you . . . to keep Pell safe from the worst excesses; but they won't have things that easy way. And I don't want to see you in their hands. We're targets. I've lived all my life in that condition. Surely it's not asking too much that I do one selfish thing—that I save my sons."

"What did Emilio say?"

"Emilio and I are still discussing it."

"He told you no. Well, so do I."

"Your mother will have a word with you."

"Are you sending her?"

Angelo frowned. "You know that's not possible."

"So. I know that. And I'm not going, and I don't think Emilio will choose to either. My blessing to him if he does, but I'm not."

"Then you don't know anything," Angelo said shortly. "We'll talk about it later."

"We won't," Damon said. "If *we* pulled out, panic would set in here. You know that. You know how it would look, besides that I won't do it in the first place."

It was true; he knew that it was.

"No," Damon said again, and laid his hand atop his father's, rose and left.

Angelo sat, looked toward the wall, toward the portraits which stood on the shelf, a succession of tridee figures . . . Alicia before her accident; young Alicia and himself; a succession of Damons and Emilios from infancy to manhood, to wives and hopes of grandchildren. He looked at all the figures assembled there, at all the gathered ages of them, and reckoned that the good days hereafter would be fewer.

After a fashion he was angry with his boys; and after another . . . proud. He had brought them up what they were.

*Emilio,* he wrote to the succession of images, and the son on Downbelow, *your brother sends his love. Send me what skilled Downers you can spare. I'm sending you a thousand volunteers from the station; go ahead with the new base if they have to backpack equipment in. Appeal to the Downers for help, trade for native foodstuffs. All love.*

And to security: *Process out the assuredly nonviolent. We're going to shift them to Downbelow as volunteers.*

He reckoned, even as he did it, where that led; the worst would stay on station, next the heart and brain of Pell. Transfer the outlaws down and keep the heel on them; some kept urging it. But fragile agreements with the natives, fragile self-respect for the techs who had been persuaded to go down there in the mud and the primitive conditions . . . it could not be turned into a penal colony. It was life. It was the body of Pell, and he refused to violate it, to ruin all the dreams they had had for its future.

There were dark hours when he thought of arranging an accident in which all of Q might decompress. It was an unspeakable idea, a madman's solution, to kill thousands of innocent along with the undesirables . . . to take in these shiploads one after the other, and have accident after accident, keeping Pell free of the burden, keeping Pell what it was. Damon lost sleep over five men. He had begun to meditate on utter horror.

For that reason too he wanted his sons gone from Pell. He thought sometimes that he might actually be capable of applying the measures some urged, that it was weakness that prevented him, that he was endangering what was good and whole to save a polluted rabble, out of which reports of rape and murder came daily.

Then he considered where it led, and what kind of life they all faced when they had made a police state of Pell, and recoiled from it with all the convictions Pell had ever had.

"Sir," a voice cut in, with the sharper tone of transmissions from central. "Sir, we have inbound traffic."

"Give it here," he said, and swallowed heavily as the schematic reached his screen. Nine of them. "Who are they?"

"The carrier *Atlantic,*" the voice of central returned. "Sir, they have eight freighters in convoy. They ask to dock. They advise of dangerous conditions aboard."

"Denied," Angelo said. "Not till we get an understanding." They could not take so many; could not; not another lot like Mallory's. His heart sped, hurting him. "Get me Kreshov on *Atlantic*. Get me contact."

Contact was refused from the other end. The warship would do as it pleased. There was nothing they could do to prevent it.

The convoy moved in, silent, ominous with the load it bore, and he reached for the alert for security.

## iii
## Downbelow: main base: 5/28/52

The rain still came down, the thunder dying. Tam-utsa-pitan watched the humans come and go, arms locked about her knees, her bare feet sunk in mire, the water trickling slowly off her fur. Much that humans did made no sense; much that humans made was of no visible use, perhaps for the gods, perhaps that they were mad; but graves . . . this sad thing the hisa understood. Tears, shed behind masks, the hisa understood. She watched, rocking slightly, until the last humans had gone, leaving only the mud and the rain in this place where humans laid their dead.

And in due time she gathered herself to her feet and walked to the place of cylinders and graves, her bare toes squelching in the mud. They had put the earth over Bennett Jacint and the two others. The rain made of the place one large lake, but she had watched; she knew nothing of the marks humans made for signs to themselves, but she knew the one.

She carried a tall stick with her, which Old One had made. She came naked in the rain, but for the beads and the skins which she bore on a string about her shoulder. She stopped above the grave, took the stick in both her hands and drove it hard into the soft mud; the spirit-face she slanted so that it looked up as much as possible, and about its projections she hung the beads and the skins, arranging them with care, despite the rain which sheeted down.

Steps sounded near her in the puddles, the hiss of human breath. She spun and leapt aside, appalled that a human had surprised her ears, and stared into a breather-masked face.

"What are you doing?" the man demanded.

She straightened, wiped her muddy hands on her thighs. To be naked thus embarrassed her, for it upset humans. She had no answer for a human. He looked at the spirit-stick, at the grave offerings . . . at her. What she could see of his face seemed less angry than his voice had promised.

"Bennett?" the man asked of her.

She bobbed a yes, distressed still. Tears filled her eyes, to hear the name, but the rain washed them away. Anger . . . that too she felt, that Bennett should die and not others.

"I'm Emilio Konstantin," he said, and she stood straight at once, relaxed out of her fight-flight tenseness. "Thank you for Bennett Jacint; he would thank you."

"Konstantin-man." She amended all her manner and touched him, this very tall one of a tall kind. "Love Bennett-man, all love Bennett-man. Good man. Say he friend. All Downers are sad." He put a hand on her shoulder, this tall Konstantin-man, and she turned and put her arm about him and her head against his chest, hugged him solemnly, about the wet, awful-feeling yellow clothes. "Good Bennett make Lukas mad. Good friend for Downers. Too bad he gone. Too, too bad, Konstantin-man."

"I've heard," he said. "I've heard how it was here."

"Konstantin-man good friend." She lifted her face at his touch, looked fearlessly into the strange mask which made him very horrible to see. "Love good mans. Downers work hard, work hard, hard for Konstantin. Give you gifts. Go no more away."

She meant it. They had learned how Lukases were. It was said in all the camp that they should do good for the Konstantins, who had always been the best humans, gift-bringers more than the hisa could give.

"What's your name?" he asked, stroking her cheek. "What do we call you?"

She grinned suddenly, warm in his kindness, stroked her own sleek hide, which was her vanity, wet as it was now. "Humans call me Satin," she said, and laughed, for her true name was her own, a hisa thing, but Bennett had given her this, for her vanity, this and a bright bit of red cloth, which she had worn to rags and still treasured among her spirit-gifts.

"Will you walk back with me?" he asked, meaning to the human camp. "I'd like to talk with you."

She was tempted, for this meant favor. And then she sadly thought of duty and pulled away, folded her arms, dejected at the loss of love. "I sit," she said.

"With Bennett."

"Make he spirit look at the sky," she said, showing the spirit-stick, explaining a thing the hisa did not explain. "Look at he home."

"Come tomorrow," he said. "I need to talk to the hisa."

She tilted back her head, looked at him in startlement. Few humans called them what they were. It was strange to hear it. "Bring others?"

"All the high ones if they will come. We need hisa Upabove, good hands, good work. We need trade Downbelow, place for more men."

She extended her hand toward the hills and the open plain, which went on forever.

"There is place."

"But the high ones would have to say."

She laughed. "Say spirit-things. I-Satin give this to Konstantin-man. All ours. I give, you take. All trade, much good things; all happy."

"Come tomorrow," he said, and walked away, a tall strange figure in the slanting rain. Satin-Tam-utsa-pitan sat down on her heels with the rain beating upon her bowed back and pouring over her body, and regarded the grave, with the rain making pocked puddles above it.

She waited. Eventually others came, less accustomed to men. Dalut-hos-me was one such, who did not share her optimism of them; but even he had loved Bennett.

There were men and men. This much the hisa had learned.

She leaned against Dalut-hos-me, Sun-shining-through-clouds, in the dark evening of their long watch, and by this gesture pleased him. He had begun laying gifts before her mat in this winter season, hoping for spring.

"The want hisa Upabove," she said. "I want to see the Upabove. I want this."

She had always wanted it, from the time that she had heard Bennett talk of it. From this place came Konstantins (and Lukases, but she dismissed that thought). She reckoned it as bright and full of gifts and good things as all the ships which came down from it, bringing them goods and good ideas. Bennett had told them of a great metal place holding out arms to the Sun, to drink his power, where ships vaster than they had ever imagined came and went like giants.

All things flowed to this place and from it; and Bennett had gone away now, making a Time in her life under the Sun. It was a manner of pilgrimage, this journey she desired to mark this Time, like going to the images of the plain, like the sleep-night in the shadow of the images.

They had given humans images for the Upabove too, to watch there. It was fit, to call it pilgrimage. And the Time regarded Bennett, who came from that journey.

"Why do you tell me?" Dalut-hos-me asked.

"My spring will be there, on Upabove."

He nestled closer. She could feel his heat. His arm went about her. "I will go," he said.

It was cruel, but the desire was on her for her first traveling; and his was on him, for her, would grow, as gray winter passed and they began to think toward spring, toward warm winds and the breaking of the clouds. And Bennett, cold in the ground, would have laughed his strange human laughter and bidden them be happy.

So always the hisa wandered, of springs, and the nesting.

## iv

## Pell: sector blue five: 5/28/52

It was frozen dinner again. Neither of them had gotten in till late, numb with the stresses of the day—more refugees, more chaos. Damon ate, looked up finally realizing his self-absorbed silence, found Elene sunk in one of her own . . . a habit, lately, between them. He was disturbed to think of that, and reached across the table to lay his hand on hers, which rested beside her plate. Her hand turned, curled up to weave with his. She looked as tired as he. She had been working too long hours—more than today. It was a remedy of sorts . . . not to think. She never spoke of *Estelle.* She did not speak much at all. Perhaps, he thought, she was so much at work there was little to say.

"I saw Talley today," he said hoarsely, seeking to fill the silence, to distract her, however grim the topic. "He seemed . . . quiet. No pain. No pain at all."

Her hand tightened. "Then you did right by him after all, didn't you?"

"I don't know. I don't think there is a way to know."

"He asked."

"He asked," he echoed.

"You did all you could to be right. That's all you can do."

"I love you."

She smiled. Her lips trembled until they could no longer hold the smile.

"Elene?"

She drew back her hand. "Do you think we're going to hold Pell?"

"Are you afraid not?"

"I'm afraid you don't believe it."

"What kind of reasoning is that?"

"Things you won't discuss with me."

"Don't give me riddles. I'm not good at them. I never was."

"I want a child. I'm not on the treatment now. I think you still are."

Heat rose to his face. For half a heartbeat he thought of lying. "I am. I didn't think it was time to discuss it. Not yet."

She pressed her lips tightly together, distraught.

"I don't know what you want," he said. "I don't know. If Elene Quen wants a baby, all right. Ask. It's all right. Anything is. But I'd hoped it would be for reasons I'd know."

"I don't know what you're talking about."

"You've done a lot of thinking. I've watched you. But you haven't done any of it aloud. What do you want?

What do I do? Get you pregnant and let you go? I'd help you if I knew how. What do I say?"

"I don't want to fight. I don't want a fight. I told you what I want."

*"Why?"*

She shrugged. "I don't want to wait anymore." Her brow furrowed. For the first time in days he had the feeling of contact with her eyes. Of Elene, as she was. Of something gentle. "You care," she said. "I see that."

"Sometimes I know I don't hear all you say."

"On ship . . . it's my business, having a child or not. Ship family is closer in some things and further apart in others. But you with your own family . . . I understand that. I respect it."

"Your home too. It's yours."

She managed the faintest of smiles, an offering, perhaps. "So what do you say to it?"

Offices of station planning were giving out dire warnings, advice otherwise, *pleadings* otherwise. It was not only the establishment of Q. There was the war, getting nearer. All rules applied to Konstantins first.

He simply nodded. "So we're through waiting."

It was like a shadow lifting. *Estelle*'s ghost fled the place, the small apartment they had drawn in blue five, which was smaller, into which their furnishings did not fit, where everything was out of order. It was all at once home, the hall with the dishes stowed in the clothing lockers and the living room which was bedroom by night, with boxes lashed in the corner, Downer wickerwork, with what should have gone into the hall lockers.

They lay in the bed that was the daytime couch. And she talked, lying in his arms, for the first time in weeks talked, late into the night, a flow of memories she had never shared with him, in all their being together.

He tried to reckon what she had lost in *Estelle:* her ship; she still called it that. Brotherhood, kinship. Merchanter morals, the stationer proverb ran; but he could not see Elene among the others, like them, rowdy merchanters offship for a dockside binge and a sleepover with anyone willing. Could never believe that.

"Believe it," she said, her breath stirring against his shoulder. "That's the way we live. What do you want instead? In-breeding? They were my cousins on that ship."

"You were different," he insisted. He remembered her as he had first seen her, in his office on a matter involving a cousin's troubles . . . always quieter than the others. A conversation, a re-meeting; another; a second voyage . . . and Pell again. She had never gone bar-haunting with her cousins, had not made the merchanter hangouts; had come to him, had spent those days on station with him. Failed to board again. Merchanters rarely married. Elene had.

"No," she said, "*You* were different."

"You'd take anyone's baby?" The thought troubled him. Some things he had never asked Elene because he thought he knew. And Elene had never talked that way. He began, belatedly, to revise all he thought he knew; to be hurt, and to fight that. She was Elene; that quantity he still believed in, trusted.

"Where else could we get them?" she asked, making strange, clear sense. "We love them, do you think not? They belong to the whole ship. Only now there aren't any." She could talk of that suddenly. He felt the tension ebb, a sigh against him. "They're all gone."

"You called Elt Quen your father; Tia James your mother. Was it that way?"

"He was. She knew." And a moment later. "She left a station to go with him. Not many will."

She had never asked him to. That thought had never clearly occurred to him. Ask a Konstantin to leave Pell . . . he asked himself if he would have, and felt a deep unease. *I would have,* he insisted. *I might have.* "It would be hard," he admitted aloud. "It was hard for you."

She nodded, a movement against his arm.

"Are you sorry, Elene?"

A small shake of her head.

"It's late to talk about things like this," he said. "I wish we had. I wish we'd known enough to talk to each other. So many things we didn't know."

"It bother you?"

He hugged her against him, kissed her through a veil of hair, brushed it aside. He thought for a moment of saying no, decided then to say nothing. "You've seen Pell. You realize I've never set foot on a ship bigger than a shuttle? Never been out from this station? Some things I don't know how to look at, or even how to imagine the question. You understand me?"

"Some things I don't know how to ask you either."

"What would you ask for?"

"I just did."

"I don't know how to say yes or no. Elene, I don't know if I could have left Pell. I *love* you, but I don't know that I could have done that—after so short a time. And that bothers me. *That* bothers me, if it's something in me that it never occurred to me . . . that I spent all my planning trying to think how to make you happy on Pell . . ."

"Easier for me to stay a time . . . than for a Konstantin to uproot himself from Pell; pausing's easy, we do it all the time. Only losing *Estelle* I never planned. Like what's out there, you never planned. You've answered me."

"How did I answer you?"

"By what it is that bothers you."

That puzzled him. *We do it all the time.* That frightened him. But she talked more, lying against him, about more than things . . . deep feelings; the way childhood was for a merchanter; the first time she had set foot on a station, aged twelve and frightened by rude stationers who assumed any merchanter was fair game. How a cousin had died on Mariner years back, knifed in a stationer quarrel, not even comprehending a stationer's jealousy that had killed him.

And an incredible thing . . . that in the loss of her ship, Elene's pride had suffered; *pride* . . . the idea set him back, so that for some time he lay staring at the dark ceiling, thinking about it.

The *name* was diminished . . . a possession like the ship. Someone had diminished it and too anonymously to give her an enemy to get it back from. For a moment he thought of Mallory, the hard arrogance of an elite breed, the aristocracy of privilege. Sealed worlds and a law unto itself, where no one had property, and everyone had it: the ship and all who belonged to it. Merchanters who would spit in a dockmaster's eye made grumbling retreat when a Mallory or a Quen ordered it. She felt grief at losing *Estelle*. That had to be. But shame too . . . that she had not been there when it mattered. That Pell had set her in the dockside offices where she could use that reputation the Quens had; but now there was nothing at her back, nothing but the reputation she had not been there to pay for. A dead name. A dead ship. Maybe she detected pity from other merchanters. That would be bitterest of all.

One thing she had asked of him. He had cheated her of it without discussing it. Without seeing.

"The first child," he murmured, turning his head on the pillow to look at her, "goes by Quen. You hear me, Elene? Pell has Konstantins enough. My father may sulk; but he'll understand. My mother will. I think it's important it be that way."

She began to cry, as she had never cried in his presence, not without resisting it. She put her arms about him and stayed there, till morning.

# 10

## Viking station: 6/5/52

Viking hung in view, agleam in the light of an angry star. Mining, industry regarding metals and minerals . . . that was its support. Segust Ayres watched, from the vantage of the freighter's bridge, the image on the screens.

And something was wrong. The bridge whispered with alarm passed from station to station, frowns on faces and troubled looks. Ayres glanced at his three companions. They had caught it too, stood uneasily, all of them trying to keep out of the way of procedures that had officers darting from this station to that to supervise.

Another ship was coming in with them. Ayres knew enough to interpret that. It moved up until it was visual on the screens, and ships were not supposed to ride that close, not at this distance from station; it was big, many-vaned.

"It's in our lane," delegate Marsh said.

The ship moved closer still to them, and the merchanter captain rose from his place, walked across to them. "We have trouble," he said. "We're being escorted in. I don't recognize the ship that's riding us. It's military. Frankly, I don't think we're in Company space anymore."

"Are you going to break and run?" Ayres asked.

"No. You may order it, but we're not about to do it. You don't understand the way of things. It's wide space. Sometimes ships get surprises. Something's happened here. We've wandered into it. I'm sending a steady no-fire. We'll go in peaceably. And if we're lucky, they'll let us go again."

"You think Union is here."

"There's only them and us, sir."

"And *our* situation?'"

"Very uncomfortable, sir. But those are the chances you took. I won't give odds you people won't be detained. No, sir. Sorry."

Marsh started to protest. Ayres put out a hand. "No. I'd suggest we go have a drink in the main room and simply wait it out. We'll talk about it."

Guns made Ayres nervous. Marched by rifle-carrying juveniles across a dock much the same as Pell's, crowded into a lift with them, these too-same young revolutionaries, he felt a certain shortness of breath and worried for his companions, who were still under guard near the ship's berth. All the soldiers he had seen in crossing the Viking dock were of the same stamp, green coveralls for a uniform, a sea of green on that dockside, overwhelming the few civilians visible. Guns everywhere. And emptiness, along the upward curve of the docks beyond, deserted distances. There were not enough people. Far from the number of residents who had been at Pell, in spite of the fact that there were freighters docked all about Viking Station. Trapped, he surmised; merchanters perhaps dealt with courteously enough—the soldiers who had boarded their own ship had been coldly courteous—but it was a good bet that ship was not going to be leaving.

Not the ship that had brought them in, not any of the others out there.

The lift stopped on some upper level. "Out," the young captain said, and ordered him left down the hall with a wave of the rifle barrel. The officer was no more than eighteen at most. Crop-headed, male and female, they all looked the same age. They spilled out before and after him, more guards than a man of his age and physical condition warranted. The corridor leading to windowed offices ahead of them was lined with more such, rifles all fixed at a precise attitude. All eighteen or thereabouts, all with close-clipped hair, all—

—attractive. That was what urged at his attention. There was an uncommon, fresh-faced pleasantness about them, as if beauty were dead, as if there were no more distinction of the plain and the lovely. In that company, a scar, a disfigurement of any kind, would have stood out as bizarre. There was no place for the ordinary among them. Male and female, the proportions were all within a certain tolerance, all similar, though they varied in color and features. Like mannequins. He remembered *Norway*'s scarred troops, and *Norway*'s gray-haired captain, the disrepute of their equipment, the manner of them, who seemed to know no discipline. Dirt. Scars. Age. There was no such taint on these. No such imprecision.

He shuddered inwardly, felt cold gathered at his belly as he walked in among the mannequins, into offices, and further, into another chamber and before a table where sat older men and women. He was relieved to see gray hair and blemishes and overweight, deliriously relieved.

"Mr. Ayres," A mannequin announced him, rifle in hand. "Company delegate." The mannequin advanced to lay his confiscated credentials on the desk in front of the central figure, a heavy-bodied woman, gray-haired. She leafed through them, lifted her head with a slight frown. "Mr. Ayres . . . Ines Andilin," she said. "A sorry surprise for you, isn't it? But such things happen. You'll now give us a Company reprimand for seizing your ship? Feel free to do so."

"No, citizen Andilin. It was, in fact, a surprise, but hardly devastating. I came to see what I might see and I have seen plenty."

"And what have you seen, citizen Ayres?"

"Citizen Andilin." He walked forward a few paces, as far as the anxious faces and sudden movement of rifles would allow. "I'm second secretary to the Security Council on Earth. My companions are of the Earth Company's highest levels. Our inspection of the situation has shown us disorder and a militarism in the Company Fleet which has passed all limit of Company responsibility. We are dismayed at what we find. We disown Mazian; we do not wish to hold any territories in which the citizens have determined they wish to be otherwise governed; we are anxious to be quit of a burdensome conflict and an unprofitable venture. You know well enough that you possess this territory. The line is stretched too thin; we can't possibly enforce what residents of the Beyond don't want; and in fact, why should we be interested to do so? We don't regard this meeting at this station as a disaster. We were, in fact, looking for you."

There was a settling in the council, a perplexity on their faces.

"We are prepared," Ayres said in a loud voice, "to cede formally all the disputed territories. We frankly have no further interest beyond present limits. The star-faring arm of the Company is dissolved by vote of the Company directorates; the sole interest we have now is to see to our orderly disengagement—our withdrawal—and the establishment of a firm border which will give us both reasonable latitude."

Heads bent. The council murmured together, one way and the other. Even the mannequins about the edges of the chamber seemed disturbed.

"We are a local authority," said Andilin at last. "You'll have opportunity to carry your offers higher. Can you leash the Mazianni and guarantee our security?"

Ayres drew in his breath. "Mazian's Fleet? No, if his captains are an example."

"You're in from Pell."

"Yes."

"And claim experience with Mazian's captains, do you?"

He blanked for the instant . . . was not accustomed to such slips. Neither was he accustomed to distances over which such comings and goings would be news. But the merchanters, he reasoned at once, would know and tell as much as he could. Withholding information was more than pointless; it was dangerous. "I met," he confessed, "with *Norway*'s captain, one Mallory."

Andilin's head inclined solemnly. "Signy Mallory. A unique privilege."

"None to me. The Company refuses responsibility for *Norway*."

"Disorder, mismanagement; denial of responsibility . . . and yet Pell is well reputed for order. I am amazed at your report. What happened there?"

"I do not serve as your intelligence."

"You do, however, disown Mazian and the Fleet. This is a radical step."

"I don't disown the safety of Pell. That's our territory."

"Then you are not prepared to cede *all* the disputed territories."

"By disputed territories, of course, we mean those starting with Fargone."

"Ah. And what is your price, citizen Ayres?"

"An orderly transition of power, certain agreements assuring the safeguarding of our interests."

Andilin's face relaxed in laughter. "You seek a treaty with *us*. You throw aside your own forces, and seek a treaty with *us*."

"A reasonable solution to a mutual difficulty. Ten years since the last reliable report out of the Beyond. Many more years than that with a fleet out of our control, refusing our direction, in a war which consumes what could be a mutually profitable trade. *That* is what brings us here."

There was deathly silence in the room.

At last Andilin nodded, her chins doubling. "Mr. Ayres, we shall wrap you in cotton wool and hand you on most gently, most, most gently, to Cyteen. With great hope that at last someone on Earth has come to his senses. A last question, rephrased. Was Mallory alone at Pell?"

"I can't answer."

"You have not yet disowned the Fleet, then."

"I retain that option in negotiations."

Andilin pursed her lips. "You need not worry about giving us critical information. The merchanters will deny us nothing. Were it possible for you to restrain the Mazianni from their immediate maneuvers, I would suggest you try. I'd suggest that to demonstrate the seriousness of your proposal . . . you at least make a token gesture toward that restaint during negotiations."

"We cannot control Mazian."

"You know that you will lose," said Andilin. "In fact, that

you have already lost, and you're attempting to hand us what we have already won . . . and get concessions for it."

"There's little interest for us in pursuing hostilities, win or lose. It seems to us that our original object was to make sure the stars were a viable commercial venture; and you patently are viable. You have an economy worth trading with, in a different kind of economic relationship from what we had before, saving us the entanglements with the Beyond we don't want. We can agree on a route, a meeting point where your ships and ours can come and go as a matter of common right. What you do on your side doesn't interest us; direct the development of the Beyond as you like. Likewise we will be withdrawing some jump freighters home for the commencement of that trade. If we can possibly secure some restraint on Conrad Mazian, we'll recall those ships as well. I'm being very blunt with you. The interests we pursue are so far from each other, there's no sane reason to continue hostilities. You're being recognized in all points as the legitimate government of the outer colonies. I am the negotiator and the interim ambassador if the negotiations are successful. We don't consider it defeat, if the will of the majority of the colonies has supported you; the fact that you are the government in these regions is persuasive of that fact. We extend you formal recognition from the new administration which has taken charge in our own affairs . . . a situation I will explain further to your central authorities; and we are prepared to open trade negotiations at the same time. All military operations within our power to control will be stopped. Unfortunately . . . it isn't within our power to stop them, only to withdraw support and approval."

"I am a regional administrator, a step removed from our central directorate, but I don't think, *ambassador* Ayres, that the directorate will have any hesitancy in opening discussion on these matters. At least, as a regional administrator sees things, this is the case. I extend you a cordial welcome."

"Haste—will save lives."

"Haste indeed. These troops will conduct you to a safe lodging. Your companions will join you."

"Arrest?"

"Absolutely the contrary. The station is newly taken and insecure as yet. We want to be sure no hazard confronts you. Cotton wool, Mr. Ambassador. Walk where you will, but with a security escort at all times; and by my earnest advice, rest. You'll be shipping out as soon as a vessel can be cleared. It's even uncertain whether you'll have a night's sleep before that departure. You agree, sir?"

"Agreed," he said, and Andilin called the young officer over and spoke to him. The officer gestured, with his hand this time; he took his leave with nods of courtesy from all the table, walked out, with a cold feeling at his back.

Practicalities, he reckoned. He did not like the look of what he saw, the too-alike guards, the coldness everywhere. Security Council on Earth had not seen such things when it gave its orders and laid its plans. The lack of intermediate Earthward stations, since the dismantling of the Hinder Star bases, made the spread of the war logistically unlikely, but Mazian had failed to prevent it from spreading all across the Beyond . . . had aggravated the situation, escalated hostilities to dangerous levels. The sudden prospect of having Mazian's forces reactivate those Hinder Star stations in a retrenching action behind Pell turned him sick with the mere contemplation of the possibilities.

The Isolationists had had their way . . . too long. Now there were bitter decisions to be taken . . . reapproachment to this thing called Union; agreements, borders, barriers . . . containment.

If the line were not held, disaster loomed . . . the possibility of having Union itself activating those abandoned Earthward stations, convenient bases. There was a fleet building at Sol Station; it had to have time. Mazian was fodder for Union guns until then. Sol itself had to be in command of the next resistance, Sol, and not the headless thing the Company Fleet had become, refusing Company orders, doing as they would.

Most of all they had to keep Pell, had to keep that one base.

Ayres walked where he was led, settled into the apartment they gave him several levels down, which was excellent in comforts, and the comfort reassured him. He forced himself to sit and appear relaxed to await his companions, that they assured him would come . . . and they did come finally, in a group and unnerved by their situation. Ayres thrust their escort out, closed the door, made a shifting of his eyes toward the peripheries of the compartment, silent warning against free speech. The others, Ted Marsh, Karl Bela, Ramona Dias, understood, and said nothing, as he hoped they had not spoken their minds elsewhere.

Someone on Viking Station, a freighter crew, was in great difficulty, he had no doubt. Supposedly merchanters were able to pass the battle lines, with no worse than occasional shepherding to different ports than they had planned; or sometimes, if it was one of Mazian's ships that stopped them, confiscation of part of the cargo or a man or woman of the crew. The merchanters lived with it. And the merchanters who had brought them to Viking would survive detention until what they had seen at Pell and here ceased to be of military value. He hoped for their sakes that this was the case. He could do nothing for them.

He did not sleep well that night, and before morning of mainday, as Andilin had warned him, they were roused out of bed to take ship further into Union territory. They were promised their destination was Cyteen, the center of the rebel command. It was begun. There was no retreat.

# 11

## Pell: Detention; red sector: 6/27/52

*He* was back. Josh Talley looked at the window of his room and met the face which was so often there . . . remembered, after the vague fashion in which he remembered anything recent, that he had known this man, and that this man was part of all that had happened to him. He met the eyes this time and, feeling more of definite curiosity than he was wont, moved from his cot, walking with difficulty, for the general weakness of his limbs—

advanced to the window and confronted the young man at closer range. He put out his hand to the window, wishing, for others kept far from him, and he lived entirely in white limbo, where all things were suspended, where touch was not keen and tastes all bland, where words came at distance. He drifted in this whiteness, detached and isolated.

*Come out,* his doctors told him. *Come out whenever you feel inclined. The world is out here. You can come when you're ready.*

It was a womblike safety. He grew stronger in it. Once he had lain on his cot, disinclined even to move, leaden-limbed and weary. He was much, much stronger; he could feel moved to rise and investigate this stranger. He grew brave again. For the first time he knew that he was getting well, and that made him braver still.

The man behind the pane moved, reached out his hand, matched it to his on the window, and his numbed nerves tingled with excitement, expecting touch, expecting the numb sensation of another hand. The universe existed beyond a sheet of plastic, all there to touch, unfelt, insulated, cut off. He was hypnotized by this revelation. He stared into dark eyes and a lean young face, of a man in a brown suit; and wondered was it he, himself, as he was outside the womb, that hands matched so perfectly, touching and not touched.

But he wore white, and it was no mirror.

Nor was it his face. He dimly remembered his own face, but it was a boy his memory saw, an old picture of himself: he could not recover the man. It was not a boy's hand that he reached out; not a boy's hand that reached back to him, independent of his willing it. A great deal had happened to him and he could not put it all together. Did not want to. He remembered fear.

The face behind the window smiled at him, a faint, kindly smile. He gave it back, reached with his other hand to touch the face as well, barriered by cold plastic.

"Come out," a voice said from the wall. He remembered that he could. He hesitated, but the stranger kept inviting him. He saw the lips move with the sound which came from elsewhere.

And cautiously he moved to the door which was always, they said, open when he wanted it.

It did open to him. Of a sudden he must face the universe without safety. He saw the man standing there, staring back at him; and if he touched, it would be cold plastic; and if the man should frown there was no hiding.

"Josh Talley," the young man said, "I'm Damon Konstantin. Do you remember me at all?"

*Konstantin.* The name was a powerful one. It meant Pell, and power. What else it had meant would not come to him, save that once they had been enemies, and were no longer. It was all wiped clean, all forgiven. *Josh Talley.* The man knew him. He felt personally obligated to remember this Damon and could not. It embarrassed him.

"How are you feeling?" Damon asked.

That was complicated. He tried to summarize and could not; it required associating his thoughts, and his strayed in all directions at once.

"Do you want anything?" Damon asked.

"Pudding," he said. "With fruit." That was his favorite. He had it every meal but breakfast; they gave him what he asked for.

"What about books? Would you like some books?"

He had not been offered that. "Yes," he said, brightening with the memory that he had loved books. "Thank you."

"Do you remember me?" Damon asked.

Josh shook his head. "I'm sorry," he said miserably. "We've probably met, but, you see, I don't remember things clearly. I think we must have met after I came here."

"It's natural you'd forget. They tell me you're doing very well. I've been here several times to see about you."

"I remember."

"Do you? When you get well I want you to come to my apartment for a visit sometime. My wife and I would like that."

He considered it and the universe widened, doubling, multiplying itself so that he was not sure of his footing. "Do I know her too?"

"No. But she knows about you. I've talked to her about you. She says she wants you to come."

"What's her name?"

"Elene. Elene Quen."

He repeated it with his lips, not to let it leave him. It was a merchanter name. He had not thought of ships. Now he did. Remembered dark, and stars. He stared fixedly at Damon's face, not to lose contact with it, this point of reality in a shifting white world. He might blink and be alone again. He might wake in his room, in his bed, and not have any of this to hold onto. He clenched his mind about it with all his strength. "You'll come again," he said, "even if I forget. Please come and remind me."

"You'll remember," Damon said. "But I'll come if you don't."

Josh wept, which he did easily and often, the tears sliding down his face, a mere outwelling of emotion, not of grief, or joy, only profound relief. A cleansing.

"Are you all right?" Damon asked.

"I'm tired," he said, for his legs were weak from standing, and he knew he should go back to his bed before he became dizzy. "Will you come in?"

"I have to stay in this area," Damon said. "I'll send you the books, though."

He had forgotten the books already. He nodded, pleased and embarrassed at once.

"Go back," Damon said, releasing him. Josh turned and walked back inside.

The door closed. He went to his bed, dizzier than he had thought. He must walk more. Enough of lying still, if he walked he would get well faster.

Damon. Elene. Damon. Elene.

There was a place outside which became real to him, to which for the first time he wanted to go, a place to reach for when he turned loose of this.

He looked to the window. It was empty. For a terrible, lonely moment he thought that he had imagined it all, that it was a part of the dream world which shaped itself in this whiteness, and that he had created it. But it had given him names; it had detail and substance independent of himself; it was real or he was going mad.

The books came, four cassettes to use in the player, and he held them close to his chest and rocked to and fro smiling to himself and laughing, cross-legged on his bed, for it *was* true. He had touched the real outside and it had touched him.

He looked about him, and it was only a room, with walls he no longer needed.

# BOOK TWO

# 1

## i

## Downbelow main base: 9/2/52

The skies were clear for the morning, only a few fleecy puffs overhead and a line of them marshaling themselves across the northern horizon, beyond the river. It was a long view; it usually needed a day and a half for the horizon clouds to come down to Downbelow base, and they planned to take advantage of that break, patching the washout which had cut them off from base four and all the further camps down the chain. It was, they hoped, the last of the storms of winter. The buds on the trees were swelling to bursting, and the grain sprouts, crowded by flood against the crossed-beam lattices in the fields, would soon want thinning and transplanting to their permanent beds. Main base would be the first to dry out; and then the bases downriver. The river was some bit lower today, so the report came in from the mill.

Emilio saw the supply crawler off on its way down the muddy road downriver, and turned his back, walked the slow, well-trampled way toward higher ground and the domes sunk in the hills, domes which had gotten to be twice as numerous as before, not to mention those that had transferred down the road. Compressors thunked along out of rhythm, the unending pulse of humanity on Downbelow. Pumps labored, adding to the thumping, belching out the water which had seeped into the domes despite their best efforts to waterproof the floors, more pumps working down by the mill dikes and over by the fields. They would not cease until the logs in the fields stood clear.

Spring. Probably the air smelled delightful to a native. Humans had little impression of it, breathing in wet hisses and stops through the masks. Emilio found the sun pleasant on his back, enjoying that much of the day. Downers skipped about, carrying out their tasks with less address than exuberance, would rather make ten scurrying trips with a handful than one uncomfortable, laden passage to anywhere. They laughed, dropped what light loads they bore to play pranks on any excuse. He was frankly surprised that they were still at work with spring coming on so in earnest. The first clear night they had kept all the camp awake with their chatter, their happy pointing at the starry heavens and talking to the stars; the first clear dawn they had waved their arms to the rising sun and shouted and cheered for the coming light—but humans had gone about with a brighter mood that day too, with the first clear sign of winter's ending. Now it was markedly warmer. The females had turned smugly alluring and the males had turned giddy; there was a good deal of what might be Downer singing from the thickets and the budding trees on the hills, trills and chatter and whistles soft and sultry.

It was not as giddy as it would get when the trees sprang into full bloom. There would come a time that the hisa would lose all interest in work, would set off on their wanderings, females first and solitary, and the males doggedly following, to places where humans did not intrude. A good number of the third-season females would spend the summer getting rounder and rounder—at least as round as the wiry hisa became—to give birth in winter, snugged away in hillside tunnels, little mites all limbs and ruddy baby fur, who would be scampering about on their own in the next spring, what little humans saw of them.

He passed the hisa games, walked up the crushed rock path way to Operations, the dome highest on the hill. His ears picked up a crunching on the rocks behind him, and he looked back to find Satin limping along in his wake, arms out for balance, bare feet on sharp stones and her imp's face screwed up in pain from the path designed for human boots. He grinned at the imitation of his strides. She stood and grinned at him, unusually splendid in soft pelts and beads and a red rag of synthetic cloth.

"Shuttle comes, Konstantin-man."

It was so. There was a landing due on this clear day. He had promised her, despite good sense, despite axioms that world-synched pairs were unstable in the spring season, that she and her mate might work a term on-station. If there was a Downer who *had* staggered about under too-heavy loads, it was Satin. She had tried desperately to impress him . . . *See, Konstantin-man, I work good.*

"Packed to go," he observed of her. She displayed the several small bags of no-knowing-what which she had hung about her person, patted them and grinned delightedly.

"I packed." And then her face went sad, and she held out her open arms. "Come love you Konstantin-man, you and you friend."

*Wife.* The hisa had never figured out husband and wife. "Come in," he bade her, touched by such a gesture. Her eyes lit with pleasure. Downers were discouraged even from the vicinity of the Operations dome. It was very rare that one was invited inside. He walked down the wooden steps, wiped his boots on the matting, held the door for her and waited for her to adjust her own breather from about her neck before he opened the inner seal.

A few working humans looked up, stared, some frowning at the presence, went back to their jobs. A number of the techs had offices in the dome, divided off by low wicker screens; the area he shared with Miliko was farthest back, where the only solid wall in the great dome afforded him and Miliko private residential space, a ten-foot section with a woven mat floor, sleeping quarters and office at once. He opened that door beside the lockers and Satin followed him in, staring about her as if she could not absorb the half of what she saw. *Not used to roofs,* he thought, imagining how great a change it was going to be for a Downer suddenly shipped to station. *No winds, no sun, only steel about, poor Satin.*

"Well," Miliko exclaimed, looking up from the spread of charts on their bed.

"Love you," Satin said, and came with absolute confidence, embraced Miliko, hugged her cheek-to-cheek around the obstacle of the breather.

"You're going away," said Miliko.

"Go to you home," she said. "See Bennett home." She hesitated, folded hands diffidently behind her, bobbed a little, looking from one to the other of them. "Love Bennett-man. See he home. Fill up eyes he home. Make warm, warm we eyes."

Sometimes Downer talk made little sense; sometimes meanings shot through the babble with astonishing clarity. Emilio gazed on her with somewhat of guilt, that for as long as they had dealt with Downers, there was none of them who could manage more than a few of the chattering Downer words. Bennett had been best at it.

The hisa loved gifts. He thought of one, on the shelf by the bed, a shell he had found by the riverside. He got it and gave it to her and her dark eyes shone. She flung her arms about him.

"Love you," she announced.

"Love you too, Satin," he told her. And he put his arms about her shoulders, walked her out through the outer offices to the lock, set her through. Beyond the plastic she opened the outer door, took her mask off and grinned at him, waved her hand.

"I go work," she told him. The shuttle was due. A human worker would not have been working on the day he was leaving assignment; but Satin headed away with a slam of the flimsy door and anxious enthusiasm, as if at this late date someone's mind could be changed.

Or perhaps it was unfair to attach to her any human motives. Perhaps it was joy, or gratitude. Downers understood no wages; *gifts,* they said.

Bennett Jacint had understood them. The Downers tended that grave. Laid shells there, perfect ones, skins, set up the strange knobby sculptures that meant something important to them.

He turned, walked back through the operations center, to his own quarters and Miliko. He took off his jacket, hung it on the peg, breather still about his neck, an ornament they all wore from the time clothing went on in the morning till it went off at night.

"Got the weather report from station," Miliko said. "We're going to catch it again in a day or so after the next one hits us. There's a big storm brewing out to sea."

He swore; so much for hopes of spring. She made a place for him among the charts on the bed and he sat down and looked at the damages she had red-penciled, flood areas station was able to show them, down the long chains of beads which were the camps they had established, along unpaved, hand-hacked roads.

"Oh, it's going to get worse," Miliko said, showing him

the topographical chart. "Comp projects enough rain with this one to get us flood in the blue zones again. Right up to base two's doorstep. But most of the roadbed should be above the floodline."

Emilio scowled, expelled a soft breath. "We'll hope." The road was the important thing; the fields would flood for weeks more without harm except to their schedules. Local grains thrived on the water, depended on it in the initial stages of their natural cycles. The lattices kept young plants from going downriver. It was human machinery and human tempers which suffered most. "Downers have the right idea," he said. "Give up during the winter rains, wander off when the trees bloom, make love, nest high and wait for the grain to ripen."

Miliko grinned, still marking her charts.

He sighed, unregarded, pulled over the slab of plastic which served him as a writing desk and started making out personnel assignments, rearranging priorities with the equipment. Perhaps, he thought, perhaps if he pleaded with the Downers, arranged some special gifts, they would hang on a little longer before their seasonal desertion. He regretted losing Satin and Bluetooth; the pair of them had been of enormous help, persuading their fellows in outright argument when it came to something their Konstantin-man wanted very badly. But that went both ways; Satin and Bluetooth wanted to go; *They* wanted something now in his power to give, and it was their time to have their way, before their spring came on them and they passed all self-control.

They were dispersing old hands and trainees and Q assignees down the road to each of the new bases, trying to keep proportions which would not leave staff vulnerable to riot; trying to make the Q folk into workers, against their belief that they were being used; tried to work with morale—it was the willing ones they moved out, and the surliest main base had to keep, in that one huge dome, many times enlarged and patched onto until dome was a misnomer—it spread irregularly over the next hill, a constant difficulty to them. Human workers occupied the several domes next; choice ones, comfortable ones—they were always reluctant to be transferred out to more primitive conditions at the wells or the new camps, alone with the forest and the floods and Q and strange hisa.

Communication was always the problem. They were linked by com; but it was still lonely out there. Ideally they wanted aircraft links; but the one flimsy aircraft they had built some years back had crashed on the landing field two years ago . . . light aircraft and Downbelow's storms did not agree. Hacking a landing site for shuttles . . . that was on the schedule, at least for base three, but the cutting of trees had to be worked out with the Downers, and that was touchy. With the tech level they managed onworld, crawlers were still the most efficient way of getting about, patient and slow as the pace of life on Downbelow had always been, chugging away through mud and flood to the wonderment and delight of Downers. Petrol and grains, wood and winter vegetables, dried fish, an experiment in domesticating the knee-high *pitsu,* which Downers hunted . . . *(You bad,* Downers had declared in the matter, *make they warm in you camp and you eat, no good this thing.* But Downers at base one had become herders, and they had all learned to eat domestic meat. Lukas had ordered it, and this was one Lukas project that had worked well.) Humans on Downbelow fared well enough equipped and fed themselves and station, even with the influx they had gotten. That was no small task. The manufacturies up on station and the manufacturies here on Downbelow were working nonstop. Self-sufficiency, to duplicate every item they normally imported, to fill every quota not alone for themselves but for the overburdened station, and to stockpile what they could . . . it was all falling into their laps here on Downbelow, the excess population, the burden of station-bred people, their own and refugees, who had never set foot on a world. They could no longer depend on the trade which had once woven Viking and Mariner, Esperance and Pan-Paris and Russell's and Voyager and others into a Great Circle of their own, supplying each others' needs. None of the other stations could have gone it alone; none had the living world it took—a living world and hands to manage it. There were plans on the board now, the first crews moved, to go for the onworld mining they had long delayed, duplicating materials already available in Pell system at large . . . just in case things got worse than anyone wanted to think. They would get massive new programs underway this summer, when Downers were receptive to approach again; get it well moving in fall, when the Downers hit their working season, when cool winds made them think of winter again and they seemed never to rest, working for humans and working to carry soft mosses into their tunnels in the wooded hills.

Downbelow was due to change. Its human population had quadrupled. He mourned it; Miliko did. They had gridded off areas already . . . Miliko's ever-present charts—places which no human should ever touch, the beautiful places, the sites they knew for holy and the places vital to the cycles of hisa and wild things alike.

Ram it through council in their own generation, even this year, before the pressures mounted. Set up protections for the things which had to endure. The pressure was already with them. Scars were already on the land, the smoke of the mill, the stumps of trees, the ugly domes and fields imposed on the riverside and being hacked out all along the muddy roads. They had wanted to beautify it as they went, make gardens, camouflage roads and domes—and that chance was gone.

They would not, he and Miliko were resolved together, would not let more damage happen. They loved Downbelow, the best and the worst of it, the maddening hisa and the violence of the storms. There was always the station for human refuge; antiseptic corridors and soft furniture were always waiting. But Miliko thrived here as he did; they made pleasant love at night with the rain pattering away on the plastic dome, with the compressors thumping away in the dark and Downbelow's night creatures singing madly just outside. They enjoyed the changes the sky made hour by hour, and the sound of the wind in the grass and the forest about them, laughed at Downer pranks and ruled the whole world, with power to solve everything but the weather.

They missed home, missed family and that different, wider world; but they talked otherwise . . . had talked even of building a dome to themselves, in their spare time, in years to come, when homes could be built here, a hope which had been closer a year or so ago, when the Downbelow establishment had been quiet and easy, before Mallory and the others had come, before Q.

Now they simply figured how to survive at the level at which they were living. Moved population about under guard for fear of what that population might try to do. Opened new bases at the most primitive level, ill-prepared. Tried to care for the land and the Downers at once, and to pretend that nothing was amiss on station.

He finished the assignments, walked out and handed them to the dispatcher, Ernst, who was also accountant and comp man . . . they all did a multitude of jobs. He walked back again into his bedroom office, surveyed Miliko and her lapful of charts. "Want lunch?" he asked. He reckoned on going to the mill in the afternoon, hoped now for a quiet cup of coffee and first access to the microwave which was the dome's other luxury of rank . . . time to sit and relax.

"I'm nearly done," she said.

A bell rang, three sharp pulses, disarranging the day. The shuttle was coming in early; he had assumed it for the evening slot. He shook his head. "There's still time for lunch," he said.

The shuttle was down before they were done. Everyone in Operations had come to the same conclusion, and the dispatcher, Ernst, directed things between bites of sandwich. It was a hard day for everyone.

Emilio swallowed the last bite, drank the last of his coffee and gathered up his jacket. Miliko was putting hers on.

"Got us some more Q types," Jim Ernst said from the dispatch desk; and moment later, loudly enough to carry through all the dome: "Two *hundred* of them. They've got them jammed in that frigging hold like dried fish. Shuttle, what are we supposed to do with them?"

The answer crackled back, garble and a few intelligible words. Emilio shook his head in exasperation and walked over to lean above Jim Ernst. "Advise Q dome they're going to have to accept some crowding until we can make some more transfers down the road."

"Most of Q is home at lunch," Ernst reminded him. As policy, they avoided announcements when all of Q was gathered. They were inclined to irrational hysteria. "Do it," he told Ernst, and Ernst relayed the information.

Emilio pulled the breather up and started out, Miliko close behind him.

* * *

The biggest shuttle had come down, disgorging the few items of supply they had requested from station. Most of the goods flowed in the other direction, canisters of Downbelow products waiting in the warehouse domes to be loaded and taken up to feed Pell.

The first of the passengers came down the ramp as they reached the landing circle beyond the hill, crushed-looking folk in coveralls, who had probably been frightened to death in transfer, jammed into a cargo hold in greater number than should have been . . . certainly in greater number than they needed on Downbelow all at one moment. There were a few more prosperous-looking volunteers . . . losers in the lottery process; they walked aside. But guards off the shuttle waited with rifles to herd the Q assignees into a group. There were old people with them, and a dozen young children at least, families and fragments of families if it held to form, all such folk as did not survive well in station quarantine. Humanitarian transfer. People like this took up space and used a compressor, and by their classification could not be trusted near the lighter jobs, those tasks involving critical machinery. They had to be assigned manual labor, such of it as they could bear. And the children—at least there were none too young to work, or too young to understand about wearing the breathers or how to change a breather cylinder in a hurry.

"So many fragile ones," Miliko said. "What does your father think we are down here?"

He shrugged. "Better than Q Upabove, I suppose. Easier. I hope those new compressors are in the load; and the plastic sheeting."

"Bet they're not," Miliko said dourly.

There was a shrieking from over the hill toward base and the domes, Downer screeches, not an uncommon thing; he looked over his shoulder and saw nothing, and paid it no mind. The disembarking refugees had stopped at the sound. Staff moved them on.

The shrieking kept up. That was not normal. He turned, and Miliko did. "Stay here," he said, "and keep a hand on matters."

He started running up the path over the hill, dizzy at once with the breather's limitations. He crested the rise and the domes came into sight, and there was in front of huge Q dome, what had the look of a fight, a ring of Downers enclosing a human disturbance, more and more Q folk boiling out of the dome. He sucked air and ran all out, and one of the Downers broke from the group below, came running with all-out haste . . . Satin's Bluetooth: he knew the fellow by the color of him, which was uncommonly red-brown for an adult. "Lukas-man," Bluetooth hissed, falling in by him as he ran, bobbing and dancing in his anxiety. "Lukas-mans all mad."

That took no translation. He knew the game when he saw the guards there . . . Bran Hale and crew, the field supervisors; there was a knot of shouting Q folk and the guards had guns leveled. Hale and his men had gotten one youth away from the group, ripped his breather off so that he was choking, would stop breathing if it kept up. They held the fainting boy among them as hostage, a gun on him, holding rifles on the others, and the Q folk and the Downers on the edges were screaming.

"Stop that!" Emilio shouted. "Break it up!" No one regarded him, and he waded in alone, Bluetooth hanging back from him. He pushed men with rifles and had to push more than once, realizing all at once that he had no gun, that he was bare-handed and alone and that there were no witnesses but Downers and Q.

They gave ground. He snatched the boy from those who held him and the boy collapsed to the ground; he knelt down, feeling his own back naked, picked up the breather that lay there and got it over the boy's face, pressed it there. Some of the Q folk tried to close in and one of Hale's men fired at their feet.

"No more of that!" Emilio shouted. He stood up, shaking in every muscle, staring at the several score Q workers outside, at others still jammed by their own numbers within the dome. At ten armed men who had rifles leveled. He was shaking in every muscle, thinking of riot, of Miliko just over the hill, of having them close in on him. "Back up," he yelled at Q. "Ease off!" And rounded on Bran Hale . . . young, sullen and insolent. "What happened here?"

"Tried to escape," Hale said. "Mask fell off in the fight. Tried to get a gun."

"That's a lie," the Q folk shouted in a babble of variants, and tried to drown Hale's voice.

"Truth," Hale said. "They don't want more refugees in their dome. A fight started and this troublemaker tried to bolt. We caught him."

There was a chorus of protest from the Q folk. A woman in the fore was crying.

Emilio looked about him, having difficulty with his own breathing. At his feet the boy had seemed to come to, writing and coughing. The Downers clustered together, dark eyes solemn.

"Bluetooth," he said, "what happened?"

Bluetooth's eyes shifted to Bran Hale's man. No more than that.

"Me eyes see," said another voice. Satin strode through, braced herself with several bobs of distress. Her voice was high-pitched, brittle. "Hale push he friend, hard with gun. Bad push she."

There were shouts from Hale's side, derision; shouts from the Q side. He yelled for quiet. It was not a lie. He knew Downers and he knew Hale. It was not a lie. "They took his breather?"

"Take." Satin said, and clamped her mouth firmly shut. Her eyes showed fear.

"All right." Emilio sucked in a deep breath, looked directly at Bran Hale's hard face. "We'd better continue this discussion in my office."

"We talk right here," Hale said. He had his crowd about him. His advantage. Emilio matched him stare for stare; it was all he could do, with no weapons and no force to back him."Downer's word," Hale said, "isn't testimony. You don't insult me on any Downer's word, Mr. Konstantin, no sir."

He could walk away, back down. Surely Operations and the regular workers could see what was going on. Maybe they had looked out from their domes and preferred not to see. Accidents could happen, in this place, even to a Konstantin. For a long time the authority on Downbelow had been Jon Lukas and his hand-picked men. He could walk away, maybe reach Operations, call help for himself from the shuttle, if Hale let him; and it would be told for the rest of his life how Emilio Konstantin handled threats. "You pack," he said softly, "and you be on that shuttle when it leaves. All of you."

"On a Downer bitch's word?" Hale lost his dignity,

chose to shout. He could afford to. Some of the rifles had turned *his* way.

"Get out," Emilio said, "on *my* word. Be on that shuttle. Your tour here is over."

He saw Hale's tension, the shift of eyes. Someone did move. A rifle went off, sizzled into the mud. One of the Q men had struck it down. There was a second when it looked like riot.

"Out!" Emilio repeated. Suddenly the balance of power was shifted. Young workers were to the fore of Q, and their own gang boss, Wei. Hale shifted eyes left and right, remeasured things, finally gave a curt nod to his companions. They moved out. Emilio stood watching them in their swaggering retreat to the common barracks, even yet not believing that trouble was over. Beside him, Bluetooth let out a long hiss, and Satin made a spitting sound. His own muscles were quivering with the fight that had not happened. He heard a sough of air, the dome sagging as the rest of Q surged out, all three hundred of them, breaching their lock wide open. He looked at them, alone with them. "You take those new transfers into your dome and you take them in without bickering and without argument. We'll make new diggings; you will and they will, quick as possible. You want them to sleep in the open? Don't you give me any nonsense about it."

"Yes, *sir,*" Wei answered after a moment. The woman who had been crying edged forward. Emilio stepped back and she bent down to help the stricken boy, who was struggling to sit up: mother, he reckoned. Others came and helped the boy up. There was a good deal of commotion about it.

Emilio grasped the youth's arm. "Want you in for a medical," he said. "Two of you take him over to Operations."

They hesitated. Guards were supposed to escort them. There were no guards, he realized in that instant. He had just ordered all the security forces in main base offworld.

"Go on inside," he said to the rest. "Get that dome normalized; I'll talk to you about it later." And while he had their attention: "Look around you. There's all of a *world* here, blast you all. Give us help. Talk to me if there's some complaint. I'll see you get access. We're all crowded here. All of us. Come look at my quarters if you think otherwise; I'll give some of you the tour if you don't believe me. We live like this because we're building. Help us build, and it can be good here, for all of us."

Frightened eyes stared at him . . . no belief. They had come in on overcrowded, dying ships; had been in Q on-station; lived here, in mud and close quarters, moved about under guns. He let go his breath and his anger.

"Go on," he said. "Break it up. Get about your business. Make room for those people."

They moved, the boy and a couple of the young men toward Operations, the rest back into their dome. The flimsy doors closed in sequence this time, locking them through, group after group, until all were gone, and the deflated dome crest began to lose some of its wrinkles as the compressor thumped away.

There was a soft chattering, a bobbing of bodies. The Downers were still with him. He put out his hand and touched Bluetooth. The Downer touched his hand in turn, a calloused brush of flesh, bobbed several times in the residue of excitement. At his other side stood Satin, arms clenched about her, her dark eyes darker still, and wide.

All about him, Downers, with that same disturbed look. Human quarrel, violence, alien to them. Downers would strike in a moment's anger, but only to sting. He had never seen them quarrel in groups, had never seen weapons . . . their knives were only tools and hunting implements. They killed only game. What did they think, he wondered; what did they imagine at such a sight, humans turning guns on each other?

"We go Upabove," Satin said.

"Yes," he agreed. "You still go. It was good, Satin, Bluetooth, all of you, it was good you came to tell me."

There was a general bobbing, expressions of relief among all the hisa, as if they had not been sure. The thought occurred to him that he had ordered Hale and his men off on that same shuttle . . . that human spite might still make things uncomfortable.

"I'll talk to the man in charge of the ship," he told them. "You and Hale will be in different parts of the ship. No trouble for you. I promise."

"Good-good-good," Satin breathed, and hugged him. He stroked her shoulder, turned and received an embrace from Bluetooth as well, patted his rougher pelt. He left them and started toward the crest of the hill, on the track to the landing site, and stopped at the sight of several figures standing there.

Miliko. Two others. All had rifles. He felt a sudden surge of relief to think he had had someone at his back after all. He waved his hand that it was all right, hastened toward them. Miliko came quickest, and he hugged her. Miliko's two companions caught up, two guards off the shuttle. "I'm sending some personnel up with you," he said to them. "Discharged, and I'm filing charges. I don't want them armed. I'm also sending up some Downers, and I don't want the two groups near each other, not at any time."

"Yes, sir." The two guards were blank of comment, objected to nothing.

"You can go back," he said. "Start moving the assignees this way; it's all right."

They went about their orders. Miliko kept the rifle she had borrowed of someone, stood against his side, her arm tight about him, his about her.

"Hale's lot," he said. "I'm packing them all off."

"That leaves us no guards."

"Q wasn't the trouble. I'm calling station about this one." His stomach tightened, reaction beginning to settle on him. "I guess they saw you on the ridge. Maybe that changed their minds."

"Station's got a crisis alert. I thought sure it was Q. Shuttle called station central."

"Better get to Operations then and cancel it." He drew her about; they walked down the slope in the direction of the dome. His knees were water.

"I wasn't up there," she said.

"Where?"

"On the ridge. By the time we arrived up there, there were just Downers and Q."

He swore, marveling then that he had won that bluff. "We're well rid of Bran Hale," he said.

They reached the trough among the hills, walked the bridge over the water hoses and up again, across to Operations. Inside, the boy was submitting to the medic's attention and a pair of techs was standing armed with pistols, keeping a nervous watch on the Q folk who had brought him in. Emilio motioned a negative to them. They cautiously put them away, looked unhappily with the whole situation.

Carefully neutral, Emilio thought. They would have gone with any winner of the quarrel out there, no help to him. He was not angry for it, only disappointed.

"You all right, sir?" Jim Ernst asked.

He nodded, stood watching, with Miliko beside him. "Call station," he said after a moment. "Report it settled."

## ii

They nestled in together, in the dark space humans had found for them, in the great empty belly of the ship, a place which echoed fearfully with machinery. They had to use the breathers, first of what might be many discomforts. They tied themselves to the handholds, as humans had warned them they must, to be safe, and Satin hugged Bluetooth-Dalut-hos-me, hating the feel of the place and the cold and the discomfort of the breathers, and most of all fearing because they were told that they must tie themselves for safety. She had not thought of ships in terms of walls and roofs, which frightened her. Never had she imagined the flight of the ships as something so violent they might be dashed to death, but as something free as the soaring birds, grand and delirious. She shivered with her back against the cushions humans had given them, shivered and tried to cease, felt Bluetooth shiver too.

"We could go back," he said, for this was not of his choosing.

She said nothing, clamped her jaw against the urge to cry that yes, they should, that they should call the humans and tell them that two very small, very unhappy Downers had changed their minds.

Then there was the sound of the engines. She knew what that was . . . had heard it often. *Felt* it now, a terror in her bones.

"We will see great Sun," she said, now that it was irrevocable. "We will see Bennett's home."

Bluetooth held her tighter. "Bennett," he repeated, a name which comforted them both. "Bennett Jacint."

"We will see the spirit-images of the Upabove," she said.

"We will see the Sun." There was a great weight on them, a sense of moving, of being crushed at once. His grip hurt her; she held to him no less tightly. The thought came to her that they might be crushed unnoticed by the great power which humans endured; that perhaps humans had forgotten them here in the deep dark of the ship. But no, Downers came and went; hisa survived this great force, and flew, and saw all the wonders which inhabited the Upabove, walked where they might look down on the stars and looked into the face of great Sun, filled their eyes with good things.

This waited for them. It was now the spring, and the heat had begun in her and in him; and she had chosen the Journey she would make, longer than all journeys, and the high place higher than all high places, where she would spend her first spring.

The pressure eased; they still held to each other, still feeling motion. It was a very far flight, they had been warned so; they must not loose themselves until a man came and told them. The Konstantin had told them what to do and they would surely be safe. Satin felt so with a faith which increased as the force grew less and she knew that they had lived. They were on their way. They *flew*.

She clutched the shell which Konstantin had given her, the gift which marked this Time for her, and about her was the red cloth which was her special treasure, the best thing, the honor that Bennett himself had given her a name. She felt the more secure for these things, and for Bluetooth, for whom she felt an increasing fondness, true affection, not the springtime heat of mating. He was not the biggest and far from the handsomest, but he was clever and clear-headed.

Not wholly. He dug in one of the pouches he carried, brought out a small bit of twig, on which the buds had burst . . . moved his breather to smell it, offered it to her. It brought with them the world, the riverside, and promises.

She felt a flood of heat which turned her sweating despite the chill. It was unnatural, being so close to him and not having the freedom of the land, places to run, the restlessness which would lead her further and further into the lonely lands where only the images stood. They were traveling, in a strange and different way, in a way that great Sun looked down upon all the same, and so she needed do nothing. She accepted Bluetooth's attentions, nervously at first, and then with increasing easiness, for it was right. The games they would have played on the face of the land, until he was the last male determined enough to follow where she led . . . were not needed. He was the one who had come farthest, and he was here, and it was very right.

The motion of the ship changed; they held each other a moment in fear, but this men had warned them of, and they had heard that there was a time of great strangeness. They laughed, and joined, and ceased, giddy and delirious. They marveled at the bit of blossoming twig which floated by them in the air, which moved when they batted at it by turns. She reached carefully and plucked it from the air, and laughed again, letting it free.

"This is where Sun lives," Bluetooth surmised. She thought that it must be so, imagined Sun drifting majestically through the light of his power, and themselves swimming in it, toward the Upabove, the metal home of humans, which held out arms for them. They joined, and joined again, in spasms of joy.

After long and long came another change, little stresses at the bindings, very gentle, and by and by they began to feel heavy again.

"We are coming down," Satin thought aloud. But they stayed quiet, remembering what they had been told, that they must wait on a man to tell them it was safe.

And there was a series of jolts and terrible noises, so that their arms clenched about each other; but the ground was solid under them now. The speaker overhead rang with human voices giving instructions and none of them sounded frightened, rather as humans usually sounded, in a hurry and humorless. "I think we are all right," Bluetooth said.

"We must stay still," she reminded him.

"They will forget us."

"They will not," she said, but she had doubts herself, so dark the place was and so desolate, just a little light where they were, above them.

There was a terrible clash of metal. The door through which they had come in opened, and there was no view of hills and forest now, but of a ribbed throatlike passage which blasted cold air at them.

A man came up it, dressed in brown, carrying one of the handspeakers. "Come on," he told them, and they made haste to untie themselves. Satin stood up and found her legs shaking; she leaned on Bluetooth and he staggered too.

The man gave them gifts, silver cords to wear. "Your numbers," he said. "Always wear them." He took their names and gestured out the passage. "Come with me. We'll get you checked in."

They followed, down the frightening passage, out into a place like the ship belly where they had been, metal and cold, but very, very huge. Satin stared about her, shivering. "We are in a bigger ship," she said. "This is a ship, too." And to the human: "Man, we in Upabove?"

"This is the station," the human said.

A hint of cold settled on Satin's heart. She had hoped for sights, for the warmth of Sun. She chided herself to patience, that these things would come, that it would yet be beautiful.

## iii
## Pell: blue sector five: 9/2/52

The apartment was tidied, the odds and ends tucked into hampers. Damon shrugged into his jacket, straightened his collar. Elene was still dressing, fussing at a waistline that—perhaps—bound a little. It was the second suit she had tried. She looked frustrated with this one too. He walked up behind her and gave her a gentle hug about the middle, met her eyes in the mirror. "You look fine. So what if it shows a little?"

She studied them both in the mirror, put her hand on his. "It looks more like I'm gaining weight."

"You look wonderful," he said, expecting a smile. Her mirrored face stayed anxious. He lingered a moment, held her because she seemed to want that. "Is it all right?" he asked. She had, perhaps, overdone, had gone out of her way to look right, had gotten special items from commissary . . . was nervous about the whole evening, he thought. Therefore the effort. Therefore the fretting about small things. "Does having Talley come here bother you?"

Her fingers traced his slowly. "I don't think it does. But I'm not sure I know what to say to him. I've never entertained a Unioner."

He dropped his arms, looked her in the eyes when she

turned about. The exhausting preparations . . . all the anxiety to please. It was not enthusiasm. He had feared so. "You suggested it; I asked were you sure. Elene, if you felt in the least awkward in it—"

"He's ridden your conscience for over three months. Forget my qualms. I'm curious; shouldn't I be?"

He suspected things . . . a more-than-willingness to accommodate him, that balance sheet Elene kept; gratitude, maybe; or her way of trying to tell him she cared. He remembered the long evenings, Elene brooding on her side of the table, he on his, her burden *Estelle* and his—the lives he handled. He had talked about Talley a certain night he ended up listening to her instead; and when the chance came—such gestures were like Elene: he could not remember bringing her another problem but that. So she took it, tried to solve it, however hard it was. Unioner. He had no way of knowing what she felt under those circumstances. He had thought he knew.

"Don't look that way," she said. "I'm curious, I said. But it's the social situation. What do you say? Talk over old times? *Have we possibly met before, Mr. Talley? Exchanged fire, maybe?* Or maybe we talk over family . . . *How's yours, Mr. Talley?* Or maybe we talk about hospital. *How have you enjoyed your stay on Pell, Mr. Talley?*"

"Elene. . . ."

"You asked."

"I wish I'd known how you felt about it."

"How do you feel about it—honestly?"

"Awkward," he confessed, leaned against the counter. "But, Elene. . . ."

"If you want to know what I feel about it—I'm uneasy, just uneasy. He's coming here, and he'll be here for us to entertain, and frankly, I don't know what we're going to do with him." She turned to the mirror and tugged at the waistline. "All of which is what I *think*. I'm hoping he'll be at ease and we'll all have a pleasant evening."

He could see it otherwise . . . long silences. "I've got to go get him," he said. "He'll be waiting." And then with a happier thought: "Why don't we go up to the concourse? Never mind the things here; it might make things easier all round, neither of us having to play host."

Her eyes lightened. "Meet you there? I'll get a table. There's nothing that can't go in the freeze."

"Do it." He kissed her on the ear, all that was available, and gave her a pat, headed out in haste to make up the time.

The security desk sent a call back for Talley and he was quick in coming down the hall . . . a new suit, everything new. Damon met him and held out his hand. Talley's face took on a different smile as he took it, quickly faded.

"You're already checked out," Damon told him, and gathered up a small plastic wallet from the desk, gave it to him. "When you check in again, this makes it all automatic. Those are your ID papers and your credit card, and a chit with your comp number. You memorize the comp number and destroy the chit."

Talley looked at the papers inside, visibly moved. "I'm discharged?" Evidently staff had not gotten around to telling him. His hands trembled, slender fingers shaking in their course over the fine-printed words. He stared at them, taking time to absorb the matter, until Damon touched his sleeve, drew him from the desk and down the corridor.

"You look well," Damon said. It was so. Their images reflected back from the transport doors ahead, dark and light, his own solid, aquiline darkness and Talley's pallor like illusions. Of a sudden he thought of Elene, felt the least insecurity in Talley's presence, the comparison in which he felt all his faults . . . not alone the look of him, but the look from inside, that stared at him guiltless . . . which had always been guiltless.

*What do I say to him?* He echoed Elene's ugly questions. *Sorry? Sorry I never got around to reading your folder? Sorry I executed you . . . we were pressed for time? Forgive me . . . usually we do better?*

He opened the door and Talley met his eyes in passing through. No accusations, no bitterness. *He doesn't remember. Can't.*

"Your pass," Damon said as they walked toward the lift, "is what's called white-tagged. See the colored circles by the door there? There's a white one too. Your card is a key; so's your comp number. If you see a white circle you have access by card or number. The computer will accept it. Don't try anything where there's no white.

You'll have alarms sounding and security running in a hurry. You *know* such systems, don't you?"

"I understand."

"You recall your comp skills?"

A few spaces of silence. "Armscomp is specialized. But I recall some theory."

"Much of it?"

"If I sat in front of a board . . . probably I would remember."

"Do you remember me?"

They had reached the lift. Damon punched the buttons for private call, privilege of his security clearance: he wanted no crowd. He turned, met Talley's too-open gaze. Normal adults flinched, moved the eyes, glanced this way and that, focused on one and the other detail. Talley's stare lacked such movements, like a madman's, or a child's, or a graven god's.

"I remember you asking that before," Talley said. "You're one of the Konstantins. You own Pell, don't you?"

"Not own. But we've been here a long time."

"I haven't, have I?"

An undertone of worry. *What is it,* Damon wondered with a crawling of his own skin, *what is it to know bits of your mind are gone? How can anything make sense?* "We met when you came here. You ought to know . . . I'm the one who agreed to the Adjustment. Legal Affairs office. I signed the commitment papers."

There was then a little flinching. The car arrived; Damon put his hand inside to hold the door. "You gave me the papers," Talley said. He stepped inside, and Damon followed, let the door close. The car started moving to the green he had coded. "You kept coming to see me. You were the one who was there so often . . . weren't you?"

Damon shrugged. "I didn't want what happened; I didn't think it was right. You understand that."

"Do you want something of me?" Willingness was implicit in the tone—at least acquiescence—in all things, anyway.

Damon returned the stare. "Forgiveness, maybe," he said, cynical.

"That's easy."

"Is it?"

"That's why you came? That's why you came to see me? Why you asked me to come with you now?"

"What did you suppose?"

The wide-field stare clouded a bit, seemed to focus. "I have no way to know. It's kind of you to come."

"Did you think it might not be kind?"

"I don't know how much memory I have. I know there are gaps. I could have known you before. I could remember things that aren't so. It's all the same. You did nothing to me, did you?"

"I could have stopped it."

"I asked for Adjustment . . . didn't I? I thought that I asked."

"You asked, yes."

"Then I remember something right. Or they told me. I don't know. Shall go on with you? Or is that all you wanted?"

"You'd rather not go?"

A series of blinks. "I thought—when I wasn't so well—that I might have known you. I had no memory at all then. I was glad you came. It was someone . . . outside the walls. And the books . . . thank you for the books. I was very glad to have them."

"Look at me."

Talley did so, an instant centering, a touch of apprehension.

"I want you to come. I'd *like* you to come. That's all."

"To where you said? To meet your wife?"

"To meet Elene. And to see Pell. The better side of it."

"All right." Talley's regard stayed with him. The drifting, he thought . . . that was defense; retreat. The direct gaze trusted. From a man with gaps in his memory, trust was all-encompassing.

"I know you," Damon said. "I've read the hospital proceedings. I know things about you I don't know about my own brother. I think it's fair to tell you that."

"Everyone's read them."

"Who—*everyone*?"

"Everyone I know. The doctors . . . all of them in the center."

He thought that over. Hated the thought that anyone should submit to that much intrusion. "The transcripts will be erased."

"Like me." The ghost of a smile quirked Talley's mouth, sadness.

"It wasn't a total restruct," Damon said. "Do you understand that?"

"I know as much as they told me."

The car was coming slowly to rest in green one. The doors opened on one of the busiest corridors in Pell. Other passengers wanted in; Damon took Talley's arm, shepherded him through. Some few heads turned at their presence in the crowd, the sight of a stranger of unusual aspect, or the face of a Konstantin . . . mild curiosity. Voices babbled, undisturbed. Music drifted from the concourse, thin, sweet notes. A few of the Downer workers were in the corridor, tending the plants which grew there. He and Talley walked with the general flow of traffic, anonymous within it.

The hall opened onto the concourse, a darkness, the only light in it coming from the huge projection screens which were its walls: views of stars, of Downbelow's crescent, of the blaze of the filtered sun, the docks viewed from outside cameras. The music was leisurely, an enchantment of electronics and chimes and sometime quiver of bass, balanced moment by moment to the soft tenor of conversation at the tables which filled the center of the curving hall. The screens changed with the ceaseless spin of Pell itself, and images switched in time from one to another to the screens which extended from floor to lofty ceiling. The floor and the tiny human figures and the tables alone were dark.

"Quen-Konstantin," he said to the young woman at the counter by the entry. A waiter at once moved to guide them to the reserved table.

But Talley had stopped. Damon looked back, found him staring about at the screens with a heart-open look on his face. "Josh," Damon said, and when he did not react, gently took his arm. "This way." Balance deserted some newcomers to the concourse, difficulty with the slow spin of the images which dwarfed the tables. He kept the grip all the way to the table, a prime one on the margin, with unimpeded view of the screens.

Elene rose at their arrival. "Josh Talley," Damon said. "Elene Quen, my wife."

Elene blinked. Most reacted to Talley. Slowly she extended her hand, which he took. "Josh, is it? Elene."

She settled back to her chair and they took theirs. The waiter stood expectantly. "Another," she said.

"Special," Damon said, looked at Talley. "Any preference? Or trust me."

Talley shrugged, looking uncomfortable.

"Two," Damon said, and the waiter vanished. He looked at Elene. "Crowded, this evening."

"Not many residents go to the dockside lately," Elene said. That was so; the beached merchanters had staked out a couple of the bars exclusively, a running problem with security.

"They serve dinner here," Damon said, looking at Talley. "Sandwiches, at least."

"I've eaten," he said in a remote tone, fit to stop any conversation.

"Have you," Elene asked, "spent much time on stations?"

Damon reached for her hand under the table, but Talley shook his head quite undisturbed.

"Only Russell's."

"Pell is the best of them." She slid past that pit without looking at it. *One shot declined,* Damon thought, wondering if Elene meant what she did. "Nothing like this at the others."

"Quen . . . is a merchanter name."

"*Was.* They were destroyed at Mariner."

Damon clenched his hand on hers in her lap. Talley stared at her stricken. "I'm sorry."

Elene shook her head. "Not your fault, I'm sure. Merchanters get it from both sides. Bad luck, that's all."

"He can't remember," Damon said.

"*Can* you?" Elene asked.

Talley shook his head slightly.

"So," Elene said, "It's neither here nor there. I'm glad you could come. The Deep spat you out; only a stationer'd dice with you?"

Damon remained perplexed, but Talley smiled wanly, some remote joke he seemed to comprehend.

"I suppose so."

"Luck and luck," Elene said, glanced aside at him and tightened her hand. "You can dice and win on dockside, but old Deep loads his. Carry a man like that for luck. Touch him for it. Here's to survivors, Josh Talley."

Bitter irony? Or an effort at welcome? It was merchanters' humor, impenetrable as another language. Talley seemed relaxed by it. Damon drew back his hand, and settled back. "Did they discuss the matter of a job, Josh?"

"No."

"You *are* discharged. If you can't work, station will carry you for a while. But I did arrange something tentatively, that you can go to of mornings, work as long as you feel able, go back home by noon, maindays. Would that appeal to you?"

Talley said nothing, but the look on his face, half-lit in the image of the sun . . . it was nearest now, in the slow rotation . . . wanted it, hung on it. Damon leaned his arms on the table, embarrassed now to give the little that he had arranged. "A disappointment, perhaps. You have higher qualifications. Small machine salvage, a job, at least . . . on your way to something else. And I've found a room for you, in the old merchanter's central hospice, bath but no kitchen . . . things are incredibly tight. Your job credit is guaranteed by station law to cover basic food and lodging. Since you don't have a kitchen, your card's good in any restaurant up to a certain limit. There are things you have to pay for above that . . . but there's always a schedule in comp to list volunteer service jobs, that you can apply for to get extras. Eventually station will demand a full day's work for board and room, but not till you're certified able. Is that all right with you?"

"I'm free?"

"For all reasonable purposes, yes." The drinks arrived. Damon picked up his frothy concoction of summer fruit and alcohol, watched with interest as Talley sampled one of the delicacies of Pell and reacted with pleasure. He sipped at his own.

"You're no stationer," Elene observed after some silence. Talley was gazing beyond them, to the walls, the slow ballet of stars. *You don't get much view on a ship,* Elene had said once, trying to explain to him. *Not what you'd think. It's the being there; the working of it; the feel of moving through what could surprise you at any moment. It's being a dust speck in that scale and pushing your way through all that Empty on your own terms, that no world can do and nothing spinning around one. It's doing that, and knowing all the time old goblin Deep is just the other side of the metal you're leaning on. You stationers like your illusions. And world folk, blue-skyers, don't even know what real is.*

He felt a chill suddenly, felt apart, with Elene and a stranger across the table making a set of two. His wife and the god-image that was Talley. It was not jealousy. It was a sense of panic. He drank slowly. Watched Talley, who looked at the screens as no stationer did. Like a man remembering breathing.

*Forget station,* he had heard in Elene's voice. *You'll never be content here.* As if she and Talley spoke a language he did not, even using the same words. As if a merchanter who had lost her ship to Union could pity a Unioner who had lost his, beached, like her. Damon reached out beneath the table, sought Elene's hand, closed it in his. "Maybe I can't give you what you most want," he said to Talley, resisting hurt, deliberately courteous. "Pell won't hold you forever now, and if you can find some merchanter to take you on after your papers are entirely clear . . . that's open too someday in the future. But take my advice, plan for a long stay here. Things aren't settled and the merchanters are moving nowhere but to the mines and back."

"The long-haulers are drinking themselves blind on dockside," Elene muttered. "We'll run out of liquor before we run out of bread on Pell. No, not for a while. Things will get better. God help us, we can't contain what we've swallowed forever."

"Elene."

"Isn't he on Pell, too?" she asked. "And aren't we all? His living is tied up with it."

"I would not," Talley said, "harm Pell." His hand moved on the table, a slight tic. It was one of the few implants, that aversion. Damon kept his mouth shut on the knowledge of the psych block; it was no less real for being deep-taught. Talley was intelligent; possibly even he could figure eventually what had been done to him.

"I—" Talley made another random motion of his hand, "don't know this place. I need help. Sometimes I'm not sure how I got into this. Do you know? Did I know?"

Bizarre connection of data. Damon stared at him disquietedly, for a moment afraid that Talley was lapsing into some embarrassing sort of hysteria, not sure what he was going to do with him in this public place.

"I have the records," he answered Talley's question. "That's all the knowledge I have of it."

"Am I your enemy?"

"I don't think so."

"I remember Cyteen."

"You're making connections I'm not following, Josh."

Lips trembled. "I don't follow them either."

"You said you needed help. In what, Josh?"

"Here. The station. You won't stop coming by. . . ."

"You mean visiting you. You won't be in the hospital anymore." Suddenly the sense of it dawned on him, that Talley knew that. "You mean do I set you up with a job and cut you loose on your own? No. I'll call you next week, depend on it."

"I was going to suggest," Elene said smoothly, "that you give Josh comp clearance to get a call through to the apartment. Troubles don't keep office hours and one or the other of us would be able to untangle situations. We are, legally, your sponsors. If you can't get hold of Damon, call my office."

Talley accepted that with a nod of his head. The shifting screens kept their dizzying course. They did not say much for a long time, listened to the music and nursed that round of drinks into a second.

"It would be nice," Elene said finally, "if you'd come to dinner at the end of the week . . . chance my cooking. Have a game of cards. You play cards, surely."

Talley's eyes shifted subtly in *his* direction, as if to ask approval. "It's a long-standing card night," Damon said. "Once a month my brother and his wife would cross shifts with ours. They were on alterday . . . transferred to Downbelow since the crisis. Josh does play," he said to Elene.

"Good."

"Not superstitious," Talley said.

"We won't bet," Elene said.

"I'll come."

"Fine," she said; and a moment later Josh's eyes half-lidded. He was fighting it, came around in an instant. All the tension was out of him.

"Josh," Damon said, "you think you can walk out of here?"

"I'm not sure," he said, distressed.

Damon rose, and Elene did; very carefully Talley pushed back from the table and navigated between them . . . not the two drinks, Damon thought, which had been mild, but the screens and exhaustion. Talley steadied once in the corridor and seemed to catch his breath in the light and stability out there. A trio of Downers stared at them round-eyed above the masks.

They both walked him to the lift and rode with him back to the facility in red, returned him through the glass doors and into the custody of the security desk. They were into alterday now and the guard on duty was one of the Mullers.

"See he gets settled all right," Damon said. Beyond the desk, Talley paused, looked back at them with curious intensity, until the guard came back and drew him down the corridor.

Damon put his arm about Elene and they started their own walk home. "It was a good thought to ask him," he said.

"He's awkward," Elene said, "but who wouldn't be?" She followed him through the doors into the corridor, walked hand in hand with him down the hall. "The war has nasty casualties," she said. "If any Quens could have come through Mariner . . . it would be that, just the other side of the mirror, wouldn't it?—for one of my own. So, God help us, help him. He could as well be one of ours."

She had drunk rather more than he . . . grew morose whenever she did so. He thought of the baby; but it was not the moment to say anything hard with her. He gave her hand a squeeze, ruffled her hair, and they headed home.

# 2

## Cyteen Station: security area; 9/8/52

Marsh had not yet arrived, not baggage or man. Ayres settled in with the others, chose his room of the four which opened by sliding partitions onto a central area, the whole thing an affair of movable panels, white, on silver tracks. The furniture was on tracks, spare, efficient, not comfortable. It was the fourth such change of lodging they had suffered in the last ten days, lodging not far removed from the last, not visibly different from the last, no less guarded by the young mannequins, ubiquitous, and armed, in the corridors . . . the same for the months they had been at this place before the shifting about started.

They did not, in effect, know where they were, whether on some station near the first or orbiting Cyteen itself. Questions obtained only evasions. *Security,* they said of the moves, and: *Patience.* Ayres maintained calm before his companion delegates, the same as he did before the various dignitaries and agencies, both military and civilian—if that had any distinction in Union—which questioned them, interrogations and discussions both singly and in a group. He had stated the reasons and the conditions of their appeal for peace until the inflections of his voice became automatic, until he had memorized the responses of his companions to the same questions; until the performance became just that, performance, an end in itself, something which they might do endlessly, to the limit of the patience of their hosts/interrogators. Had they been negotiating on Earth, they would have long since given up, declared disgust, applied other tactics; that was not an option here. They were vulnerable; they did as they could. His companions had borne themselves well in this distressing circumstance . . . save Marsh. Marsh grew nervous, restless, tense.

And it was of course Marsh the Unionists singled out for particular attention. When they were in single session, Marsh was gone from their midst longest; in the four times they had been shifted lately, Marsh was the last to move in. Bela and Dias had not commented on this; they did not discuss or speculate on anything. Ayres did not remark on it, settling in one of the several chairs in the living area of their suite and picking up from the inevitable vid set the latest propaganda the Unionists provided for their entertainment: either closed-circuit, or if it were station vid, it indicated mentalities incredibly tolerant of boredom—histories years old, accounts cataloging the alleged atrocities committed by the Company and the Company Fleet.

He had seen it all before. They had requested access to the transcripts of their own interviews with the local authorities, but these were denied them. Their own facilities for making such records, even writing materials, had been stolen from their luggage, and their protests were deferred and ignored. These folk had an utter lack of respect for diplomatic conventions . . . typical, Ayres thought, of the situation, of authority upheld by rifle-bearing juveniles with mad eyes and ready recitations of regulations. They most frightened him, the young, the mad-eyed, the too-same young ones. Fanatic, because they knew only what was poured into their heads. Put in on tape, likely, beyond reason. *Don't talk with them,* he had warned his companions. *Do whatever they ask and make your arguments only to their superiors.*

He had long since lost the thread of the broadcast. He cast a look up and about, where Dias sat with her eyes fixed on the screen, where Bela played a game of logic with makeshift pieces. Surreptitiously Ayres looked at his watch, which he had tried to synch with the hours of the Unionists, which were not Earth's hours, nor Pell's, nor the standard kept by the Company. An hour late now. An hour since they had arrived here.

He bit at his lips, doggedly turned his mind to the material on the screen, which was no more than anesthetic, and not even effective at that: the slanders, they had gotten used to. If this was supposed to annoy them, it did not.

There was, eventually, a touch at the door. It opened. Ted Marsh slipped in, carrying his two bags; there was a glimpse of two young guards in the corridor, armed. The door closed. Marsh walked through with his eyes downcast, but all the bedroom doors were slid closed. "Which?" he asked, compelled to stop and ask of them.

"Other side, other way," Ayres said. Marsh slung back across the room and set his bags down at that door. His brown hair fell in disorder, thin strands about his ears; his collar was rumpled. He would not look at them. All his movements were small and nervous.

"Where have you been?" Ayres asked sharply, before he could escape.

Marsh darted a look back. "Foulup in my assignment here. Their computer had me listed somewhere else."

The others had looked up, listened. Marsh stared at him and sweated.

*Challenge the lie? Show distress?* The rooms were all monitored; they were sure of it. He could call Marsh a lair, and make clear that the game was reaching another level. They could . . . his instincts shrank from it . . . take the man into the bathroom and drown the truth out of him as efficiently as Union could question him. Marsh's nerves could hardly stand up to them if they did so. The gain was questionable on all fronts.

Perhaps . . . pity urged at him . . . Marsh was keeping his ordered silence. Perhaps Marsh wanted to confide in them and obeyed his orders for silence instead, suffering in loyalty. He doubted it. Of course the Unionists had settled on him . . . not a weak man, but the weakest of their four. Marsh glanced aside, carried his bags into his room, slid the door shut.

Ayres refused even to exchange glances with the others. The monitoring was probably visual as well, and continuous. He faced the screen and watched the vid.

Time was what they wanted, time gained by this means or gained by negotiations. The stress was thus far bearable. They daily argued with Union, a changing parade of officials. Union agreed to their proposals in principle, professed interest, talked and discussed, sent them to this and that committee, quibbled on points of protocol. On protocol, when materials were stolen from their luggage! It was all stalling, on both sides, and he wished he knew why, on theirs.

Military action was surely proceeding, something which might not benefit their side in negotiation. They would get the outcome dropped in their laps at some properly critical phase, would be expected to cede something further.

Pell, of course. Pell was the most likely cession to ask; and that could not be allowed. The surrender of Company officers to Union's revolutionary justice was another likely item. Not feasible in fact, although some meaningless document could be arranged in compromise: outlawry, perhaps. He had no intention of signing Fleet personnel lives away if he could help it, but a yielding of objection on prosection of some station officials classed as state enemies . . . that might have to be. Union would do as it wished anyway. And what happened this far remote would have little political impact on Earth. What the visual media could not carry into living rooms, the general public could not long remain exercised about. Statistically, a majority of the electorate could not or did not read complicated issues; no pictures, no news; no news, no event; no great sympathy on the part of the public nor sustained interest from the media: safe politics for the Company. Above all they could not jeopardize the majority they had won on other issues, the half century of careful maneuvering, the discrediting of Isolationist leaders . . . the sacrifices already made. Others were inevitable.

He listened to the idiot vid, searched the propaganda for evidence to clarify the situation, listened to the reports of Union's alleged benefits to its citizens, its vast programs of internal improvement. Of other things he would wish to know, the extent of Union territory in directions other than Earthward, the number of bases in their possession, what had happened at the fallen stations, whether they were actively developing further territories or whether the war had effectively engaged their resources to the utmost . . .these pieces of information were not available. Nor was there information to indicate just how extensive the rumored birth-labs were, what proportion of the citizenry they produced, or what treatment those individuals received. A thousand times he cursed the recalcitrance of the Fleet, of Signy Mallory in particular. No knowing ultimately whether his course had been the right one, to exclude the Fleet from his operation. No knowing what would have happened had the Fleet fallen in line. They were now where they must be, even if it was this white set of rooms like all the other white sets of rooms they had experienced; they were doing what they had to—without the Fleet, which could have given them negotiating strength (minor), or proven a frighteningly random third side in the negotiations. The stubbornness of Pell had not helped; Pell, which chose to placate the Fleet. With support from the station they might have had some impact on the mentality of such as Mallory.

Which still returned to the question whether a Fleet which considered its own interests paramount could be persuaded to anything. Mazian and his like could never be controlled for the length of time it would take Earth to prepare defense. They were not, he reminded himself, *not* Earthborn; not regulation-followers, to judge by his sight of them. Like the scientific personnel who had reacted to Earth's emigration bans and summons homeward back in the old days . . . by deserting further Beyond. To Union, ultimately. Or to be like the Konstantins, who had been tyrants so long in their own little empire that they felt precious little responsibility toward Earth.

And . . . this terrified him, when he let himself think about it . . . he had not expected the *difference* out there, had not expected the Union mentality, which seemed to slant off toward some angle of behavior neither parallel nor quite opposite to their own. Union tried to break them down . . . this bizarre game with Marsh, which was surely a case of divide and conquer. Therefore he refused to engage Marsh. Marsh, Bela, and Dias did not have detailed information in them; they were simply Company officers, and what they knew was not that dangerous. He had sent back to Earth the two delegates who, like himself, knew too much; sent them back to say that the Fleet could not be managed, and that stations were collapsing. That much was done. He and his companions here played the game they were given, maintained monastic silence at all times, suffered without comment the shifts in lodging and the disarrangements which were meant to unbalance them—a tactic merely aimed at weakening them in negotiation, Ayres hoped, and not that more dire possibility, that it presaged a seizure of their own persons for interrogation. They went through the motions, hoped that they were closer to success on the treaty than they had been.

And Marsh moved through their midst, sat in their sessions, regarded them in private with a bruised, disheveled look, without their moral support . . . because to ask reasons or offer comfort was to breach the silence which was their defensive wall. *Why?* Ayres had written once on a plastic tabletop by Marsh's arm. In the oil of his fingertip, something he trusted no lens could pick up. And when that had gained no reaction: *What?* Marsh had erased both, and written nothing, turned his face away, his lips trembling in imminent breakdown. Ayres had not repeated the question.

Now at length he rose, walked to Marsh's door, slid it open without knocking.

Marsh sat on his bed, fully clothed, arms locked across his ribs, staring at the wall, or beyond it.

Ayres walked over to him, bent down by his ear. "Concisely," he said in the faintest of whispers, not sure even that would fail to be heard, "what do you think is going on? Have they been questioning you? Answer me."

A moment passed. Marsh shook his head slowly.

"Answer," Ayres said.

"I am singled out for delays," Marsh said, a whisper that stammered. "My assignments are never in order. There's always some mixup. They keep me sitting and waiting for hours. That's *all,* sir."

"I believe you," Ayres said. He was not sure he did, but he offered it all the same, and patted Marsh's shoulder. Marsh broke down and cried, tears pouring down a face which struggled to be composed. The supposed cameras . . . they were eternally conscious of the cameras they believed to be present.

Ayres was shaken by this, the suspicion that they themselves were Marsh's tormentors, as much as Union. He left the room and walked back into the other. And swelling with anger he stopped amid the room, turned his face up to the complicated crystal light fixture which was his chiefest suspicion of monitoring. "I protest," he said sharply, "this deliberate and unwarranted harassment."

Then he turned and sat down, watched the vid again. His companions had reacted no more than to look up. The silence resumed.

There was no acknowledgment of the incident the next morning, in the arrival of the day's schedule, carried by a gun-wearing mannequin.

*Meeting 0800,* it informed them. The day was starting early. There was no other information, not topic nor with whom nor where, not even mention for arrangements of lunch, which were usually included. Marsh came out of his room, shadow-eyed as if he had not slept. "We don't have much time for breakfast," Ayres said; it was usually delivered to their quarters at 0730, and it was within a few minutes of that time.

The light at the door flashed a second time. It opened

from the outside, no breakfast, rather a trio of the mannequin-guards.

"Ayres," one said. Just that, without courtesies. "Come."

He bit back a reply. There was no arguing with them; he had told his people so. He looked at the others, went back and got his jacket, playing the same game, taking time and deliberately irritating those waiting on him. When he reckoned that he had delayed as long as made the point he came alone to the door and into the custody of the young guards.

*Marsh,* he could not help thinking. *What was their game with Marsh?*

They brought him down the corridor in the correct direction for the lift, through the lift-sequence and halls without marking or designation, into the conference rooms and offices, which relieved his immediate apprehensions. They entered a familiar room, and passed through into one of the three interview rooms they used. Military this time. The silver-haired man at the small circular table had metal enough studding the pocket-flap of his black uniform to have made up the ranks of the last several he had talked to combined. Insane pattern of insignia. No knowing what, precisely, the intricate emblems represented . . . amusing on one level, that Union had managed to evolve so complex a system of medals and insignia, as if all that metal were meant to impress. But it *was* authority, and power; and that was not amusing at all.

"Delegate Ayres." The gray-haired man . . . gray with rejuv, by the scarcely lined vigor of the face, a drug entirely common out here . . . available on Earth only in inferior substitutes . . . rose and offered his hand. Ayres took it solemnly. "Seb Azov," the man introduced himself. "From the Directorate. Pleasure to meet you, sir."

The central government; the Directorate was, he had learned, now a body of three hundred twelve: whether this related to the number of stations and worlds in some proportion, he was not aware. It met not only on Cyteen but elsewhere; and how one got into it, he did not know. This man was, beyond doubt, military.

"I regret," Ayres said coldly, "to begin our acquaintance with a protest, citizen Azov, but I refuse to talk until a certain matter is cleared up."

Azov lifted bland brows, sat down again. "The matter, sir?"

"The harassment to which one of my party is being subjected."

"Harassment, sir?"

He was, he knew, supposed to lose his composure, give way to nervousness or anger. He refused either. "Delegate Marsh and your computer seem to find difficulty locating his room assignments, remarkable, since we are inevitably lodged together. I rate your technical competency above that. I am unable to name it anything but harassment that this man is kept waiting hours while alleged discrepancies are sorted out. I maintain that this is harassment designed to lessen our efficiency through exhaustion. I complain of other tactics, such as the inability of your staff to provide us recreational opportunity or room for exercise, such as the inevitable insistence of your staff that they lack authorizations, such as the evasive responses of your staff when we make an inquiry regarding the name of this base. We were promised Cyteen. How are we to know whether we are speaking to authorized persons or merely to low-level functionaries of no competency or authority to negotiate the serious matters on which we have come? We have traveled a far distance, citizen, to settle a grievous and dangerous situation, and we have received precious little cooperation from the persons we have met here."

It was not improvisation. He had prepared the speech for an occasion of opportunity, and the visible brass presented the target. Clearly, Azov was a little taken aback by the attack. Ayres maintained a front of anger, the best miming he had yet done, for he was terrified. His heart hammered against his ribs and he hoped his color had not changed perceptibly.

"It will be attended," Azov said after a moment.

"I should prefer," said Ayres, "stronger assurance."

Azov sat staring at him a moment. "Take my word," he said in a tone that quivered with force, "you will be satisfied. Will you sit, sir? We have some business at hand. Accept my personal apology for the inconvenience to delegate Marsh; it will be investigated and remedied."

He considered walking out, considered further argument, considered the man in front of him, and took the offered chair. Azov's eyes fixed on him with, he thought, some measure of respect.

"On your word, sir," Ayres said.

"I regret the matter; I can say little more at the moment. There is a pressing matter regarding the negotiations; we've come upon what you might call . . . a situation." He pressed a button on the table console. "Kindly send in Mr. Jacoby."

Ayres looked toward the door, slowly, betraying no strong anxiety, although he felt it. The door opened; a man in civilian clothing came in . . . civilian, not the uniforms or uniform-like suits which had distinguished all who had previously dealt with them.

"Mr. Segust Ayres, Mr. Dayin Jacoby of Pell Station. I understand you've met."

Ayres rose, extended his hand to this arrival in cold courtesy, liking it all less and less. "A casual meeting, perhaps; forgive me, I don't remember you."

"Council, Mr. Ayres." The hand gripped his and withdrew without warmth. Jacoby accepted the gestured offer of the third chair at the round table.

"A three-cornered conference," Azov murmured. "Your terms, Mr. Ayres, claim Pell and stations in advance of it as the territory you wish to protect. This doesn't seem to be in accord with the wishes of the citizens of that station . . . and you are on record as supporting the principle of self-determination."

"This man," Ayres said without looking at Jacoby, "is no one of consequence on Pell and has no authority to make agreements. I suggest you consult with Mr. Angelo Konstantin, and send appropriate inquiries to the station council. I don't in fact know this person, and as for any claim he makes to be on the council, I can't attest to their validity."

Azov smiled. "We have an offer from Pell which we are accepting. This does throw into question the proposals under discussion, since without Pell, you would be laying claim to an island *within* Union territory—stations which, I must tell you, are already part of Union territory, by similar decisions. You have no territory in the Beyond. None."

Ayres sat still, feeling the blood draining from his extremities. "This is not negotiation in good faith."

"Your Fleet is now without a single base, sir. We have utterly cut them off. We call on you to perform a humanitarian act; you should inform them of the fact and of their alternatives. There's no need for the loss of ships and lives in defense of a territory which no longer exists. Your cooperation will be appreciated, sir."

"I am outraged," Ayres exclaimed.

"That may be," Azov said. "But in the interest of saving lives, you may choose to send that message."

"Pell has not ceded itself. You're likely to find the real situation different from what you imagine, citizen Azov, and when you wish better terms from us, when you want that trade which might profit us both, consider what you're throwing away."

"Earth is *one world.*"

He said nothing. Had nothing to say. He did not want to argue the desirability of Earth.

"The matter of Pell," said Azov, "is an easy one. Do you know the vulnerability of a station? And when the will of the citizenry supports those outside, a very simple matter. No destruction; that's not our purpose. But the Fleet will not operate successfully in the absence of a base . . . and you hold none. We sign the articles you ask, including the arrangement of Pell as a common meeting point—but in our hands, not yours. No difference, really . . . save in the observance of the will of the people . . . which you claim to hold so dear."

It was better than it might have been; but it was designed to appear so. "There are," he said, "*no* representatives of the citizens of Pell here, only a self-appointed spokesman. I would like to see his letters of authorization."

Azov gathered up a leather-bound folder from before him. "You might be interested in this, sir: the document you offered us . . . *signed* by the government and Directorate of Union, and the council, precisely as you worded it . . . abstracting the control of stations which are now in our hands, and a few minor words regarding the status of Pell: the words 'under Company management' have been struck, here and on the trade document. Three small words. All else is yours, precisely as you gave it. I understand that you are, due to distances, empowered to sign on behalf of your governments and the Company."

Refusal was on his lips. He considered it, as he was in

the habit of considering what slipped from him. "Subject to ratification by my government. The absence of those words would cause distress."

"I hope that you will urge them to acceptance, sir, after reflection." Azov laid the folder on the table and slid it toward him. "Examine it at your leisure. From our side, it *is* firm. All the provisions you desired, all the provisions, to put it frankly, that you can possibly ask, since your territories do not exist."

"I frankly doubt that."

"Ah. That is your privilege. But doubt doesn't alter fact, sir. I suggest that you content yourself with what you *have* won . . . trade agreements which will profit us all, and heal a long breach. Mr. Ayres, what more in reason do you think you can ask? That we cede what the citizens of Pell are willing to give us?"

"Misrepresentation."

"Yet you lack any means to investigate, thus confessing your own limitations of control and possession. You say the government which sent you from Earth has undergone profound changes, and that we must deal with you as a new entity, forgetting all past grievances as irrelevant. Does this new entity . . . propose to meet our signing of their document with further demands? I would suggest, sir, that your military strength is at a low ebb . . . that you have no means to verify anything, that you were obliged to come here in a series of freighters at the whim of merchanters. That a hostile posture is not to the good of your government."

"You are making threats?"

"Stating realities. A government without ships, without control of its own military and without resources . . . is not in a position to insist that its document be signed without changes. We have abstracted meaningless clauses and three words, leaving the government of Pell essentially in the hands of whatever government the citizens of Pell choose to establish; and is this a fit matter for objection on the part of the interest you represent?"

Ayres sat still a moment. "I have to consult with others of my delegation. I don't choose to do so with monitoring in progress."

"There is no monitoring."

"We believe to the contrary."

"Again you are without means to verify this one way or the other. You must proceed as best you can."

Ayres took the folder. "Don't expect me or my staff at any meetings today. We'll be in conference."

"As you will." Azov rose, extended his hand. Jacoby remained seated and offered no courtesy.

"I don't promise signature."

"A conference. I quite understand, sir. Pursue your own course; but I should suggest that you seriously consider the effects of refusing this agreement. Presently we consider our border to be Pell. We're leaving you the Hinder Stars, which you may, if you wish, develop to your profit. In case of failure of this agreement, we shall set our own boundaries, and we will be direct neighbors."

His heart was beating very hard. This was nearing ground he did not want to discuss at all.

"Further," said Azov, "should you wish to save the lives of your Fleet and recover those ships, we've added to that folder a document of our own. Contingent on your agreement to attempt recall of the Fleet, and your order to them to withdraw to the territories you have taken for your boundary by the signature of this treaty, we will drop all charges against them and against other enemies of the state which you may name. We'll permit them to withdraw under our escort and to accompany you home, although we understand that this is at considerable hazard to our side."

"We are not aggressive."

"We could better believe that did you not refuse to call off your ships, which are presently attacking our citizens."

"I've told you flatly that I have no command over the Fleet and no power to recall it."

"We believe that you might use considerable influence. We will make facilities available to you for the transmission of a message . . . the cessation of hostilities will follow the Fleet ceasefire."

"We'll consider the matter."

"Sir."

Ayres bowed, turned, walked out, met by the ever-present young guards, who began to guide him elsewhere among the offices. "The other meeting has been canceled," he informed them. "We go back to my quarters. All my companions do."

"We have our orders," the foremost said, which was all they ever said. It would be straightened out only when they reached the site of the 0800 meeting and gathered the whole party, a new group of young guards then to guide them back, long waiting in between while things were cleared through channels. This was always the way of things, inefficiency meant to drive them mad.

His hand sweated on the leather of the folder he was given, the folder with the documents signed by the government of Union. Pell, lost. A chance to recover at least the Fleet and a proposal which might destroy it. He much feared that the government of Union was planning further ahead than Earth imagined. The Long View. Union had been born with it. Earth was only now acquiring it. He felt transparent and vulnerable. *We know you're stalling,* he imagined the thoughts behind Azov's broad, powerful face. *We know you want to gain time; and why; and for now it suits us too, a trifling agreement we and you will abrogate at earliest convenience.*

Union had swallowed all it meant to digest . . . for now.

They could not afford debate, could not raise deadly issues in a privacy they probably did not have. Sign it and carry it home. What he had in his head was the important matter. They had learned the Beyond; it was about them in the person of soldiers with a single face and virtually a single mind; in the defiance of *Norway's* captain, the arrogance of the Konstantins, the merchanters who ignored a war that had been going on all about them for generations . . . attitudes Earth had never understood, that different powers rule out here, different logic.

Generations which had shaken the dust of Earth from off their feet.

Getting home—by signing a meaningless paper Mazian would never heed, no more than Mallory would come to heel for the asking—getting back alive was the important thing, to make understood what he had seen. For that he would do the necessary things, sign a lie and hope.

# 3

## i

## Pell: stationmaster's office, sector blue one; 9/9/52; 1100 hrs.

The daily toll of disasters extended even to regions beyond station. Angelo Konstantin rested his head on his hand and studied the printout in front of him. A seal blown on Centaur Mine, on Pell IV's third moon . . . fourteen men killed. Fourteen—he could not help the thought—skilled, cleared workers. They had humanity rotting in its own filth the other side of Q line, and they had to lose the like of these instead. Lack of supply, old parts, things which should have been replaced being rigged to keep working. A quarter credit seal gave way and fourteen men died in vacuum. He typed through a memo to locate workers among Pell techs who could replace the lost ones; their own docks were going idle . . . jammed with ships on main berths and auxiliaries, but very little moving in or out . . . and the men were better out there in the mines where their expertise could do some good.

Not all the transferred workers had necessary skills at what they were set to do. A worker had been killed on Downbelow, crushed trying to direct a crawler out of the mud where an inexperienced partner had driven it. Condolences had to be added to those Emilio had already written to the family on-station.

There were two more murders known in Q, and a body had been found adrift in the vicinity of the docks. Supposedly the victim had been vented alive. Q was blamed. Security was trying to get ID on the victim, but there was considerable mutilation of the body.

There was a case of another kind, a lawsuit involving two longtime resident families sharing quarters in alter-day rotation. The original inhabitants accused the newcomers of pilferage and conversion. Damon sent him the case as an example of a growing problem. Some council action was going to have to be taken in legislation to make responsibilities clear in such cases.

A docksider newly assigned to his post was in hospital, half killed by the crew of the militarized merchanter *Janus*. The militarized crews demanded merchanter privileges and access to bars, against some stationer authorities who tried to put them under military discipline. The bones would mend; the relations between station-side officers and the merchanter crews were in worse condition. The next stationer officer who went out with the patrols was looking to get his throat cut. Merchanter families were not used to strangers aboard.

*No station personnel to be assigned to militia ships without permission of ship's captain,* he sent to the militia office. *Militia ships will patrol under their own officers pending resolution of morale difficulties.*

That would create anguish in some quarters. It would create less than a mutiny would, a merchanter ship against the station authority which tried to direct it. Elene had warned him. He found occasion now to take that advice, an emergency in which stationmaster could override council's ill-advised desire to keep its thumb on the armed freighters.

There were petty crises in supply. He stamped authorizations where needed, some after the fact, approval on local supervisors' ingenuity, particularly in the mines. He blessed skilled subordinates who had learned to ferret hidden surpluses out of other departments.

There was need for repair in Q and security asked authorization for armed forces to seal and clear orange three up to the forties, for the duration of the construction, which meant moving out barracksful of residents. It was rated urgent but not life-threatening; taking a repair crew in without sealing the area was. He stamped it Authorized. Shutting down the plumbing in that sector instead threatened them with disease.

"A merchanter captain Ilyko to see you, sir."

He drew in his breath, stabbed at the button on the console, calling the woman in. The door opened, admitted a huge woman, grayed and seamed with years rejuv had not caught in time. Or perhaps she was in the decline . . . the drugs would not hold it off forever. He gestured to a chair; the captain took it gratefully. She had sent the interview request an hour ago, while the ship was coming in. She came from *Swan's Eye,* a can-hauler out of Mariner. He knew the locals, but not this woman. She was one of their own now, militarized; the blue sleeve cord was the insignia she wore to indicate as much.

"What's the message," he asked, "and from whom?"

The old woman searched her jacket and extracted an envelope, leaned heavily forward to lay it on his desk. "From the Olvigs' *Hammer,*" she said. "Out of Viking. Flashed us out there and gave us this hand-to-hand. They're going to lie out of station scan a while . . . afraid, sir. They don't like what they see at all."

"Viking." Word of that disaster had come in long ago. "And where have they been since then?"

"Their message might make it clearer; but they claim to have taken damage clearing Viking. Short-jumped and hung out in nowhere. That's their story. And they're scarred up for sure, but they've got a load. We should have been so lucky when we ran. Then we wouldn't be running militia service, would we, sir, for dock charges?"

"You know what's in this?"

"I know," she said. "There's something on the move. Push is coming to shove, Mr. Konstantin. The way I reckon it . . . *Hammer* tried a jump Unionside and didn't find it so good over there after all; Union tried to grab her, it seems, and she ran for it. She's scared of the same thing here. Wanted me to come in ahead of her and bring the message, so's she won't have her hands dirty with it. Consider her position if Union figures she blew the whistle on them. Union's moving."

Angelo regarded the woman, the round face and deep-sunken dark eyes. Nodded slowly. "You know what happens here if your crew talks on station or elsewhere. Makes it very hard on us."

"Family," she said. "We don't talk to outsiders." The black eyes fixed steadily on him. "I'm militia, Mr. Konstantin, because we had the bad luck to come in with no load and you laid a charge on us; and because there's nowhere else. *Swan's Eye* isn't one of the combine haulers; got no reserve and no credit here like some. But what's credit, eh, Mr. Konstantin, if Pell folds? From here on, never mind the credits in your bank; I want supplies in my hold."

"Blackmail, captain?"

"I'm taking my crew back out there on patrol and we're going to watch your perimeter for you. If we see any Union ships we'll flash you word in a hurry and jump fast. A canhauler isn't up to seek-and-dodge with a rider ship, and I'm not going to do any heroics. I want the same advantage Pell crews have, that have food and water hoarded up off the manifests."

"You charge there's hoarding?"

"Mr. stationmaster, you *know* there's hoarding by every ship that's attached to some station-side concern, and you're not going to antagonize those combines by investigating, are you? How many of your station-side officers get their uniforms dirty checking the holds and tanks visually, eh? I'm flat and I'm asking the same break for my family the others got by being combine. Supplies. Then I go back out on the line."

"You'll get them." He turned then and there and keyed it through on priority. "Be off this station as quickly as possible."

She nodded when he had done and faced her again. "Fair done, Mr. Konstantin."

"Where will you jump, captain, if you have to?"

"The cold Deep. Got me a place I know, out in the dark. Lots of freighters do, you know that, Mr. Konstantin? Long, lean years coming if the push breaks through. Union will patronize them that were Union long before. Lie low and hope they need ships bad, if it comes. New territories would stretch them thin and they'd need it. Or slink Earthward. Some would."

Angelo frowned. "You think it's really coming."

She shrugged. "Feel the draft, stationmaster. Wouldn't be on this station for any bribe if the line don't hold."

"A lot of the merchanters hold your opinions?"

"We've been ready," she said in a low voice, "for half a hundred years. Ask Quen, stationmaster. You looking for a place, too?"

"No, captain."

She leaned back and nodded slowly. "My respects to you for it, stationmaster. You can believe we won't jump without giving an alarm, and that's more than some of our class will do."

"I know that it's a heavy risk for you. And you've got your supplies, all you need. Anything more?"

She shook her head, a slight flexing of her bulk. She gathered herself to her wide-braced feet. "Wish you luck," she said, and offered her hand. "Wish you luck. All the merchanters that are here and not on the other side of the line—picked their side against the odds; them that still meet out in the dark and get you supplies right out of Union—they don't do it all for profit. No profit here. You know that, Mr. stationmaster? It would have been easier on the other side . . . in some ways."

He shook her thick hand. "Thank you, captain."

"Huh," she said, and shrugged self-consciously, waddled out.

He took the message, opened it. It was a handwritten note, a scrawl. *Back from Unionside. Carriers orbiting at Viking, four, maybe more. Rumor says Mazian's on the run, ships lost:* Egypt, France, United States, *maybe others. Situation falling apart.* It was not signed, had no ship's name attached. He studied the message a moment, then rose and finger-keyed the safe, put the paper in, and locked it. His stomach was unsettled. Observers could be wrong. Information could be planted, rumors started deliberately. This ship would not come in. *Hammer* would observe a while, possibly come in, possibly run; any attempt to drag them in for direct questioning would be bad politics with other merchanters. Freighters circled Pell, hoping for food, for water, consuming station supplies, using up combine credit, which they had to honor for fear of riot: old debts, to vanished stations. Using up station supplies rather than the precious hoards which they had conserved aboard . . . against the day they might have to run. Some brought *in* supplies, true; but more consumed them.

He keyed through to the desk outside. "I'm closing up for the day," he said. "I can be reached at home. If it can't wait, I'll come back."

"Yes, sir," the murmur came back. He gathered up a few of his less disturbing papers, put them in his case, put on his jacket, and walked out with a nod of courtesy to his secretary, to the several officials who had their offices in the same room, and entered the corridor outside.

He had been working late the last several days; was due at least the chance to work in greater comfort, to read the caseful of documents without interruption. He had had trouble on Downbelow: Emilio had shipped it all stationside last week with a scathing denunciation of the personnel involved and the policies they represented. Damon had urged the troublemakers shipped out to the mining posts—a quick way to fill up the needed number of workers. Counsel for the defense protested prejudice in the Legal Affairs office, and urged clearing of the tainted service records with full reinstatment. It had flared into something bitter. Jon Lukas had made offers, made demands; they finally had *that* settled. Presently he had fifty files on Q residents being processed out as provisionals. He thought of stopping by the executive lounge for a drink on the way, doing some of the paperwork there, taking his mind off what still had him sweating. He had a pager in his pocket, was never without it, even with com to rely on. He thought about it.

He went home, that little distance down blue one twelve, quietly opened the door.

"Angelo?"

Alicia was awake, then. He shed his case and his jacket on the chair by the door. "I'm home," he said, smiled dutifully at the old Downer female who came out of Alicia's room to pat his hand and welcome him. "Good day, Lily?"

"Have good day," Lily affirmed, grinning her gentle smile. She made herself noiseless in gathering up what he had put down, and he walked back into Alicia's room, leaned down over her bed and kissed her. Alicia smiled, still as she was always still on the immaculate linens, with Lily to tend her, to turn her, to love her with the devotion of many years. The walls were screens. About the bed the view was of stars, as if they hung in mid-space; stars, and sometimes the sun, the docks, the corridors of Pell; or pictures of Downbelow woods, the base, of the family, of all such things as gave her pleasure. Lily changed the sequences for her.

"Damon came by," Alicia murmured. "He and Elene.

For breakfast. It was nice. Elene's looking well. So happy."

Often they stopped by, one or the other of them . . . especially with Emilio and Miliko out of reach. He remembered a surprise, a tape he had dropped into his jacket pocket for fear of forgetting it. "Had a message from Emilio. I'll play it for you."

"Angelo, is something wrong?"

He stopped in mid-breath and shook his head ruefully. "You're sharp, love."

"I know your face, love. Bad news?"

"Not from Emilio. Things are going very well down there; much better. He reports considerable progress with the new camps. They haven't had any trouble out of Q personnel, the road is through to two, and there's a number willing to transfer down the line."

"I think I get only the better side of the reports. I watch the halls. I get that too, Angelo."

He gently turned her head for her, so that she could look at him more easily. "War's heating up," he said. "Is that grim enough?"

The beautiful eyes . . . still beautiful, in a thin, pale face . . . were vital and steady. "How close now?"

"Just merchanters getting nervous. Not at all close; there's no sign of that. But I'm concerned about morale."

She moved her eyes about, a gesture at the walls. "You make all my world beautiful. *Is* it beautiful . . . out there?"

"No harm has come to Pell. There's nothing imminent. You know I can't lie to you." He sat down on the edge of the bed, the clean, smooth sheets, took her hand. "We've seen the war get hot before and we're still here."

"How bad is it?"

"I talked to a merchanter a few moments ago, who talked about merchanter attitudes; spoke about places out in the Deep, good for sitting and waiting. Thought comes to me, do you know, that there *are* other stations of a kind, more than Pell left; chunks of rock in unlikely places . . . things merchanters know about. Maybe Mazian; surely Mazian. Just places where ships know to go. So if there are storms . . . there are havens, aren't there? If it comes down to any bad situation, we do have some choices."

"You'd leave?"

He shook his head. "Never. Never. But there's still a chance of talking the boys into it, isn't there? We persuaded one to Downbelow; work on your youngest; work on Elene . . . she's your best hope. She has friends out there; she knows, and she could persuade Damon." He pressed her hand. Alicia Lukas-Konstantin needed Pell, needed the machinery, equipment a ship could not easily maintain. She was wedded to Pell and the machines. Any transfer of her entourage of metal and experts would be public, doomsday headlined on vid. She had reminded him of that. *I am Pell,* she had laughed, not laughing. She had been, once, beside him. He was not leaving. In no wise did he consider that, without her, abandoning what his family had built over the years, what they had built, together. "It's not close," he said again. But he feared it was.

## ii

## Pell: White Dock: Lukas Company offices; 1100 hrs.

Jon Lukas gathered the pertinent papers together, glared up at the men who crowded his dock-front office. Glared for a long moment to make the point. He laid the papers down on the front of the desk and Bran Hale gathered them up and passed them to the rest of the men.

"We appreciate it," Hale said.

"Lukas Company has no need of employees. You understand that. *Make* yourselves useful. This is a personal favor, a debt, if you like. I appreciate loyalty."

"There'll be no trouble," Hale said.

"Just stay low. Temper cost you your security clearance. You won't exercise that temper working for me. I warned you. I warned you when we worked together on Downbelow . . ."

"I remember," Hale said. "But we were run off, Mr. Lukas, for personal reasons. Konstantin was looking for an excuse. He's changing your policies, tearing up things, disarranging everything you've done. And we tried, sir."

"Can't help that," Jon said. "I'm not down there. I'm not running things. And now you're not. I'd rather Jacoby could have gotten you off with something lighter, but there you are. You're in private employ now." He leaned back at the desk. "I could need you," he said soberly.

"Figure on that too. So it could have turned out worse for you . . . station life now, no more mud, no more headaches from bad air. You work for the company at whatever comes up and you use your heads. You'll do all right."

"Yes, sir," Hale said.

"And, Lee . . ." Jon looked at Lee Quale, a level, sober stare. "You may be standing guard on Lukas property from time to time. You just may have a gun on your person. And you don't fire it. You know how close you came to Adjustment on that account?"

"Bastard hit the barrel," Quale muttered.

"*Damon* Konstantin runs Legal Affairs. Emilio's brother, man. Angelo's got it all in his pocket. If he'd had a better case he'd have sent you through the mill. Think about the odds the next time you cross the Konstantins on your own."

The door opened. Vittorio slipped in, ignoring his instant frown of discouragement. Vittorio came up beside his chair, leaned close to his ear.

"Man came in," Vittorio whispered. "Off a ship named *Swan's Eye*."

"I don't know any *Swan's Eye*," he hissed back. "He can wait."

"No," Vittorio persisted, leaned close a second time. "Listen to me. I'm not sure he's authorized."

"How, not authorized?"

"*Papers*. I'm not sure he's supposed to be on station at all. He's out there. I don't know what to do with him."

Jon drew a quick breath, suddenly cold. An office full of witnesses. A dock full of them. "Send him in," he said. And to Hale and the others: "Go on outside. Fill out the papers and hand them to personnel. Take whatever they give you for today. *Go on*."

There were dark looks from them, suspicion of offense. "Come on," Hale said, shepherding the others out. Vittorio hastened out after them, vanished, leaving the door open.

A moment later a man merchanter-clad slipped through and closed it. Like that, closed it. No fear, no furtiveness in that move. As if *he* commanded. An ordinary face, a thirtyish man of no distinction at all. His manner was cold and quiet.

"Mr. Jon Lukas," the newcomer said.

"I'm Jon Lukas."

Eyes lifted meaningfully to the overhead, about the walls.

"No monitoring," Jon said, short of breath. "You walk in here in public and you're afraid of monitoring?"

"I need a cover."

"What's your name. Who *are* you?"

The man walked forward and wrenched a gold ring from his finger, took a station ID card from his pocket, laid both on the desk in front of him.

*Dayin's.*

"You made a proposal," the man said.

Jon sat frozen.

"Get me cover, Mr. Lukas."

"Who are you?"

"I came on *Swan's Eye*. Time's limited. They'll take on supplies and head out."

"Name, man. I don't deal with nonentities."

"Give me a name. A man of your own to walk onto *Swan's Eye*. A hostage, one who can deal in your name if need be. You have a son."

"Vittorio."

"Send him."

"He'd be missed."

The newcomer stared at him, coldly adament. Jon pocketed card and ring, reached a numb hand for the intercom. "Vittorio."

The door opened. Vittorio slipped in, eyes quick with apprehension, let the door close again.

"The ship that brought me," the man said, "will take you, Vittorio Lukas, to a ship called *Hammer,* out on the peripheries; and you needn't have apprehensions of the crew of either. They're trusted, all of them. Even the captain of *Swan's Eye* has a powerful interest in your safety . . . wanting her own family back. You'll be safe enough."

"Do as he says," Jon said. Vittorio's face was the color of paste.

"*Go?* Like that?"

"You're safe," Jon said. "You're precious well safe . . . safer than you'd be here, not when it comes to what it's coming to. Your papers, your card, your key. Give them to him. Go on *Swan's Eye* with one of the deliveries. Just don't look guilty and don't get off. It's easy enough."

Vittorio simply stared at him.

"You're safe, I assure you," the stranger said. "You go out there, sit, wait. Act as liaison with our operations."

"Our."

"I'm told you understand me."

Vittorio reached to his pocket, handed over all his papers. There was a numb terror on his face. "Comp number," the other prompted; Vittorio wrote it down for him on the desk-pad.

"You're all right," Jon said. "I'm telling you you're better off there than here."

"That's what you told Dayin."

"Dayin Jacoby is quite well," the stranger said.

"Don't foul it up," Jon said. "Get your wits together. You foul it up out there and we'll all be in for Adjustment. You read me clear?"

"Yes, sir," Vittorio said faintly. Jon gave him a nod toward the door, dismissal. Vittorio tentatively held out a hand toward him. He took it perfunctorily—could not, even now, *like* this son of his. Came closest in this moment, perhaps, that Vittorio proved of some real service to him.

"I appreciate it," he muttered, feeling some courtesy would salve wounds. Vittorio nodded.

"This dock," the stranger said, sorting through Vittorio's papers. "Berth two. And hurry about it."

Vittorio left. The stranger slipped the papers and the comp number into his own pocket.

"Use of the number periodically should satisfy comp," the man said.

"Who are you?"

"Jessad will do," the man replied. "Vittorio Lukas, I suppose, when it come to comp. What's his residence?"

"Lives with me," Jon said, wishing otherwise.

"Anyone else? Any woman, close friends who'll not be sympathetic . . . ?"

"The two of us."

"Jacoby indicated as much. Residence with you . . . very convenient. Will it excite comment if I walk there in this clothing?"

Jon sat down on the edge of his desk, mopped his face with his hand.

"No need to be distressed, Mr. Lukas."

"They—the Union Fleet—they're moving in?"

"I'm to arrange certain things. I'm a consultant, Mr. Lukas. That would be an apt term. Expendable. A man, a ship or two . . . small risk against the gain. But I do want to live, you understand, and I propose not to be expended . . . without satisfaction for it. Just so you don't suffer a change of heart, Mr. Lukas."

"They've sent you in here . . . with no backing—"

"Backing in plenty when it comes. We'll talk tonight, in residence. I'm quite in your hands. I understand there's no strong bond between yourself and your son."

Heat flushed his face. "No business of yours, Mr. Jessad."

"No?" Jessad looked him slowly up and down. "It's coming, you can be sure of that. You've bid to be on the winning side. To do certain services . . . in return for position. I'll be evaluating you. Very businesslike. You take my meaning. But you'll do well to take my orders, to do nothing without my advice. I have a certain expertise in this situation. I'm advised that you don't permit domestic monitoring; that Pell is very adamant on this point; that there's no apparatus."

"There isn't," Jon said, swallowing heavily. "It's very much against the law."

"Convenient. I'd hate to walk in under camera. The clothes, Mr. Lukas. Acceptable in your corridors?"

Jon turned, searched his desk, found the appropriate form, his heart pounding all the while. If the man should be stopped, if there were suspicion, his signature on the document . . . but it was already too late. If *Swan's Eye* were boarded and searched, if someone noticed that Vittorio failed to leave it before it undocked . . . "Here," he said, tearing off the pass. "This isn't to show anyone unless you're stopped by security." He pushed the com buttom and leaned over the mike. "Bran Hale still out there? Get him in here. Alone."

"Mr. Lukas," Jessad said, "we don't need other parties to this."

"You asked advice about the corridors. Take it. If you're stopped, your story is that you're a merchanter whose papers were stolen. You're on your way to talk to administration about it, and Hale's your escort. Give me Vittorio's papers. *I* can carry them. You daren't be caught with them, with that story. I'll straighten it all out when I get to the apartment this evening."

Jessad handed them over in return for the pass. "And what do they do with merchanters whose papers get stolen?"

"They call in their whole ship's family and it's a very great deal of commotion. You could end up in detention and Adjustment if things go that far, Mr. Jessad. But stolen papers are known here, and it's a better cover than your plan. If it happens, go along with everything and trust my judgment. I have ships. I can arrange something. Claim you're off *Sheba*. I know the family."

The door opened. Bran Hale stood there, and Jessad shut his mouth on whatever he would have said.

"Trust me," Jon repeated, relishing his discomfiture. "Bran, you're useful already. Walk this man to my apartment." He fished in his pocket after the manual guest key. "See him there and inside and sit with my guest until I come, will you? Could be a long while. Make yourself free in the place. And if you get stopped, he has a different story. You just follow his cue, all right?"

Hale's eyes took in Jessad, flicked back to him. Intelligent man, Hale. He nodded, without asking questions.

"Mr. Jessad," Jon murmured, "you can trust this man to see you there."

Jessad smiled tautly, offered his hand. Jon took it, a dry grip of a man of no normal nerves. Hale showed him out and Jon stood by his desk, watching both of them depart. The staff in the outer office were all like Hale, Lukas people, administrative level and trustworthy. Men and women he had chosen . . . and not one of them was likely to be doubling on the Konstantin payroll: he had always seen to that. He was still anxious. He turned from the view of the door to the sideboard, poured himself a drink, for however unruffled Jessad was, his own hands were shaking from the encounter and the possibilities in it. A Unionist agent. It was farce, a too elaborate result of his intrigue with Jacoby. He had sent out a tentative feeler and someone had raised the stakes in the game to a ridiculous level.

Union ships were coming. Were very close, that they would take the enormous chance of sending in someone like Jessad. He resumed his seat at his desk, holding the drink, sipped at it, trying to pull his thoughts into coherency. The proposed deception of comp could not go on. He reckoned the life of the Jessad/Vittorio charade in days, and if something went wrong he would be the one quickest caught, not Jessad, who was not in comp. Jessad was expendable in Union plans, perhaps, but he was more so.

He drank, trying to think.

Seized up paper with sudden inspiration, more forms, started the call-up procedure for a short-hauler. There were crews in Lukas employ who would not talk, like *Sheba,* men who would take a ship out and carry a ghost aboard, falsify manifests, falsify crew or passenger listings . . . the tracing of the black market routes had turned up all manner of interesting data that some captains did not want known. So this afternoon another ship would go out to the mines, and Vittorio's comp number could be changed into the station log.

A little ripple, a ship moving; no one paid attention to short-haulers. Out to the mines and back again, a ship incapable of threatening security because it lacked speed and star capacity and weapons. He might still have some questions to answer from Angelo, but he knew all the right answers to give. He transmitted the order to comp, watched in satisfaction as comp swallowed the order and sent out notification to Lukas Company that any ship moving had to carry some station items to the mines free-freighted. Ordinarily he would have kicked hard at the size of the assessment for free transport; it was outrageous. He keyed back at it: *Accepted 1/4 station lading; will depart 1700md.*

Comp took it. He leaned back with a great sigh of relief, his heart settling down to a more reasonable rhythm. Personnel was an easy matter; he knew his better men.

He set to work again, pulling names from comp, choosing the crew, a merchanter family long in Lukas's pay. "Send the Kulins in the moment they hit the office," he told his secretary over the com. "There's a commission waiting for them. Make it out and hurry about it. Scramble together *anything* we've meant to freight out, and get it going; then get an extra dock crew to make a pickup from station lading for free-freighting, no quarrels, take whatever they're given and get back here. You make sure those papers are flawless and that there's no snag . . . absolutely no snag . . . in comp entries. You understand me?"

"Yes, sir," the answer came back. And a moment later: "Contact made with the Kulins. They're on their way and thank you for the commission, sir."

*Annie* was convenient, a ship comfortable enough for a prolonged tour of Lukas mine interests. Small enough for obscurity. He had taken such tours in his youth, learning the business. So Vittorio might. He sipped at his drink and thumbed the papers on his desk, fretting.

## iii

## Pell: Central Cylinder; 9/9/52; 1200 hrs.

Josh sank down to the matting, sat, collapsed backward, in the gym's reduced G. Damon leaned over him, hands on bare knees, the suspicion of amusement on his face.

"I'm done," Josh said when he had a breath; his sides hurt. "I'd exercised, but not this much."

Damon sank to his knees by him on the mat, hunched and himself hard-breathing. "Doing all right, anyhow. I'm ready to call it." He sucked air and let out a slower breath, grinned at him. "Need help?"

Josh grunted and rolled over, heaved himself up on one arm, gathered himself gracelessly to his feet, shaking in every muscle and conscious of the men and women in better form who passed them on the steep track which belted all Pell's inner core. It was a crowded place, echoing with shouted conversation. It was freedom, and the worst there was to fear here was a little laughter. He would have kept going if he could . . . had already run longer than he should, but he hated to have the time end.

His knees shook, and his belly ached. "Come on," Damon said, rising with more ease. Damon caught his arm and guided him toward the dressing rooms. "Take a steam bath, a chance to get the knots out at least. I've got a little while before I have to get back to the office."

They went into the chaotic locker room, stripped and tossed the clothing into the common laundry. Towels were stacked there for the taking. Damon tossed a couple at him and showed him into the door marked STEAM, through a quick shower into a series of cubbyholes obscured by vapor, down a long aisle. Most places were occupied. They found a few vacant toward the end of the row, took one in the middle and sat down on the wooden benches. So much water to waste . . . Josh watched Damon dip up water and pour it on his head, cast the rest on a plate of hot metal until the steam boiled up and obscured him in a white cloud. Josh doused himself after similar fashion, mopped with the towel, short of breath and dizzy in the heat.

"You all right?" Damon asked him.

He nodded, anxious not to spoil the time, anxious all the while he was with Damon. He desperately tried to maintain his balance, walking the line of too much trust on the one side and on the other—a terror of trusting anyone. He hated being alone . . . had never . . . sometimes certainties flashed out of his tattered memory, firm as truth . . . had never liked being alone. Damon would tire of him. The novelty would wear off. Such company as his had to pall after a while.

And then he would be alone, with half his mind and a token freedom, in this prison that was Pell.

"Something bothering you?"

"No." And desperately, to change the subject, for Damon had complained he lacked company coming to the gym: "I'd thought Elene would meet us here."

"Pregnancy is beginning to slow her down a little. She's not feeling up to it."

"Oh." He blinked, looked away. It was an intimacy, such a question; he felt like an intruder—naïve in such things. Women, he thought he had known, but not pregnant ones, not a relationship—as it was between Damon and Elene—full of permanencies. He remembered someone he had loved. Older. Dryer. Past such things. A boy's love. He had been the child. He tried to follow the threads where they led, but they tangled. He did not want to think of Elene in that regard. Could not. He recalled warnings . . . psychological impairment, they had called it. Impairment . . .

"Josh . . . are you all right?"

He blinked again, which could become a nervous tic if he let it.

"Something's eating at you."

He made a helpless gesture in reply, not wanting to be trapped into discussion. "I don't know."

"You're worried about something."

"Nothing."

"Don't trust me?"

The blink obscured his vision. Sweat was dripping into his eyes. He mopped his face.

"All right," Damon said, as if it were.

He got up, walked to the door of the wooden cubicle, anything to put distance between them. His stomach was heaving.

"Josh."

A dark place, a close place . . . he could run, clear this closeness, these demands on him. That would get him arrested, sent back to hospital, into the white walls.

"Are you scared?" Damon asked him plainly.

It hit as close to the mark as any other word. He made a helpless gesture, uncomfortable. Elsewhere the noise of other voices became like silence, a roar in which their own cell was remote.

"You figure what?" Damon asked. "That I'm not honest with you?"

"No."

"That you can't trust me?"

"No."

"What, then?"

He was close to being sick. He hit that barrier when he crossed his conditioning . . . knew what it was.

"I wish," Damon said, "that you'd talk."

He looked back, his back to the wooden partition. "You'll stop," he said numbly, "when you get tired of the project."

"Stop what? Are you back on that desertion theme again?"

"Then what do you want?"

"You think you're a curiosity," Damon asked him, "or what?"

He swallowed the bile risen in his throat.

"You get that impression, do you," Damon asked, "from Elene and me?"

"Don't want to think that," he managed to say finally. "But I am a curiosity, whatever else."

"No," Damon said.

A muscle in his face began to jerk. He reached for the bench, sat down, tried to stop the tic. There were pills; he was no longer on them. He wished he were, to be still and not to think. To get out of here, break off this probing at him.

"We like you," Damon said. "Is something wrong with that?"

He sat there, paralyzed, his heart hammering.

"Come on," Damon said, gathering himself up. "You've had enough heat."

Josh pulled himself to his feet, finding his knees weak, his sight blurring from the sweat and the temperature and the reduced *G.* Damon offered a hand. He flinched from it, walked after Damon down the aisle and into the showers at the end of the room.

The cooler mist cleared his head somewhat; he stayed in the stall a few moments longer than need be, inhaled the cooling air, came out again somewhat calmed, walked towel-wrapped into the locker room again. Damon was behind him. "I'm sorry," he told Damon, for things in general.

"Reflexes," Damon said. He frowned intensely, caught his arm before he could turn aside. Josh flinched back against the locker so hard it echoed.

A dark place. A chaos of bodies. Hands on him. He jerked his mind away from it, leaned shivering against the metal, staring into Damon's anxious face.

"Josh?"

"I'm sorry," he said again. "I'm sorry."

"You look like you're going to pass out. Was it the heat?"

"Don't know," he murmured. "Don't know." He reached toward the bench, sat down to catch his breath. It was better after a moment. The dark receded. "I *am* sorry." He was depressed, convinced Damon would not long tolerate him. The depression spread. "Maybe I'd better check back into the facility."

"That bad?"

He did not want to think of his own room, the barren apartment in hospice, blank-walled, cheerless. There were people he knew in the hospital, doctors who knew him, who could deal with these things, and whose motives he knew were limited to duty.

"I'll call the office," Damon said, "and tell them I'm going to be late. I'll take you to the hospital if you feel you need it."

He rested his head on his hands. "I don't know why I do this," he said. "I'm remembering something. I don't know what. It hits me in the stomach."

Damon sat down astride the bench, just sat, and waited on him.

"I can figure," Damon said finally, and he looked up, recalling uneasily that Damon had had access to all his records.

"*What* do you figure?"

"Maybe it was a little close in there. A lot of the refugees panic at crowding. It's scarred into them."

"But I didn't come in with the refugees," he said. "I remember that."

"And what else?"

A tic jerked at his face. He rose, began to dress, and after a moment Damon did likewise. Other men came and went about them. Shouts from outside reached into the room when the door opened, the ordinary noise of the gym.

"Do you really want me to take you to the hospital?" Damon asked finally.

He shrugged into his jacket. "No. I'll be all right." He judged that such was the case, although his skin was still drawn in chill the clothes should have warmed away. Damon frowned, gestured toward the door. They walked out into the cold outer chamber, entered the lift with half a dozen others, rode it the dizzying straight drop into outershell *G*. Josh drew a deep breath, staggered a little in walking off, stopped as the flow of traffic swirled about him.

Damon's hand closed on his elbow, moved him gently in the direction of a seat along the corridor wall. He was glad to sit down, to rest a moment and watch the people pass them. They were not on Damon's office level, but on a green one. The strains of music from the concourse floated out to them from the far end. They should have ridden it on down . . . had stopped, Damon's idea. Near the track around to the hospital, he reasoned. Or just a place to rest. He sat, taking his breath.

"A little dizzy," he confessed.

"Maybe it would be better if you went back at least for a checkup. I should never have encouraged you to this."

"It's not the exercise." He bent, rested his head in his hands, drew several quiet breaths, straightened finally.

"Damon, the names . . . you know the names in my records. Where was I born?"

"Cyteen."

"My mother's name . . . do you know it?"

Damon frowned. "No. You didn't say; mostly you talked about an aunt. Her name was Maevis."

The older woman's face came to him again, a warm rush of familiarity. "I remember."

"Had you forgotten even that?"

The tic came back to his face. He tried not to acknowledge it, desperate for normalcy. "I have no way to know, you understand, what's memory and what's imagination, or dreams. Try dealing with things when you don't know the difference and can't tell."

"The name was Maevis."

"Yes. You lived on a farm."

He nodded, treasuring a sudden glimpse of sunlit road, a weathered fence—he was often on that road in his dreams, bare feet in slick dust, a house, a prefab and peeling dome . . . many such, field upon field, ripe gold in the sun. "Plantation. A lot larger than a farm. I lived there . . . I lived there until I went into the service school. That was the last time I was ever on a world—wasn't it?"

"You never mentioned any other."

He sat still a moment, holding onto the image, excited by it, by something beautiful and warm and real. He tried to recover details. The size of the sun in the sky, the color of sunsets, the dusty road that led to and from the small settlement. A large, soft, comfortable woman and a thin, worried man who spent a lot of time cursing the weather. The pieces fit, settled into place. Home. That was home. He ached after it. "Damon," he said, gathering courage—for there was more than the pleasant dream. "You don't have any reason to lie to me, do you? But you did—when I asked you for the truth a while ago—about the nightmare. Why?"

Damon looked uncomfortable.

"I'm scared, Damon. I'm scared of lies. Do you understand that? Scared of other things." He stammered uncontrollably, impatient with himself, with muscles that jerked and a tongue that would not frame things and a mind like a sieve. "Give me names, Damon. You've read the record. I know you have. Tell me how I got to Pell."

"When Russell's collapsed. Like everyone else."

"No. Starting with Cyteen. Give me names."

Damon laid an arm along the back of the bench, faced him, frowning. "The first service you mentioned was a ship named *Kite*. I don't know how many years; maybe it was the only ship. You'd been taken off the farm, I take it, into the service school, whatever you call the place, and you were trained in armscomp. I take it that the ship was a very small one."

"Scout and recon," he murmured, and saw in his mind the exact boards, the cramped interior of *Kite,* where the crew had to hand-over-hand their way in zero *G*. A lot of time at Fargone Station; a lot of time there—and out on patrol; out on missions just looking for what they could see. Kitha . . . Kitha and Lee . . . childlike Kitha—he had had particular affection for her. And Ulf. He recovered faces, glad to remember them. They had worked close—in more than one sense, for the dartships had no cabins, no privacy. They had been together . . . years. Years.

Dead now. It was like losing them again.

*Watch it!* Kitha had yelled; he had yelled something too, realizing they were blind-spotted; Ulf's mistake. He sat helpless at his board, no guns that would bear on the threat. He flinched from it.

"They picked me up," he said. "Someone did."

"A ship named *Tigris* hit you," Damon said. "Ridership. But it was a freighter in the area that homed in on your capsule signal."

"Go on."

Damon stayed silent a moment as if he were thinking on it, as if he would not. He grew more and more anxious, his stomach taut. "You were brought onto station," Damon said finally, "aboard a merchanter—a stretcher case, but no injuries. Shock, cold, I suppose . . . your life-support had started to fade, and they nearly lost you."

He shook his head. That much was blank, remote and cold. He recalled docks, doctors; interrogation, endless questions.

Mobs. Shouting mobs. Docks and a guard falling. Someone had coldly shot the man in the face, while he lay on the ground stunned. Dead everywhere, trampled, a surge of bodies before him and men about him—armored troops.

*They've got guns!* someone had shouted. And panic broke out.

"You were picked up at Mariner," Damon said. "After it blew, when they were hunting Mariner survivors."

"Elene—"

"They questioned you at Russell's," Damon said softly, doggedly. "They were facing—I don't know what. They were frightened, in a hurry. They used illegal techniques . . . like Adjustment. They wanted information out of you, timetables, ship movements, the whole thing. But you couldn't give it to them. You were on Russell's when the evacuation began, and you were moved to this station. That's what happened."

A dark umbilical from station to ship. Troops and guns.

"On a warship," he said.

*"Norway."*

His stomach knotted. Mallory. Mallory and *Norway*. Graff. He remembered. Pride . . . died there. He became a nothing. Who he was, what he was . . . they had not cared, among the troops, the crew. It was not even hate, but bitterness and boredom, cruelty in which *he* did not matter, a living thing that felt pain, felt shame . . . screamed when the horror became overwhelming, and realizing that there was no one at all who cared—stopped screaming, or feeling, or fighting.

*Want to go back to them?* He could hear even the tone of Mallory's voice. *Want to go back?* He had not wanted that. Had wanted nothing, then, but to feel nothing.

This was the source of the nightmares, the dark, confused figures, the thing that wakened him in the night.

He nodded slowly, accepting that.

"You entered detention here," Damon said. "You were picked up; Russell's; *Norway;* here. If you think we've thrown anything false into your Adjustment . . . no. Believe me. Josh?"

He was sweating. Felt it. "I'm all right," he said, although it was hard, for a moment, to draw breath. His stomach kept heaving. Closeness—emotional or physical—was going to do this to him; he identified it now. Tried to control it.

"Sit there," Damon said, rose before he could object, and went into one of the shops along the hall. He rested there obediently, head against the wall behind him, his pulse easing finally. It occurred to him that it was the first time he had been loose alone, save for the track between his job and his room in the old hospice. Being so gave him a peculiarly naked feeling. He wondered if those who passed knew who he was. The idea frightened him.

*You will remember some things,* the doctor had told him, when they stopped the pills. *But you can get distance from them.* Remember *some* things.

Damon came back, bringing two cups of something, sat down, and offered one to him. It was fruit juice and something else, iced and sugared, which soothed his stomach. "You're going to be late getting back," he recalled.

Damon shrugged and said nothing.

"I'd like—" To his intense shame, he stammered. "—to take you and Elene to dinner. I have my job now. I have some credit above my hours."

Damon studied him a moment. "All right. I'll ask Elene."

It made him feel a great deal better. "I'd like," he said further, "to walk back home from here. Alone."

"All right."

"I needed to know . . . *what* I remember. I apologize."

"I'm worried for you," Damon said, and that profoundly touched him.

"But I walk by myself."

"What night for dinner?"

"You and Elene decide. My schedule is rather open."

It was poor humor. Damon dutifully smiled at it, finished his drink. Josh sipped the last of his and stood up. "Thank you."

"I'll talk to Elene. Let you know the date tomorrow. Take it easy. And call me if you need."

Josh nodded, turned, walked away, among the crowds who . . . might . . . know his face. Like those on the docks, in his memory: crowds. It was not the same. It was a different world and he walked in it, down his own portion of hall as the newfound owner of it . . . walked to the lift along with those born to Pell, stood with them waiting on the lift car as if he were ordinary.

It came. "Green seven." He spoke up for himself when the press inside cut him off from the controls and someone kindly pressed it for him. Shoulder to shoulder in the car. He was all right. It whisked him down to his own level. He excused his way past passengers who gave him not a second glance, stood in his own corridor, near the hospice.

"Talley," someone said, startling him. He glanced to his right, at uniformed security guards. One nodded pleasantly to him. His pulse raced and settled. The face was distantly familiar. "You live here now?" the guard asked him.

"Yes," he said, and in apology: "I don't remember well . . . from before. Maybe you were there when I came in."

"I was," the guard said. "Good to see you came out all right."

He seemed to mean it. "Thank you," Josh said, walked on his way and the guards on theirs. The dark which had advanced retreated.

He had thought them all dreams. *But I don't dream it,* he thought. *It happened.* He walked past the desk at the entry to the hospice, down the corridor inside to number 18. He used his card. The door slid aside and he walked into his own refuge, a plain, windowless place . . . a rare privilege, from what he had heard of vid about the overcrowding everywhere. More of Damon's arranging.

Ordinarily he would turn on the vid, using its noise to fill the place with voices, for dreams filled the silences.

He sat down now on the bed, simply sat there a time in the silence, probing the dreams and the memories like half-healed wounds. *Norway.*

Signy Mallory.

Mallory.

## iv

## Pell: White Dock: Lukas Company offices; 1830 hrs; 0630 hrs. alterday: alterdawn

There were no disasters. Jon stayed in the office, rearmost of all the offices, took normal calls, worked his routine of warehousing reports and records, trying in one harried corner of his mind to map out what to do if the worst happened.

He stayed later than usual, after the lights had dimmed slightly on the docks, after a good deal of the first shift staff had left for the day and the mainday activity had settled down . . . just a few clerks out in the other offices to answer com and tend things till the alterday staff came in. *Swan's Eye* went out unchallenged at 1446; *Annie* and the Kulins left with Vittorio's papers at 1703, without question or commotion more than the usual close inquiries about schedules and routing, for the militia. He breathed easier then.

And when *Annie* had long since cleared the vicinity of the station, beyond any reasonable chance of protest, he took his jacket, locked up, and headed home.

He used his card at the door, to have every minutest record in comp as it should be . . . found Jessad and Hale sitting opposite one another in silence, in his living room. There was coffee, soothing aroma after the afternoon tension. He sank into a third chair and leaned back, taking possession of his own home.

"I'll have some coffee," he told Bran Hale. Hale frowned and rose to go fetch it. And to Jessad: "A tedious afternoon?"

"Gratefully tedious," Jessad said softly. "But Mr. Hale has done his best to entertain."

"Any trouble getting here?"

"None," Hale said from the kitchen. He brought back the coffee, and Jon sipped at it, realized Hale was waiting.

Dismiss him . . . and sit alone with Jessad. He was not eager for that. Neither was he eager to have Hale talking too freely, here or elsewhere. "I appreciate your discretion," he told Hale. And with a careful consideration: "You know there's something up. You'll find it worth your while more than monetarily. Only see you keep Lee Quale from indiscretions. I'll fill you in on it as soon as I find out more. Vittorio's gone. Dayin's . . . lost. I've need of some reliable, intelligent assistance. You read me, Bran?"

Hale nodded.

"I'll talk with you about this tomorrow," he said then very quietly. "Thank you."

"You all right here?" Hale asked.

"If I'm not," he said, "you take care of it. Hear?"

Hale nodded, discreetly left. Jon settled back with somewhat more assurance, looked at his guest, who sat easily in front of him.

"I take it you trust this person," Jessad said, "and that you want to promote him in your affairs. Choose your allies wisely, Mr. Lukas."

"I know my own." He drank a sip of the scalding coffee. "I don't know you, Mr. Jessad or whatever your name is. Your plan to use my son's ID I can't permit. I've arranged a different cover . . . for him. A tour of Lukas interests: a ship's outbound for the mines and his papers are on it."

He expected outrage. There was only a polite lift of the brows. "I have no objection. But I shall need papers, and I don't think it wise to expose myself to interrogation obtaining them."

"Papers can be gotten. That's the least of our problems."

"And the greatest, Mr. Lukas?"

"I want some answers. Where's Dayin?"

"Safe behind the lines. No cause for worry. I'm sent as a contingency . . . an assumption that this offer is valid. If not, I shall die . . . and I hope that's not the case."

"What can you offer me?"

"Pell," Jessad said softly. "Pell, Mr. Lukas."

"And you're prepared to hand it to me."

Jessad shook his head. "You're going to hand it to us, Mr. Lukas. That's the proposal. I'll direct you. Mine is the expertise . . . yours the precise knowledge of this place. You'll brief me on the situation here."

"And what protection have I?"

"My approval."

"Your rank?"

Jessad shrugged. "Unofficial. I want details. Everything from your shipping schedules to the deployment of your ships to the proceedings of your council . . . to the least detail of the management of your own offices."

"You plan to live in my apartment the whole time?"

"I find little reason to stir forth. Your social schedule may suffer for it. But is there a safer place to be? This Bran Hale—a discreet man?"

"Worked for me on Downbelow. He was fired down there for upholding my policies against the Konstantins. Loyal."

"Reliable?"

"Hale is. Of some of his crew I have some small doubt . . . at least regarding judgment."

"You must take care, then."

"I am."

Jessad nodded slowly. "But find me papers, Mr. Lukas. I feel much more secure with them than without."

"And what happens to my son?"

"Concerned? I'd thought there was little love lost there."

"I asked the question."

"There's a ship holding far out . . . one we've taken, registered to the Olvig merchanter family, but in fact military. The Olvigs are all in detention . . . as are most of the people of *Swan's Eye*. The Olvig ship, *Hammer,* will give us advance warning. And there's not that much time, Mr. Lukas. First . . . will you show me a sketch of the station itself?"

*Mine is the expertise.* An expert in such affairs, a man trained for this. A terrible and chilling thought came on him, that Viking had fallen from the inside; that Mariner on the other hand . . . had been blown. Sabotage. From the inside. Someone mad enough to kill the station he was on . . . or leaving.

He stared into Jessad's nondescript face, into eyes quite, quite implacable, and reckoned that on Mariner there had been such a person as this.

Then the Fleet had shown up, and the station had been deliberately destroyed.

## V

## Pell: Q zone: orange nine; 1900 hrs.

There were still people standing in line outside, a queue stretching down the niner hall out onto the dock. Vassily Kressich rested his head against the heels of his hands as the most recent went out in the ungentle care of one of Coledy's men, a woman who had shouted at him, who had complained of theft and named one of Coledy's gang. His head ached; his back ached. He abhorred these sessions, which he held, nevertheless, every five days. It was at least a pressure valve, this illusion that the councillor of Q listened to the problems, took down complaints, *tried* to get something done.

About the woman's complaint . . . little remedy. He knew the man she had named. Likely it was true. He would ask Nino Coledy to put the lid on him, perhaps save her from worse. The woman was mad to have complained. A bizarre hysteria, perhaps, that point which many reached here, when anger was all that mattered. It led to self-destruction.

A man was shown in. Redding, next in line. Kressich braced himself inwardly, leaned back in his chair, prepared for the weekly encounter. "We're still trying," he told the big man.

"I paid," Redding said. "I paid plenty for my pass."

"There are no guarantees in Downbelow applications, Mr. Redding. The station simply takes those it has current need of. Please put your new application on my desk and I'll keep running it through the process. Sooner or later there'll be an opening—"

"I want out!"

*"James!"* Kressich shouted in panic.

Security was there instantly. Redding looked about wildly, and to Kressich's dismay, reached for his waistband. A short blade flashed into his hand, not for security . . . Redding turned from James—for *him.*

Kressich flung himself backward on the chair's track. Des James hurled himself on Redding's back. Redding sprawled facedown on the desk, sending papers everywhere, slashing wildly as Kressich scrambled from the chair and against the wall. Shouting erupted outside, panic, and more people poured into the room.

Kressich edged over as the struggle came near him. Redding hit the wall. Nino Coledy was there with the others. Some wrestled Redding to the ground, some pushed back the torrent of curious and desperate petitioners. The mob waved forms they hoped to turn in. "My turn!" some woman was shrieking, brandishing a paper and trying to reach the desk. They herded her out with the others.

Redding was down, pinned by three of them. A fourth kicked him in the head and he grew quieter.

Coledy had the knife, examined it thoughtfully and pocketed it, a smile on his scarred young face.

"No station police for him," James said.

"You hurt, Mr. Kressich?" Coledy asked.

"No." He discounted bruises, felt his way to his desk. There was still shouting outside. He pulled the chair up to the desk again and sat down, his legs shaking. "He talked about having paid money," he said, knowing full well what was going on, that the forms came from Coledy and cost whatever the traffic would bear. "He's got a bad record with station and I can't get him a pass. What do you mean selling him an assurance?"

Coledy turned a slow look from him to the man on the floor and back again. "Well, now he's got a bad mark with us, and that's worse. Get him out of here. Take him out down the hall, the other way."

"I can't see any more people," Kressich moaned, resting his head against his hands. "Get them out of here."

Coledy walked into the outer corridor. "Clear it out!" Kressich could hear him shouting above the cries of protest and the sobbing. Some of Coledy's men began to make them move . . . armed, some of them, with metal bars. The crowd gave back, and Coledy returned to the office. They were taking Redding out the other door, shaking him to make him walk, for he was beginning to recover, bleeding from the temple in a red wash which obscured his face.

*They'll kill him,* Kressich thought. Somewhere in the less trafficked hours, a body would find its way somewhere to be found by station. Redding surely knew it. He was trying to fight again, but they got him out and the door closed.

"Mop that up," Coledy told one of those who remained, and the man searched for something to clean the floor. Coledy sat down again on the edge of the desk.

Kressich reached under it, brought out one of the bottles of wine with which Coledy supplied him. Glasses. He poured two, sipped at the Downer wine and tried to warm the tremors from his limbs, the twinges of pain from his chest. "I'm too old for this," he complained.

"You don't have to worry about Redding," Coledy told him, picking up his glass.

"You can't create situations like that," Kressich snapped. "I know what you're up to. But don't sell the passes where there's no chance I'll be able to get them."

Coledy grinned, an exceedingly unpleasant expression. "Redding would ask for it sooner or later. This way he paid for the privilege."

"I don't want to know," Kressich said sourly. He drank a large mouthful of the wine. "Don't give me the details."

"We'd better get you to your apartment, Mr. Kressich.

Keep a little watch on you. Just till this matter is straightened out."

He finished the wine at his own rate. One of the youths in Coledy's group had gathered up the stack of papers the struggle had scattered about the floor, and laid it on his desk. Kressich stood up then, his knees still weak, averted his eyes from the blood which had tracked on the matting.

Coledy and four of his men escorted him, through that same back door which had received Redding and his guards. They walked down the corridor into the sector in which he maintained his small apartment, and he used his manual key . . . comp had cut them off and nothing worked here but manual controls.

"I don't need your company," he said shortly. Coledy gave him a wry and mocking smile, parodied a bow.

"Talk with you later," Coledy said.

Kressich went inside, closed the door again by manual, stood there with nausea threatening him. He sat down finally, in the chair by the door, tried to stay still a moment.

Madness accelerated in Q. The passes which were hope for some to get out of Q only increased the despair of those left behind. The roughest were left, so that the temperature of the whole was rising. The gangs ruled. No one was safe who did not belong to one of the organizations . . . man or woman, no one could walk the halls safely unless it was known he had protection; and protection was sold . . . for food or favors or bodies, whatever the currency available. Drugs . . . medical and otherwise . . . made it in; wine did; precious metals, anything of value . . . made it out of Q and into station. Guards at the barriers made profits.

And Coledy sold applications for passes out of Q, for Downbelow residency. Sold even the right to stand in the lines for justice. And anything else that Coledy and his police found profitable. The protections gang reported to Coledy for license.

There was only the diminishing hope of Downbelow, and those rejected or deferred became hysterical with the suspicion that there were lies recorded about them in station files, black marks which would keep them forever in Q. There were a rising number of suicides; some gave themselves to excesses in the barracks halls which became sinks of every vice. Some committed the crimes, perhaps, of which they feared they were accused; and some became the victims.

"They kill them down there," one young man had cried, rejected. "They don't go to Downbelow at all; they take them out of here and kill them, that's where they go. They don't take workers, they don't take young men, they take old people and children out, and they get rid of them."

"Shut up!" others had cried, and the youth had been beaten bloody by three others in the line before Coledy's police could pull him out; but others wept, and still stood in line with their applications for passes clutched in their hands.

*He* could not apply to go. He feared some leak getting back to Coledy if he put in an application for himself. The guards were trading with Coledy, and he feared too much. He had his black market wine, had his present safety, had Coledy's guards about him so that if anyone was harmed in Q, it would not be Vassily Kressich, not until Coledy suspected he might be trying to break from him.

Good came of what he did, he persuaded himself. While he stayed in Q, while he held the fifth-day sessions, while he at least remained in a position to object to the worst excesses. Some things Coledy would stop. Some things Coledy's men would think twice about rather than have an issue made of them. He saved something of order in Q. Saved some lives. Saved a little bit from the thing Q would become without his influence.

And *he* had access to the outside . . . had that hope, always, if the situation here became truly unbearable, when the inevitable crisis came . . . he could plead for asylum. Might get out. They would not put him back to die. Would not.

He rose finally, hunted out the bottle of wine he had in the kitchen, poured himself a quarter of it, trying not to think of what had happened, did happen, would happen.

Redding would be dead by morning. He could not pity him, saw only the mad eyes of the man staring at him as he lunged across the desk, scattering papers, slashing at him with the knife . . . at *him,* and not at Coledy's guards.

As if *he* were the enemy.

He shuddered, and drank his wine.

## vi

## Pell: Downer residence; 2300 hrs.

Change of workers. Satin stretched aching muscles as she entered the dimly lit habitat, stripped off the mask and washed fastidiously in the cool water of the basin provided for them. Bluetooth (never far from her, day or night) followed and squatted down on her mat, rested his hand on her shoulder, his head against her. They were tired, very tired, for there had been a great load to move this day, and although the big machines did most of the work, it was Downer muscle which set the loads on the machines and humans who did the shouting. She took his other hand and turned it palm up, mouthed the sore spots, leaned close and gave a lick to his cheek where the mask had roughed the fur.

"Lukas-men," Bluetooth snarled. His eyes were fixed straight forward and his face was angry. They had worked for Lukas-men this day, some who had given the trouble Downbelow, at the base. Satin's own hands hurt and shoulders ached, but it was Bluetooth she worried for, with this look in his eye. It took much to stir Bluetooth to real temper. He tended to think a great deal, and while he was thinking, found no chance to be angry, but this time, she reckoned he was doing both, and when he did lose his temper, it would be bad for him, among humans, with Lukas-men about. She stroked his coarse coat and groomed him until he seemed calmer.

"Eat," she said. "Come eat."

He turned his head to her, lipped her cheek, licked the fur straight and put his arm about her. "Come," he agreed, and they got up and walked through the metal tunnel to the big room, where there was always food ready. The young ones in charge here gave them each a generous bowlful, and they retreated to a quiet corner to eat. Bluetooth managed good humor at last, with his belly full, sucked the porridge off his fingers in contentment. Another male came trailing in, got his bowl and sat down by them, young Bigfellow, who grinned companionably at them, consumed one bowl of porridge and went back after his second.

They liked Bigfellow, who was not too long ago from Downbelow himself, from their own riverside, although from another camp and other hills. Others gathered when Bigfellow came back, more and more of them, a bow of warmth facing the corner they sat in. Most among them were seasonal workers, who came to the Upabove and returned to Downbelow again, working with their hands and not knowing much of the machines: these were warm toward them. There were other hisa, beyond this gathering of friends, the permanent workers, who did not much speak to them, who sat to themselves in the far corner, who sat much and stared, as if their long sojourning among humans had made them into something other than hisa. Most were old. They knew the mystery of the machines, wandered the deep tunnels and knew the secrets of the dark places. They always stayed apart.

"Speak of Bennett," Bigfellow asked, for he, like the others who came and went, whatever the camp which had sent them on Downbelow, had passed through the human camp, had known Bennett Jacint; and there had been great mourning in the Upabove when the news of Bennett's death had come to them.

"I speak," Satin said, for she, newest here, had the telling of this tale, among tales that the hisa told in this place, and she warmed quickly to the story. Every evening since their coming, the talk had not been of the small doings of the hisa, whose lives were always the same, but of the doings of the Konstantins, and how Emilio and his friend Miliko had made the hisa smile again . . . and of Bennett who had died the hisa's friend. Of all who had come to the Upabove to tell this tale, there was none to tell it who had *seen*, and they made her tell it again and again.

"He went down to the mill," she said, when she came to that sad time in the story, "and he tells the hisa there no, no, please run, humans will do, humans will work so river takes no hisa. And he works with his own hands, always, always, Bennett-man would work with his own hands, never shout, no, loves the hisa. We gave him a name—I gave, because he gave me my human name and my good spirit. I call him Comes-from-bright."

There was a murmuring at this, appreciation and not censure, although it was a spirit-word for Sun himself. Hisa wrapped their arms about themselves in a shiver, as they did each time she told this.

"And the hisa do not leave Bennett-man, no, no. They work with him to save the mill. Then old river, she is angry with humans and with hisa, always angry, but most angry because Lukas-mans make bare her banks and take her water. And we warn Bennett-man he must not trust old river, and he hears us and come back; but we hisa, we work, so the mill will not be lost and Bennett not be sad. Old river, she come higher, and takes the posts away; and we shout quick, quick, come back! for the hisa who work. I-Satin, I work there, *I* see." She thumped her chest and touched Bluetooth, embellishing her tale. "Bluetooth and Satin, we see, we run to help the hisa, and Bennett and good mans his friends, all, all run to help them. But old river, she drinks them down, and we come too late in running, all too late. The mill breaks, ssst! And Bennett he reaches for hisa in arms of old river. She takes him too, with mans who help. We shout, we cry, we beg old river give Bennett back; but she takes him all the same. All hisa she gives back, but she takes Bennett-man and his friends. Our eyes are filled with this. He dies. He dies when he holds out arms for the hisa, his good heart makes him die, and old river, bad old river she drink him down. Humans find him and bury him. I set the spirit-sticks above him and gave him gifts. I come here, and my friend Bluetooth comes, because it is a Time. I come here on pilgrimage, where is Bennett's home."

There was a murmured approval, a general swaying of the bodies which ringed them. Eyes glistened with tears.

And a strange and fearful thing had happened, for some of the strange Upabove hisa had moved into the back fringes of the crowd, themselves swaying and watching.

"He loves," one of them said, startling others. "He loves the hisa."

"So," she agreed. A knot swelled into her throat at this admission from one of the terrible strange ones, that they listened to the burden of her heart. She felt among her pouches, her spirit-gifts. She brought out the bright cloth, and held it in gentle fingers. "This is my spirit-gift, my name he gives me."

Another swaying and a murmur of approval.

"What is your name, storyteller?"

She hugged her spirit-gift close to her breast and stared at the strange one who had asked, drew in a great breath. Storyteller. Her skin prickled at such an honor from the strange Old One. "I am Sky-sees-her. Humans call me Satin." She reached a caressing hand to Bluetooth.

"I am Sun-shining-through-clouds," Bluetooth said, "friend of Sky-sees-her."

The strange one rocked on his haunches, and by now all the strange hisa had gathered, to a muttering of awe among the others, who gave way to leave an open space between them and her.

"We hear you speak of this Comes-from-bright, this Bennett-man. Good, good, was this human, and good you gave him gifts. We make your journey welcome, and honor your pilgrimage, Sky-sees-her. Your words make us warm, make warm our eyes. Long time we wait."

She rocked forward, respecting the age of the speaker, and his great courtesy. There were increasing murmurs among the others. "This is the Old One," Bigfellow whispered at her shoulder. "He does not *speak* to us."

The Old One spat, brushed his coat disdainfully. "The storyteller speaks sense. She marks a Time with her journey. She walks with her eyes open, not only her hands."

"Ah," the others murmured, taken aback, and Satin sat dismayed.

"We praise Bennett Jacint," the Old One said. "He makes us warm to hear these things."

"Bennett-man is *our* human," Bigfellow said staunchly. "Downbelow human: he sent me here."

"Loved us," another said, and another: "All loved him."

"He defended us from Lukases," Satin said. "And Konstantin-man is his friend, sends me here for my spring, for pilgrimage; we meet by Bennett's grave. I come for great Sun, to see his face, to see the Upabove. But, Old One, we see only machines, no great brightness. We work hard, hard. We do not have the blossoms or the hills, my friend and I, no, but we still hope. Bennett says here is good, here is beautiful; he says great Sun is near this place. We wait to see, Old One. We asked for the images of the Upabove, and no one here has seen them. They say that humans hide them away from us. But we still wait, Old One."

There was long silence, while Old One rocked to and fro. Finally he ceased, and held up a bony hand. "Sky-sees-her, the things you seek are here. *We* visit there. The images stand in the place where human Old Ones meet, and we have seen them. Sun watches over this place, yes, that is true. Your Bennett-man did not deceive you. But there are things here that will make your bones cold, storyteller. We do not speak these secret things. How will hisa Downbelow understand them? How will they bear them? Their eyes do not see. But this Bennett-man made warm your eyes and called you. Ah! long we wait, long, long, and you make warm our hearts to welcome you.

"Ssst! Upabove is not what it seems. The images of the plain we remember. *I* have seen them. *I* have slept by them and dreamed dreams. But the images of Upabove . . . they are not for our dreaming. You tell us of Bennett Jacint, and we tell you, storyteller, of one of us you do not see: Lily, humans call her. Her name is Sun-smiles-on-her, and *she* is the Great Old One, many more than my seasons. The images we gave humans have become human images, and near them a human dreams in the secret places of the Upabove, in a place all bright. Great Sun comes to visit her . . . never moves she, no, for the dream is good. She lies all in bright, her eyes are warm with Sun; the stars dance for her; she watches all the Upabove on her walls, perhaps watches us in this moment. *She* is the image which watches us. The Great Old One cares for her, loves her, this holy one. Good, good is her love, and she dreams us all, all the Upabove, and her face smiles forever upon great Sun. She is *ours*. We call her Sun-her-friend."

*"Ah,"* the gathering murmured, stunned at such a thing, one mated to great Sun himself. "Ah," Satin murmured with the others, hugged herself and shivering, leaned forward. "Shall we see this good human?"

"No," said Old One shortly. "Only Lily goes there. And myself. Once. Once I saw."

Satin sank back, profoundly disappointed.

"Perhaps there *is* no such human," Bluetooth said.

Now Old One's ears lay back, and there was an intake of breath all about them.

"It is a Time," said Satin, "and my journey. We come very far, Old One, and we cannot see the images and we cannot see the dreamer; we have not yet found the face of Sun."

Old One's lips pursed and relaxed several times. "You come. We show you. This night you come; next night others . . . if you are not afraid. We show you a place. It has no humans in it for a short time. *One hour*. Human counting. I know how to reckon. You come?"

From Bluetooth there was not a sound. "Come," Satin said, and felt his reluctance as she tugged at his arm. Others would not. There were none so daring . . . or so trusting of the strange Old One.

Old One stood up, and two of his company with him. Satin did, and Bluetooth stood up more slowly.

"I go too," Bigfellow said, but none of his companions came with him to join them.

Old One surveyed them with a curious mockery, and motioned them to come, down the tunnels, into the further ways, tunnels where hisa could move without masks, dark places where one must climb far on thin metal and where even hisa must bend to walk.

"He is mad," Bluetooth hissed finally into her ear, panting. "And we are mad to follow this deranged Old One. They are all strange who have been here long."

Satin said nothing, not knowing any argument but her desire. She feared, but she followed, and Bluetooth followed her. Bigfellow trailed along after all of them. They panted when they must go a long way bent or climb far. It was a mad strength that the Old One and his two fellows had, as if they were used to such things and knew where they were going.

Or perhaps—the thought chilled her bones—it was some bizarre humor of the Old One to strand them deep in the dark ways, where they might wander and die lost, to teach the others a lesson.

And just as she was becoming convinced of that fear, the Old One and his companions reached a stopping place and drew up their masks, indicating that they were at a place which would break into human air. Satin swept hers up to her face and Bluetooth and Bigfellow did so only just in time, for the door behind them closed and the door before them opened on a bright hall, white floors and the green of growing things, and here and there scattered humans coming and going in the lonely large space . . . nothing like the docks. Here was cleanliness and light, and vast dark beyond them, where Old One wished to lead them.

Satin felt Bluetooth slip his hand into hers, and Bigfellow hovered close to both of them as they followed, into a darkness even vaster than the bright place they had left, where there were no walls, only sky.

Stars shifted about them, dazzling them with the motion, magical stars which changed from place to place, burning clear and more steadily than ever Downbelow saw them. Satin let go the hand which held hers and walked forward in awe, gazing about her.

And suddenly light blazed forth, a great burning disc spotted with dark, flaring with fires.

"Sun," Old One intoned.

There was no brightness, no blue, only dark and stars and the terrible close fire. Satin trembled.

"There is dark," Bluetooth objected. "How can there be night where Sun is?"

"All stars are kindred of great Sun," said Old One. "This is a truth. The brightness is illusion. This is a truth. Great Sun shines in darkness and he is large, so large we are dust. He is terrible, and his fires frighten the dark. This is truth. Sky-sees-her, this is the true sky: this is your name. The stars are like great Sun, but far, far from us. This we have learned. See! The walls show us the Upabove itself, and the great ships, the outside of the docks. And there is Downbelow. We are looking on it now."

"Where is the human camp?" Bigfellow asked. "Where is old river?"

"The world is round like an egg, and some of it faces away from Sun; this makes night on that side. Perhaps if you looked closely you might see old river; I have thought so. But never the human camp. It is too small on the face of Downbelow."

Bigfellow hugged himself and shivered.

But Satin walked among the tables, walked into the clear place, where great Sun shone in his truth, overcoming the dark . . . terrible he was, orange like fire, and filling all with his terror.

She thought of the dreaming human called Sun-her-friend, whose eyes were forever warmed with that sight, and the hair lifted on her nape.

And she stretched wide her arms and turned, embracing all the Sun, and his far kindred, lost in them, for she had come to the Place which she had journeyed to find. She filled her eyes with the sight, as Sun looked at her, and she could never be the same again, forever.

# 4

## Aboard Norway: null point, Union space; 9/10/52

Omicron Point.

*Norway* was not the first to come flashing into the vicinity of that dark, planet-sized piece of rock and ice, visible only as it occluded stars. Others had preceded her to this sunless rendezvous. Omicron was a wanderer, a bit of debris between stars, but its location was predictable and it provided mass enough to home in on out of jump . . . a place as nowhere as it was possible to be, a chance finding by Sung of *Pacific* long ago, used by the Fleet since then. It was one of those bits that the sublight freighters had dreaded, which jumpships with private business to conduct . . . cherished and kept secret.

Sensors were picking up activity, multiple ship presence, transmissions out of this forever-night. Computer talked to computer as they came in; and Signy Mallory kept her eyes flickering from one to the other bit of telemetry, fighting the hypnotism that so easily set in from jump and the necessary drugs. She hurled *Norway* into realspace max, heading for those signals and out of the jump range with the sense of something on her tail, trusted her crew's accuracy and aimed with the ship underway, the flickering few minutes of heart-in-throat transit near *C,* where all they had was approximation.

She cut it back quickly, started dumping velocity, no comfortable process, and the slightly speed-mad telemetry and slightly drug-mad human brain fought for precise location; overestimate that dump and she could take *Norway* right into that rock or into another ship.

"Clear, clear, all in now but *Europe* and *Libya,*" com reported.

No mean feat of navigation, to find Omicron so accurately, to come in within middle scan, right in the jump range, after a start from near Russell's, far away. Fail their time, and they would have been in the jump range when something else came in, and that was disaster. "Good job," she sent to all stations, looking at the reckoning Graff flashed to her center screen: "Two minutes off mark but dead on distance; can't cut it much closer at our starting range. Good signals being received. Stand by."

She took her pattern in relation to Omicron, checked through data; within the half hour there was a signal from *Libya,* which had just come in. *Europe* came in a quarter hour after that, from another plane.

That was the tale of them, then. They were in one place, at one time, which they had not been since their earliest operations. Unlikely as it was Union would come on them in strength here, they were still nervous.

Computer signal came in from *Europe.* They were given breathing space, to rest. Signy leaned back, took the com plug from her ear, unharnessed and got up finally while Graff moved to the post she had vacated. They were not at the disadvantage of some: *Norway* was one of the mainday ships . . . her main command staff on the schedule they were following now. Others, *Atlantic, Africa,* and *Libya,* were alterday, so that strike hours were never remotely predictable, so that there were ships with their main crews available on either schedule. But they were all mainday now, a synchronization they had never undergone, and the alterday captains did the suffering, jump and reversed hours combined.

"Take over," she bade Graff, wandered back through the aisle, touched a shoulder here and there, walked back to her own nook in the corridor . . . passed it by. She walked on back instead to crew quarters, looked in on them, alterday crew, most drugged senseless, to get their rest despite jump. A few, having an aversion to that procedure, were awake, sat in the crew mainroom looking better than they probably felt. "All stable," she told them. "Everyone all right?"

They avowed so. They would drug out now, safe and peacefully. She left them to do that, took the lift down to the outershell and the troop quarters, walked the main corridor behind the suiting area, stopped in one barracks after another, where she interrupted knot after knot of men and women sitting and trading speculations on their prospects . . . guilty looks and startled ones, troopers springing to their feet in dismay to find themselves under her scrutiny, a frantic groping after bits of clothing, a hiding of this and that which might be disapproved; she did not, but the crew and troops had some quaint reticences. Some here too slept drugged, unconscious in their bunks; most did not . . . gambled, in many a compartment, while the ship shot her own dice with the Deep, while flesh and ship seemed to dissolve and the game continued on the other side of a far-stretched moment.

"Going to be a bit slow down here," she would say in each case. "We're in pattern and we're all stable; at your ease down here, but keep yourselves within a minute's prep for moving. No reason to think there's a problem, but we take no chances."

Di Janz intercepted her in the main corridor after the third such visit, nodded courtesy, walked with her through this private domain of his, seeming pleased in her presence among his command. Troops braced when Di walked with her, came to blank attention. Best, she thought, to pull the pretended inspection, just to let them know command had not forgotten them down here. What was coming was the kind of operation the troops dreaded, a multiple-ship strike, which raised the hazard of getting hit. And the troops had to ride it out blind, useless, jammed in the small safety the inner structure of the ship could afford them. There were no braver when it came to walking into possible fire, boarding a stopped merchanter, landing in some ground raid; and they took in stride the usual strike, *Norway* sweeping in alone, hit and run. But they were nervous now . . . she had heard it in the muttered comments which filtered over open com—always open: *Norway* tradition, that they all knew what was going on, down to the newest troopers. They obeyed, would obey, but their pride was hurt in this new phase of the war, in which they had no use. Important to be down here now, to make the gesture. Queasy as they were with jump and drugs, they were at their lowest, and she saw eyes brighten at a word, a touch on the shoulder in passing. She knew them by name, every one, called them by name, one and another of them. There was Mahler, whom she had taken from Russell's refugees, looking particularly sober and no little frightened; Kee, from a merchanter; Di had come years ago, the same way. Many, many more. Some of them were rejuved, like her, had known her for years . . . knew the score as well, too, she reckoned, as well as any of them knew it. Bitter to them that this critical phase was not theirs, could not be.

She walked the dark limbo of the forward hold, round the cylinder rim, into the eitherway world of the ridership crews, a place like home, a memory of other days, when she had had her quarters in such a place, this bizarre section where the crews of the insystem fighters, their mechanics, prep crews, lived in their own private world. A whole other command existed here, right way up at the moment, under rotation, ceiling down the rare times they were docked. Two of the eight crews were here, Quevedo's and Almarshad's, of *Odin* and *Thor;* four were off duty; two were riding null up in the frame . . . or inside their ships, because locking crews through the special lift out of the rotation cylinder took one rotation of the hull, and they could not spare that time if they jumped into trouble. Riding null through jump—she recalled that experience well enough. Not the pleasantest way to travel, but it was always someone's job. They had no intent to deploy the riders here at Omicron, or two more sets of them would have been up there in the can, as they called it, in that exile. "All's as it should be," she said to those in demi-prep. "Rest, relax, keep off the liquor; we're still on standby and will be while we're here. Don't know when we'll be ordered out or with how much warning. Could have to scramble, but far from likely. My guess is we don't make mission jump without some time for rest. This operation is on our timetable, not Union's."

There was no quibble. She took the lift up to main level, walked the shorter distance around to number one corridor, her legs still rubbery, but the drugs were losing their numbing effect. She went to her own office/quarters, paced the floor a time, finally lay down on the cot and rested, just to shut her eyes and let the tension ebb, the nervous energy that jump always threw into her, because usually it meant coming out into combat, snapping decisions rapidly, kill or die.

Not this time; this was the planned one, the thing to which they had been moving for months of small strikes, raids that had taken out vital installations, that had harried and destroyed where possible.

Rest a while; sleep if they could. She could not. She was glad when the summons came.

It was a strange feeling, to stand again in the corridors of *Europe,* stranger still to find herself in the company of all the others seated in the flagship's council room . . . an eerie and panicky feeling, this meeting of all of them who had been working together unmet these many years, who had so zealously avoided each other's vicinities except for brief rendezvous for the passing of orders ship to ship. In recent years it was unlikely that Mazian himself had known where all his fleet was, whether particular ships survived the missions on which they were sent . . . or what mad operations they might be undertaking solo. They had been less a fleet than a guerrilla operation, skulking and striking and running.

Now they were here, the last ten, the survivors of the maneuvers—herself; Tom Edger of *Australia,* lean and grim-faced; big Mika Kreshov of *Atlantic,* perpetually scowling; Carlo Mendez of *North Pole,* a small, dark man of quiet manner. There was Chenel of *Libya,* who had gone on rejuv—his hair had turned entirely silver since she had seen him a year ago; there was dark-skinned Porey of *Africa,* an incredibly grim man . . . cosmetic surgery after wounds was not available in the Fleet. Keu of *India,* silk-soft and confident; Sung of *Pacific,* all efficiency; Kant of *Tibet,* another of Sung's stamp.

And Conrad Mazian. Silver-haired with rejuv, a tall, handsome man in dark blue, who leaned his arms on the table and swept a slow glance over them. It was intended for effect; possibly it was sincere affection, that open look. Dramatic sense and Mazian were inseparable; the man lived by it. Knowing him, knowing the manner of him, Signy still found herself drawn in by the old excitement.

No preliminaries, no statement of welcome, just that look and a nod. "Folders are in front of you," Mazian said. "Closest security: codes and coordinates are in those. Carry them back with you and familiarize your key personnel with the details, but don't discuss anything ship to ship. Key your comps for alternatives A, B, C, and so on, and go to them by that according to the situation. But we don't reckon to be using those alternatives. Things are set up as they should be. Schematic—" He called an image to the screen before them, showed them the familiar area of their recent operations, which by stripping away vital personnel and leaving chaos on the stations left one lone untampered station like the narrowing of a funnel toward Pell, toward the wide straggle of Hinder Stars. One station. Viking. Signy had figured the pattern long since, the tactic old as Earth, old as war, impossible for Union to resist, for they could not allow vacuum in power, could not allow the stations they had struggled to gain to fall into disorder, plundered of technicians and directors and security forces, deliberately allowed to collapse. Union had started this game of station-taking. So they had rammed stations down Union's throat; Union had then to move in or have stations lost, had to supply techs and other skilled personnel, to replace the ones evacuated. And ships to guard them, quickly, one after the other. Union had had to stretch even its monster capacity to hold what it had been given to digest.

It had had to take Viking whole, with all the internal complications of a station never evacuated . . . take it latest, because by ramming stations down Union's gullet in their own rapid sequence, they had dictated the sequence and direction of Union's moves of ships and personnel.

Viking had been last.

Central to the others, with desolation about it, stations struggling to survive.

"All indication is," Mazian said softly, "that they have decided to fortify Viking; logical choice: Viking's the only one with its comp files complete, the only one where they've had a chance to round up all the dissidents, all the resistance, where they could apply their police tactics and card everyone, instantly. Now it's all clean, all sanitary for their base of operations; we've let them throw a lot into it; we take *out* Viking, and hit at the others, that are hanging by a thread in terms of viability . . . and then there's nothing but far waste between us and Fargone; between Pell and Union. We make expansion inconvenient, costly; we herd the beast to its wider pastures in the other direction . . . while we can. You have your specific instructions in the folders. The fine details may have to be improvised within certain limits, according to what might turn up in your sectors. *Norway, Libya, India,* unit one; *Europe, Tibet, Pacific,* two; *North Pole, Atlantic, Africa,* three; *Australia* has its own business. If we're lucky we won't face anything at our rear, but every contingency is covered. This is going to be a long session; that's why I let you rest. We'll simulate until there are no more questions."

Signy drew a slow breath and released it, opened the folder and in the silence Mazian afforded them to do so, scanned the operation as it was set up, her lips pressed to a thinner and thinner line. No need for drill: they knew what they were about, variations on old themes they had all run separately. But this was navigation that would try all their skill, a mass strike, a precision of arrival not synched, but separate, disaster if jumpships came near each other, if an object of mass like the enemy just happened to be in the vicinity. They were going to flash in close enough to Viking to give the opposition no options, skin the hair off disaster. The presence of any enemy ship where it statistically ought not to be, the deployment of ships out from station in unusual configurations . . . all manner of contingencies. They took into account too the positions of worlds and satellites in the system on their arrival date, to screen themselves where possible. To flash out of jump space with nerves still sluggish, to haul dazed minds into action and try to plot instantly the location of friend and enemy, to coordinate an attack so precisely that some of them were going to overjump Viking and some underjump it, come in from all sides at once, from the same start—

They had one advantage over Union's sleek, new ships, the fine equipment, the unscarred young crews, tape-trained, deeptaught with all the answers. The Fleet had experience, could move their patched ships with a precision Union's fine equipment had not yet matched, with nerve Union conservatism and adherence to the book discouraged in its captains.

They might lose a carrier in this kind of operation, maybe more than one, come jolting in too close, take each other out. The odds were in favor of its happening. They rode Mazian's Luck . . . that it would not. That was their edge, that they would do what no one sane could do, and shock aided them.

The schematics appeared, one after the other. They argued, for the most part listened and accepted, for there was little to which they wished to object. They shared a meal, returned to the briefing room, argued the last round.

"One day for rest," Mazian said. "We go at maindawn, day after tomorrow. Set it up in comp; check and doublecheck."

They nodded, parted company, each to his own ship, and there was a peculiar flavor to the parting as well . . . that when next they met, they would be fewer.

"See you in hell," Chenel muttered, and Porey grinned.

A day to get it all into comp; and the appointment was waiting.

# 5

## Cyteen Station: Security area: 9/14/52

Ayres awoke, not sure what had wakened him in the quiet of their apartments. Marsh had gotten back . . . the latest fright they had had, when he failed to rejoin them after recreation. Tension afflicted Ayres. He realized that for some time he had slept tense, for his shoulders hurt and his hands were clenched, and he lay still now with sweat gathered on his face, not sure what had caused it.

The war of nerves had not ceased. Azov had what he wanted, a message calling Mazian in. They quibbled now over some points of secondary agreements, for the future of Pell, which Jacoby professed to hand to Union. They had their recreation time, that much, but they were detained in conferences, harassed by petty tactics the same as before. It was as if all his appeal to Azov had only aggravated the situation, for Azov was not accessible for the last five days . . . gone, the lesser authorities insisted, and the difficulties raised for them now had the taint of malice.

Someone was astir outside. Soft footsteps. The door slid back unannounced. Dias's silhouette leaned into it. "Segust," she said. "Come. You must come. It's Marsh."

He rose and reached for his robe, then followed Dias. Karl Bela was stirring him from his room likewise, next door to him. Marsh's room was across the sitting room, next to Dias's, and the door was open.

Marsh hung, gently turning, by his belt looped from a hook which had held a movable light. The face was horrible. Ayres froze an instant, then dragged back the chair which had slid on its track, climbed up, and tried to get the body down. They had no knife, had nothing with which they might cut the belt. It was imbedded in Marsh's throat and he could not get it free and support the body at once. Bela and Dias tried to help, holding the knees, but that was no good.

"We've got to call security," Dias said.

Ayres climbed down from the chair, hard-breathing, stared at them.

"I might have stopped him," Dias said. "I was still awake. I heard the moving about, a great deal of noise. Then strange sounds. When they had stopped so suddenly and so long—I finally got up to see."

Ayres shook his head, looked at Bela then stalked out to the sitting room and the com panel by the door, punched through a request to security. "One of us is dead," he said. "Put me through to someone in charge."

"Request will be relayed," the answer came back. "Security is on its way."

The contact went dead, no more informative than usual.

Ayres sat down, head in hands, tried not to think of Marsh's horrible corpse slowly spinning in the next compartment. It had been coming; he had feared worse, that Marsh would break down in his tormentors' hands. A brave man after his own fashion, he had not broken. Ayres tried earnestly to believe that he had not.

Or guilt, perhaps? Remorse might have driven him to suicide.

Dias and Bela sat down nearby, waited with him, faces stark and somber, hair disordered from sleep. He tried to comb his own with his fingers.

Marsh's eyes. He did not want to think of them.

A long time passed. "What's keeping them?" Bela

wondered, and Ayres recovered sense enough to glance up harshly at Bela, reprimand for that show of humanity. It was the old war; it continued even in this, especially after this.

"Maybe we should go back to bed," Dias said.

At other times, in other places, a mad suggestion. Here it was sanity. They needed their rest. A systematic effort was being made to deprive them of it. A little more and they would all be like Marsh.

"Probably they will be late," he agreed aloud. "We might as well."

They quietly, as if it were the sanest thing in the world, retired to their separate rooms. Ayres took off his robe and hung it over the chair by his bed, reckoning anew that he was proud of his companions, who held up so well, and that he hated—*hated* Union. It was not his business to hate, only to get results. Marsh at least was free. He wondered what Union did with their dead. Ground them up, perhaps, for fertilizer. That would be typical of such a society. Economical. Poor Marsh.

It was guaranteed that Union would be perverse. He had no sooner settled into bed, reduced his mind to a level that excluded clear thought, closed his eyes in an attempt at sleep, than the outer door whisked open, the tread of booted feet sounded in the sitting room, his door was rudely pulled back and armed soldiers stood silhouetted against the light.

With studied calm, he rose to his feet.

"Dress," a soldier said.

He did so. There was no arguing with the mannequins.

"Ayres," the soldier said, motioning with his rifle. They had been moved out of the apartment to one of the offices, he and Bela and Dias, made to sit for at least an hour on hard benches, waiting for someone of authority, who was promised them. Presumably security needed to examine the apartment in detail. "Ayres," the soldier said a second time, this time harshly, indicating that he should rise and follow.

He did so, leaving Dias and Bela with a touch of apprehension in the parting. They would be bullied, he thought, perhaps even accused of Marsh's murder. *He* was about to be, perhaps.

Another means of breaking their resistance, only, he thought. He might be in Marsh's place; he was the one separated from the others.

He was taken out of the office, brought among a squad of soldiers in the outer corridor, hastened farther and farther from the offices, from all the ordinary places, taken down in a lift, marched along another hall. He did not protest. If he stopped, they would carry him; there was no arguing with these mentalities, and he was too old to submit to being dragged down a hall.

It was the docks . . . the *docks,* crowded with military, squad upon squad of armed troops, and ships loading. "No," he said, forgetting all his policy, but a rifle barrel slammed against his shoulders, and moved him on, across the ugly utilitarian decking, up to the ramp and umbilical which linked some ship to the dock. Inside, then; the air was, if anything, colder than it was on the docks.

They passed three corridors, a lift, numerous doors. The door at the end was open and lighted, and they brought him in, into the steel and plastic of shipboard furnishings, sloping shapes, chairs of ambiguous design, fixed benches, decks of far more obvious curve than those of the station, everything cramped and angles strange. He staggered, unused to the footing, looked in surprise at the man seated at the table.

Dayin Jacoby rose from a chair to welcome him.

"What's going on?" he asked of Jacoby.

"I really don't know," Jacoby told him, and it seemed the truth. "I was roused out last night and brought aboard. I've been waiting in *this* place half an hour."

"Who's in charge here?" Ayres demanded of the mannequins. "Inform him I want to speak with him."

They did nothing, only stood, rifles braced all at the same drill angle. Ayres slowly sat down, as Jacoby did. He was frightened. Perhaps Jacoby himself was. He lapsed into his long habit of silence, finding nothing to say to a traitor at any event. There was no polite conversation possible.

The ship moved, a crash echoing through the hull and the corridors and disturbing them from their calm. Soldiers reached for handholds as the moment of queasy null came on them. Freed of station's grav, they had a moment yet to acquire their own, as ship's systems took over. Clothes crawled unpleasantly, stomachs churned; they were convinced of imminent falling, and the falling when it came was a slow settling.

"We've left," Jacoby muttered. "It's come, then."

Ayres said nothing, thinking in panic of Bela and Dias, left behind. *Left.*

A black-clad officer appeared in the doorway, and another behind him.

Azov.

"Dismissed," Azov said to the mannequins, and they went out in silent order. Ayres and Jacoby rose at once.

"What's going on?" Ayres asked directly. "What is this?"

"Citizen Ayres," said Azov, "we are on defensive maneuvers."

"My companions—what about them?"

"They are in a most secure place, Mr. Ayres. You've provided us the message we desired; it may prove of use, and therefore you're with us. Your quarters are adjoining, just down that corridor. Kindly confine yourself there."

"What's happening?" he demanded, but the aide took him by the arm and escorted him to the door. He seized the frame and resisted, casting a look back at Azov. "What's happening?"

"We are preparing," Azov said, "to deliver Mazian your message. And it seems fit for you to be at hand . . . if further questions are raised. The attack is coming; I make my guess where, and that it will be a major one. Mazian doesn't give up stations for nothing; and we're going, Mr. Ayres, to put ourselves where he has obliged us to stand . . . up the wager, as it were. He's left us no choice, and he knows it; but of course, it's earnestly to be hoped that he will regard the authority you have to recall him. Should you wish to prepare a second, even more forceful message, facilities will be provided you."

"To be edited by your experts."

Azov smiled tautly. "Do you want the Fleet intact? Frankly I doubt you can recover it. I don't think Mazian will regard your message; but as he finds himself deprived of bases, you may yet have a humanitarian role to fill."

Ayres said nothing. He reckoned silence even now the wisest course. The aide took him by the arm and drew him back down the corridor, showed him into a barren compartment of plastic furniture, and locked the door.

He paced a time, what few paces the compartment allowed. In time he yielded to the weariness in his knees and sat down. He had managed badly, he thought. Dias and Bela were . . . wherever they were—on a ship or still on the station, and what station they had been on he still did not know. Anything might happen. He sat shivering, suddenly realizing that they were lost, that soldiers and ships were aimed at Pell and Mazian . . . for Jacoby was brought along too. Another—humanitarian—function. In his own stupidity he had played to stay alive, to get home. It looked less and less likely. They were about to lose it all.

"A peace has been concluded," he had said in the simple statement he had permitted to be recorded, lacking essential codes. "Security council representative Segust Ayres by authority of the Earth Company and the security council requests the Fleet make contact for negotiation."

It was the worst of all times for major battle to be joined. Earth needed Mazian where he was, with all his ships, striking at random at Union, a nuisance, making it difficult for Union to extend its arm Earthward.

Mazian had gone mad . . . against Union's vast extent, to launch the few ships he had, and to engage on a massive scale and *lose.* If the Fleet was wiped out, then Earth was suddenly out of the time he had come here to win. No Mazian, no Pell, and everything fell apart.

And might not a message of the sort he had framed provoke some rash action, or confound maneuvers already in progress, lessening the chance of Mazian's success even further?

He rose, paced again the bowed floor of what looked to be his final prison. A second message then. An outrageous demand. If Union was as self-convinced as the mannequins, as humorlessly convinced of their purpose, they might let it pass if it fit their demands.

"Considering merger of Company interest with Union in trade agreements," he composed in his head. "Negotiations far advanced; as earnest of good faith in negotiations, cease all military operations; cease fire and accept truce. Stand by for further instructions."

Treachery . . . to drive Mazian into retreat, into the kind of scattered resistance Earth needed at this stage. It was the only hope.

# BOOK THREE

# 1

## i

## In approach to Pell: 10/4/52; 1145 hrs.

Pell.

*Norway* moved as the Fleet moved, hurling their mass into realspace in synch. Com and scan flurried into action, searching for the mote which was giant *Tibet,* which had jumped in before them, advance guard, in this rout.

"Affirmative," com sent to command with comforting swiftness. *Tibet* was where she was supposed to be, intact, probe untouched by any hostile activity. Ships were scattered about the system, commerce, quickly evaporating bluster from some self-claimed militia. *Tibet* had had one merchanter skip out in panic, and that was bad news. They needed no tale-bearers running to Union; but possibly that was the last place a merchanter wanted to head at the moment.

And a moment later confirmation snapped out from *Europe,* from the flagship's operations: they were in safe space with no action probable.

"Getting com out of Pell itself now," Graff relayed to her post at controls, still listening. "Sounds good."

Signy reached across the board and keyed signal to the rider-captains, advising them. Fast to *Norway*'s hull, so many parasites, they did not kick loose. Com was receiving direct and frantic ID's from the militia ships scrambling out of their projected course as they came insystem dangerously fast, out of system plane. The Fleet itself was more than nervous, running as they were in one body, probing their way into the last secure area they hoped to have left.

They were nine now. Chenel's *Libya* was debris and vapor, and Keu's *India* had lost two of its four riders.

They were in full retreat, had run from the debacle at

Viking, seeking a place to draw breath. They all had scars; *Norway* had a vane trailing a cloud of metallic viscera, if they still had the vane at all after jump. There were dead aboard, three techs who had been in that section. They had not had time to vent them, not even to clean up the area, had run, saved the ship, the Fleet, such as remained of Company power. Signy's boards still flashed with red lights. She passed the order to damage control to dispose of the corpses, whatever of them they could find.

Here too there might have been an ambush—was not, would not be. She stared at the lights in front of her, looked at the board, with the drugs still weighting her senses, numbing her fingers as she manipulated controls to take back *Norway*'s governance from comp synch. They had scarcely engaged at Viking, had turned tail and run—Mazian's decision. She had never questioned, had respected the man for strategic genius—for years. They had lost a ship, and he had pulled them, after months of planning, after maneuvers that had taken four months and unreckoned lives to set up.

Had pulled them from a fight from which their nerves were still jangled, from a fight which they could have won.

She had not the heart to look beside her to meet Graff's eyes, or Di's, or the faces of the others on the bridge; and no answer for them. Had none for herself. Mazian had another idea . . . something. She was desperate to believe that there was sane reason for the abort.

Get out quickly, redo it. Replan it. Only this time they had been pushed out of all their supply lines, had given up all the stations from which they had drawn goods.

It was possible Mazian's nerve had broken. She insisted otherwise to herself, but reckoned inwardly what moves she would have called, what she would have done, in command of the Fleet. What any of them could have done better than had been done. Everything had worked according to plan. And Mazian had aborted. *Mazian,* that they worshipped.

Blood was in her mouth. She had bitten her lip through.

"Receiving approach instructions from Pell via *Europe,*" com told her.

"Graff," she said, "take it over." She reserved her own

attention to the screens and the emergency com link she had plugged into her ear, direct link with Mazian when he should decide finally to use it, when he should decide to communicate with the Fleet, which he had not, silent since the orders which had hurled them out of a battle they had not lost.

It was a routine approach, all routine. She received clearance through Mazian's com, keyed the order to her rider captains, scattering *Norway*'s fighters as other ships of the Fleet were shedding their own, backup crews manning them this time. The riders would keep an eye on the militia, blast any that threatened to bolt, then come and dock to them after the great carriers were safely berthed at station.

Com chatter continued out of Pell; go slow, station pleaded with them, Pell was a crowded vicinity. There was nothing from Mazian himself.

## ii
## Pell: Blue Dock; 1200 hrs.

Mazian—Mazian himself, and not Union, not another convoy. The whole Fleet was coming in.

Word ran through the station corridors with the speed of every uncontrolled channel, through the station offices and the smallest gathering on the docks, through Q as well, for there were leaks at the barriers, and screens showed the situation there. Emotion ran from outright panic while there had been the possibility of Union ships . . . to panic of a different flavor when they knew it for what it was.

Damon studied the monitors and intermittently paced the floors of dock command blue. Elene was there, seated at the com console, holding the plug to her ear and frowning in concentrated dispute with someone. Merchanters were in a state of panic; the militarized ones were an impulse away from bolting entirely, in dread of being swept up by the Fleet, crews and ships as well impressed to service. Others dreaded confiscations, of supplies, of arms, of equipment and personnel. Such fears and complaints were his concern; he talked to some of them, when he could offer any assurance. Legal Affairs was supposed to prevent such confiscations by injunction, by writs and decrees. Decrees . . . against Mazian. Merchanters knew what that was worth. He paced and fretted, finally went to com and took another channel, contacting security.

"Dean," he hailed the man in charge, "call me alterday shift. If we can't pull them off Q, we still can't leave those freighter docks open to easy intrusion. Put some live bodies in the way. Uniform some of the supervisory staff if you haven't enough. General call-up; get those docks secure and make sure you keep the Downers out of there."

"Your office authorizes it."

"It authorizes it." There was hesitation on the other end; there were supposed to be papers, counter-signatures from the main office. Stationmaster could do it; stationmaster's office had its hands full trying to make sense out of this situation. His father was on com trying to stall off the Fleet with argument.

"Get me a signed paper when you can," Dean Gihan said. "I'll get them there."

Damon breathed a soft hiss, shut down the contact, paced more, paused again behind Elene's chair, leaning on the back of it. She leaned back in a moment's lull, half-turned to touch his hand. Her face had been white when he had come into the room. She had recovered her color and her composure. Techs kept busy, dispensing the finer details of orders to the dock crews below, preparations for station central to start shifting freighters out of berth to accommodate the Fleet. Chaos—there were not only freighters in dock; there were a hundred merchanters assigned permanent orbit with the station about Downbelow, a drifting cloud of freighters for which there had been no room. Nine ships of vast size were moving in on that, sending ships off dock out into it. Mazian's com was firing a steady catechism of questions and authorizations at Pell, as yet refusing to specify what he wanted or where he meant to dock, if he meant to dock at all.

*Us next?* The nightmare was with them. Evacuation. Pregnancy was no state in which to contemplate a refugee journey to God knew where, through jump—to some long-abandoned Hinder Star station; to Sol, to Earth. . . . He thought of *Hansford*. Thought of Elene . . . in that.

Of what had been civilized men when they started.

"Maybe we won," a tech said. He blinked, realized that too for a possibility, but not possible . . . they had always known at heart that it was impossible, that Union had grown too big, that the Fleet could give them years, as it had until now, but not victory, never that. The carriers would not have come in in this number, not for any other reason than retreat.

He reckoned their chances if Pell refused evacuation; reckoned what awaited any Konstantin in Union hands. The military would never let him stay behind. He set his hand on Elene's shoulder, his heart beating fit to break, realizing the possibility of being separated, losing her and the baby. He would be put aboard under arrest if there were an evacuation, the same way as it had happened on other stations, to get vital personnel out of Union hands, people put on whatever ship they could reach. His father . . . his mother . . . Pell was their lives; was life itself to his mother—and Emilio and Miliko. He felt sick inside, stationer, out of generations of stationers, who had never asked for war.

For Elene, for Pell, for all the dreams they had had, he would have fought.

But he did not know where to begin.

## iii
## Norway: 1300 hrs.

Signy had it visual now, the hubbed ring of Pell's Station, the distant moon, the bright jewel of Downbelow, cloud-swirled. They had long since dumped velocity, moved in with dreamlike slowness compared to their former speed, as the station's smooth shape resolved itself into the chaos of angles its surface was.

Freighters were jammed into every berth of the visible side, docking and standby. There was incredible clutter on scan, and they were moving slowly because it took that long for these sluggish ships to clear an approach for them. Every merchanter which had not been swept into Union hands had to be hereabouts, at station, in pattern, or farther out, or hovering off in the deep just out of system. Graff still had controls, a tedious business now. Unprecedented crowding and traffic. Chaos indeed. She was afraid, when she analyzed the growing tautness at her gut. Anger had cooled and she was afraid with a helplessness she was not accustomed to feel . . . a wish that by someone very wise and at some time long ago, other choices had been made, which would have saved them all from this moment, and this place, and the choices they had left.

"Carriers *North Pole* and *Tibet* will stand off from station," the notification came from *Europe*. "Assume patrol."

That was mortally necessary; and on this particular approach, Signy wished herself and her crew on that assignment. There was bitter choice ahead. She did not look forward to another operation like Russell's Station, where civ panic had anticipated the military action for the station's dismantling, mobs at the docks . . . her crew had had enough of that. *She* had, and disliked the thought of letting troops loose on a station when they were in the mood hers were in now.

Another message came through. Pell Station advised that it had shifted a number of freighters out of berths to accommodate the warships in one sequence and without immediate neighbors on the docks. The dislodged freighters would be moving through the pattern of the orbiting ships in a direction opposite to their entry of that pattern. Mazian's voice cut in, deep and harsh, a repeated advisement that, whatever disruption in the patterns of ships about Pell, if any freighter tried to jump system they would be blown without warning.

Station acknowledged; it was all they could do.

## iv
## Pell: Q; 1300 hrs.

Nothing worked. In Q nothing ever seemed to. Vassily Kressich punched buttons totally dead and punched them again, hit the com unit with the heel of his hand and still had no response from station com central. He paced the limits of his small apartment. The breakdowns infuriated him, drove him almost to tears. They happened daily; the water, the fans, the com, vid, supplies, shortages driving home over and over again the misery of his living, the decay, the pressure of bodies, the senseless violence of people driven mad by crowding and uncertainty. He had the apartment. He had his possessions; he kept these things meticulously in order, scrubbed often and obsessively. The smell of Q clung to him, no matter how he washed and how diligently he scrubbed the floors and sealed the closet against the pervading smell. It was an antiseptic reek, of cheap astringents and whatever chemicals the station used to combat disease and crowding and keep the life-support in balance.

He paced the floor, tried the com again, hoping, and it did not work. He could hear commotion outside in the corridor, trusted that Nino Coledy and his boys would have things under some control . . . hoped so. There were times when he could not get out of Q, in the occasional disturbances, when the gates sealed and even his council pass did not suffice to make an exception. He knew where he ought to be—outside, restoring order, managing Coledy, trying to restrain the Q police from some of their excesses.

And he could not go. His flesh cringed at the mere thought of confronting the mobs and the shouting and the hate and the ugliness of Q . . . of more blood, and more things to disturb his sleep. He dreamed of Redding. Of others. Of people he had known who turned up dead in the corridors, or vented. He knew that this cowardice was ultimately fatal. He fought it, knowing where it led, that when once he appeared to come apart, he was lost . . . and knowing that, there were days when it was difficult to walk those halls, when he felt his courage inadequate. He was one of them, no different from the rest; and given shelter, he did not want to come out of it, did not want to cross even that brief space necessary to reach the security post and the doors.

They would kill him, Coledy or one of the rival powers. Or someone with no motive at all. Someday in the madness of rumor which swept Q, they would kill him, someone disappointed in an application, someone who hated and found him a symbol of authority. His stomach knotted now every time he opened the door of his apartment. There were questions outside and he had no answers; there were demands, and he could not meet them; eyes, and he could not face them. If he went out this day, he had to come back, when the disorder might be worse; he was never permitted out of Q more than one shift at a time. He had tried, tested his credit with them—finally gathered the courage to *ask* for papers, to ask for release, days after the last disturbance—asked, knowing it might get back to Coledy; asked knowing it might cost him his life. And they had denied him. The great, the powerful council of which he was a member . . . would not hear him. He had, Angelo Konstantin said, too great a value where he was, privately made a show of pleading with him to stay where he was. He said nothing more of it, fearing it would go more public, and he would not live long after that.

He had been a good man, a brave man once. He had reckoned himself so, at least, before the voyage; before the war; while there was Jen, and Romy. He had twice been mobbed in Q, once beaten senseless. Redding had tried to kill him and would not be the last. He was tied and sick, and rejuv was not working for him; he suspected the quality of what he had gotten, suspected the strain was killing him. He had watched his face acquire new lines, a hollowed hopelessness; he no longer recognized the man he had been a year ago. He feared obsessively for his health, knowing the quality of medical care they had in Q, where any medicines were stolen and might be adulterated, where he was dependent on Coledy's largesse for drugs as well as wine and decent food. He no longer thought of home, no longer mourned, no longer thought of the future. There was only today, as horrible as yesterday; and if there was one desire he had left, it was to have some assurance it would not be worse.

Again he tried com, and this time not even the red light came on. Vandals dismantled things in Q as fast as their own repair crews could get them working . . . their own crews. It took days to get Pell workmen in here, and some things stayed broken. He had nightmares of such an end for them all, sabotage of something vital by a maniac who did not consider personal suicide enough, the whole section voided.

It could be done.

In crisis.

Or at any moment.

He paced the floor, faster and faster, clenched his arms across his stomach, which hurt constantly when he was under stress. The pain grew, wiping out other fears.

He gathered his nerve at last, put on his jacket, weaponless as most of Q was not, for he had to pass checkpoint scan. He fought nausea, setting his hand on the door release, finally nerved himself to step out into the dark, graffiti-marred corridor. He locked the door after him. He had not yet been robbed, but he expected to be, despite Coledy's protection; everyone was robbed. Safest to have little; he was known to have much. If he was safe it was that what he had belonged to Coledy in his men's eyes, that *he* did—if word of his application to leave had not gotten to their ears.

Through the hall and past the guards . . . Coledy's men. He walked onto the dock, among crowds which stank of sweat and unchanged clothes and antiseptic sprays. People recognized him and snatched at him with grimy hands, asking news of what was happening over in the main station.

"I don't know, I don't know yet; com's dead in my quarters. I'm on my way to learn. Yes, I'll ask. I'll ask, sir." He repeated it over and over, tearing from one pair of clutching hands to the next, one questioner to the other, some wild-eyed and far gone in the madness of drugs. He did not run; running was panic, panic was mobs, mobs were death; and there were the section doors ahead, the promise of safety, a place beyond which Q could not reach, where no one could go without the precious pass he carried.

"It's Mazian," the rumor was running Q dockside. And with it: "They're pulling out. All Pell's pulling out and leaving us behind."

"Councillor Kressich." A hand caught his arm and meant business. The grip pulled him abruptly about. He stared into the face of Sax Chambers, one of Coledy's men, felt threat in the grip which hurt his arm. "Going *where,* councillor?"

"Other side," he said, breathless. They knew. His stomach hurt the more. "Council will be meeting in the crisis. Tell Coledy. I'd better be there. No telling what council will hand us otherwise."

Sax said nothing—did nothing for a moment. Intimidation was a skill of his. He simply stared, long enough to remind Kressich that he had other skills. He let go, and Kressich pulled away.

Not running. He must not run. Must not look back. Must not make his terror evident. He was composed on the outside, though his belly was tied in knots.

A crowd was gathered about the doors. He worked his way through them, ordered them back. They moved, sullenly, and he used his pass to open their side of the access, stepped through quickly and used the card to seal the door before any could gather the nerve to follow. For a moment then he was alone on the upward ramp, the narrow access, in bright light and a lingering smell of Q. He leaned against the wall, trembling, his stomach heaving. After a moment he walked on down the ramp on the other side and pressed the button which should attract the guards on the other side of Q line.

This button worked. The guards opened, accepted his card, and noted his presence in Pell proper. He passed decontamination, and one of the guards left his post to walk with him, routine, whenever the councillor from Q was admitted to station, until he had passed the limits of the border zone; then he was allowed to walk alone.

He straightened his clothes as he went, trying to shed the smell and the memory and the thoughts of Q. But there was alarm sounding, red lights blinking in all the corridors, and security personnel and police were everywhere evident. There was no peace this side either.

v

## Pell: station central, com central office; 1300 hrs.

The boards in central com were lit from end to end, jammed with calls from every region of the station at once. Residential use had shut itself down in crisis; situation red was flashing in all zones, advising all residents to stay put.

They were not all regarding that instruction. Some halls of the halls on monitor were vacant; others were full of panicked residents. What showed now on Q monitor was worse.

"Security call," Jon Lukas ordered, watching the screens. "Blue three." The division chief leaned over the board and gave directions to the dispatcher. Jon walked over to the main board, behind the harried com chief's post. The whole of council had been called to take whatever emergency posts they could reach, to provide policy, not specifics. He had been closest, had run, reaching this post, through the chaos outside. Hale . . . Hale, he fervently hoped, had done what he was told, was sitting in his apartment, with Jessad. He watched the confusion in the center, paced from board to board, watched one and another hall in confusion. The com chief kept trying to call through to the stationmaster's office, but even he could not get through; tried to route it through station command com, and kept getting a CHANNEL UNAVAILABLE blinking on the screen.

The chief swore, accepted the protests of his subordinates, a harried man in the eye of a crisis.

"What's happening?" Jon asked. When the man ignored the question for a moment to handle a subordinate's query, he waited. "What are you doing?"

"Councillor Lukas," the chief said in a thin voice, "we have our hands full. There's no time."

"You can't get through."

"No, sir, I can't get through. They're tied up with command transmission. Excuse me."

"Let it foul," he said, when the supervisor started to turn back to the board, and when the man looked at him, startled: "Give me general broadcast."

"I need the authorization," the com chief said. Behind him, red lights began to flash and multiply. "It's the authorization I need, councillor. Stationmaster has to give it."

*"Do it!"*

The man hesitated, looked about him as if there were advice to be had from some other quarter. Jon seized him by the shoulder and faced him to the board while more and more lights flashed on the jammed boards.

"Hurry it," Jon ordered him, and the chief reached for an internal channel and punched in a mike.

"General override to number one," he ordered, and had the acknowledgment back in an instant. "Override on vid and com." The com center main screen lit, camera active.

Jon drew a deep breath and leaned into the field. The

image was going everywhere, not least to his own apartment, to the man named Jessad. "This is Councillor Jon Lukas," he said to all Pell, breaking into every channel, operations and residential, from the stations busy directing incoming ships to the barracks of Q to the least and greatest residence in the station. "I have a general announcement. The fleet presently in our vicinity is confirmed to be that of Mazian, proceeding in under normal operations for docking. This station is secure, but will remain under condition red until the all-clear is given. Operations in the com center and elsewhere will proceed more smoothly if each citizen will refrain from the use of communications except in the most extreme necessity. All points of the station are secure and there has been no damage or crisis. Records will be made of calls, and failure to regard this official request will be noted. All Downer work crews, report to your section habitats at once and wait for someone to direct you. Stay off the docks. All other workers continue about your assigned business. If you can solve problems without calling central, do so. As yet we have nothing but operations contact with the Fleet; as soon as information becomes available, we will make it public. Please stay by your receivers; this will be the quickest and most accurate source of news."

He leaned out of the field. The warning lights went off the console camera. He looked about him to find the chaos on the boards much less, as the whole station had been otherwise occupied for a moment. Some calls returned at once, presumably necessary and urgent; most did not. He drew a deep breath, thinking in one part of his mind of what might be happening in his apartment, or worse, away from it—hoping that Jessad was there, and fearing that he would be discovered there. *Mazian.* Military presence, which might start checking records, asking close questions. And to be found harboring Jessad. . . .

"Sir." It was the com chief. The third screen from the left was alight. Angelo Konstantin, angry and flushed. Jon punched the call through.

"Use procedures," Angelo spat, and broke off. The screen went dark, as Jon stood clenching his hands and trying to reckon whether that was because he had caught Angelo with no good answer or because Angelo was occupied.

*Let it come,* he thought in an access of hate, the pulse

pounding in his veins. Let Mazian evacuate all who would go. Union would come in after . . . would have need of those who knew the station. Understandings could be reached; his understanding with Jessad paved the way for that. It was no time to be timid. He was in it and there was no retreat now.

The first step . . . to become visible, a reassuring voice, and let Jessad see him doing it. Become known, have his face familiar all over the station. That was the advantage the Konstantins had always had, monopoly of public visibility, handsomeness. Angelo looked the vital patriarch; he did not. He had not the manner, the lifelong habit of authority. But ability—that he had; and once his heart had begun to settle out of the initial dread of the disorder out there, he found advantage in the disorder; in any events that went against the Konstantins.

Only Jessad . . . he remembered Mariner, which had died when Mazian had crowded in on the situation there. Only one thing protected them now . . . that Jessad had to rely on him and on Hale as his arms and legs, having no network yet of his own; and at the moment Jessad was neatly imprisoned, *having* to trust him, because he dared not try the halls without papers—dared not be out there with Mazian coming in.

He drew in a breath, expanded with the thought of the power he actually had. He was in the best of positions. Jessad could provide insurance . . . or what was another body vented, another paperless body, as they sometimes ended up vented out of Q? He had never killed before, but he had known from the time he accepted Jessad's presence that it was a possibility.

# 2

## Norway: 1400 hrs.

It was a slow process, to berth in so many ships: *Pacific* first, then *Africa; Atlantic; India. Norway* received clearance and Signy, from her vantage at the post central to the bridge, passed the order to Graff at controls. *Norway* moved in with impatient dispatch, having waited so long; was opening the ports of Pell dock crews to attach the umbilicals while *Australia* began its move; was completing secure-for-stay while the super-carrier *Europe* glided into dock, disdaining the pushed assist which station wanted to give.

"Doesn't look like trouble here," Graff said. "I'm getting an all-quiet on dockside. Stationmaster's security is thick out there. No sign of panicked civs. They've got the lid on it."

That was some comfort. Signy relaxed slightly, beginning to hope for sanity, at least while the Fleet sorted out its own business.

"Message," com said then. "General hail from Pell stationmaster to Fleet at dock: welcome aboard and will you come to station council at earliest?"

"*Europe* will respond," she murmured, and in a moment *Europe*'s com officer did so, requesting a small delay.

"All captains," she heard at last on the emergency channel she had been monitoring for hours, Mazian's own low voice, "private conference in the briefing room at once. Leave all command decisions to your lieutenants and get over here."

"Graff." She hurled herself out of her cushion. "Take over. Di, get me ten men for escort, double-quick."

Other orders were pouring over com from *Europe*, from the deployment of fifty troopers from each ship to dockside, full combat rig; for passing Fleet command to *Australia*'s second, Jan Meyis, for the interim; for riders of docked ships to apply to station control for approach instructions, to come in for reattachment. Coping with those details was Graff's job now. Mazian had something to tell them, explanations, long-awaited.

She went to her office, delayed only to slip a pistol into her pocket, hastened to the lift and out into the access corridor amid the rush of troops Graff was ordering to the dockside . . . combat-rigged from the moment they had gone into station approach, headed for the hatch before the echoes of Graff's voice had died in *Norway*'s steel corridors. Di was with them, and her own escort sorted itself out and attached itself as she passed through.

The whole dock was theirs. They poured out at the same moment as troops from other ships hit the dockside, and station security faded back in confusion before the businesslike advance of armored troops who knew precisely the perimeter they wanted and established it. Dockworkers scrambled this way and that, uncertain where they were wanted: "Get to work!" Di Janz shouted. "Get those waterlines over here!" And they made up their minds at once . . . little threat from them, who were standing too close and too vulnerable compared to the troops. Signy's eyes were for the armed security guards beyond the lines, at their attitude, and at the shadowed tangles of lines and gantries which might shelter a sniper. Her detachment surrounded her, with Bihan as officer. She swept them with her, moving rapidly, up the row of ship-berths, where a mob of umbilicals and gantries and ramps stretched as far as the eye could see up the ascending curve of the dock, like mirror reflections impeded only by the occasional arch of a section-seal and the upward horizon . . . merchanters docked beyond them. Troops made themselves a screen all along the route between *Norway* and *Europe*. She followed after *Australia*'s Tom Edger and his escort. The other captains would be at her back, coming as quickly as they could.

She overtook Edger on the ramp up to *Europe*'s access; they walked together. Keu of *India* caught them up when they had passed the ribbed tube and reached the lift, and Porey of *Africa* was hard on Keu's heels. They said nothing, each of them gone silent, perhaps with the same thoughts and the same anger. No speculations. They took only a pair apiece of their guards, jammed the lift car and rode up in silence, walked down the main-level corridor to the council room, steps ringing hollowly up here, in corridors wider than *Norway*'s, everything larger-scaled. Deserted: only a few *Europe* troops stood rigid guard here.

The council room likewise was empty, no sign of Mazian, just the bright lights of the room ablaze to tell them that they were expected at that circular table. "Outside," Signy bade her escort, as the others went. She and the others took their seats by precedence of seniority, Tom Edger first, herself, three vacancies, then Keu and Porey. Sung of *Pacific* arrived, ninth among the chairs. *Atlantic*'s Kreshov arrived, settled into the number four seat by Signy's other side.

"Where is he?" Kreshov asked finally, at the end of patience. Signy shrugged and folded her arms on the table, staring across at Sung without seeing him. Haste . . . and then wait. Pulled out of battle, kept in long silence . . . and now wait again to be told why. She focused on Sung's face, on a classic aged mask which never admitted impatience; but the eyes were dark. Nerves, she reminded herself. They were exhausted, had been yanked out of combat, through jump, into this. Not a time to make profound or far-reaching judgments.

Mazian came in finally, quietly, passed them and took his place at the head of the table, face downcast, haggard as the rest of them. Defeat? Signy wondered, with a knot in the pit of her stomach, like something which would not digest. And then he looked up and she saw that small tautness about Mazian's mouth and knew otherwise . . . sucked in her breath with a flare of anger. She recognized the little tension, a mask—Conrad Mazian played parts, staged his appearances as he staged ambushes and battles, played the elegant or the coarse by turns. This was humility, the falsest face of all, quiet dress, no show of brass; the hair, that silver of rejuv, was immaculate, the lean face, the tragic eyes . . . the eyes lied most of all, facile as an actor's. She watched the play of expressions, the marvelous fluidity that would have seduced a saint. He prepared to maneuver them. Her lips drew tight.

"You all right?" he asked them. "All of you—"

"*Why* were we pulled out?" she asked forthwith, surprised a direct contact from those eyes, a reflection of anger in return. "What can't go over com?" She never questioned, had never objected to an order of Mazian's in her whole career. She did now, and watched the expression go from anger to something like affection.

"All right," he said. "All right." He slid a glance around the room . . . again there were seats vacant. They were nine, with two out on patrol. The glance centered on each of them in turn. "Something you have to hear," Mazian said. "Something we have to reckon with." He pushed buttons at the console before his seat, activated the screens on the four walls, identical. Signy looked up at the schematic they had last seen at Omicron Point, the taste of bile in her mouth, watched the area widen, familiar stars shrinking in wider scale. There was no more Company territory; it was not theirs any more; only Pell. On wider view, they could see the Hinder Stars. Not Sol. But that was in the reckoning too now. She knew well enough where it was, if the schematic kept widening. It froze, ceased to grow.

"What is this?" Kreshov asked.

Mazian only let them look.

Long.

"What is this?" Kreshov asked again.

Signy breathed; it took conscious effort in that silence. Time seemed at a halt, while Mazian showed them in dead silence what was graven in their minds already.

They had lost. They had ruled there once, and they had lost.

"From one living world," Mazian said, almost a whisper, "from one living world of our beginning, humankind reached out as far as we've ever gone. One narrow reach of space here, thrust far back from what Union has . . . the Hinder Stars; Pell . . . and the Hinder Stars. Tenable, and with the personnel overloading Pell . . . possible."

"And run again?" Porey asked.

A muscle jerked in Mazian's jaw. Signy found her heart beating hard and her palms sweating. It was close to falling apart . . . all of it.

"Listen," Mazian hissed, mask dropped. *"Listen!"*

He stabbed another button. A voice began to speak, distant, recorded. She knew it, knew the foreign inflection . . . knew it.

"Captain Conrad Mazian," the recording began, "this is second secretary Segust Ayres of the Security Council, authorization code Omar series three, with authority of the Council and the Company; cease fire. Cease fire. Peace is being negotiated. As earnest of good faith require you cease all operations and await orders. This is a Company directive. All efforts are being made to guarantee safety of Company personnel, both civilian and military, during this negotiation. Repeat: Captain Conrad Mazian, this is second secretary Segust Ayres. . . ."

The voice died abruptly with the push of a key. Silence lingered after it. Faces were stark with dismay.

"War's over," Mazian whispered. "War's *over,* do you understand?"

A chill ran through Signy's blood. All about them was the image of what they had lost, the situation in which they were cast.

"Company's finally showed up to do something," Mazian said. "To hand them . . . this." He lifted a hand to the screens, a gesture which included the universe. "I recorded that message relayed from the Union flagship, *that message*. From Seb Azov's flagship. Do you understand? The code designation is valid. Mallory, those Company men who wanted passage . . . that's what they've done to us."

She drew in her breath. All warmth had fled. "If I'd taken them aboard. . . ."

"You couldn't have stopped them, you understand. Company men don't make solitary decisions. It was already decided elsewhere. If you'd shot them on the spot, you couldn't have stopped it . . . only delayed it."

"Until we'd drawn a different line," she replied. She stared into Mazian's pale eyes and recalled every word she had spoken with Ayres, every move, every intonation. She had let the man go, to do this.

"So they got their passage somehow," Mazian said. "The question is, what agreement they've made first, at Pell—and just how much they've signed over to Union. There's the possibility too that those so-named negotiators aren't intact. Mind-wiped, they'd sign and say right into Union's anxious fingers, knowing the company signal codes—and no knowing what else they spilled, no knowing what codes, what information, what was compromised, how much of everything they've handed over; our internal codes, no, but we don't know what of the Pell codes went . . . all the kind of thing that would let them come right in here. *That's* why the abort. Months of planning; yes; stations gone; ships and friends gone; vast human suffering—all of that, for nothing. But I had to make a fast decision. The Fleet is intact; so is Pell; we've got that much, right or wrong. We could have won at Viking; and gotten ourselves pinned there, lost Pell . . . all source of supply. That's why we pulled out."

There was not a sound, not a move. It suddenly made full sense.

"That's what I didn't want on com," Mazian said. "It's your choice. We're at Pell, where we have a choice. Do we assume it's Company men who sent that . . . in their right minds? Unforced? That Earth still backs us—? It's in question. But—old friends, does that really matter?"

"How, matter?" Sung asked.

"Look at the map, old friends, look at it again. Here . . . here is a world. Pell. And does a power survive without it. What is Earth . . . but that? You have your choice here: follow what may be Company orders, or we hold here, gather resources, take action. *Europe*'s staying regardless of orders. If enough do, we can make Union think twice about putting its nose in here. They don't have crews that can fight our style of fight; we've got supply here; we have resources. But make up your minds—I won't stop you—or you can stay and do what I think you might do. And when history writes what happened to the Company out here, it can write what it likes about Conrad Mazian. I made my choice."

"Two of us," Edger said.

"Three," Signy said, no faster than the murmur from the others. Mazian passed a slow glance from one to the other, nodded.

"Then we hold here, but we have to take it. Maybe we'll have cooperation here and maybe we won't. We're going to find out.—And we're not all in on this yet. Sung, I want you personally to go out to *North Pole* and *Tibet* and put it to them. Explain it any way you like. And if there's any large number of dissenters in any crew, or among the troops, we'll give them our blessing and let them go, take one of the merchanter ships here and ship them out. I leave it to individual captains to handle that."

"There won't be any dissent," Keu said.

"*If* there are," Mazian said. "The station, now—we move out and disperse our own security throughout, put our own personnel in key spots. Half an hour is enough for you to break this to your own commands. Whatever they ultimately decide to do, there's no question that we need to hold Pell securely before we can take any action, either to clear a ship for some to leave, or to hold onto it."

"Go?" Kreshov asked when silence lingered.

"Go," Mazian said softly, dismissing them.

Signy pushed back and moved, first after Sung, past Mazian's own security at the door, gathered her two-man escort and went, aware of others hard at her heels. Uncertainty still weighted her conscience. She had been Company all her life—cursed it, hated its policies and its blindness—but she felt suddenly naked, standing outside it.

Timidity, she reasoned with herself. She was a student of history, valued the lessons of it. The worst atrocities began with half-measures, with apologies, compromising with the wrong side, shrinking from what had to be done. The Deep and its demands were absolutes; and the compromise the Company had come to the Beyond to try would not hold longer than the convenience of the stronger . . . and that was Union.

They served Earth, she persuaded herself, better by what they did than the Company agents did by what they traded away.

# 3

## i
## Pell: sector white two; 1530 hrs.

The warning lights must still be on outside in the corridor. The salvage center kept to a deliberate pace. The supervisor walked the aisles between the machines and silenced any talk by his presence. Josh carefully kept his head down, unfastened a plastic seal from a small, worn-out motor, dropped it into a tray for further sorting, dropped clamps into yet another tray, disassembled the components into varied categories, for reuse or recycling according to wear and type of material.

There had been, since the original com announcement, no further word from the screen on the forward wall. No discussion was allowed after the initial murmur of dismay at the news. Josh kept his eyes averted from the screen, and from the station policeman at the door. He was more than three hours past his shift's quitting time. They should all have been dismissed, all those on partial. Other workers should have arrived. He had been here over six hours. There was no provision for meals here. The supervisor had finally sent out for sandwiches and drinks for them. There was still a cup of ice on the bench in front of him. He did not touch it, wishing to seem completely busy.

The supervisor stopped a moment behind him. He did not react, did not break the rhythm of his actions. He heard the supervisor move on, and did not look to see.

They did not treat him differently from the others here. It was his own troubled mind, he persuaded himself, which made him suspect they might be watching him in particular. They were all closely supervised. The girl by him, a solemn, slow-moving child and ever so careful, was doing the most complex job of which she was capable, and nature had cheated her of much capacity.

Many here in the salvage center were of that category. There were some who entered here young, perhaps to seek a track up through the job classifications, to gain elementary mechanical skills and to go higher, into technical positions or manufacture. And there were some whose nervous behavior indicated other reasons for being here, anxious, obsessive concentration . . . strange to observe the symptoms in others.

Only he had never been a criminal as they might have been, and perhaps they trusted him less for that. He cherished his job here, which kept his mind busy, which gave him independence . . . quite as the sober girl beside him cherished her place, he thought. At first, in his zeal for demonstrating his skill, he had worked with feverish quickness; and then he saw that it upset the child beside him, and that distressed him, because she could not do more, could never do more. He compromised then, and did not make his efficiency obvious. It was enough to survive. It had looked to be enough for a long time.

Only now he felt sick to his stomach and wished he had not eaten all his sandwich, but even in that matter he had not wanted to seem different from those about him.

The war had gotten to Pell. Mazianni. The Fleet was at hand.

*Norway,* and Mallory.

He did not think some thoughts. When the dark crowded him, he worked the harder and blinked the memories away. Only . . . *war* . . . Someone near him whispered about having to evacuate the station.

It was not possible. It could not happen.

*Damon!* he thought, wishing that he could get up and leave, go to the office, be reassured. Only there was no reassurance to be found, and he was afraid to try it.

Mazian's Fleet. Martial law.

*She* was with them.

He might break, if he was not careful; the balance of his mind was delicate and he knew it. Perhaps to have asked for this oblivion was in itself insane, and Adjustment had made him no more unbalanced than he had ever been. He suspected every emotion he felt, and therefore tried to feel as few as possible.

"Rest," the supervisor said. "Ten-minute break."

He kept working, as he had through previous rest periods. So did the girl beside him.

## ii
## Norway: 1530 hrs.

"We hold Pell," Signy told her crew and the troops, those present with her on the bridge and those scattered throughout the ship. "Our decision—Mazian's, mine, the other captains—is to hold Pell. Company agents have signed a treaty with Union . . . handed them everything in the Beyond and called for us to stand aside while they do it; they turned our contact code over to Union. *That's* why we aborted the strike . . . why we took out. No knowing what of our codes is betrayed." She let that sink in, watching grim faces all about her, aware of the whole body of the ship and all the listeners elsewhere within it. "Pell . . . the Hinder Stars, this whole edge of the Beyond . . . this is what we have left secure. We aren't going to take that order from the Company; we aren't going to accept surrender, however it's cloaked. We're off the leash, and this time we fight the war our own way. We've got ourselves a world and a station; and the whole Beyond began from that. We can rebuild the Hinder Star stations, all that used to exist between here and the Sun itself. We can do it. The Company may not be smart enough to want a buffer now between themselves and Union, but they will, believe me they will, and they'll be smart enough at least not to trifle with us. Pell's *our* world now. We've got nine carriers to hold it. We're not Company anymore. We're Mazian's Fleet, and Pell is *ours*. Any contrary opinions?"

She waited for some, although she knew her people like family . . . for some might have other opinions, might have second thoughts about this. There was reason they should.

A sudden cheer erupted off the troop decks, found echo, all channels open. People on the bridge were hugging one another and grinning. Graff embraced her; armscomper Tiho did; and others of her officers of many years. Some were crying. There were tears in Graff's eyes. None in her own; might have been, but that she felt guilt . . . still, irrationally, the habit of an outworn loyalty. She embraced Graff a second time, pushed back, looked around her. "Get all of us ready," she said. It was going all over the ship, open com. "We're moving in to take station central before they know what's hit them. Di, hurry it."

Graff started giving orders. She heard Di doing so, down in the troop corridors, distinctive echo. The bridge moved into activity, techs jostling one another in the narrow aisles getting to posts. "Ten minutes," she shouted, "full armament, all available troops arm and out."

There was shouting elsewhere, the com giving evidence of troops rushing to suit even before the orders were officially passed. The commands began echoing through the corridors. Signy walked back to her small office/quarters and took the precaution of helmet and body armor, none for her limbs, trading risk for freedom of motion. Five minutes. She heard Di counting over the open com, with outright chaos feeding out from various command stations. No matter. This crew and the troops knew their business in the dark and upside down. All family here. The incompatible met early accidents and those left were close as brothers, as children, as lovers.

She headed out, slipping her pistol openly into the armor-holster, rode the lift down; armored troops pouring down the corridor at a rattling run hit the wall to give her room the instant they recognized her coming through, so that she could run to the fore, where she belonged.

"Signy!" they cried after her, jubilant. "Bravo, *Signy!*"

They were alive again, and felt it.

### iii

## Pell council: sector blue one

"No," Angelo said at once. "*No,* don't try to stop them. Pull back. Pull back our forces immediately."

Station command acknowledged and turned to its business. Screens in the council chamber began to reflect new orders; the muffled voice of security command gave reports. Angelo sank back in his chair, at the table in the center of council, amid the partially filled tiers, the soft murmurings of panic among those who had contrived to get back here through the halls. He propped his mouth against his steepled hands and sat studying the incoming reports which cut across the screens in rapid sequence, views of the docks, where armored troops boiled out.

Some of the council had waited too long, could not get out of the sections where they worked or where they had taken up an emergency post. Damon and Elene came in together, for refuge, out of breath, hesitated at the door. Angelo beckoned his son and daughter-in-law in on personal privilege, and they approached at his urging and settled at two of the vacant places at the table. "Had to leave dock office in a hurry," Damon said quietly. "Took the lift up." Hard behind them came Jon Lukas and his clutch of friends to seat themselves, the friends in the tiers and Jon at the table. Two of the Jacobys made it, hair disheveled and faces glistening with sweat. It was not council; it was a sanctuary from what was happening outside.

On the screens matters were worsening, the troops headed in toward the heart of the station, security trying to keep up with the situation by remote, switching from one camera to the next in haste, a rapid flickering of images.

"Staff wants to know if we lock the control-center doors," a councillor said from the doorway.

"Against rifles?" Angelo moistened his lips, slowly shook his head, staring at the flick of images from camera to camera to camera.

"Call Mazian," Dee said, a new arrival. "Protest this."

"I have, sir. I have no answer. I reckon he's with them."

*Q disorder,* a screen advised them. *Three known dead; numerous injured. . . .*

"Sir," a call broke through the message. "They're mobbing the doors in Q, trying to batter them down. Shall we shoot?"

"Don't open," Angelo said, his heart pounding at the acceleration of insanity where there had been order. "Negative, don't fire unless the doors are breached. What do you want—to let them loose?"

"No, sir."

"Then don't." The contact went dead. He wiped his face, feeling ill.

"I'll get down that way," Damon offered, half out of his chair.

"You're not going anywhere," Angelo said. "I don't want you gathered up in any military sweep."

"Sir," an urgent voice came at his elbow, a presence which had come down from the tiers. "Sir—"

Kressich.

*"Sir,"* Kressich said.

"Q com is down," security command advised. "They've got it out again. We can splice something in. They can't have reached the dock speakers."

Angelo looked at the man Kressich, a haggard, grayed individual, who had gotten more so in the passing months. "Hear that?"

"They're afraid," Kressich said, "that you're going to leave here and let the Fleet leave them for Union."

"We don't know what the Fleet's intention may be, Mr. Kressich, but if a mob tries to breach those doors into our side of the docks, it's going to be beyond our power to do anything but shoot. I suggest you get on the com link to that section when they get it patched, and if there's a speaker they haven't broken, make that clear to them."

"We know we're pariahs whatever happens," Kressich returned, lips trembling. "We asked, we asked over and over, speed up the checks, run ID's, purify our records, do it faster. Now it's too late, isn't it?"

"Not necessarily, Mr. Kressich."

"You're going to see to your own people first, get them on the available ships in comfort. You're going to take our ships."

"Mr. Kressich—"

"Work has been progressing," said Jon Lukas. "*Some* of you may have clear papers. I wouldn't jeopardize them, sir."

There was sudden silence from Kressich, an uncertain look, his face an unwholesome color. His lips trembled and the tremor spread to his chin, his hands locked upon each other.

*Amazing,* Angelo thought sourly, *how easily it comes down to small concerns; and how accurately he does it. Congratulations, Jon.*

Easy to deal with the refugees of Q. Offer all their leaders clear paper and reason with them. Some had, in fact, proposed that.

"They've got blue three," Damon muttered. Angelo followed his gaze to the monitors, on which the flow of armored troops and their stationing along the corridors had become a rapid, mechanical process.

"Mazian," said Jon. "Mazian himself."

Angelo stared at the silver-haired man in the lead, mentally counting off the moments it would take that tide of soldiery to flow up the spiraling emergency ramps to their level, to the doors of the council itself.

That long, he still held the station.

## iv
## Sector blue one; number 0475

The images changed. Lily fretted, sprang up and walked back and forth, a step toward the buttons on the box, a step toward the dreamer, whose eyes were troubled.

Finally she dared reach for the box, to change the dream.

"No," the dreamer told her sharply, and she looked back and saw the pain . . . the dark, lovely eyes in the pale face, the white, white sheets, all about her light, save the eyes, which gazed on the sights in the halls. Lily came back to her, interposed her body between dream and dreamer, smoothed the pillow.

"I turn you," she offered.

"No."

She stroked the brow, touched so, so gently. "Dal-tes-elan, love you, love you."

They are troops," Sun-her-friend said, in that voice so still and calm that it shed peace on others. "Men-with-guns, Lily. It's trouble. I don't know what may happen."

"Dream them gone," Lily pleaded.

"I have no power to do that, Lily. But see, there is no using the guns. No one is hurt."

Lily shivered, and stayed close. From time to time on the ever-changing walls the face of Sun appeared, reassuring them, and stars danced, and the face of the world shone for them like the crescent moon. And the line of men-in-shells grew, filling all the ways of the station.

## v

There was no resistance. Signy had not drawn her gun, although her hand was on it. Neither had Mazian or Kreshov or Keu. Threat was for the troops, leveled rifles with the safeties off. They had fired one warning burst on the docks, nothing since. They moved quickly, giving no time for thought in those who met them now, no hint that there was argument possible. And there were few who lingered to meet them at all in these sections. Angelo Konstantin had given orders, Signy reckoned—the only sensible course.

They changed levels, up a ramp at the end of the main hall. Boots rang in complete vacancy; the sharp report of troops in their wake filing off to station themselves at the appointed line-of-sight intervals sent up other echoes. They passed from the emergency ramp to the area of station control; troops moved in there too, under officers, lowered rifles, while other detachments headed down the side halls to invade other offices: no shooting, not here. They kept moving down the center corridors, passed from cold steel and plastics to the sound-deadening matting, entered the hall of the bizarre wooden sculptures, whose eyes looked no less shocked now than before.

And the human faces, the small group gathered in the anteroom of the council chambers, were as round-eyed.

Troopers swept through, pushed at the ornate doors to open them. The leaved doors swung to either side and two troopers braced like statues facing inward, rifles leveled. The councillors inside, in a chamber far from filled, rose and faced the guns as Signy and Mazian and the others walked through. There was dignity in their posture, if not defiance.

"Captain Mazian," said Angelo Konstantin, "can I offer you to sit and talk this over with us . . . you and your captains?"

Mazian stood still a moment. Signy stood between him and Keu, Kreshov on the other side, surveying faces. Not the full council, not by half. "We don't take that much of your time," Mazian said. "You asked us here, so we're here."

No one had moved, not to sit, not to shift position.

"We'd like an explanation," Konstantin said, "of this—operation."

"Martial law," Mazian said, "for the duration of the emergency. And questions . . . direct questions, Mr. Konstantin, regarding agreements you may have made with certain Company agents. Understandings . . . with Union, and the flow of classified information to Union intelligence. Treason, Mr. Konstantin."

Blood left faces all about the room.

"No such understandings," Konstantin said. "No such understandings exist, captain. This station is neutral. We are a Company station, but we do not permit ourselves to be drawn into military action, or used as a base."

"And this . . . militia . . . you have scattered about you?"

"Sometimes neutrality needs reinforcement, captain. Captain Mallory herself warned us of random refugee flights."

"You claim ignorance that information . . . was handed to Union by civilian Company agents. You aren't party to any agreements, arrangements, or concessions which those agents may have made with the enemy?"

There was a moment of heavy silence. "We know of no such agreements. If there were any agreements to be made, Pell was not informed of them; and if we had been we would have discouraged them."

"You're informed now," Mazian said. "Information was passed, including code words and signals which jeopardize the security of this station. You've been handed to Union, stationmaster, by the Company. Earth is folding up its interests out here. You're one. We're another. We don't accept such a situation. Because of what's already been turned over, other stations have been lost. You're the border. With what forces we have, Pell is both necessary to us and tenable. Do you understand me?"

"You'll have every cooperation," Konstantin said.

"Access to your records. Every security problem should be weeded out and set under quarantine."

Konstantin's eyes shifted to Signy and back again. "We've followed all your procedures as outlined by captain Mallory. Meticulously."

"There'll be no section of this station, no record, no machine, no apartment, if need be, where my people don't have instant access. I would prefer to withdraw most of my forces and leave yours in charge, if we can have this clearly understood: that if there are security problems, if there are leaks, if a ship bolts from pattern out there, or if order breaks down in any particular, we have our own procedures, and they involve shooting. Is that clear?"

"It is," Konstantin said. "abundantly clear."

"My people will come and go at will, Mr. Konstantin, and they'll shoot if they judge it necessary; and if we have to come in shooting to clear the way for one of ours, we will, every man and woman in the Fleet. But that won't happen. Your own security *will* see to it—or your security with the help of ours. You tell me which way."

Konstantin's jaw clenched. "So we are plain on both sides, Captain Mazian, we recognize your obligation to protect your forces and to protect this station. We will cooperate; we will expect cooperation from you. When I send a message hereafter, it goes *through*."

"Absolutely," Mazian said easily. He looked to right and left of him, moved finally, walked a space toward the doors while Signy and the others still faced council. "Captain Keu," he said, "you may discuss matters further with council. Captain Mallory, take the operations center. Captain Kreshov, check through security records and procedures."

"I'll want someone knowlegeable," Kreshov said.

"The security director will assist you," Konstantin said. "I'll call that order ahead."

"I also," Signy said, glancing at a familiar face at the central table, the younger Konstantin. The young man's expression altered at that look, and the young woman by him reached a hand to his.

"Captain," he said.

"Damon Konstantin . . . yourself, if you will. You can be of help."

Mazian left, taking a few of the escort with him, for a general tour of the area, or more than likely, further operations, the taking of other sections, like the core and its machinery. Jan Meyis, *Australia*'s second in command, was on that delicate task. Keu drew back a chair at the council table, taking possession of it and the chamber; Kreshov followed Mazian out. "Come on," Signy said, and young Damon paused for a glance at his father, who was thin-lipped and upset, at parting with the young woman at his side. They did not, Signy reckoned, think much of her company. She waited, then walked with him to the door where she gathered up two of her own troopers for escort, Kuhn and Dektin.

"The command center," she directed Konstantin, and he showed her out the door with incongruous and natural courtesy, tending the way they had come in.

Not a word from him; his face was set and hard.

"Your wife back there?" Signy asked. She collected details . . . on those of consequence. "Who?"

"My wife."

"Who?"

"Elene Quen."

That startled her. "Station family?"

"The Quens. Off *Estelle*. Married me and stayed off her last run."

"She's lost. You know that."

"We know."

"Pity. Children, you two?"

It was a moment before he answered that one. "On the way."

"Ah." The woman had been a little heavy. "There are two of you Konstantin boys, aren't there?"

"I have a brother."

"Where is he?"

"On Downbelow." The expression was more and more anxious.

"There's nothing to worry about."

"I'm not worrying."

She smiled, mocking him.

"Are your forces on Downbelow too?" he asked.

She kept the smile, saying nothing. "I recall you're from Legal Affairs."

"Yes."

"So you'd know quite a few of the comp accesses for personnel records, wouldn't you?"

He shot her a look that wasn't frightened. Angry. She looked to the corridor ahead, where troops guarded the windowed complex of central. "We're assured your cooperation," she reminded him.

"Is it true that we were ceded?"

She smiled still, reckoning the Konstantins, if anyone, to have their wits about them, to know their value and that of Pell. "Trust me," she said with irony. COMMAND CENTRAL, a sign said, with an arrow pointing; COMMUNICATIONS, another; BLUE ONE, 01-0122. "Those signs," she said, "come down. Everywhere."

"Can't."

"And the color keys."

"The station is too confusing—even residents could get lost—the halls mirror-image, and without our color-keys. . . ."

"So in my ship, Mr. Konstantin, we don't mark corridors for intruders."

"We have children on this station. Without the colors. . . ."

"They can learn," she said. "And the signs all come off."

Station central lay open before them . . . occupied by troops. Rifles swung anxiously as they entered, then recentered. She looked all about the command center, the row upon row of control consoles, the technicians and station officers who worked there. Troops visibly relaxed at her presence. Civs at their posts looked relieved as well—at that of young Konstantin, she reckoned; for that purpose she had brought him.

"It's all right," Signy said to the troops and the civs. "We've reached an accommodation with the stationmaster and the council. We're not evacuating Pell. The Fleet is setting up a base here, one we're not going to give up. No way Union's coming in here."

A murmur went among the civs, eyes meeting eyes with subdued looks of relief. From hostages they were suddenly allies. The troops had grounded their rifles.

"*Mallory,*" she heard whispered from point to point of the room. "That's Mallory." In *that* tone, which was not love . . . nor was it disrespect.

"Show me about," she said to Damon Konstantin.

He walked about the control center with her, quietly named the posts, the personnel who filled them, many of whom she would remember; she was good at that when she wanted to be. She stopped a moment and looked about her, at the screens, the rotating schematic Downbelow, dotted with green and red points. "Bases?" she asked.

"We've got several auxiliary sites," he said, "trying to absorb and feed what you left us."

"Q?" She saw the monitor on that section too, seething human mass battering at a sealed door. Smoke. Debris. "What do you do with them?"

"You didn't give us that answer," he replied. Few took that tone with her. It amused her.

She listened, looked about her at the grand complex, bank upon bank, boards with functions alien to those of a starship. This was commerce and the maintenance of a centuries-old orbit, cataloging of goods and manufacture, of internal and onworld populations, native and human

. . . a colony, busy with mundane life. She surveyed it with a slow intake of breath, a sense of ownership. This was what they had fought to keep alive.

Com central came through suddenly, an announcement from council. ". . . wish to assure station residents," said Angelo Konstantin, with council chambers in the background, "that no evacuation of this station will take place. The Fleet is here for our protection. . . ."

Their world.

It only remained to put it in order.

# 4

## Downbelow: main base: 1600 hrs. station standard Local Dawn*

Morning was near, a red line on the horizon. Emilio stood in the open, breath paced evenly through the mask, wearing a heavy jacket against the perpetual chill of nights at this latitude and elevation. The lines moved in the dark, quietly, bowed figures hastening with loads like insects saving eggs from flood, outward, out of all the storage domes.

The human workers still slept, those in Q and those of the residents' domes. Only a few staff helped in this. His eyes could spot them here and there about the landscape of low domes and hills, tall shadows among the others.

A small, panting figure scurried up to him, gasped a naked breath. "Yes? Yes, you send, Konstantin-man?"

"Bounder?"

*Seasonal variation in daylit hours and difference in rotational period from station (Earth) standard results in daily progressing time difference: station and world pass only rarely into relative synch.

"I Bounder." The voice hissed around a grin. "Good runner, Konstantin-man."

He touched a wiry, furred shoulder, felt a spidery arm twine with his. He took a folder paper from his pocket, gave it into the hisa's callused hand. "Run, then," he said. "Carry this to all human camps, let their eyes see, you understand? And tell all the hisa. Tell them all, from the river to the plain; tell them all send their runners, even to hisa who don't come in human camps. Tell them be careful of men, trust no strangers. Tell them what we do here. Watch, watch, but don't come near until a call they know. Do the hisa understand?"

"Lukases come," the hisa said. "Yes. Understand, Konstantin-man. I *Bounder*. I am wind. No one catches."

"Go," he said. "Run, Bounder."

Hard arms hugged him, with that frightening easy strength of the hisa. The shadow left him into the dark, flitted, *ran* . . .

Word sped. It could not be recalled, not so easily.

He stood still, watched the other human figures on the hillside. He had given his staff orders and refused to confide in them, wishing to spare them responsibility. The storage domes were mostly empty now, all the supplies they had contained taken deep into the bush. Word sped along the river, by ways which had nothing to do with modern communications, nothing which listeners could monitor, word which sped with a hisa's speed and would not be stopped at any order from the station or those who held it. Camp to camp, human and hisa, wherever hisa were in touch one with the other.

A thought struck him . . . that perhaps never before Man had the hisa had reason to talk to others of their kind in this way; that never to their knowledge was there war, never unity among the scattered tribes, but somehow knowledge of Man had gotten from one place to the other. And now humans sent a message through that strange network. He imagined it passing on riverbanks and in the brush, by chance meetings and by purpose, with whatever purpose moved the gentle, bewildered hisa.

And over all the area of contact, hisa would steal, who had no concept of theft; and leave their work, who had no concept of wages or of rebellion.

He felt cold, wrapped as he was in layers of clothing,

well insulated against the chill breeze. He could not, like Bounder, run away. Being Konstantin and human, he stood waiting, while advancing dawn picked out the lines of burdened workers, while humans from the other domes began to stir out of sleep to discover the systematic pilferage of stores and equipment, while his staff stood by watching it happen. Lights went on under the transparent domes . . . workers came out, more and more of them, standing in shock.

A siren sounded. He looked skyward, saw only the last few stars as yet, but com had wind of something. And a presence disturbed the rocks near him, and a slim arm slipped around his waist. He hugged Miliko against him, cherishing the contact.

There was a call from across the slope; arms lifted, pointed up. The light of the descending ship was visible in the paling sky . . . sooner than they had wanted.

"Minx!" He called one of the hisa to him, and she came, a female with the white blaze of an old burn on her arm; came burdened as she was and panting. "Hide now," he told her, and she ran back to the line, chattering to her fellows as she went.

"Where are they going?" Miliko asked. "Did they say?"

"They know," he said. "Only they know." He hugged her the tighter against the wind. "And their coming back again—that depends on who does the asking."

"If they take us away. . . ."

"We do what we can. But there'll be no outsiders giving them orders."

The light of the ship brightened, intense. Not one of their shuttles, but something bigger and more ominous.

Military, Emilio reckoned; a carrier's landing probe.

"Mr. Konstantin." One of the workers came running up, stopped with a bewildered spreading of his hands. "Is it true? Is it true that Mazian's up there?"

"We were sent word that's what it is. We don't know what's going on up there; indications are things are quiet. Keep it calm; pass the word . . . we keep our wits about us, ride events as they come. No one says anything about the missing supplies; no one mentions them, you understand? But we aren't going to have the Fleet strip us down here and then go off to leave the station to starve; *that's* what's going on. You pass that word too. And you take your orders only from me and from Miliko, hear?"

"Sir," the man breathed, and at his dismissal, ran off to carry the news.

"Better put it to Q," Miliko said.

He nodded, started that way, from the hillside on which they stood. Over the hill a glow flared up, field lights on to guide the landing. He and Miliko walked the path over to Q, found Wei there. "Fleet's up there," Emilio said. And at the quick, panicked murmur: "We're trying to keep food for station and ourselves; trying to stop a Fleet takeover down here. You saw nothing. You heard nothing. You're deaf and blind, and you don't have responsibility for anything; *I* do."

There was murmuring, from the resident workers, from Q. He turned, he and Miliko, headed by the path from there to the landing site; a crowd of his own staff and resident workers formed about him . . . Q folk too; no one stopped them. They had no guards anymore, not here, not at the other camps; Q worked by posted schedules like other workers. It was not without its arguments, its difficulties; but they were less a threat than what descended on them all, which would make its demands for provisions for troop-laden carriers, and possibly demands for live bodies.

The ship came down in thunder, settled into the landing area and overfilled it, and on the hillside they stopped their ears in its sound and turned their faces from its reeking wind until the engines had shut down. It rested there in the breaking day, foreign and ungainly, and bristling with war. The hatch opened, lowered a jaw to the ground, and armored troops walked down onto the soil of the world as they on their hillside stood still in a line of their own, armorless and weaponless. The troops braced, aimed rifles. An officer came down the ramp into the light, a dark-skinned man with a breathing mask only, no helmet.

"That's Porey," Miliko whispered. "That has to be Porey himself."

He felt the burden on himself to go down and answer the posed threat, let go Miliko's hand; but she did not let go his. They walked down the hill together, to meet the legendary captain . . . stopped at speaking range, all too conscious of the rifles now much closer to them.

"Who's in charge of this base?" Porey demanded.

"Emilio Konstantin and Miliko Dee, captain."

"Before me?"

"Yes, captain."

"Receive a decree of martial law. All supplies at this base are confiscated. All civilian government, human and native, is suspended. You will turn over all records of equipment, personnel, and supplies immediately."

Emilio made an ironic sweep of his free hand, offering the domes, plundered domes. Porey would not be amused, he reckoned. Certain hand-kept books had disappeared too. He was afraid, for himself, for Miliko . . . for the men and women of this base and others; not least of all for the hisa, who had never seen war.

"You will remain on this world," Porey said, "to assist us in whatever ways are necessary."

Emilio smiled tautly and pressed Miliko's hand. It was arrest, nothing less than that. His father's message, rousing him out of sleep, had given him time. About him were workers who had never asked to be put in this position, who had been volunteered for this service. He relied less on their silence than on the hisa's speed. It was even possible that the military would put him under more direct restraint. He thought of his family on the station, the possibility of Pell being evacuated, and of Mazian's men making deliberate ruin of Downbelow itself in a pullout, destroying what they did not want Union to get their hands on, impressing all the able-bodied into the Fleet. They would put guns in hisa's hands if it would get them lives to throw against Union.

"We'll discuss the matter," he answered, "captain."

"Arms will be turned over to my troops. Personnel will submit to search."

"I suggest discussion, captain."

Porey gestured sharply. "Bring them inside."

The troops started for them. Miliko's hand clenched on his. He took the initiative and they walked forward on their own, suffered themselves to be spot-searched and brought up the ramp into the glare of the ship's interior, where Porey waited.

Emilio stopped at the upper end of the ramp, with Miliko

beside him. "We have the responsibility for this base," he said. "I don't want to make public issue of it. Very quietly, I'll comply with reasonable needs of your forces."
"You are making threats, Mr. Konstantin."
"I'm making a statement, sir. Tell us what you want. I know this world. Military intervention in a working system would have to take valuable time to establish its own ways, and in some cases, intervention could be destructive."
He stared into Porey's scar-edged eyes, well read that this was a man who did not like to be defied. Who was personally dangerous.
"My officers will go with you," Porey said, "to get the records."

# 5

## i

## Pell: sector white two; 1700 hrs.

Police had come in, quiet men, who stood by the door and talked to the supervisor. Josh saw them from under his brows and kept his head down, his fingers never missing a turn of the piece he was removing. The young girl by him had stopped outright, nudged him hard in the ribs.
"Hey," she said, "Hey, it's *police*."
Five of them. Josh ignored the blows in his ribs and she only jabbed him the harder.
Above them the com screen came on. The light caught his eyes and he looked up for an instant at another general announcement, for the return of limited freedom of passage in green section. He ducked his head and resumed work.
"They're looking this way," the girl said.
They were. They were making gestures in this direction. Josh shot a look up and down again, up once more, for troops had come in, armored. Company soldiers. Mazianni. "Look," the girl said. He set himself back to

work. The silken voice of central continued over the com, promising that it was all safe. He stopped believing it.

Footsteps were in the aisle, coming from the other side, heavy steps and many of them. They reached him and stopped behind him. He kept working in a last, feverish hope. *Damon,* he thought, wished. *Damon!*

A hand touched his shoulder and made him turn. He stared up into the supervisor's face, unfocused, on the security police from the station and a soldier in the armor and insignia of Mazian's Fleet.

"Mr. Talley," said one of the police, "will you come with us, please?"

He realized the wrench in his hand as a weapon, carefully laid it on the counter, wiped his hand on his overalls, and stood up.

"Where are you going?" the girl beside him asked. He had never known her name. Her plain face was distressed. "Where are you going?"

He did not answer, not knowing. One of the police took him by the arm and brought him away down the aisle and up the side of the shop to the door. They were all staring. "Quiet," the supervisor said. There was a general murmuring. The police and the troops brought him outside into the corridor and stopped there. The door closed, and a troop officer, in body armor only, faced him to the wall and searched him.

The man took his papers from his pocket. He faced about again when they let him and stood with his back against the wall, watching the officer go through the papers. *Atlantic,* their insignia said. A sick terror worked in him. Company soldiers had the papers in their hands, and they were all his claim to harmlessness, proof of what he had been through, that he was no danger to anyone. He reached out to recover them and the officer held them out of reach. Mazianni. The shadow came back. He withdrew his hand, remembering other encounters, his heart pounding.

"I have a pass," he said, trying to keep the tic from his face, which came when he was upset. "It's with the papers. You can see I work here. I'm supposed to be here."

"Mornings only."

"We were all held," he said. "We were all held over. Check the others. We're all from morning shift."

"You'll come with us," one of the troopers said.

"Ask Damon Konstantin. He'll tell you. I know him. He'll tell you that I'm all right."

That delayed them. "I'll make a note of that," the officer said.

"It's possibly true," said one of the station police. "I've heard something like that. He's a special case."

"We have our orders. Comp spat him out; we have to clear the matter. You lock him up in your facilities or we lock him up in ours."

Josh opened his mouth to state a preference. "We'll take him," the policeman said before he could plead.

"My papers," Josh said. He stammered and flushed with shame. Some reactions were still too much to control. He held out a demanding hand for his papers and it shook visibly. "Sir."

The officer folded them and carefully put them into his belt-kit. "He doesn't need them. He's not going anywhere. You take him and put him away, and you have him available if any of us want him, you understand that? He may go into Q later, but not till command's had a chance to review it."

"Understood," the policeman said crisply. He seized Josh's arm, led him down the corridor. The troops walked behind, and finally, at an intersection of corridors, their path and that of the troops diverged.

But there were Mazianni at every visible hallway. He felt cold and exposed . . . felt profound relief when the police stopped at a lift and took him into the car alone; they were, for that ride up and around to red sector one, without the troops.

"Please call Damon Konstantin," he asked of them. "Or Elene Quen. Or anyone in their offices. I know the numbers."

There was silence for most of the ride.

"We'll report it through channels," one said finally, without looking at him.

The lift stopped, red one. Security zone. He walked out between them, through the transparent partition and to the desk at the entry. Troops were inside this office too, armored and armed, and that sent a wave of panic through him, for he had hoped that in this place at least he was under station authority.

"Please," he said at the desk, while they were checking

him in. He knew the young officer in charge; he had been here when he was a prisoner. He *remembered*. He leaned forward toward him and lowered his voice, desperately. "Please call the Konstantins. Let them know I'm here."

Here too there was no answer, only an uncomfortable shift of the eyes away from him. They were afraid, all the stationers—terrified of the armed troops. Soldiers drew him away from the desk, led him down the corridor to the detention cells, put him into one, barren and white and furnished only with sanitary facilities and a white bench extruded from the walls. They delayed to search him again, strip search this time, and left him his clothing on the floor.

He dressed, sank down finally onto the bench, tucked his feet up and rested his head against his knees, tired from his long working and knotted up with fear.

## ii

## Merchanter ship Hammer: in deep space; 1700 hrs.

Vittorio Lukas rose from his seat and walked the curve of *Hammer*'s dingy bridge, hesitated at the twitch of the stick in the hand of the Unioner who continually kept an eye on him. They would not let him come within reach of controls; in this tiny, steeply curved rotation cylinder—most of *Hammer*'s unlovely mass was a null-*G* belly, aft—there was a line on the tiles, marked in tape, which circumscribed his prison. He had not discovered yet what would happen if he crossed it without being called; he never meant to find out. He was allowed most of the circuit of the cylinder, the crew quarters where he slept; the tiny main-room section . . . and this far into the operations area. From here he could make out one of the screens and see scan past the tech's soldier; he lingered, staring at it, at the backs of men and women in merchanter dress who were not merchanters, his belly still queasy from drugs and his nerves crawling from jump. He had spent most of the day throwing up his insides.

The captain was standing watching the screens, saw him, beckoned him. Vittorio hesitated; at a second signal came walking ahead into that forbidden operations zone, not without a backward glance at the man with the stick. He accepted the captain's friendly hand on his shoulder as he took a closer look at scan; prosperous looking sort, this man . . . might have been a Pell businessman, urged his crew rather than snapping orders. They all treated him well enough, even with politeness. It was his situation and the potentials in it which had him terrified. *Coward,* his father would say in disgust. It was true. He was. This was no place and no company for him.

"We're moving back soon now," the man said . . . Blass, his name was, Abe Blass. "Didn't jump far, just enough to stay out of Mazian's way. Relax, Mr. Lukas. Your stomach treating you better now?"

He said nothing. The mention of his malaise brought a spasm to his gut.

Nothing's wrong," Blass said softly, hand still on his shoulder. "Absolutely nothing, Mr. Lukas. Mazian's arrival doesn't trouble us."

He looked at the man. "And what if the Fleet spots us when we come in again?"

"We can always jump," Blass said. "*Swan's Eye* won't have strayed from her post; and Ilyko won't talk; she knows where her interests lie. Just rest easy, Mr. Lukas. You still seem to have some apprehensions of us."

"If my father on Pell is compromised . . ."

"That won't be likely to happen. Jessad knows what he's doing. Believe me. It's all planned for. And Union takes care of its friends." Blass patted the shoulder. "You're doing very well for a first jump. Take an old timer's advice and don't push yourself. Just relax. Go on back to the main room and I'll talk to you as soon as our move in is plotted."

"Sir," he murmured, and did as he was told, wandering past the guard back up the curving deck to the deserted main room. He took a seat at the molded table/bench arrangement, leaned his arm on the table, swallowed heavily.

It was not all nausea from jump. He was terrified. *Make a man of you,* he could hear his father saying. He seethed with misery. He was what he was, and he did not belong here, with the likes of Abe Blass and these grim verysame people. His father had made him expendable. If he were ambitious he would try to make points for himself in these circumstances, ingratiate himself with Union. He did not. He knew his abilities and his limits, and he wanted Roseen, wanted his comforts, wanted a good drink he could not have with the drugs filling his system.

It was not going to work, none of it; and they would snatch him Unionside where everyone walked in step, and that would be the end of everything he knew. He feared changes. What he had at Pell was good enough. He had never asked much of life or of anyone, and the thought of being out here in the center of nothing at all . . . gave him nightmares.

But he had no choices. His father had seen to that.

Blass came finally, sat down and solemnly spread charts on the table and explained things to him as if he were someone of consequence to the mission. He looked at the diagram and tried to understand the premises of this shifting about through nothing, when he could not in fact understand where they were, which was essentially nowhere.

"You should feel very confident," Blass said. "I assure you you're in a far safer place than the station is right now."

"You're a very high officer in Union," he said, "aren't you? They wouldn't send you like this . . . otherwise."

Blass shrugged.

"*Hammer* and *Swan's Eye* . . . all the ships you've got near Pell?"

Blass shrugged again. That was his answer.

# 6

## i

## Maintenance access white 9-1042; 2100 hrs.

The men had come and gone for a long time, men-in-shells, carrying guns. Satin shivered and tucked further back into the shadows by the cargo lift. They were many who had run when the Lukas directed, who had run again when the stranger men came by the ways that the hisa could use, the narrow ways, the dark tunnels where hisa could breathe without masks and the men could not. Men of the Upabove knew these ways but they had not yet shown them to the strangers, and hisa were safe, though some of them cried deep in the dark, deep, deep below, so that men would not hear.

There was no hope here. Satin pursed her lips and sidled backward in a crouch, waited while the air changed, scampered back into safe darkness. Hands touched her. There was male-scent. She hissed in reproof and smelt after the one who was hers. Arms folded her about. She laid her head wearily against a hard shoulder, comforting as she was comforted. Bluetooth offered her no questions. He knew that there was no better news, for he had said as much when she had insisted on going out to see.

It was trouble, bad trouble. Lukases spoke and gave orders, and strangers threatened. Old One was not here . . . none of the long-timers were, having gone somewhere about their own business, to the protection of important things, Satin reckoned. To duties ordered by important humans and perhaps duties which regarded hisa.

But they had disobeyed, had not gone to the supervisors, no more than the Old Ones had gone, who also hated Lukases.

"Go back?" someone asked finally.

They would be in trouble if they turned themselves in after running. Men would be angry with them, and the men had guns. "No," she said, and when there was muttering to the contrary, Bluetooth turned his head to spit a surlier negative. "Think," he said. "We go there, men can be there, bad trouble."

"Hungry," another protested.

No one answered.

Men might take their friendship from them for what they had done. They realized that clearly now. And without that friendship, they might be on Downbelow always. Satin thought of the fields of Downbelow, the soft clouds she had once thought solid enough to sit on, the rain and the blue sky and the gray-green-blue leaves, the flowers and soft mosses . . . most of all the air which smelled of home. Bluetooth dreamed of that, perhaps, as the heat of her spring faded, and she had not quickened, being young, in her first adult season. Bluetooth saw things now with a clearer head. He mourned the world at times. At times she did. But to be there always and forever. . . .

Sky-sees-her, that was her name; and she had seen truth. The blue was false, a cover stretched out like a blanket; truth was black distances, and the face of great Sun shining in the dark. Truth would always hang above them. Without the favor of humans, they would return to Downbelow without hope, forever and ever to know themselves shut off from the sky. There was no home now, not now that they had looked upon Sun.

"Lukases go away sometime," Bluetooth murmured against her ear.

She burrowed her head against him, trying to forget that she was hungry and thirsty, and did not answer him.

"Guns," said another voice, near them. "They will shoot us and we will lose ourselves forever."

"Not if we stay here," said Bluetooth, "and do what I said."

"They are not our humans," said Bigfellow's deep voice. "Hurt our humans, these."

"This is a man-fight," Bluetooth returned. "Nothing for the hisa."

A thought came. Satin lifted her head. "Konstantins. Konstantin-fight, this. We will find Konstantins, ask what to do. Find Konstantins, find Old Ones too, near Sun's Place."

"Ask Sun-her-friend," another exclaimed. "*She* must know."

"Where *is* Sun-her-friend?"

There was silence. No one knew. The Old Ones preserved that secret.

"*I* will find her." That was Bigfellow. He wriggled close to them, reached out a hand to her shoulder in the dark. "I go many places. Come. Come."

She drew in her breath, lipped uncertainly at Bluetooth's cheek.

"Come," Bluetooth agreed, suddenly, drawing her by the hand. Bigfellow hastened off just ahead, a pattering of feet in the dark. They went after him and others followed, up the dark corridors and the ladders and the narrow places where sometimes there was light and most times not. Some fell behind, for they went among pipes and in cold places and places which burned their bare feet, and past machinery which thundered with ominous powers.

Bluetooth pushed into the lead at times, letting go her hand; at times Bigfellow shoved him aside and went first again. Satin doubted in fact that Bluetooth had the least idea where he was going or what way would lead them to Sun-her-friend; to the Sun's Place they had been, and dimly she had that sense she had on the earth, that said in her heart what way a place should be . . . up was true; she thought that it should be left . . . but sometimes the tunnels did not bend left; and they wound. The two males pushed ahead, one and then the other, until they were all panting and stumbling; more and more fell behind; and at last the one behind her caught her hand, pleaded by that gesture . . . but Bluetooth and Bigfellow pushed on and she was losing them. She parted from the last of their followers and kept going, trying to overtake them.

"No more," she pleaded when she had caught them on the metal steps. "No more, let us go back. You are lost."

Bigfellow would not heed. Panting, he edged higher; she tugged at Bluetooth and he hissed in frustration and went after Bigfellow. Madness. Madness had settled on them. "You show me *nothing!*" she wailed. She bounced in despair and hastened after, panting, trying to reason with them, who had passed beyond reasoning. They passed panels and doors where they might have gotten out into the open; all these they rejected . . . but at last they came to a place where they were faced with choices, where a light burned blue above a door; where the ladders extended everywhere, up and down and in three other directions.

"Here," Bigfellow said after a little hesitation, feeling of the buttons at the lighted door. "Here is a way."

"No," Satin moaned. "No," Bluetooth objected too, perhaps recovering his senses; but Bigfellow pushed the first button and slipped into the air chamber when the door opened. "Come back," Bluetooth exclaimed, and they scrambled to stop him, who was mad with the rivalry, who did this for *her,* and for nothing else. They went in after him; the door closed at their backs. The second door opened under Bigfellow's hand as they caught up with him, and there was light—it blinded.

And suddenly guns fired and Bigfellow went down in the doorway with a smell of burning. He cried and shrieked horribly, and Bluetooth whirled and hit the other door button, his hard arm carrying her with him as the door opened and wind surged about them. Man-voices bellowed over a sudden wail of alarms, silenced as the door closed. They hit the ladders and ran, ran blindly down and through the darkways, deep, deep into the dark. They dragged their breathers down, but the air smelt wrong. They finally stopped their running, sweating and shivering. Bluetooth rocked and moaned with pain in the dark, and Satin searched him for a wound, found his fingers locked on his upper arm. She licked the sore place, which was hot and burned, soothed it as best she could, hugged him and tried to still the rage which had him trembling. They were lost, both lost in the darkways; and Bigfellow was horribly dead, and Bluetooth sat and hissed with pain and anger, muscles hard and quivering. But in a moment he shook himself, lipped at her cheek, shivered as she put her arms about him.

"O let us go home," he whispered. "O let us go home, Tam-utsa-pitan, and no more see humans. No machines, no fields, no man-work, only hisa always and always. Let us go home."

She said nothing. The disaster was hers, for *she* had suggested, and Bigfellow had wanted her and Bluetooth had risen to the challenge of his daring, as if they had been in the high hills. Her disaster, her doing. Now Bluetooth himself spoke of leaving her dream, unwilling to follow her further. Tears filled her eyes, doubts for herself, loneliness, that she had walked too far. Now they were in worse trouble, for to find themselves they must go up again to the man-places and open a door and beg help, and they had seen the result of that. They held each other and did not stir from where they were.

## ii

Mallory looked tired, a hollowness to her eyes as she paced the aisles of command central, countless circuits of it, while her troops stood guard. Damon watched her, himself leaning against a counter, hungry and tired himself, but it was, he reckoned, nothing to what the Fleet personnel must be feeling, having gone through jump, passing from that to this tedious police duty; workers, never relieved at their posts, looked haggard, muttered timid complaints . . . but there was no other shift for these troops.

"Are you going to stay here all night?" he asked her.

She turned a cold look on him, said nothing, walked on.

He had watched her for some hours, a foreboding presence in the center. She had a way of moving that made no noise, no swagger, no, but it was, perhaps, the unconscious assumption that anyone in her way would move. They did. Any tech who had to get up did so only when Mallory was patroling some other aisle. She had never made a threat—spoke seldom, mostly to the troopers, about what, only she and they knew. She was even, occasionally and before the hours wore on, pleasant. But there was no question the threat was there. Most residents on-station had never seen close up the kind of gear that surrounded Mallory and her troops; had never touched a gun with their own hands, would be hard put to describe what they saw. He noted three different models in this small selection alone, light pistol; long-barreled ones; heavy rifles, all black plastics and ominous symmetries; armor, to diffuse the burn of such weapons . . . that gave the troops the same deadly machined look as the rest of the gear, no longer human. It was impossible to relax with such among them.

A tech rose at the far side of the room, looked over her shoulder as if to see if any of the guns had moved . . . walked down the aisle as if it were mined. Gave him a printed message, retreated at once. Damon held the message in his hand unread, conscious of Mallory's interest. She had stopped pacing. He found no way to avoid attention, unfolded the paper and read it.

> PSSCIA/PACPAKONSTANT INDAMON/AU1-1-1-1-1/1030/10/4/52/2136MD/0936A/START/TALLEY PAPERS CONFISCATED AND TALLEY ARRESTED BY FLEET ORDER/SEC OFFICE GIVEN CHOICE LOCAL DETENTION OR MILITARY INTERVENTION/TALLEY CONFINED THIS POST/TALLEY REQUEST MESSAGE SENT KONSTANTIN FAMILY/HEREIN COMPLIED/REQUEST INSTRUCTION/REQUEST POLICY CLARIFICATION/SAUNDERSREDONESECCOM/ENDITENDITENDIT.

He looked up, pulse racing, caught between relief it was nothing worse and distress for what it was. Mallory was looking straight at him, a curious, challenging interest on her face. She walked over to him. He considered an outright lie, hoping she would not insist on the message and make an issue of it. He considered what he knew of her and reckoned otherwise.

"There's a friend of mine in trouble," he said. "I need to leave and go see about him."

"Trouble with us?"

He considered the lie a second time. "Something like."

She held out her hand. He did not offer the message.

"Perhaps I can help." Her eyes were cold and her hand stayed extended, palm up. "Do we assume," she asked when it was not forthcoming, "that this is something embarrassing to station? Or do we make further assumptions?"

He handed over the paper, while there were choices at all. She scanned it, seemed perplexed for a moment, and gradually her face changed.

"Talley," she said. "Josh Talley?"

He nodded, and she pursed her lips.

"A friend of the Konstantins. How times do change."

"He's Adjusted."

The eyes flickered.

"His own request," he said. "What else did Russell's leave him?"

She kept looking at him, and he wished that there were somewhere else to look, and somewhere else to be. Adjustment spilled things. It thrust Pell and her into an intimacy he did not want . . . which too clearly she did not want—those records on station.

"How is he?" she asked.

He found even the asking bizarrely ugly, and simply stared.

"Friendship," she said. "Friendship, and from such opposite poles. Or is it patronage? He asked for Adjustment, and you gave it to him; finished what Russell's started . . . I detect offended sensibilities, do I not?"

"We're not Russell's."

A smile to which the eyes gave the lie. "How bright a world, Mr. Konstantin, where there's still such outrage. And where Q exists . . . on the same station. Within arm's reach one of the other, and administered by your office. Or maybe Q itself is misplaced compassion. I suspect you must have created that hell by half-measures. By exercise of your sensibilities. Your private object of outrage, this

Unioner? Your apology to morality . . . or your statement on the war, Mr. Konstantin?"

"I want him out of detention. I want his papers back. He has no politics any longer."

No one talked to Mallory that way; plainly no one did. After a long moment she broke contact with his eyes, a dismissal, nodded slowly. "You're accountable?"

"I make myself accountable."

"On that understanding . . . No. No, Mr. Konstantin, *you* don't go. You don't need to go in person. I'll clear him through Fleet channels, send him home . . . on your assurance things are as you say."

"You can see the records if you want."

"I'm sure they'd contain nothing of news." She waved a hand, a signal to someone behind him, a tiny move. His spine crawled with the sudden realization there had been a gun at his back. She walked over to the com console, leaned over the tech and keyed through to the Fleet channel. "This is Mallory. Release the papers and person of Joshua Talley, in station detention. Relay to appropriate authorities, Fleet and station. Over."

The acknowledgment came back, impersonal and uninterested.

"May I," Damon asked her, "may I send a call to him? He'll need some clear instruction. . . ."

"Sir," one of the techs nearby said, facing about in her place. "Sir—"

He glanced distractedly at the anguished face.

"A Downer's been shot, sir, in green four."

The breath went out of him. For a moment his mind refused to work.

"He's *dead,* sir."

He shook his head, sick at his stomach, turned and glared at Mallory. "They don't hurt anything. No Downer ever lifted a hand to a human except to escape, in panic. *Ever.*"

Mallory shrugged. "Past mending now, Mr. Konstantin. Get on about your own business. Someone slipped and fired; there was a no-shoot order. It's our business, not yours. Our own people will take care of it."

"They're *people,* captain."

"We've shot people too," Mallory said, unruffled. "Get

on about your business, I say. This matter is under martial law, and I'll settle it."

He stood still. Everywhere in the center faces were turned toward them, and the boards flashed with neglected lights. "Get to work," he ordered them sharply, and backs turned at once. "Get a station medic to that area."

"You try my patience," Mallory said.

"They are our citizens."

"Your citizenship is broad, Mr. Konstantin."

"I'm telling you—they're terrified of violence. If you want chaos on this station, captain, panic the Downers."

She considered the point, nodded finally, without rancor. "If you can mend the situation, Mr. Konstantin, see to it. And go where you choose."

Just that. *Go.* He started away, glanced back with sudden dread of Mallory, who could cast away a public argument. He had lost, had let anger get the better of him . . . and *go,* she said, as if her pride were nothing.

He left, with the disturbed feeling that he had done something desperately dangerous.

*"Clear Damon Konstantin for passage,"* Mallory's voice thundered through the corridors, and troops who had made to challenge him did not.

## iii

He ran, leaving the lift on green four, his ID and card in hand, flashed both at a zealous trooper who tried to bar his way, and won through. Troops were gathered ahead, blocking off all view. He ran up and, roughly seized, showed the card and pushed his way past the troopers.

"Damon." He heard Elene's voice before he saw her, swung about and met her arms in the press of armored troops, hugged her in relief.

"It's one of the temporaries," she said, "a male named Bigfellow. Dead."

"Get out of here," he wished her, not trusting the troops' good sense. He looked beyond her. There was a good deal of blood on the floor at the access doorway. They had gotten the dead Downer into a bodybag and onto a stretcher for removal. Elene, her arm linked with his, showed no inclination to leave.

"Doors got him," she said. "But the shot may have

killed him first.—Lt. Vanars, off *India,*" she murmured, for a young officer urged his way toward them. "In charge of this unit."

"What happened?" Damon asked the lieutenant. "What happened here?"

"Mr. Konstantin? A regrettable error. The Downer appeared unexpectedly."

"This is *Pell,* lieutenant, full of civilians. The station will want a full report on this."

"For the safety of your station, Mr. Konstantin, I'd urge you to review your security procedures. Your workers blew the lock. *That* cut the Downer in half, when the emergency seal went; someone had that inner door open out of sequence. How far do these tunnels go? Everywhere?"

"They've run," Elene said quickly, "down, away from here. They're probably temporaries and they don't know the tunnels well. And they're not about to come out again with the threat of guns out here. They'll hide down there till they die."

"Order them out," Vanars said.

"You don't understand the Downers," Damon said.

"Get them all out of the tunnels. Seal them up."

"Pell's maintenance is in those tunnels, lieutenant; and our Downer workers *live* in that network, with their own atmospheric system. The tunnels can't shut down. I'm going in there," he said to Elene. "They may answer."

She bit her lip. "I'm staying right here," she said, "till you come out."

There were objections he would have made. It was not the place for them. He shot a look at Vanars. "It may take me a while. Downers aren't a negotiable matter on Pell. They're frightened, and they can get into places they can die in and cause us real trouble. *If* I get into trouble, contact station authorities, don't send troops in; we can deal with them. If another gun goes off in their vicinity we may not *have* a maintenance system, sir. Our life-support and theirs are linked, a system in precise balance."

Vanars said nothing. Did not react. It was impossible to know if reason meant anything with him or the rest of them. He squeezed Elene's hand, drew away, and shouldered his way past the armored troops, tried to avoid stepping in a dark pool of blood as he carded open the lock.

The door opened, closed behind him, started its cycle

automatically. He reached for the human breathing gear which always hung on the right of entry of such chambers, slipped it on before the effects became severe. His breath took on the suck and hiss he associated subconsciously with Downer presence, loud in the metal chamber. He opened the inner door and the echo came back out of far depths. He had a dim blue light where he was, but he paused to unlock the compartment by the door and take out a lamp. The powerful beam cut through the dark into a web of steel.

"Downers!" he called, his voice echoing hollowly down and down. He felt the cold as he walked through the door and let it seal, stood on the joining platform from which the ladders ran in all directions. "Downers! It's Damon Konstantin! Do you hear me? Call out if you hear me."

The echoes died very slowly, depth upon depth.

"Downers?"

A moan drifted up out of the dark, an echoing keening which stirred the hairs at his nape. Anger?

He went further, gripping the light with one hand, the thin rail with the other, stopped and listened. "Downers?"

Something moved in the dark depths. Soft footfalls rang very softly on metal far below. "Konstantin?" an alien voice lisped. "Konstantin-man?"

"It's Damon Konstantin," he called again. "Please come up. No guns. It's safe."

He stayed still, feeling the slight tremor in the scaffolding as feet trod it far down in the dark. He heard breathing, and his eyes caught the light far below, shimmer like illusion. There was an impression of fur, and another glimmer of eyes, ascending by stages. He stayed very still, one man, and fragile in these dark places. They were not dangerous . . . but no one had attacked them with guns before.

They came, more distinct in his hand-held light, bedraggled and struggling up the last stage, panting, the one hurt and the other wide-eyed with terror.

"Konstantin-man," that one said with a quavering lisp. "Help, help, help."

They held out hands, pleading. He set the lamp down on the grating on which he stood and accepted them as children, touched the male very carefully, for the poor fellow was bleeding all down his arm and drew back his lips in a fretful snarl.

"All right," he assured them. "You're safe, you're safe now. I'll get you out."

"Scared, Konstantin-man." The female stroked her mate's shoulder and looked from one to the other of them with round, shadowed eyes. "All hide gone find no path."

"I don't understand you."

"More, more, more we, dead hungry, dead 'fraid. Please help we."

"Call them."

She touched the male, a gesture eloquent of worry. The male chattered something to her, pushed at her, and she reached and touched at Damon.

"I'll wait," Damon assured her. "I wait here. All safe."

"Love you," she said in a breath, and scrambled back down with a ringing of the metal steps, lost at once in the dark. In a moment more, shrieks and trills sounded out into the depths until the echoes redoubled; voices woke out of other places, male and female, deep and high, until all the depths and dark went mad. A shriek erupted by him: the male shouted something down.

They came in the silence which followed, ringings of steps on the metal deep below, callings occasionally echoing sharply and moanings rising which stirred the scalp. The female came running back to stroke her mate's shoulder and to touch his hands. "I Satin, I call. Make he all right, Konstantin-man."

"They have to come through the lock few at a time, you understand, careful of the lock."

"I know lock," she said. "I careful. Go, go, I bring they."

She was already hastening down again. Damon put his arm about the male and brought him into the lock, dragged his mask up for him, for the fellow was muzzy with shock, snarling with pain but making no attempt to snap or strike. The next door opened, on the flare of light and armed men, and the Downer started within the circle of his arm, snarled and spat, yielded to a reassuring hug. Elene was there, breaking through the troops, holding her hands out to help.

"Get the troops back," Damon snapped, light-blinded and unable to distinguish Vanars. "Out of the way. Quit waving guns at them." He urged the Downer to sit on the floor by the wall, and Elene was ordering the medic over. "Back these troops out of here!" Damon said again. "Leave us to it!"

An order was passed. To his great relief the *India* troopers began to pull back, and the Downer sat still, with some persuasion yielded his injured arm to examination as the medic knelt down with his kit. Damon tugged his own mask down, stifling in it, squeezed Elene's hand as she bent down beside him. The air stank of sweating, frightened Downer, a pungent muskiness.

"Name's Bluetooth," the medic said, checking the tag. He made a few swift notes and began gently to treat the injury. "Burn and hemorrhage. Minor, except for shock."

"Drink," Bluetooth pleaded, and reached for the kit. The medic rescued it and quietly promised him water when they could find some.

The lock opened, yielded up a near dozen Downers. Damon stood up, reading panic in their looks. "I'm Konstantin," he said at once, for the name carried importance with the Downers. He met them with outstretched hands, suffered himself to be hugged by sweating, shock-hazed Downers, gentle enfoldings of powerful furred arms. Elene welcomed them likewise, and in a moment another lockful had spilled out, making a knot which filled the corridor and outnumbered the troops who stood in the end of the hall. The Downers cast anxious looks in that direction, but kept together. Another lockful, and Bluetooth's mate was with them, chattering anxiously until she had found him. Vanars came among them, quite without swagger in this brown-furred flood.

"You're requested to get them to a secure area as quickly as possible," Vanars said.

"Use your com and clear us passage via the emergency ramps via four through nine to the docks," Damon said. "Their habitat is accessible from there; we'll escort them back. That's quickest and safest for all concerned."

He did not wait for Vanars's comment in the matter, but waved an arm at the Downers. "Come," he said, and they fell silent and began to move. Bluetooth, his arm done up in a white bandage, scrambled up not to be left, and chattered something to the others. Satin added her own voice, and there was a general and sudden cheerfulness among the Downers. He walked, hand in hand with

Elene, and the Downers strode along about and behind them with the peculiar accompaniment of the breather-sounds, moving gladly and quickly. The few guards along their route stayed very still, suddenly in the minority, and Downers chattered with increasing freedom among themselves as they reached the end of the hall and entered the spiraling broad ramp which led to doors on all the nine levels. An arm snaked about Damon's left as they descended; he looked and it was Bluetooth, and Satin was with him, so that they came four abreast down the ramp, bizarre company . . . five, for another had joined hands with Elene on the right. Satin cried something. A chorus answered. Again she spoke, her voice echoing in the heights and depths; and again the chattering chorus thundered out, with a bounce in steps about them. Another yelled from the rear; and voices answered; and a second time. Damon tightened his hand on Elene's, at once stirred and alarmed at this behavior, but the Downers were content to walk with him, shouting what had begun to sound like a marching chant.

They broke into green nine, and marched down the long hall . . . entered the docks with a great shout, and the echoes rang. The line of troops which guarded the ship accesses stirred ominously, but no more than that. "Stay with me," Damon ordered his companions sternly, and they did so, up the curving horizon into the area of their habitat, and there to a parting. "Go," he told them. "Go and mind you be careful. Don't scare the men with guns."

He had expected them to run, scampering free as they had begun to do about him. But one by one they came and wished to hug him and Elene, with tender care, so that the parting took some little time.

Last, Satin and Bluetooth, who hugged and patted them. "Love you," Bluetooth said. "Love you," said Satin, in her turn.

No word, no question about the dead one. "Bigfellow was lost," Damon told them, although he was sure by Bluetooth's burn that they had been somewhere involved in the matter. "Dead."

Satin bobbed a solemn agreement. "You send he home, Konstantin-man."

"I'll send," he promised. Humans died, and did not merit transport. They had no strong ties to this soil, or to any soil, a vague distressed desire toward burying, but not at inconvenience. This was inconvenient, but so was it to be murdered far from home. "I'll see it's done."

"Love you," she said solemnly, and hugged him a second time, laid her hand most gently on Elene's belly, and walked away with Bluetooth, running after a moment to the lock which led to their own tunnels.

It left Elene standing with her own hand to her stomach and a dazed stare at him. "How could she know?" Elene asked with a bewildered laugh. It disturbed him too.

"It shows a little," he said.

"To one of them?"

"They don't get large," he said. And looking past her, to the docks, and the lines of troops. "Come on. I don't like this area."

She looked where he had, to the soldiers and the more motley groups which ranged the upcurving horizon of the docks, near the bars and restaurants. Merchanters, keeping an eye on the military, on a dock which had been taken away from them.

"Merchanters have owned this place since Pell began," she said, "and the bars and the sleepovers. Establishments are shutting down, and Mazian's troops won't be happy. Freighter crews and Mazian's . . . in one bar, in one sleepover—station security had better be tight when any of those troops go on liberty."

"Come on," he said, taking her arm. "I want you out of this. Running out here, going out into that corridor with the Downers—"

"Where were you?" she shot back. "Down *in* the tunnels."

"I know them."

"So I know the docks."

"So what were you doing up in four?"

"I was down here when the call came; I asked Keu for a pass and got one, got his lieutenant to cooperate with dock offices; I was doing my job, thank you; and when the call came through Fleet com, I got Vanars up there before someone else got shot."

He hugged her gratefully, walked with her around the turn into blue nine, another barren vista of troops stationed at intervals and no one in the corridors.

"Josh," he said suddenly, dropping his arm.

"What?"

He kept his pace, headed for the lift, gathered his papers from his pocket, but they were *India* troops, and they were waved through. "Josh got picked up. Mallory knows he's here and where he is."

"What are you going to do about it?"

"Mallory agreed to release him. They may have let him loose already. I've got to check comp and find out where he is, whether still in detention or back at his apartment."

"He could sleepover with us."

He said nothing, thinking about that.

"Which of us," she asked, "is really going to sleep easy otherwise?"

"Not much sleep with him around either. We'll be jammed up in that apartment. As good have him in bed with us."

"So I've slept crowded. So it could drag on more than one night. If they get their hands on him—"

"Elene. It's one thing if station handles a protest. There are things in this, personal things with Josh . . ."

"Secrets?"

"Things that don't bear the light. Things Mallory might not want out, you understand me? She's dangerous. I've talked to multiple murderers less cold-blooded."

"Fleet captain. It's a breed, Damon. Ask any merchanter. You know there's probably kin of the merchanters on-station standing in those lines, but they'll not break information to hail their own mothers, no. What the Fleet takes . . . doesn't come back. You don't tell me anything I don't know about the Fleet. I can tell you that if we want to do something we should do it. Now."

"If we bring him in with us, we risk having that act in Fleet files . . ."

"I think I know what you *want* to do."

She had her own stubbornness. He reckoned matters, stopped at the lift, his hand on the button. "I figured we'd better get him," he said.

"So," she said. "Thought so."

# 7

## i

### Pell: sector white four: 2230 hrs.

Jon Lukas walked nervously through the vacant halls, despite the pass Keu had given to all of them in the council chambers. Troops might be withdrawn progressively starting at maindawn, they had been promised. Had to, he reckoned. Some of them were already being rotated off to rest, some Fleet crew, armorless, taking up guard in their places. It was all quiet; he was not even challenged but once, at the lift exit, and he walked to his door, used his card to open it.

The front room was deserted. His heart lurched with the immediate fear that his unbidden guest had strayed; but then Bran Hale appeared in the hall by the kitchen and looked re-relieved to see him.

"All right," Hale said, and Jessad came out, and two others of Hale's men after him.

"About time," Jessad said. "This was growing tedious."

"It's going to stay that way," Jon said peevishly. "Everyone has to stay here tonight: Hale, Daniels, Clay . . . I'm not having my apartment door pour a horde of visitors out under the troops' noses. They'll be gone come morning."

"The Fleet?" Hale asked.

"The troops in the halls." Jon went to the kitchen bar, examined a bottle which had been full when he left it and which now had two fingers remaining. He poured himself a drink and sipped it with a sigh, his eyes stinging with exhaustion. He walked over to the chair he favored and sank down as Jessad took his place opposite, across the low table, and Hale and his men rummaged at the bar for another bottle. "I'm glad you were prudent," he said to Jessad. "I was worried."

Jessad smiled, cat-eyed. "I surmise you were. That for a moment or two you thought of solutions. Maybe you're still thinking in that line. Shall we discuss it?"

Jon frowned, slid a glance at Hale and his men. "I trust them more than you, and that's a fact."

"It's likely you thought of being rid of me," Jessad said. "And I wouldn't be surprised if you aren't right now more concerned about where rather than if. You might get away with it entirely. Probably you would."

The directness disturbed him. "Since you bring it up yourself, I suppose you've got a counter proposal."

The smile persisted. "One: I'm no present hazard; you may want to think matters over. Two: I am undismayed by Mazian's arrival."

"Why?"

"Because that contingency is covered."

Jon lifted the glass to his lips and took a stinging swallow. "By what?"

"When you jump to land in the Deep, Mr. Lukas, you can do it three safe ways: not throw much into the jump in the first place . . . if you're in regions you know very, very well; or use a star's G to pull you up; or—if you're good—the mass in some null point. A lot of junk in Pell's vicinity, you know that? Nothing very big, but big enough."

"What are you talking about?"

"The Union Fleet, Mr. Lukas. Do you think there's no reason Mazian has his ships grouped for the first time in decades? Pell's all they have left; and the Union Fleet is out there, just as they sent me ahead, knowing where they'd come."

Hale and his men had gathered, settled on the couch and along the back of it. Jon shaped the situation in his mind, Pell a battle zone, the worst of all scenarios.

"And what happens to us when it's discovered there's no way to dislodge Mazian?"

"Mazian can be driven off. And when that's done he has no bases at all. He's done; and we have *peace,* Mr. Lukas, with all the rewards of it. That's why I'm here."

"I'm listening."

"Officials have to be taken out. The *Konstantins* have to be taken out. You have to be set in their place. Have you the nerve for that, Mr. Lukas, despite relationships? I understand there's a—kinship involved here; yourself, Konstantin's wife—"

He clamped his lips together, flinching as he always did, from the thought of Alicia as she was now. Could not face that. Had never been able to stomach it. It was not life, linked to those machines. Not life. He wiped at his face. "My sister and I don't speak. Haven't, for years. She's an invalid; Dayin would have told you that."

"I'm aware of it. I'm talking about her husband, her sons. Have you the nerve, Mr. Lukas?"

"Nerve, yes, if the planning makes sense."

"There's a man on this station named Kressich."

He sucked in a slow breath, the drink resting in his hand against the chair arm. "Vassily Kressich, elected councillor of Q. How do you know him?"

"Dayin Jacoby gave us the name . . . as the concillor from that zone; and we have files. This man Kressich . . . comes from Q when the council meets. He then has a pass which will let him do so, or is it visual inspection?"

"Both. There are guards."

"Can those who do the inspecting be bribed?"

"For some things, yes. But stationers, Mr. Whoever-you-are, have a natural reluctance to doing anything to damage the station they're living in. You can get drugs and liquor into Q; but a man . . . a guard's conscience about a case of liquor and his instinct for self-preservation are two different things."

"Then we'll have to keep any conference with him brief, won't we?"

"Not *here*."

"That's up to you. Perhaps the lending of an ID and papers. I'm sure among your many faithful employees something can be arranged, some apartment near the Q zone. . . ."

"What kind of conference are you talking about? And what are you looking for from Kressich? The man is spineless."

"How many employees do you have in all," Jessad asked, "as faithful and trusted as these men here? Men who might take risks, who might kill? We have need of that sort."

Jon cast a look at Bran Hale, feeling short of breath. Back again. "Well, Kressich isn't the type, I'll tell you."

"Kressich has contacts. Can a man stay seated atop that monster of Q without them?"

## ii

## Pell: sector green seven: merchanter's hospice; 2241 hrs.

Com buzzed. The light was on, a call coming through. Josh looked at it across his room, stopped in his pacing. They had let him go. *Go home,* they had said, and he had done so, through corridors guarded by police and Mazianni. They knew at this moment where he was. And now someone was calling his room, hard after his arrival.

The caller insisted; the red light stayed on, blinking. He did not want to answer, but it might be detention checking to be sure he had gotten here. He was afraid not to respond to it. He crossed the room and pushed the reply button.

"Josh Talley," he said into the mike.

"Josh. Josh, it's Damon. Good to hear your voice. Are you all right?"

He leaned against the wall, caught his breath.

"Josh?"

"I'm all right. Damon, you know what happened."

"I know. Your message got to me. I've taken personal responsibility for you. You're coming to our apartment tonight. Pack what you need. I'm coming there after you."

"Damon, no. *No.* Stay out of this."

"We've talked it over; it's all right. No argument."

"Damon, don't. Don't let it get on their records. . . ."

"We're your legal sponsors as it is, Josh. It's already on the records."

"Don't."

"Elene and I are on our way."

The contact went dead. He wiped his face. The knot which had been at his stomach had risen into his throat. He saw no walls, nothing of where he was. It was all metal, and Signy Mallory, young face and age-silvered hair, and eyes dead and oldest of all. Damon and Elene and the child they wanted . . . they prepared to put everything at risk. For him.

He had no weapons. Needed none, if it were to be himself and her alone, as it had been in her quarters. He had been dead then, inside. Had existed, hating his existence. The same kind of paralysis beckoned now . . . to let things be, accept, take cover where it was offered; it was always easier. He had not threatened Mallory, having had nothing to fight for.

He pushed from the wall, felt of his pocket, making sure his papers were there. He walked into the hall and through it past the unmanned front desk of the hospice, out into the open where the guards stood. One of the local security started to challenge him. He looked frantically down the corridor where a trooper stood.

*"You!"* he shouted, disturbing the vacant quiet of the hall. Police and trooper reacted, the trooper with leveled rifle and a suddenness which had almost been a pulled trigger. Josh swallowed tightly, held his hands in plain view. "I want to talk with you."

The rifle motioned. He walked with hands still wide at his sides, toward the armored trooper and the dark muzzle. "Far enough," the trooper said. "What is it?"

The insignia was *Atlantic*'s. "Mallory of *Norway,*" he said. We're good friends. Tell her Josh Talley wants to talk with her. Now."

The trooper had a disbelieving look, a scowl finally. But he balanced the rifle in the crook of his arm and reached for his com button. "I'll relay to the *Norway* duty officer," he said. "You'll be going in, in either case—your way, if she does know you, and on general investigation if she doesn't."

"She'll see me," he said.

The trooper pushed the com button and queried. What came back came privately over his helmet com, but his eyes flickered. "Check it, then," he said to *Norway.* And after a moment more: "Command central. Got it. Out." He hooked the com unit to his belt again, and motioned with the rifle barrel. "Keep walking down that hall and go up the ramp. That trooper down there will take you in charge and see you talk to Mallory."

He went, walking quickly, for he did not reckon it would take Damon and Elene long to reach the hospice.

They searched him. Of course they would do so. He endured it for the third time this day, and this time it did not bother him. He was cold inside, and outer things did not trouble him. He straightened his clothes and walked with them up the ramp, past sentries at every level. On green two they entered a lift and rode it the short rise and traverse into blue one. They had not even asked for his papers, had scarcely looked at them more than to be sure that the folder held nothing but papers.

They walked a short distance back along the matting-carpeted hall. There was a reek of chemicals in the air. Workmen were busy peeling all the location signs. The windowed section further, crammed with comp equipment and with a few techs moving about, was specially guarded. *Norway* troops. They opened the door and let him and his guards in, into station central, among the aisles of busy technicians.

Mallory, seated at the end of the counters, rose to meet him, smiled coldly at him, her face haggard. "Well?" she said.

He had thought the sight of her would not affect him. It did. His stomach wrenched. "I want to come back," he said, "on *Norway*."

"Do you?"

"I'm no stationer; I don't belong here. Who else would take me?"

Mallory looked at him and said nothing. A tremor started in his left knee; he wished he might sit down. They would shoot him if he made a move; he thoroughly believed that they would. The tic threatened his composure, jerked at the side of his mouth when she turned away a moment and glanced back again. She laughed, a dry chuckle. "Konstantin put you up to this?"

"No."

"You've been Adjusted. That so?"

The stammer tied his tongue. He nodded.

"And Konstantin makes himself responsible for your good behavior."

It was all going wrong. "No one's responsible for me," he said, stumbling on the words. "I want a ship. If *Norway* is all I've got, then I'll take it." He had to look at her directly, at eyes which flickered with imagined thoughts, things which were not going to be said here, before the troopers.

"You search him?" she asked the guards.

"Yes, ma'am."

She stood thinking a long moment, and there was no smile, no laughter. "Where are you staying?"

"A room in the old hospice."

"The Konstantins provide it?"

"I work. I pay for it."

"What's your job?"

"Small salvage."

An expression of surprise, of derision.

"So I want out of it," he said. "I figure you owe me that."

There was interruption, movement behind him, which stopped. Mallory laughed, a bored, weary laugh, and beckoned to someone. "Konstantin. Come on in. Come get your friend."

Josh turned. Damon and Elene were both there, flushed and upset and out of breath. They had followed him. "If he's confused," Damon said, "he belongs in the hospital." He came and laid a hand on Josh's shoulder. "Come on. Come on, Josh."

"He's not confused," Mallory said. "He came here to kill me. Take your friend home, Mr. Konstantin. And keep a watch on him, or I'll handle matters my way."

There was stark silence.

"I'll see to it," Damon said after a moment. His fingers bit into Josh's shoulder. "Come on. Come *on*."

Josh moved, walked with him and Elene, past the guards, out and down the long corridor with the work crews and the chemical smell; the doors of central closed behind him. Neither of them said anything. Damon's grip shifted to his elbow and they took him into a lift, rode it down the short distance to five. There were more guards in this hall, and station police. They passed unchallenged into the residential halls, to Damon's own door. They brought him inside and closed the door. He stood waiting, while Damon and Elene went through the routine of turning on lights, and taking off jackets.

"I'll send for your clothes," Damon said shortly. "Come on, make yourself at home."

It was not the welcome he deserved. He picked a leather chair, mindful of his grease-stained work clothes. Elene brought him a cool drink and he sipped at it without tasting it.

Damon sat down on the arm of the chair next to his.

Temper showed. Josh accepted that, found a place at his feet to stare at.

"You ran us a circular chase," Damon said. "I don't know how you got past us but you managed it."

"I asked to go."

Whatever Damon would have wanted to say, he swallowed. Elene came over and sat down on the couch opposite him.

"So what did you have in mind?" Damon asked evenly.

"You shouldn't have gotten involved. I didn't want you involved."

"So you ran from us?"

He shrugged.

"Josh—did you mean to kill her?"

"Eventually. Somewhere. Sometime."

They found nothing to say. Damon finally shook his head and looked away, and Elene came over behind Josh's chair, laid a gentle hand on his shoulder.

"It didn't work," Josh said finally, tripping on the words. "It went everyway wrong. I'm afraid now she thinks you put me up to it. I'm sorry. I'm sorry."

Elene's hand brushed his hair, descended again to his shoulder. Damon simply stared at him as if he were looking at someone he had never seen before. "Don't you ever," Damon said, "think of doing that again."

"I didn't want you two hurt. I didn't want you taking me in with you. Think how it looks to them—you, with me."

"You think Mazian runs this station all of a sudden? And you think a captain in the Fleet is going to break relations with the Konstantins, whose cooperation Mazian needs . . . in a personal feud?"

He thought that over. It made sense in a way he wanted to believe, and therefore he suspected it.

"It's not going to happen," Damon said. "So forget about it. No trooper is about to walk into this apartment, you can depend on it. Just don't give them excuses for wanting to. And you came close. You understand that? The worst thing you can do is give them a pretext. Josh, it was Mallory's order that got you out of detention. I asked it. She did it a second time back there . . . as a favor. Don't depend on a third."

He nodded, shaken.

"Have you eaten today?"

He considered, confused, finally thought back to the sandwich, realized that at least part of his malaise was lack of food. "Missed supper," he said.

"I'll get you some clothes of mine that will fit. Wash up, relax. We'll go back to your apartment tomorrow morning and get whatever you need."

"How long am I going to stay here?" he asked, turning his head to look at Elene and back at Damon. It was a small place. He was aware of the inconvenience. "I can't move in on you."

"You stay here until it's safe," Damon said. "If we have to make further arrangements, we will. In the meantime I'm going to do some review on your papers or whatever excuse I can contrive that will excuse your spending the next few working days in my office."

"I don't go back to the shop?"

"When this is settled. Meanwhile we're not going to let you out of our sight. We made it clear they'll have to create a major incident to touch you. I'll put my father onto it too, so that no one in either office gets caught by a surprise request. Just, please, don't provoke anything."

"No," he agreed. Damon gave a jerk of his head back toward the hall. He rose and went with Damon, and Damon searched an armload of clothing out of the lockers outside the bath. He went into the bath, bathed and felt better, clean of the memory of the detention cell, wrapped himself in the soft robe Damon had lent him, and came out to the aroma of supper cooking.

They ate, crowded at the table, exchanged what they had seen in their separate sections. He could talk without anxiousness finally, now that the nightmare was on him, and he was no longer alone in it.

He chose the far corner of the kitchen, made himself a pallet on the floor, out of the amazing abundance of bedding Elene urged on him. *We'll get a cot by tomorrow,* she promised him. *At least, a hammock.* He settled down in it, heard them settle in the living room, and felt safe, believing finally what Damon had told him . . . that he was in a refuge even Mazian's Fleet could not breach.

# 8

## Downbelow: Africa landing probe, main base; 2400 hrs. md.; 1200 hrs. a; local daylight

Emilio leaned back in the chair and stared resolutely at Porey's scowl, waited, while the scarred captain made several notes on the printout before him, and pushed it back across the table at him. Emilio gathered it up, leafed through the supply request, nodded slowly.

"It may take a little time," he said.

"At the moment," said Porey, "I am simply relaying reports and acting on instructions. You and your staff are not cooperating. Go on with that as long as you please."

They sat in the small personnel area of Porey's ship, flat-decked, never meant for prolonged space flight. Porey had had his taste of Downbelow air, and of their domes and the dust and the mud, and retreated to his ship in disgust, calling him in instead of visiting the main dome. And that would have suited him well, if it had only taken the troops away as well; it had not. *They* were still outside, masked and armed. Q and the residents as well worked the fields under guns.

"I also am receiving instructions," Emilio said, "and acting on them. The best that we can do, captain, is to acknowledge that both sides are aware of the situation, and your reasonable request will be honored. We are both under orders."

A reasonable man might have been placated. Porey was not. He simply scowled. Perhaps he resented the order which had put him on Downbelow; perhaps it was his natural expression. Likely he was short of sleep; the short intervals at which the troops outside were being relieved indicated they had not come in fresh, and Porey's crew had been in evidence, not Porey—alterday crew, perhaps.

"Take your time," Porey repeated, and it was evident that he would remember the time taken—the day that he had the chance to do things his own way.

"By your leave," Emilio said, received no courtesy, and stood up and walked out. The guards let him go, down the short corridor and via lift to the ship's big belly, where lift functioned as lock, into Downbelow atmosphere. He drew up his mask and walked down the lowered ramp into the cool wind.

They had not yet sent occupation forces to the other camps. He reckoned that they would like to, but that their forces were limited, and there were no landing areas at those sites. As for Porey's demand for supplies, he reckoned he could come up with the requested amount; it scanted them, certainly scanted station, but their balking and the stripped domes, he reckoned, had at least gotten the Fleet's demand down to something tolerable.

*Situation improved,* his father's most recent message had been. *No evacuation planned. Fleet contemplating permanent base at Pell.*

That was not the best news. It was not the worst. All his life he had figured on the war as a debt which had to come due someday, in some generation. That Pell could not keep its neutrality forever. While the Company agents had been with them, he had hoped, forlornly, that some outside force might be prepared to intervene. It was not. They had Mazian, instead, who was losing the war Earth would not finance, who could not protect a station that might decide to finance him, who knew nothing of Pell, and cared nothing for Downbelow's delicate balances.

*Where are the Downers?* the troops had asked. *Frightened by strangers,* he had answered. There was no sign of them. He did not plan that there should be. He tucked Porey's supply request into his jacket pocket and walked the path up and over the hill. He could see the troops standing here and there among the domes, rifles evident; could see the workers far off among the fields, all of them, turned out to work regardless of schedules or age or health. Troops were down at the mill, at the pumping station. They were asking questions among the workers about production rates. So far it had not shaken the basic story, that station had simply absorbed what they produced. There were all those ships up there, all those merchanters orbiting station. It was not likely that even Mazian would start singling out merchanters and taking supply from them . . . not when they were that numerous.

But Mazian, the thought kept nagging at him, had not outmaneuvered Union this long to be taken in by Emilio Konstantin. Not likely.

He walked the path down over the bridge in the gully, up again, toward operations. He saw its door open, saw Miliko come outside, stand waiting for him, her black hair blowing, her arms clenched against the day's chill. She had wanted to come to the ship with him, fearing his going alone into Porey's hands, without witnesses. He had argued her out of it. She started toward him now, coming down the hill, and he waved, to let her know it was at least as all right as it was likely to be.

They were still in command of Downbelow.

# 9

## Blue one: 10/5/52; 0900

A trooper was on guard at the corner. Jon Lukas hesitated, but that was guaranteed to attract attention. The trooper made a move of his hand to the vicinity of the pistol. Jon came ahead nervously, card in hand, offered it, and the trooper—heavyset, dark-skinned—took it and frowned while looking at it. "That's a council clearance," Jon said. "Top council clearance."

"Yes, sir," the trooper said. Jon took the card back, started down the crosshall, with the feeling that the trooper was still watching his back. "Sir."

He turned.

"Mr. Konstantin's at his office, sir."

"His wife's my sister."

There was a moment of silence. "Yes, sir," the trooper

said mildly, and made himself a statue again. Jon turned and walked on.

Angelo did well for himself, he thought bitterly, no crowding here, no giving up of *his* living space. The whole end of crosshall four was Angelo's.

And Alicia's.

He stopped at the door, hesitated, his stomach tightening. He had gotten this far. There was a trooper back there who would ask questions, make an issue of unusual behavior. There was no going back. He pressed com. Waited.

"Who?" a reedy voice asked, startling him. "Who you?"

"Lukas," he said. "Jon Lukas."

The door opened. A thin, grayed Downer frowned up at him from eyes surrounded with wrinkles. "I Lily," she said.

He brushed past her, stepped in and looked about the dim living room, the costly furniture, the luxury, the space of it. The Downer Lily hovered there, anxious, let the door close. He turned, his eyes drawn to light, saw a room beyond, a white floor, with the illusion of windows open on space.

"You come see she?" Lily asked.

"Tell her I'm here."

"I tell." The old Downer bowed, walked away with a stooped, brittle step. The place was quiet, deathly hushed. He waited in the dark living room, found nothing to do with his hands, his stomach more and more upset.

There were voices from the room. "Jon," he heard in the midst of it. Alicia's voice. At least it was the human one. He shivered, feeling physically ill. He had never come to these rooms. Never. Had seen Alicia by remote, tiny, withered, a shell the machines sustained. He came now. He did not know why he came—and did know. To find out what was truth—to know—if he could face dealing with Alicia; if it was life worth living. All these years—the pictures, the transmitted, cold pictures he could somehow deal with, but to be there in the same room, to look into her face and have to talk with her. . . .

Lily came back, hands folded, bowed. "You come. You come now."

He moved. Got as far as halfway to the white-tiled room, the sterile, hushed room, and his stomach knotted.

Suddenly he turned and started for the outside door.

"You come?" The Downer's puzzled voice pursued him. "You come, sir?"

He touched the switch and left, let the door close behind him, drew a breath of the cooler, freer air of the hall outside.

He walked away from it, the place, the Konstantins.

"Mr. Lukas," the trooper on guard said as he reached the corner, his eyes asking curious questions through the courtesy.

"She was asleep," he said, swallowed, kept walking, trying with every step to put that apartment and that white room out of his mind. He remembered a child, a girl, someone else. He kept it that way.

# 10

## i

### Pell: sector blue one; council chambers; 10/6/52; 1400 hrs.

Council was breaking up early, having passed what measures were set before it to pass, with Keu of *India* sitting in grim witness of what they said and what they did, his stone-still countenance casting a pall on debate. On this third day of the crisis, Mazian made his demands, and obtained.

Kressich gathered up his notes and came down from the uppermost tier into the sunken center of the chambers, by the seats about the table, delayed there, resisting the outflow of traffic, looking anxiously toward Angelo Konstantin, who conferred with Nguyen and Landgraf and some of the other representatives. Keu still sat at the table, listening, his bronze face like a mask. He feared Keu . . . feared to raise his business in front of him.

But he went nevertheless, edged insistently as close as he could get to the head of it, into that private company about Konstantin where he knew he was not wanted, Q's representative, reminder of problems no one had time to solve. He waited, while Konstantin finished his discussion with the others, stared at Konstantin intently so that Konstantin should be aware that his particular attention was wanted.

At last Konstantin took note of him, stayed a moment from his evident intention to leave in Keu's company, for Keu had risen. "Sir," Kressich said. "Mr. Konstantin." He drew from his folder of papers one which he had prepared, proferred it to Konstantin's hand. "I have limited facilities, Mr. Konstantin. Comp and print isn't accessible to me where I live. You know that. The situation there. . . ." He moistened his lips, conscious of Konstantin's frown. "My office was nearly mobbed last night. Please, sir. Can we assure my constituents . . . that the Downbelow appointments will continue?"

"That's under negotiation, Mr. Kressich. The station is making every effort to get procedures back to normal; but programs are being reviewed; policy and directions are being reviewed."

"It's the only hope." He avoided Keu's stare, kept his eyes fixed on Konstantin. "Without that . . . we've got no hope. Our people will go to Downbelow. To the Fleet. To any place that will take them. Only the applications have to be accepted. They have to see there's hope of getting out. Please, sir."

"The nature of this?" Konstantin asked, lifting the paper to view.

"A bill I haven't the facilities to reproduce for the council to consider. I hoped your staff . . ."

"Regarding the applications."

"Regarding that, sir."

"The program remains," Keu interrupted coldly, "under discussion."

"We'll try," Konstantin said, placing the paper among the others he held. "I can't bring this up on the floor, Mr. Kressich. You understand that. Not until the basic issues in question are resolved at other levels. I'll have to hold it, and I earnestly beg that you don't bring up the question tomorrow, although of course you *can* do that. Public debate might upset negotiations. You're a man experienced in government; you understand me. But in courtesy, if we can bring this up at some future meeting . . .

I'll of course have my staff prepare this or other bills for distribution. You understand my position, sir."

"Yes, sir," he said, sick at heart. "Thank you."

He turned away. He had hoped, dimly. He had hoped also for a chance to appeal for station help, security, protection. He did not want Keu's sort of protection. Dared not ask. They had seen the Fleet's mercy, in the persons of Mallory and Sung and Kreshov. The troops would come in; take Coledy's organization apart as a beginning; his security; all the protection he had.

He walked out into the council chambers foyer, past the mocking, amazed stares of Downbelow statues, out the glass doors into the hall, and, unmolested by the guards, walked toward the lift which would take him down to the blue niner level, to go home, back to Q.

There was something like normal traffic in the corridors of main station now, thinner than usual, but station residents were back about their jobs and moving freely if cautiously; no one tended to linger anywhere.

Someone jostled him in meeting. A hand met his, pressed a card into it. He stopped, with a confused impression of a man, a face he had not bothered to see. In terror he resisted the impulse to look about. He pretended to adjust the papers in his folder, walked on, and farther down the hall examined the card: an access card, a bit of tape on its surface: green nine 0434. An address. He kept walking, dropped the hand with the card to his side, his heart hammering against his ribs.

He could ignore it, pass on back into Q. Could turn the card in, claim to have found it, or tell the truth: that someone wanted to contact him without others' knowledge. Politics. It had to be. Someone willing to take a risk wanted something from the representative of Q. A trap—or hope, a trade of influence. Someone who might be able to move obstructions.

He could reach green nine; just an accidental wrong button on the lift. He stopped in front of the lift call plate, alone, coded green and stood in front of the panel so no one passing might notice the glowing green. The car came; the doors opened. He stepped in and a woman came darting in at the last moment, punched the inside plate to code green two. Doors shut; he looked furtively at her as the car began to move, averted his eyes quickly. The car made a one-section traverse and started down. She got off at two; he stayed on, while the car picked up passengers, none that knew him. It stopped at six, at seven, acquired more. At eight, two got out; nine: he exited with four others, walked toward the docks, his fingers sweating on the card. He passed occasional troopers, who kept a general watch on the flow of traffic in the halls. None of them was likely to notice an ordinary man walking down a hall, stopping at a door, using a card to enter. It was the most natural of actions. Crossway four was coming up. There was no guard there. He slowed, thinking desperately, his heart speeding; he began to think of walking on.

A walker just behind him hooked his sleeve and brusquely swept him forward. "Come on," the man said, and turned the corner with him. He made no resistance, fearing knives, instincts bred in Q. Of course the deliverer of the card had come down too . . . or had some confederate. He moved puppetlike, walked the crosshall to the door. Let free, the walker passing on, he used the card.

He walked in. It was a small apartment, with an unmade bed, discarded clothes lying all over it. A man walked out of the nook which served as kitchen, a nondescript man in his middle thirties. "Who are you?" the man asked him.

It set him off balance. He started to pocket the card, but the man held out his hand demanding it. He surrendered it.

"Name?" the man asked.

"Kressich." And desperately: "I'm due . . . they'll miss me any minute."

"Then I won't keep you too long. You're from Russell's Star, Mr. Kressich, yes?"

"I thought you didn't know me."

"A wife, Jen Justin; a son, Romy."

He felt beside him for a littered chair, leaned on it, his heart paining him. "What are you talking about?"

"Am I correct, Vassily Kressich?"

He nodded.

"The trust your fellow citizens of Q have placed in you . . . to represent their interests. You are, of course, one whose initiative they respect . . . regarding their interests."

"Make your point."

"Your constituency is in a bad position . . . papers entangled. And when the military security gets tighter, as it will, with Mazian's force in control—I do wonder, Mr. Kressich, what kind of measures could be set up. You've all opposed Union after one fashion and the other, of course, some out of genuine dislike; some out of self-interest; some out of convenience. You, now, what sort were you?"

"Where do you get your information?"

"Official sources. I know a great deal about you that you never told this comp. I've done research. To put it finely, I've seen your wife and son, Mr. Kressich. Are you interested?"

He nodded, unable to do more than nod. He leaned on the chair, trying to breathe.

"They're well. On a station the name of which I know . . . where I saw them. Or perhaps moved by now. Union has realized their possible value, knowing the name of the man who represents so formidable a number of people on Pell. Computer search turned them up, but they'll not be lost again. Would you like to see them again, Mr. Kressich?"

"What do you want from me?"

"A little of your time. A little preparation for the future. You can protect yourself, your family, your constituents, who are pariahs under Mazian. What help could you get from Mazian in locating your family? Or how could he get you to them? And surely there are other families divided, who may now repent a rash decision, a decision Mazian forced them to take, who may understand . . . that the real interest of any Beyonder is the Beyond itself."

"You're Union," Kressich said, to have it beyond doubt.

"Mr. Kressich, I'm Beyonder. Aren't you?"

He sat down on the arm of the chair, for his knees were unsteady. "What is it you want?"

"Surely there's a power structure in Q, something you would know. Surely a man like you . . . is in contact with it."

"I have contacts."

"And influence?"

"And influence."

"You'll be in Union hands sooner or later; you realize that . . . if Mazian doesn't take measures of his own. Do you realize what he might do if he decides he wants to stay here? You think he's going to have Q near his ships? No, Mr. Kressich, you're on the one hand cheap labor; on the other a nuisance. Depending on the situation. The way things are going to go—very soon—you're going to be a liability to him. What means can I use to contact you, Mr. Kressich?"

"You contacted me today."

"Where is your office?"

"Orange nine 1001."

"Is there com?"

"Station. Just station can call through to me. And it breaks down. Anytime I want to call, I have to clear it through com central; it's set up that way. You can't—can't call through. And it's always broken."

"Q is prone to riot, is it not?"

He nodded.

"Could the councillor of Q . . . arrange one?"

A second time he nodded. Sweat was running down his face, his sides. "Can you get me off Pell?"

"When you've done what you can for me, a guaranteed ticket off, Mr. Kressich. Gather your forces. I don't even ask to know who they are. But you'll know me. A message from me will use the word Vassily. That's all. Just that word. And if such a call should come, you see that there is—immediate and widespread disturbance. And for that, you may begin to look forward to that reunion."

"Who are you?"

"Go on now. You've lost no more than ten minutes of your time. You can make up most of it. I'd hurry, Mr. Kressich."

He rose, glanced back, left in haste, the corridor air cold on his face. No one challenged him, no one noticed. He matched the pace of the main corridor, and decided that if challenged about the time, he had talked to Konstantin, talked to people in the foyer; that he had gotten ill and stopped in a restroom. Konstantin himself would attest that he had left upset. He wiped his face with his hand, his vision tending to blur, rounded the corner onto green dock, and kept walking, into blue, and toward the line.

There was a knock at the door. Hale answered it, and Jon turned tensely from his place by the kitchen bar, let go a profound sigh of relief as Jessad walked in, and the door closed behind him.

"No trouble," Jessad said. "They're covering up the signs, you know. Preparing for in-station action. Makes finding directions a little difficult."

"Kressich, confound you."

"No trouble." Jessad stripped off his coat and tossed it to Hale's man Keifer, who had appeared from the bedroom. Keifer felt the jacket pocket at once, recovered his papers with understandable relief. "You didn't get stopped," Keifer said.

"No," Jessad said. "Just walked right to your apartment, went in, sent your partner out with the card . . . all very smooth."

"He agreed?" Jon asked.

"Of course he agreed." Jessad was in an unusual mood, feeling a residue of excitement, his normally dull eyes alive with humor. He walked over to the bar and poured himself a drink.

"My clothes," Keifer objected.

Jessad laughed, sipped at the drink, then set it down and began to take off the shirt. "He's back in Q by now. And we control it."

## ii

## Union carrier, Unity, amid the Union Fleet: deep space

Ayres sat down at the table in the main room, ignored the guards, to lean his head against his hands and try to recover his balance. He remained as he was for several breaths, then rose, walked to the water dispenser on the wall, unsteady on his feet. He moistened his fingers and bathed his face with the cold water, took a paper cup and drank to settle his stomach.

Someone joined him in the room. He looked, scowled instantly, for it was Dayin Jacoby, who sat down at the only table. He would not have gone back to it, but his legs were too weak to bear long standing. He did not bear up well through jump. Jacoby fared better, and that too he held against him.

"It's close," Jacoby said. "I have a good idea where we are."

Ayres sat down, forced his eyes into focus. The drugs made everything distant. "You should be proud of yourself."

"Mazian . . . will be there."

"They don't confide in me. But it makes sense that he would . . . Is this being recorded?"

"I have no idea. What if it is? The fact is, Mr. Ayres, that you can't retain Pell for the Company, you can't protect it. You had your chance, and it's gone. And Pell doesn't want Mazian. Better Union order than Mazian."

"Tell that to my companions."

"Pell," Jacoby said, leaning forward, "deserves better than the Company can give it. Better than Mazian will give it, that's sure. I'm for *our* interest, Mr. Ayres, and we deal as we must."

"You could have dealt with us."

"We did . . . for centuries."

Ayres bit his lip, refusing to be drawn further into this argument. The drugs he had to have for jump . . . fogged his thinking. He had already talked, and he had resolved not to. They wanted something of him, or they would not have brought him out of confinement and let him up onto this level of the ship. He leaned his head against his hand and tried to reason himself out of his muzziness while there was still time.

"We're ready to go in." Jacoby pursued him. "You know that."

Jacoby was trying to frighten him. He had been prostrate with terror during the last maneuvering. He had endured jump twice now, with the feeling that his guts were twisted inside out. He refused to think of another one.

"I think they're going to have a talk with you," Jacoby said, "about a message for Pell, something to the effect that Earth has signed a treaty; that Earth supports the right of the citizens of Pell to choose their own government. That kind of thing."

He stared at Jacoby, doubting, for the fist time, where right and wrong lay. Jacoby was from Pell. Whatever Earth's interests, those interests could not be served by antagonizing a man who might, despite all wishes to the contrary, end up high in the government on Pell.

"You'll be interested, perhaps," Jacoby said, "in agreements involving Pell itself. If Earth doesn't want to be cut off . . . and you protest it seeks trades . . . it has to go *through* Pell, Mr. Ayres. We're important to you."

"I'm well aware of that fact. Talk to me when you *are* in authority over Pell. Right now the authority on Pell is Angelo Konstantin, and I have yet to see anything that says differently."

"Deal now," Jacoby said, "and expect agreement. The party I represent can assure you of safeguards for your interests. We're a jumping-off point, Mr. Ayres, for Earth and home. A quiet takeover on Pell, a quiet stay for you while you're waiting on your companions to overtake you, for a journey home in a ship easily engaged here at Pell; or difficulties . . . prolonged difficulties, resulting from a long and difficult siege. Damage . . . possibly the destruction of the station. I don't want that; I don't think you do. You're a humane man, Mr. Ayres. And I'm begging you—make it easy on Pell. Just tell the truth. Make it clear to them that there's a treaty, that their choice has to be Union. That Earth has let them go."

"You work for Union. Thoroughly."

"I want my station to survive, Mr. Ayres. Thousands upon thousands of people . . . could die. You know what it is with Mazian using it for cover? He can't hold it forever, but he can ruin it." Ayres sat staring at his hand, knowing that he could not reason accurately in his present condition, knowing that most of what he had been told in all his stay among them was a lie. "Perhaps we should work together, Mr. Jacoby, if it can assure an end to this without further bloodshed."

Jacoby blinked, perhaps surprised.

"Probably," Ayres said, "We are both realists, Mr. Jacoby . . . I suspect you of it. Self-determination is a nice term for last available choice, is it not? I comprehend your argument. Pell has no defenses. Station neutrality . . . meaning that you go with the winning side."

"You have it, Mr. Ayres."

"So do I," he said. "Order—in the Beyond—benefits trade, and that's to the Company's interest. It was inevitable that independence would come out here. It's just come sooner than Earth was ready to understand. It would have been acknowledged long ago if not for the blindness of ideologies. Brighter days, Mr. Jacoby, are possible. May we live to see them."

It was a lie as sober-faced as he had ever delivered. He leaned back in his chair with nausea urging at him from the effects of jump and from outright terror.

"Mr. Ayres."

He looked back at the doorway. It was Azov. The Union officer walked in, resplendent in black and silver.

"We are monitored," Ayres observed sourly.

"I don't delude myself with your affection, Mr. Ayres. Only with your good sense."

"I'll make your recording."

Azov shook his head. "We go heralded," he said, "but by a different warning. There's no hope that Mazian's ships will all be docked. We brought you along first for the Mazianni; and secondly because in the taking of Pell station it will be useful to have a voice of former authority."

He nodded weary assent. "If it saves lives, sir."

Azov simply stared at him. Frowned, finally. "Take time to recover your equilibrium, sirs. And to contemplate what you might do to benefit Pell."

Ayres looked to Jacoby as Azov left and saw that Jacoby was also capable of anxiety. "Doubts?" he asked Jacoby sourly.

"I have kin on that station," Jacoby said.

# BOOK FOUR

# 1

## i
## Pell 10/10/52; 1100 hrs.

The station was calmer. Queries to Legal Affairs had begun, and that was a good indication that the tension on the station was easing. The input file was full of queries about military actions, threatened lawsuits, indignant protests from merchants on-station who felt damages were due them for the continued curfew on the docks. There were protests from the merchanter ship *Finity's End* regarding a missing youth, the object of much anxiety, in the theory that one of the military crews could have swept him up in impressment. In fact the youth was probably in some station sleepover with a current infatuation from some other ship. Comp was quietly carrying out a card-use search, not an easy matter, for merchanter passes were not in such frequent use as stationer cards.

Damon entertained hopes of finding him safe, refused to take alarm until the records search had come in; he had seen too many of these come across his desk only to discover a young merchanter who had had a falling out with his family or drunk too much to listen to vid. The whole thing was more security's problem at this level, but security had its hands full, its men and women standing guard duty with haggard eyes and short tempers. LA could at least punch comp buttons and take up some of the clerical work. Another killing in Q. It was depressing, and there was absolutely nothing they could do but note the fact. There was a report of a guard under suspension, accused of smuggling a case of Downer wine into Q. Some officer had decided the problem should not wait, when it was likely there was petty smuggling going on everywhere among the merchanters out there. The man was being made an example.

He had three postponed hearings in the afternoon. They were likely to be postponed again, because the council was meeting and the board of justices was involved in that. He decided to agree with the defender to that effect, and put the message through, reserving the afternoon instead for the disposal of more queries that the lower levels of the office could not handle.

And having disposed of that, he swung his chair about and looked back at Josh, who sat dutifully reading a book on the auxiliary unit and trying not to look as bored as he ought to be. "Hey," Damon said. Josh looked at him. "Lunch? We can take a long one and work out at the gym."

"We can go there?"

"It's open."

Josh turned the machine off.

Damon rose, leaving everything on hold, walked over and gathered up his jacket, felt after cards and papers to be absolutely sure. Mazian's troops still stood guard here and there, as unreasonable as they ever had been.

Josh likewise put on a jacket . . . they were about the same size, and it was borrowed. Lending, Josh would accept, if not giving, augmenting his small wardrobe so that he could come and go in the offices without undue attention. Damon held the door button, instructed the office outside to delay calls for two hours.

"Back at one," the secretary acknowledged, and turned to take an incoming call. Damon motioned Josh on through into the outer corridor.

"A half an hour at the gym," Damon said, "then a sandwich at the concourse. I'm hungry."

"Fine," Josh said. He looked nervously about him. Damon looked too, and felt uneasy. The corridors had very little traffic even yet. People were just not trusting of the situation. Some troops stood, distantly visible.

"The troops should all be pulled back," he said to Josh, "by the end of this week. Our own security is taking over entirely in white; green maybe in two days. Have patience. We're working on it."

"They'll still do what they want," Josh said somberly.

"Huh. Did Mallory, after all?"

A shadow came on Josh's face. "I don't know. When I think about it, I still don't know."

"Believe me." They had reached the lift, alone. A

trooper stood at the corner of another corridor, a fact in the tail of the eye, nothing remarkable. He pushed the code for the core. "Had a bit of good news come in this morning. My brother called up, said things are smoothing out down there."

"I'm glad," Josh murmured.

The trooper moved suddenly. Came toward them. Damon looked. Others further down the hall started moving, all of them, at a near run. "Abort that," the first trooper snapped, reaching them. She reached for the panel herself. "We're on a call."

"I can get you a priority," Damon said—to be rid of them. The move indicated trouble; he thought of them shoving stationers around on other levels.

"Do it."

He took his card from his pocket, thrust it into the slot and coded his priority; the lights went red. The rest of the troopers arrived as the car did, and armored shoulders pushed them aside as the troops all crowded in, leaving them there. The car whisked away, nonstop for whatever destination they had coded from inside. There was not a trooper left in the corridor. Damon looked at Josh, whose face was pale and set.

"We take the next car," Damon said with a shrug. He was himself disturbed, and quietly coded in blue nine.

"Elene?" Josh asked.

"Want to get down there," he said. "You come with me. If there's trouble, it's likely to end up on the dockside. I want to get down there."

The car delayed in coming. He waited several moments and finally used his card a second time, a second priority; the lights went red, signifying a car on priority call, then blinked, signifying nothing available. He slammed his fist against the wall, cast a second look at Josh. It was far to walk; easier to wait for a car to free itself . . . quicker in the long run.

He walked over to the nearest com unit, keyed in on priority, while John stood waiting by the lift doors. "Hold the car if it comes," he said to Josh, punched the call in. "Com Central, this is Damon Konstantin on emergency. We're seeing troops pulling out on the run. What's going on?"

There was a long delay. "Mr. Konstantin," a voice came back, "this is a public com unit."

"Not at the moment, central. What's going on?"

"General alert. Emergency posts, please."

"What's going on?"

Com had cut itself off. A measured siren began to sound. Red lights began to pulse in the overheads. People came out of the offices, looked at one another as if hoping it was drill, or mistaken. His own secretary was outside, far down the hall.

"Get back inside," he shouted. "Get those doors shut." People moved backward, retreated into offices. The red light by Josh's shoulder was still blinking, indicating no car available: every car in the system must have jammed up down at the docks.

"Come on," he said to Josh, motioned toward the end of the hall. Josh looked confused and he strode over, caught Josh by the arm. "Come on."

There were others in the hall, farther on. He snapped an order at them, cleared them out, not blaming them . . . there were others besides Konstantins who had loved ones scattered about the station, children in school and nurseries, people in hospital. Some ran ahead of them, refusing orders. A station security agent shouted out another order to halt; ignored, laid a hand on his pistol.

"Let them go," Damon snapped. "Let be."

"Sir." The policeman's face relaxed from a grimace of panic. "Sir, I'm not getting anything over com."

"Keep that gun holstered. You learn those reflexes from the troops? Stand your post. Calm people down. Help them where you can. There's a scramble going on. Could even be drill. Ease up."

"Sir."

They walked on, toward the emergency ramp, in the quiet hall . . . not running; a Konstantin could not run, spread panic. He walked, trying to hold off panic in himself. "No time," Josh said under his breath. "By the time the alert gets here, the ships are on us. If Mazian's been caught at dock. . . ."

"Got militia and two carriers out from station," Damon said, and remembered all at once who Josh was. He caught his breath, gave him a desperate look, met a face as worried as his own. "Come on," he said.

They reached the emergency ramp, heard shouting, loud as they opened the doors. Runners were headed in down it from other levels. "Slow down!" Damon yelled at those who passed him, and they did, several turns, but a few became many, and suddenly there were more coming up, the noise increasing, more running . . . the transport system jammed everywhere and all the levels pouring into the spiral well. "Take it easy," Damon shouted, grabbed shoulders physically and tried to slow it, but the rush accelerated, bodies jamming in, men, women, and children, impossible now even to get out of it. The doors were full of people trying to go down.

"The docks!" he heard shouted. It spread like fire, with the red light of alarm burning in the overhead, the assumption that had been seething in Pell since the troops came—that someday it would come, that the station was under attack, that evacuation was underway. The mass pressed *down,* and there was no stopping it.

## ii

## Norway: 1105

CFX/KNIGHT/189-8989-687/EASYEASYEASY/SCORPION-TWELVE/ZEROZEROZERO/ENDIT.

Signy keyed back acknowledgment and turned to Graff with a wide sweep of her hand. "Hit it!" Graff relayed, and GO sounded throughout the ship. Warnings flared, spreading to dockside. Troops outside finished stripping the umbilicals. "We can't take them," Signy said when Di Janz fretted in com. It sat ill with her to abandon men. "They're all right."

"Umbilicals clear," Graff shouted across, off com. It was a go-when-ready from *Europe,* which had left its troops, already moving out. *Pacific* was moving. *Tibet*'s rider was still heading in behind the wave of the original message, signaling with its presence what *Tibet* had already sent; and what was happening on the fringes of Pell System was as old as the light-bound signal that came reporting it, ships inbound, more than an hour ago. The lights on *Norway*'s main board flicked green, a steady ripple of them, and Signy released clamp and set *Norway* free, with the troops who had made it aboard still hastening for security. *Norway* moved null for a moment under the gentle puffs of directionals and undocking vents, continued the roll of her frame and cut in main thrust with a margin that skimmed *Australia*'s clearance and probably set off alarms all over Pell. They acquired hard G, the inner cylinder under combat synch, rolling to compensate stresses: weight bore down, eased, slammed down again.

They came to heading, with a clutter of merchanters in lower plane; *Europe* and *Pacific* ahead of them, *Australia* breaking clear behind. *Atlantic* would be moving any second; *India*'s Keu was on-station and headed for his ship; *Africa*'s Porey was downworld. *Africa* would move out under its lieutenant's command and rendezvous with Porey shuttling up from Downbelow, running tailguard at best.

The inevitable was on them. That rider was some minutes behind *Tibet*'s message, insurance. Its message was reaching them now; and a chatter of further transmission from *Tibet* itself, and *North Pole*'s voice added itself, along with the alarm of militia ships helplessly in the path of the strike. *Tibet* was engaged, trying to make the incoming fleet dump speed to deal with them. *North Pole* was moving. Merchanter vessels serving as militia were altering course, slow ships, short-haulers, at a standstill compared to the speed of the incoming fleet. They could slow it if they had the nerve. If.

"Rider's turned," scan op said in her ear. She saw it onscreen. The rider had gotten their acknowledgment minutes ago, had put about; that scan image was meeting them now. Longscan comp had put the rest of the arc together and the comp tech had reasoned the rest by human intent . . . the yellow fuzz going off from the red approach line was longscan's new estimate of the ridership's position; the old estimate faded to faint blue, mere warning to watch that line of approach in case. They were headed right down it in outgoing plane, while the incoming rider was obliged to go nadir. And they were all streaming out together, right down the line.

Signy gnawed her lip, cautioned scan and com monitor to keep up with events all around the sphere, fretting that Mazian had hauled them out in one vector only. *Come on,* she thought with the taste of one disaster in her mouth, *no more like Viking. Give us a few options, man.*

CFX / KNIGHT / 189-9090-687 / NINERNINERNINER / SPHINX / TWOTWOTWO TRIPLET / DOUBLET / QUARTET / WISP / ENDIT.

New orders. The late ships were given the other vectors. *Pacific* and *Atlantic* and *Australia* moved onto new courses, slow motion flowering of the pattern to shield the system.

## iii
## Pell: stationmaster's offices

MERCHANTER HAMMER TO ECS IN VICINITY/MAYDAYMAYDAYMAYDAY/UNION CARRIERS MOV-/ING/TWELVE CARRIERS OUR VICINITY/GOING FOR JUMP/MAYDAYMAYDAYMAYDAY. . . .

SWAN'S EYE TO ALL SHIPS/RUNRUNRUNRUN. . . .

ECS TIBET TO ALL SHIPS/RELAY/. . . .

Over an hour old, proliferating through the system in relay through the com of every ship receiving and still going, like an echo in a madhouse. Angelo leaned to the comp console and keyed through to dockside, where the shock of a massive pullout still had crews spilling out on emergency call: military crews had handled it, their own way, undocked without interval. Central was in chaos, with a pending G crisis if the systems could not adjust to the massive kickoff. There were palpable instabilities. Com was jammed. And for nearly two hours the situation on the rim of the solar system had been in progress, while the message flashed its lightbound way toward them.

Troops were left on the dock. Most had been aboard already, barracked onship; some had not made it, and military channels on-station echoed with incomprehensible messages, angry voices. Why they had pulled the troops, why they had delayed to board those they could with attack incoming . . . the implication of that was the liberty of the Fleet to run out on them. Mazian's order. . . .

*Emilio,* he thought distractedly. The schematic of Downbelow on the left wall-screen flickered with a dot that was Porey's shuttle. He could not call; no one could—Mazian's orders . . . com silence. *Hold pattern,* traffic control was broadcasting to merchanters in orbit; it was all they could say. Com queries flowed from merchanters at dock, faster than operators could answer them with pleas for quiet.

Union was bound to have done this. *Anticipated,* Mazian had flashed him, in what direct communication he had gotten. For days the captains had stayed near the ships—troops jammed aboard in discomfort—not in courtesy to station; not in response to their requests to have the troops out of the halls.

Prepared for pullout. Despite all promises, prepared for pullout.

He reached for the com button, to call Alicia, who might be following this on her screens. . . .

"Sir." His secretary Mills came on com. "Security requests you come to com central. There's a situation down in green."

"What situation?"

"Crowds, sir."

He thrust himself from his desk, grabbed his coat.

"Sir—"

He turned. His office door opened unasked, Mills there protesting the intrusion of Jon Lukas and a companion. "Sir," Mills said. "I'm sorry. Mr. Lukas insisted . . . I told him. . . ."

Angelo frowned, vexed at the intrusion and at once hoping for assistance. Jon was able, if self-interested. "I need some help," he said, and his eyes flicked in alarm at the small movement of the other's man hand to his coat, the sudden flash of steel. Mills failed to see it . . . Angelo cried aloud as the man slashed Mills, scrambled back as the man flung himself at him. Hale: he recognized the face suddenly.

Mills shrieked, bleeding, sinking against the open doorway; there were screams from the outer office; the blow struck, a numbing shock. Angelo reached for the driving hand and met the weapon protruding from his chest, stared disbelievingly at Jon . . . at hate. There were others in the doorway.

Shock welled up in him, with the blood.

## iv
## Q

*"Vassily,"* the voice said over com. "Vassily, do you hear me?"

Kressich, at his desk, sat paralyzed. It was Coledy, of those who sat about him, hunched and waiting, who reached past him and punched the respond button. "I hear," Kressich said past the knot in his throat. He looked at Coledy. In his ears was the buzz of voices out on the docks, people already frightened, already threatening riot.

"Keep him safe," Coledy said to James, who was over the five others who waited outside. "Keep him very safe."

And Coledy went. They had waited, had hovered about com, one of them always near it, gathered here in the confusion. It was on them now. After a moment there was a rise in the noise of the mob outside, a dull, bestial sound which shook the walls.

Kressich bowed his face into his hands, stayed so for a long time, not wishing to know.

"The doors," he heard finally, a shout from outside. "The doors are open!"

## v

## Green nine

They ran, stumbling and breathless, jostling others in the corridor, a sea of panicked people, red-dyed in alarm lights. A siren still went; there was a queasiness of G as station systems struggled to keep themselves stable. "It's the docks," Damon breathed, his vision blurring. A runner hit him and he fended the body off, pushed his way, with Josh in his wake, where the ramp opened onto nine. "Mazian's peeled off." It was all that made sense.

Shrieks broke out and there was a massive backflow in the crowd that brought all the press to a stop. Of a sudden traffic began to go the other way, people retreating from something. There were frantic screams, bodies jammed against them.

*"Damon!"* Josh yelled from behind him. It was no good. They were pushed back, all of them, against the crush of bodies behind. Shots streaked overhead, and the whole jammed mass quivered and rang with screams. Damon got his arms in front of him for leverage, to keep from being suffocated . . . ribs were compressed.

Then the rear of the press turned, running in panic down some route of escape; and the crush became a battering flood. He tried to stand in it, having his own direction. A hand caught his arm, and Josh caught up with him, staggered as the mob shoved and stampeded and they tried to fight the current.

More shots. A man went down; more than one—hit. The fire was going into the crowd.

"Stop shooting!" Damon shouted, still with a wall of people in front of him, a wall diminishing as if a scythe were hitting it. "Cease fire!"

Someone grabbed him from the back, pulled him as fire came through. He got the edge of one and jerked in pain, scrambling for balance in the rout, running now—it was Josh with him, pulling him along in their retreat. A man's back exploded an arm's length ahead of them, and the man fell under the others.

"This way!" Josh yelled, jerked him left, down a side corridor where part of the rout was going. He went, that direction as good as the other . . . saw a way to double back through, redoubled his effort, to get to the docks, running through the maze of secondary corridors back again to nine.

They made it as far as three intersections, frantic people scattering everywhere, at every intersection of the corridors, staggering in the flux of G. And then screams broke out in the halls ahead.

"Look out!" Josh yelled, catching at him. He gasped air and turned, ran where the curving inner hall rose up and up into what was going to turn into a blank wall, the sector division.

Not blank. There was a way. Josh yelled and tried to drag him back when he saw the cul de sac; "Come *on,*" he snapped and caught Josh's sleeve, kept running as the wall came down off the horizon at them, became level, a blank wall with a painted mural, and at the right, the heavy door of a Downer hatchway.

He leaned up against the wall, fumbled his card out, jammed it in the slot. The hatch opened with a gust of tainted air, and he dragged Josh into it, into virtual dark, numbing cold.

The door sealed. Air exchange started and Josh looked about in panic; Damon reached for the masks in the recess, thrust one at Josh, got one over his own face and sucked a restricted breath, trembling so that he could hardly get the band adjusted.

"Where are we going?" Josh asked, voice changed by the mask. "Now what?"

There was a lamp in the recess. He took it, thumbed the

light on. He reached for the inner-door switch, opened it, a sound that echoed up and up. A slant of the beam picked out catwalks. They were on a grid, and a ladder went down farther still, into a round tube. G diminished, dizzyingly. He caught at the rail.

Elene . . . Elene would be in the worst of it; she would go to cover, get those office doors locked—had to. He was not able to get through out there; had to get to help, reach a point where he could get security forces moving in a front that could stop it. Up. Get up to the high levels; that was white sector on the other side of that partition. He tried to find an access to it, but the beam showed no way. There was no direct connection, section to section, except the docks, except on number one level. he remembered that—complicated lock systems . . . Downers knew where—he did not. Get to central, he thought; get to an upper hall and get to com. Everything was amiss, G out of balance—the Fleet had gone; maybe merchanters too, throwing them out of stability, and central was not correcting it. Something was massively *wrong* up there.

He turned, staggered as G surged sickeningly, grabbed an upslanted rail, and started climbing.

Josh followed.

## vi
## Green dock

There was no response from central; the handcom kept giving back the STANDBY, interspersed with static. Elene thumbed it off and cast a frantic look back at the lines of troops that held green nine entry. "Runner," she called. A youth came up to her on the double. They were reduced to this, with com blacked out. "Get to all the ships round the rim, one to the next as far as you can run, and tell them to pass the word on their own com if they can. *Hold where you are,* tell them. Tell them . . . you know what to say. Tell them there's trouble out there and they'll run headon into it if they bolt. Go!"

Scan might be out. She had reckoned the blackout the Fleet's doing; but *India* and *Africa* had gone, leaving troops to hold the dock, troops they had no room to take; and the signal was still being interrupted. No knowing what information the merchanters were getting, or what messages the troops might have gotten over their own com. No knowing who was in charge of the deserted troops, whether some high officer or some desperate and confused noncom. There was a wall of them at the niner entries of blue and green docks—a wall of troops facing up the curving horizons sealing off those same docks from either side, rifles braced and ready, the sealing of their square. She feared them no less than the enemy incoming. They had fired, turned one mob, *killed* people; there were still sporadic shots. She had twelve staff members and six of them were missing . . . cut off by the com blackout. The others were directing dock crew efforts to check the dumped umbilicals against a fatal seal breach; the whole section should be under precautionary seal—if her people up in blue control could get it straightened out: they had dead switches, the whole system jammed by an override. G flux still hit them at intervals; fluid mass in the tanks had to be shunted as fast as the lines could jet it their way, everything in tanks anywhere, to compensate; station had attitude controls; they might be using them. It was terrifying in a huge space like the docks, the up and down of weight, unsettling premonition that at any moment they might get a flux of more than a kilo or two.

"Ms. Quen!"

She turned. The runner had not gotten through: some ass in the line of troops must have turned him back. She started toward him in haste, toward the line that suddenly, inexplicably, was wavering, facing about toward *them,* rifles leveled.

A shout roared out at her back. She looked, to the upcurving horizon, saw an indistinct wavefront of runners coming down that apparent wall toward them, beyond the curtaining section arch. *Riot.*

"The *seal!*" she shouted into the useless handcom, dead as it had been. The troops were moving; she was between them and targets. She ran for the far side, the tangle of gantries, heart pounding, looked back again as the line of troops advanced, narrowing their perimeter, passing her by, some of them taking positions in the cover of the gantries. She thumbed the handcom and desperately tried her office: "Shut it *down!*"—but the mob was past blue control, might be *in* it. The noise of the mob swelled, a tide pouring toward them while others were still coming down off the horizon, an endless mass. She realized suddenly the aspect of the distant faces, behavior not panic, but hate; and weapons—pipes, clubs—

The troops fired. There were screams as the first rank went down. She stood paralyzed, not twenty meters from the troops' rear, seeing more and more of the mob pouring toward them over their own dead.

*Q*. Q was loose. They came waving weapons and shrieking, a sound which grew from distant roar to deafening, with no end to their numbers.

She turned, ran, staggering in the flux, in the wake of her own fleeing dock crews, of scattered Downers who saw man-trouble and sought shelter.

The noise grew behind her.

She doubled her pace, a hand to her belly, trying to cushion the shock in her stride. There were screams behind her, almost drowned in the roar. They would overrun these troops too, gain the rifles . . . coming on by the sheer weight of numbers. She looked back . . . saw green nine vomiting forth scattered runners, getting past the troops. Panic showed in their faces. She gasped for air and kept going, despite the dull ache in her pelvic arch, dog-trotting when she must, reeling in the G surges. Runners began to pass her, a scattered few at first, then others, a buffeting flood as she passed white section arch; and on the horizon ahead a tide breaking crossways from niner entries, thousands upon thousands up the sweep of the horizon, running for the merchanter ships at dock, screaming that merged with the cries behind, men and women screaming and pushing each other.

Men passed her in greater and greater numbers . . . bloody, reeking, waving weapons, shrieking. A shock hit her back, threw her to a knee and the man kept running. Another hit her . . . stumbled, kept going. She staggered up, arm numb, tried for the gantries, the shelter of supports and lines . . . shots burst out ahead of her from a ship's access.

"Quen!" someone yelled. She could not tell the source, looked about, tried to fight the human tide, and stumbled in the press.

"Quen!" She looked about; a hand caught her arm and pulled her, and a gun fired past her head. Two others grabbed her, hauled her through the press . . . a blow grazed her head and she staggered, flung her weight then with the men who were trying to pull her through, amid the web of lines and gantries. There were screams and shots; others reached out to seize them and she tensed to fight, thinking them the mob, but a wall of bodies absorbed her and the men with her, merchanter types. "Fall back," someone was yelling. "Fall back. They're through!" They were headed up a ramp, to an open hatchway, a cold ribbed tube, glowing yellow white, a ship's access.

"I'm not boarding!" she cried in protest, but she had no wind left to protest anything, and there was nowhere but the mobs. They dragged her up the tube and those who had held the entry came crowding after as they hit the lock, hurtling in. They jammed up in a crushing press as the last desperate runners surged in. The door hissed and clanged shut, and she flinched . . . by some miracle the door had taken no limbs.

The inner hatch spilled them into a lift corridor. A pair of big men pushed the others through and steadied her on her feet while a voice thundered orders over com. Her belly hurt; her thighs ached; she sank against the wall and rested there until one of them touched her shoulder, a huge man, gentle-handed.

"All right," she said. "I'm all right."

It was easing, the strain of the run . . . she pushed her hair back, looked at the men, these two who had been out there with her, heaved through the crowd, shoving rioters out of the way; knew them, and the patch they wore, black, without device: *Finity's End*. The ship that had lost a son on the station; the men she had dealt with that morning. Going for their ship, perhaps . . . and they had gone aside after one of their own, to pull a Quen out of that mob. "Thank you," she breathed. "The captain—please, I've got to talk to him . . . fast."

No objections. The big man . . . Tom—she recalled the name—got his arm about her, helped her walk. His cousin opened the lift door and hit the button inside. They walked out again into a fair-sided center, crowded at the moment by the lack of rotation. Main room and bridge were downmost, bridge forward, and the two brought her that way . . . better now, much better. She walked on her own, into the bridge, amid the rows of equipment and the gathered crew. Neihart. Neihart was the ship's family;

Viking-based. The seniors were on the bridge; some of the younger crew . . . children would be snugged away topside, out of this. She recognized Wes Neihart, captain of the family, seamed and silver-haired, sad of face.

"Quen," he said.

"Sir." She met the offered hand, declined the seat they offered, leaned against the back of it to face him. "Q's loose; com's out. Please . . . contact the other ships . . . pass word . . . don't know what's wrong in central, but Pell's in dire trouble."

"We're not taking on passengers," Neihart said. "We've seen the result of that. So have you. Don't ask it."

"Listen to me. Union's out there. We're a shell . . . around this station. Got to stay put. Will you give me com?"

She spoke for Pell, had done so, to this captain, to all the others; but this was his deck, not Pell, and she was a beggar without a ship.

"Dockmaster's privilege," he allowed suddenly, swept a hand toward the boards. "Com's yours."

She nodded gratitude, let them show her to the nearest board, sank into the cushion with a cramp in her lower belly—she put her hand there—*not the baby,* she prayed. She had a numbness in that arm, her back, where she had been hit. Instruments blurred as she reached for the ear-piece, and she blinked the board into focus, trying to focus her mind as well as her vision. She punched in the ship-to-ship. "All ships, record and relay: this is Pell dock control, Pell liaison Elene Quen aboard Neihart's *Finity's End,* white dock. Request that all docked merchanter seal locks and do not, repeat, negative, admit any stationers to your ships. Pell is not evacuating. Get this much on out-side broadcast if you can make it heard on loudspeakers; station com is blacked out. Those ships in dock, if you can safely release dock from inside shutdown, do so; but do not undock. Those ships in pattern, hold your pattern; do not leave pattern. Station will compensate and regain sta-bility. Repeat, Pell is not being evacuated. A military action is in progress in the system. Nothing will be served by evacuating the station. Please play the following sec-tion for outside broadcast where possible: Attention. By dockmaster's authority, all station law enforcers are re-quested to do their utmost to establish order in whatever areas they are. Do not attempt to go to central. Stay where you are. Citizens of Pell: you are in serious danger from riot. Establish barricades at all niner entries and all section lines and prepare to defend them to prevent the movement of destructive mobs. Quarantine has been breached. If you scatter in panic you will contribute to riot and endanger your own lives. Defend the barricades. You will be able to hold the station area by area. Station com is blacked out due to military intervention, and the G flux is due to unauthorized undock of military ships. Stability will be restored as quickly as possible. To any refugee out of quarantine: I appeal to you to contribute your efforts to the establishment of defense lines and barricades along with Pell citizens. Station will negotiate with you regarding your situation; your cooperation in this crisis will make a profound impression on Pell's gratitude, and you may be assured of favorable consideration as this situation is stabilized. Please remain where you are, defend your areas, and remember that this station supports your lives too. All merchanters: please cooperate with me in this emergency. If you have information, pass it to me on *Finity's End.* This ship will serve as dock headquarters during the emergency. Please play ship to ship and broadcast appropriate sections over exterior systems. I am standing by for your contact."

Messages flashed back, frantic queries after more information, harsh demands, threats of bolting dock at once. All about her the folk of *Finity's End* were making their own preparations for flight.

At any moment, she hoped, at any moment com might clear, station central might come through bright and sane, bringing contact with command—with Damon, who might be in central and might not. Not, she hoped, in those corridors with Q run amok. Mainday noon—the worst of all times—with most of Pell out away from jobs and shops, in the corridors. . . .

Blue dock was his emergency assignment. He might have tried to come there; would have tried. She knew him. Tears blurred her eyes. She clenched her fist on the arm of the chair, tried to think away the diminishing ache in her belly.

"White section seal just activated." Word came to them from *Sita,* which had a vantage. Other ships echoed reports of other seals in function; Pell had segmented itself in defense, the first sign that it had defensive reactions left in it.

"Scan's got something," came panicked word from a crew member behind her. "Could be a merchanter out of pattern. Can't tell."

She wiped her face and tried to concentrate on all the threads in her hands. "Just stay put," she said. "If we breach those umbilicals we've got dead in the thousands out there. Do manual seal. Don't break, don't break those connections."

"Takes time," someone said. "We may not have it."

"So start doing it," she wished them.

## vii

## Pell: sector blue one: command central

The red lights which had flared across the boards had diminished in number. Jon Lukas paced from one to the other post and watched techs' hands, watching scan, watching the activity everywhere they still had monitor. Hale stood guard beyond the windows, in central com, with Daniels; Clay was here, at one side of the room, Lee Quale on the other, and others of Lukas Company security, none of the station's own. The techs and directors questioned nothing, working feverishly at the emergencies which occupied them.

There was fear in the room, more than fear of the attack outside. The presence of guns, the lasting blackout . . . they knew, Jon reckoned, they well knew that something was amiss in Angelo Konstantin's silence, in the failure of any of the Konstantins or their lieutenants to reach this place.

A tech handed him a message and fled back to his seat without meeting his eyes. It was a repeated query from Downbelow main base. That was a problem they could defer. For now they held central, and the offices, and he did not intend to answer the query. Let Emilio figure it a military order which silenced station central.

On the screens the scan showed ominous lack of activity. They were sitting out there. Waiting. He paced the circuit of the room again, looked up abruptly as the door opened. Every tech in the room froze, duties forgotten, hands in mid-motion at the sight of the group which appeared there, civilian, with rifles leveled, with others at their backs.

Jessad, two of Hale's men, and a bloodied security agent, one of their own.

"Area's secure," Jessad reported.

"Sir." A director rose from his post. "Councillor Lukas—what's happening?"

"Set that man down," Jessad snapped, and the director gripped the back of his chair and cast Jon a look of diminishing hope.

"Angelo Konstantin is *dead,*" Jon said, scanning all the frightened faces. "Killed in the rioting, with all his staff. Assassins hit the offices. Get to your work. We're not clear of this yet."

Faces turned, backs turned, techs trying to make themselves invisible by their efficiency. No one spoke. He was heartened by this obedience. He paced the room another circuit, stopped in the middle of it.

"Keep working and listen to me," he said in a loud voice. "Lukas Company personnel are holding this sector secure. Elsewhere we have the kind of situation you see on the screens. We're going to restore com, for announcement from this center only, and only announcements I clear. There is no authority on this station at the moment but Lukas Company, and to save this station from damage I will shoot those I have to. I have men under my command who will do that without hesitation. Is that clear?"

There were no comments, not so much as the turning of a head. It was perhaps something with which they were in temporary agreement, with Pell's systems in precarious balance and Q rioting on the docks.

He drew a calmer breath and looked at Jessad, who nodded a reassuring satisfaction.

## viii

The webbery of ladders stretched before and behind, a maze of tubes across the overhead, and it was bitterly cold. Damon shone the beam one way and the other, reached for a railing, sank down on the gridwork as Josh sank down by him, the breather-sounds loud, strained. His head pounded. Not enough air, not fast enough for exertion; and the maze they were in . . . branched. There was logic to it: the angles were precise; it was a matter of counting. He tried to keep track.

"Are we lost?" Josh asked between gasps.

He shook his head, angled the beam up, the way they should go. Mad to have tried this, but they were alive, in one piece. "Next level," he said, "ought to be two. I figure . . . we go out . . . take a look, how things are out there . . ."

Josh nodded. G flux had stopped. They still heard noise, unsure in this maze where it came from. Distant shouts. Once a booming shock he thought might be the great seals. It seemed better; he hoped . . . moved, with a clattering ringing of the metal, reached for the rail again and started to climb, the last climb. He was overwhelmingly anxious, for Elene, for everything he had cut himself off from in coming this way . . . No matter the hazard, he had to get out.

There was a static sputter. It boomed through the tunnels and echoed.

"Com," he said. It was coming back together, all of it.

"This is a general announcement. We are approaching G stabilization. We ask that all citizens keep to their present areas and do not attempt to cross section lines. There is still no word from the Fleet, and none is expected yet. Scan remains clear. We do not anticipate military action in the vicinity of this station . . . It is with extreme sorrow that we report the death of Angelo Konstantin at the hand of rioters and the disappearance in violence of other members of the family. If any have reached safety, please contact station central as soon as possible, any Konstantin relative, or any knowing their whereabouts, please contact station central immediately. Councillor Jon Lukas remains acting stationmaster in this crisis. Please give full cooperation to Lukas Company personnel who are fulfilling security duties in this emergency."

Damon sank down on the steps. A cold deeper than the chill of the metal settled into him. He could not breathe. He became aware that he was crying, tears blurring the light and choking his breath.

". . . announcement," the com began to repeat. "We are approaching G stabilization. We ask that all citizens. . . ."

A hand settled on his shoulder, pulled him about. "Damon?" Josh said through the noise.

He was numb. Nothing made sense. "Dead," he said, and shuddered. "O God—"

Josh stared at him, took the lamp from his hand. Damon thrust himself for his feet, for the last climb, for the access he knew was up there.

Josh pulled him hard, turned him around against the solid wall. "Don't go," Josh pleaded with him. "Damon, don't go out there now."

Josh's paranoid nightmares. It was that look on his face. Damon leaned there, his mind going in all directions, and no clear direction. *Elene.* "My father . . . my mother . . . that's blue one. Our guards were in blue one. Our own guards."

Josh said nothing.

He tried to think. It kept coming up wrong. Troops had moved; the Fleet had pulled out. Murders instant . . . in Pell's heaviest security . . .

He turned the other way, the way they had just come, his hands shaking so he could hardly grip the railing. Josh shone the light for him, caught his elbow to stop him. He turned on the steps, looked up into Josh's masked, light-distorted face.

"Where?" Josh asked.

"I don't know who's in control up there. They *say* it's my uncle. I don't know." He reached for the lamp, to take it. Josh surrendered it reluctantly and he turned, started down the ladders as quickly as he could slide down the steps, Josh following desperately after.

Get down again. Down was easy. He hurried at the limit of breath and balance, until he was dizzy and the lamp's beam swung madly about the framework and the tunnels. He slipped, recovered, kept descending.

"Damon," Josh protested.

He had no breath for arguing. He kept going until his sight was fading from want of air, sank down on the steps trying to pull air enough through the breather to keep from fainting. He felt Josh leaning by him, heard him panting, no better off. "Docks," Damon said. "Get down there . . . get to ships. Elene would go there."

"Can't get through."

He looked at Josh, realized he was dragging another life into this. He had no choices either. He got up, started down again, felt the vibrations of Josh's steps still behind him.

The ships would be sealed. Elene would be there or locked in the offices. Or dead. If the troops had hit him . . . if for some mad reason . . . the station was being disabled in advance of a Union takeover . . .

But Jon Lukas was supposed to be up there in central.

Had some action failed? Had Jon somehow prevented them from hitting central itself?

He lost count of the stops for breath, of the levels they passed. *Down.* He hit bottom finally, a gridwork suddenly wider, did not realize what it was until he searched with the light and stopped finding downward ladders. He walked along the grid, saw the faint glimmer of a blue light, that over an access door. He reached it, pushed the switch; the door slid back with a hiss and Josh followed him into the lock's brighter light. The door closed and air exchange started. He tugged down the mask and got a full breath of air, chill and only slightly tainted. His head was pounding. He focused hazily on Josh's sweating face, marked with the mask, distraught. "Stay here," he said in pity. "Stay here. If I get this cleared up, I'll come back; if I don't—decide for yourself what to do."

Josh leaned there, eyes glazed.

Damon turned his attention to the door, got his breathing back to normal, rubbed his eyes to clear them, finally pushed the button and put the door in function. Light blinded him; there was shouting out there, screaming, the smell of smoke. *Life-support,* he thought with a chill . . . it opened on one of the minor halls, and he headed out, started running, heard running footfalls behind him and looked back.

"Get back," he wished Josh, "get back in there."

He had no time to argue with him. He ran, down the hall . . . had to be in green sector; it had to be nine in this direction . . . all the signs were gone. He saw riot ahead of him, people running scattered through the halls; and some had lengths of pipe and there was a body in the hall . . . he dodged it and kept going. The rioters he saw did not look like Pell . . . unshaven, unkempt . . . he knew suddenly *what* they were, and flung everything into his running, pelted down the hall and up a turn, headed as close to the docks as he could get without going into the main corridor. He had to break into it finally, dodged a runner among other runners. There were more bodies on the floor, and looters ran rampant. He shouldered past men who clutched pipes and knives and, some of them, guns . . .

The entry to the dock was closed, sealed. He saw that, staggered aside as a looter came swinging a pipe at him, for no reason more than that he was in the way.

The attacker kept going, a half-circle that pulled him about and ended against the wall, with Josh, who slammed his head into the wall and came up with the pipe in his hand.

Damon whirled and ran, for the sealed doors . . . reached for his pocket, for the card, to override the lock.

*"Konstantin!"* someone shouted behind him.

He turned, stared at a man, at a gun leveled at him. A length of pipe hurtled out of nowhere and hit the man, and looters scrabbled for the gun, a surging mob. In panic he whirled, thrust the card for the slot; the door whipped back, with the vast dockside beyond, and other looters. He ran, sucking in the cold air, down the dock toward white sector, where he saw other great seals in place, the dock seals, two levels tall and airtight. He stumbled from exhaustion and caught himself, pelted up the curve toward them, hearing someone close behind him and hoping it was Josh. The stitch that had started in his side unnoticed grew to a lancing pain . . . Past looted shops with dark, open doors, he reached the wall beside the huge seals, fetched up against the closed door of the small personnel lock, thrust his card into the slot.

It was dead. No response. He pushed it harder, thinking it might have failed contact, inserted it a second time. It was cut off. It should at least have lighted the buttons, given him a chance to put through a priority code, or flashed the hazard signal.

"Damon!" Josh reached the door beside him, caught at his shoulder, pulled him around. There were people moving behind them, thirty, half a hundred, from all across the docks . . . from green nine, in greater and greater number.

"They know you got a door open," Josh said. "They know you've got that kind of access."

He stared at them. Snatched his card from the slot. Useless, blanked; control had blanked his card.

*"Damon."*

He grabbed at Josh and ran, and the crowd started forward with a howl. He raced for the open doors, for the shops . . . into the dark doorway of the nearest. He whirled inside, pushed the button to seal the door. That at least worked.

The first of the mob hit the door, hammered at it. Panicked faces pressed close to the plastic, lengths of pipe hammered at it, scarring it: it was a security seal, like all the dock-front stores . . . pressure-tight, windowless, but for that double-thick circle.

"It's going to hold," Josh said.

"I don't think," he said, "that we can get out again. I don't think we can get out of here until they come to get us."

Josh looked at him across the space of the window, from the other side of the door, pale in the light that came through it.

"They blanked my card," Damon said. "It stopped working. Whoever's in station central just cut off my card use." He looked toward the plastic, on which the gouges were deepening. "I think we just trapped ourselves."

The hammering continued. Madness raged outside, not assassins, not any sane impulse toward hostage-taking, only desperate people with a focus for their desperation. Q residents with a pair of stationers within reach. The scars deepened on the plastic, almost obscuring the faces and hands and weapons. It was remotely possible they could get through it.

And if that happened there was no need of assassins.

# 2

## i

## Norway: 1300 hrs.

It was a waiting game now, probe and vanish. Ghosts. But solid enough out there, somewhere beyond system limits. *Tibet* and *North Pole* had lost contact with the incoming enemy; Union had about-faced, at the cost of one of

*Tibet*'s riders . . . at the cost of one of Union's. But it was far from over. The com flow kept up, calm and quiet out of both carriers. Signy gnawed her lip and stared at the screens before her, while Graff tended op. *Norway* held position along with the rest of the Fleet—having dumped speed, drifted, still not too remote from the mass of Pell IV and III and the star itself. Dead-stopped. They had refused to be drawn out. Had now to use mass to shelter them from an arrival close at hand. It was not likely that Union would be reckless enough to use jump for entry—not their style—but they took the precaution . . . sitting targets as they were. Wait long enough and even conservative Union commanders could circle their scan range to find new lines of attack, having probed things; wolves round the firelight, and themselves trying to sit within it, visible and dead still and vulnerable. Union had *room* out there, could get a good run started, too fast for them to handle.

And for some time there had been bad news coming out of Pell, silence broken, rumblings of serious disorder.

From Mazian . . . persistent silence, and one of them dared breach it with a communication to question. *Come on,* she wished Mazian, *turn some of us loose to hunt.* The riders hung off from *Norway* in widest deployment, like those of the other ships, twenty-seven riderships, seven carriers; and thirty-two militia ships trying to fill up their pattern—indistinguishable on longscan, some of them, from riderships; two of them from carriers. As long as the Fleet sat still, not betraying themselves by tight moves and speed, whoever looked at scan had to wonder if some of those slow, steady ships might not be warships disguising their moves. *Tibet*'s rider had gotten back to mother; and *Tibet* and *North Pole* had seven riders and eleven militia in their area, short-haulers incapable of running, turned brave by necessity: they could not get out of the way . . . so they made part of the screen. As if they could depend on attack coming from that direction. Union had felt at them. Pricked at the organism and vanished out of range. It was probably Azov out there. One of Union's oldest; one of the best. Feathertouch and feint. He had sucked in more than one commander too good to die that way.

Nerves crawled. The techs on the bridge looked at her

from time to time. Silence existed inside as well as among the ships, contagious unease.

A comtech turned at his station, looked at her. "Pell situation worsening," he said off com. There was a murmur from other stations.

"Minds on your business," she snapped, on general address. "It's likely to come from any side of us. Forget Pell or we get it in our faces, hear me? I'll vent the crewman who woolgathers."

And to Graff: "Ready status."

The blue light went on in the overhead. That would wake them up. A light flashed on her board, indicating the armscomp board lit, the armscomper and his aides fully prepared.

She reached to the comp board, punched a code for a recorded instruction. *Norway*'s sighting eye began to rove toward the reference star in question, to perform identifications and to lock in. In case. In case there was something going on unaccounted for in their plans, and Mazian, likewise receiving that Pell chatter, was thinking of running: their direct beam pickup was trained on *Europe,* and *Europe* still had nothing to say. Mazian was thinking; or had made up his mind, and trusted his captains to take precautions. She tapped a signal to the jump tech's board, as he had already to have noted the other move. The board went live, a stepped up power flow to the generation vane monitors, that gave them options other than realspace. If the Fleet broke from Pell, chances were they would not all arrive where they were instructed, at the nearest null point. That there would never again be a Fleet, nothing between Union and Sol.

The com flow from Pell became grim indeed.

## ii
## Downer access

Men-with-guns. Keen ears could still pick up the shouts outside, the terrible fighting. Satin shivered at a crash against the wall, trembled, finding no reason for this thing that happened . . . but that Lukases had done this; and Lukases gave orders, in power in the Upabove. Bluetooth hugged her, whispered to her, urged her, and she came, as silently as the others. The whispers of bare hisa feet passed above them, below. They moved in dark, a steady flow. They dared no lights, which might guide men to find them.

Some were ahead of them, some behind. Old One himself led, the strange hisa, who had come down from the high places, and commanded them without telling them why. Some had lingered, fearing the strange ones; but there were guns behind, and mad humans, and they would come in haste very soon.

A human voice rang out far below in the tunnels, echoing up. Bluetooth hissed and pushed, moved faster in his climbing, and Satin scampered along with all her might, heated by this exertion, her fur damp and her hands sliding on the rails where others had grasped them.

"Hurry," a hisa voice whispered at once of the levels, high, high in the Upabove's dark places, and hands urged them up still another climb, where a dim light shone, making a silhouette of a hisa who waited there. A lock. Satin tugged her mask into place and scrambled up to the doors, caught Bluetooth's hand, for fear of losing him where Old One should lead.

The lock received them. They jammed in with others, and the inner seal gave way on a mass of brown hisa bodies, hands which reached and drew them out in haste, other hisa, who stood facing outward, shielding them from what lay beyond.

They had weapons, lengths of pipe, like the men carried. Satin was stunned, felt backward after Bluetooth, to be sure of his presence in this milling angry throng, in the white lights of humans. There were only hisa in this hall. They filled the corridor as far as the closed doors at the end. Blood smeared one of the walls, a scent which did not reach them through the masks. Satin rolled a distraught glance in the direction the press was sweeping them, felt a soft hand which was not Bluetooth's close upon her arm and lead her. They passed a door into a human place, vast and dim, and the door closed, bringing quiet.

"Hush," their guides said. She looked about in panic to see if Bluetooth was still with her and he reached out to her, caught her hand. They walked nervously in the company of their elder guides, through this spacious manplace, oh, so carefully, for fear, and for respect to the weapons and the anger outside. Others, Old Ones, rose from the shadows and met them. "Storyteller," an Old One addressed her, touching her in welcome. Arms embraced her; others came from beyond a bright, bright doorway and embraced her and Bluetooth, and she was dazed by the honor they gave. "Come," they said, leading her, and they came into that bright place, a room without limits, with a white bed, a sleeping human, and a very old hisa who crouched by it. Dark and stars were all about, walls which were and were not, and of a sudden, great Sun peering into the room, upon them and on the Dreamer.

"Ah," Satin breathed, dismayed, but the old hisa rose up and held out hands in welcome. "The Storyteller," Old One was saying, and the oldest of all left the Dreamer a moment to embrace her. "Good, good," the Oldest said tenderly.

"Lily," the Dreamer said, and the Oldest turned, knelt by the bed to tend her, stroked her grayed head. Marvelous eyes turned on them, alive in a face white and still, her body shrouded in white, everything white, but the hisa named Lily and the blackness which expanded all about them, dusted with stars. Sun had vanished. There was only themselves.

"Lily," the Dreamer said again, "who are they?"

At *her* the Dreamer looked, at her, and Lily beckoned. Satin knelt down, and Bluetooth beside her, gazed with reverence into the warmth of the Dreamer's eyes, the Dreamer of the Upabove, the mate of great Sun, who danced upon her walls. "Love you," Satin whispered. "Love you, Sun-she friend."

"Love you," the Dreamer whispered in her turn. "How is it outside? Is there danger?"

"We make safe," Old One said firmly. "All, all the hisa make safe this place. Men-with-guns stay away."

"They're dead." The wonderful eyes filmed with tears, and sought toward Lily. "Jon's doing. Angelo—Damon—Emilio, maybe—but not me, not yet. Lily, don't leave me."

Lily so, so carefully put her arm about the Dreamer, laid her graying cheek against the Dreamer's graying hair. "No," Lily said. "Love you, no time leave, no, no, no. Dream they leave, men-with-guns. Downers all stand you place. Dream to great Sun. We you hands and feet, we many, we strong, we quick."

The walls had changed. They looked now upon violence, upon men fighting men, and all of them shrank closer together in dread. It passed, and only the Dreamer remained tranquil.

"Lily. The Upabove is in danger of dying. It will need the hisa, when the fighting is done, need you, you understand? Be strong. Hold this place. Stay with me."

"We fight, fight mans come here."

"*Live.* They daren't kill you, you understand. Men need the hisa. They don't won't come in here." The bright eyes grew dark with passion and gentle again. Sun was back, his awesome face filling all the wall, silencing angers. He reflected in the Dreamer's eyes, touched the whiteness with his color.

"Ah," Satin breathed, and swayed from side to side. Others did, one with her, making a soft moan of awe.

"She is Satin," Old One said to the Dreamer. "Bluetooth her friend. Friend of Bennett-man, see he die."

"From Downbelow," the Dreamer said. "Emilio sent you to the Upabove."

"Konstantin-man you friend? Love he, all, all Downers. Bennett-man he friend."

"Yes. He was."

"She say," Old One said, and in the language of hisa . . . "Storyteller, Sky-sees-her, make the story for the Dreamer, make bright her eyes and warm her dreams; sing it into the Dream."

Heat rose to her face and her throat grew taut for fear, for a great one she was not, only a maker of little songs, and to tell a tale in human words . . . in the presence of the Dreamer, and of great Sun, with all the stars about, to become part of the Dream. . . .

"Do it," Bluetooth urged her. His faith warmed her heart.

"I Sky-see-she," she began, "come from Downbelow, tell you Bennett-man, tell you Konstantin, sing you hisa things. Dream hisa things, Sun-she-friend, like Bennett make dream. Make he live, make he walk with hisa, ah! Love you, love he. Sun smile look at he. Long, long time we dream hisa dreams. Bennett make we see human dream, show we true things, tell we Sun he hold all

Upabove, hold all Downbelow in he arms, and Upabove she make wide she arms to Sun, tell we ships come and go, big, *big,* come and go, bring mans from the faraway dark. Make wide we eyes, make wide we dream, make we dream same as humans, Sun-she-friend. This thing Bennett give we; and he give he life. He tell we good things in Upabove, make warm we eyes with want for these good things. We come. We see. So wide, so big dark, we see Sun smile in the dark, make the dream for Downbelow, the blue sky. Bennett make we see, make we come, make we new dreams.

"Ah! I Satin, I tell you time humans come. Before humans, no time, only dream. We wait and not know we wait. We see humans and we come to Upabove. Ah! time Bennett come cold time, and old river she quiet. . . ."

The dark, lovely eyes were set upon her, interested, intent upon her words as if she had skill like the old singers. She wove the truth as best she could, making this true, and not the terrible things which were happening elsewhere, making it truer and truer, that the Dreamer might make it truth, that in the turning cycles, this truth might come round again as the flowers did, and the rains and all lasting things.

## iii
## Station central

The boards had stabilized. Station central had adjusted to panic as a perpetual condition, apparent in the fevered attention to details, the refusal of techs to acknowledge the increasing coming and going of armed men in the command center.

Jon patrolled the aisles, scowling, disapproving of any move beyond necessity. "Another call from the merchanter *Finity's End,*" a tech told him. "Elene Quen speaking, demands information."

"Denied."

"Sir—"

"Denied. Tell them to sit and wait it out. Make no more unauthorized calls. Do you expect us to broadcast information that could aid the enemy?"

The tech turned to her work, visibly trying not to see the guns.

*Quen.* Young Damon's wife, with the merchanters, already trouble, making demands, refusing to come out. The information had already proliferated, and the Fleet had to be picking it up by now from the merchanters in pattern about the station. Mazian knew by now what had happened. Quen with the merchanters and Damon on green section dock; Downers knotted about Alicia's bedside, blocking number four crosshall in that area. Let her keep her Downer guard: the section door was shut. He folded his hands behind him and tried to look calm.

A movement caught his eyes, near the door. Jessad was back after brief absence, stood there, a silent summons. Jon walked in that direction, misliking Jessad's grim sobriety.

"Any progress?" he asked Jessad, stepping outside.

"Located Mr. Kressich," Jessad said. "He's here with an escort; wants a conference."

Jon scowled, glanced down the hall where Kressich waited with a cluster of guards about him, and an equal number of their own security.

"Situation as it was with blue one four," Jessad said. "Downers still have it blocked. We've got the door; we could decompress."

"We need them," Jon said tautly. "Let it be."

"For *her* sake? Half-measures, Mr. Lukas. . . ."

"We need the Downers; she's got them. Let be, I said. It's Damon and Quen who're trouble. What are you doing in that regard?"

"Can't get anyone on that ship; she's not coming out and they're not opening. As for him, we know where he is. We're working on it."

"What do you mean you're working on it?"

"Kressich's people," Jessad hissed. "We need to get through out there, you understand me? Pull yourself together and talk to him; promise him anything. He's got the mobs in his hand. He can pull the strings. Do it."

Jon looked at the group in the hall, his thoughts scattering, Kressich, Mazian, the merchanter situation . . . Union. The Union fleet had to move soon, had to. "What do you mean, need to get through out there? Do you know where he is or don't you?"

"Not beyond doubt," Jessad admitted. "We turn that mob loose on him and there won't be enough to identify.

And we need to *know*. Believe me. Talk to Kressich. And hurry about it, Mr. Lukas."

He looked, caught Kressich's eyes, nodded, and the party came closer . . . Kressich, as gray and wretched-looking as ever. But those about him were another matter: young, arrogant, cocky in their bearing.

"The councillor wants a share of this," one said, small, dark-haired man with a scar on his face.

"You speak for him?"

"Mr. Nino Coledy," Kressich identified him, surprising him with a direct answer and a harder look than Kressich had ever mustered in council. "I advise you to listen to him, Mr. Lukas, Mr. Jessad. Mr. Coledy heads Q security. We have our own forces, and we can get order when we ask for it. Are you ready to have it?"

Jon turned a disturbed look on Jessad, obtained nothing; Jessad was blank of comment. "If you can stop the mobs—do it."

"Yes," said Jessad quietly. "Quiet as this stage would serve us. Welcome to our council, Mr. Kressich, Mr. Coledy."

"Give me com," Coledy said. "General address."

"Give it to him," Jessad said.

Jon drew a deep breath, suddenly with questions trembling on his lips, what kind of game Jessad was playing with him, pushing these two into the inner circle; Jessad's *own,* as Hale was his? He swallowed the questions, swallowed anger, remembering what was out there, how fragile it all was. "Come with me," he said, led the way inside, took Coledy to the nearest com board. Scan was visible from there, Mazian still holding steady. It was too much to hope that Mazian would be easily disposed of. Far too much, that it would be easy. The Fleet had the area pocketed . . . Mazian's ships, dotted here and there about the multi-level halo that was the merchanters' orbit about Pell.

"Move," he said to a tech, dislodged him, put Coledy in that place and himself punched through to com central. Bran Hale's face lit up the screen. "Got a call for you to send out," he told Hale. "This one goes on general override."

"Right," Hale said.

"Mr. Lukas," someone called, breaking the general

hush in central. He looked about. Scan screens were flashing intersect alert.

"Where is it?" he exclaimed. Scan had nothing definite. A peppering of yellow haze warned of something incoming, fast. Comp began to siren alarms. There were soft outcries, curses, techs reaching for boards.

*"Mr. Lukas!"* someone cried, frantic appeal.

## iv

## Finity's End

"Scan," the alarm rang out. Elene saw the flicker and cast a frantic look at Neihart.

"Break us loose," Neihart said, avoiding her eyes. *"Go!"*

The word flashed ship to ship. Elene gathered herself against the parting jolt . . . too late to run for the dock, far too late; umbilicals were long since shut off, ships grappled-to only.

A second jolt. They were free, peeling away from station as the whole row of still-docked merchanters followed, counterclockwise round the rim; as any mistake in inside shutdown might mean a ruptured umbilical, as whole sections of dock might decompress. She sat still, feeling the familiar sensations she had thought she might never feel again, free, loose, like the ship, outward bound from what was coming at them; and feeling as if part of her were torn away.

A second invader passed . . . came zenith and disrupted scan, triggered alarms . . . was gone, on its way toward the Fleet. They were alive, drifting loose at their helpless slow-motion rate, coming out on an agreed course, a general drift of all those undocking. She folded her arm across her belly and watched the screens before her in *Finity*'s command center, thinking on Damon, on all that was back there.

Dead, maybe; they said Angelo was dead; maybe Alicia was; maybe Damon—maybe. . . . She hurled the thought at herself, trying to accept it sanely, if it had to be accepted, if there was revenge to be gotten for it. She drew deep breaths, thinking on *Estelle,* on all her kin. A second time spared, then. A talent for leaving disasters. She had a life in her that was Quen and Konstantin at once, names that meant something in the Beyond; names which Union would not find comfortable for them in future, that she would give them cause to remember.

"Get us out of here," she said to Neihart, cold and furious; and when he looked at her, seeming amazed by this shift of mind: "Get us out. Run for jump. Pass the word. Matteo's Point. Flash the word system-wide. We're leaving, right through the Fleet."

She was Quen, and Konstantin, and Neihart moved. *Finity's End* overshot the station and kept going, broadcasting instruction to every merchanter near and far in the system. Mazian, Union, Pell—none of them could stop it.

Instruments blurred before her eyes, cleared again with a blink. "After Matteo's," she said to Neihart, "we jump again. There'll be others . . . in deep. Folk who've had enough, who wouldn't come to Pell. We'll find them."

"No hope of your own there, Quen."

"No," she agreed with a shake of her head. "None of mine. They're gone. But I know coordinates. So do we all. I helped you, kept your holds full and never questioned your manifests."

"Merchanters know it."

"So will the Fleet know these places. So we hang together, captain. We move together."

Neihart frowned. It was not characteristic of merchanters . . . to be together on anything but a dock-front brawl.

"Got a boy on one of Mazian's ships," he said.

"I've got a husband on Pell," she said. "What's left now but to settle accounts for this?"

Neihart considered it a moment, finally nodded. "The Neiharts will stand by your word."

She leaned back, stared at the screen before her. They had scan image, Union insystem, ghosts ripping across scan. It was nightmare. Like Mariner, where *Estelle* and all the other Quens had died, holding to a doomed station too late . . . where the Fleet had let something through or something had gotten them from within. It was the same thing . . . only this time merchanters were not sitting still for it.

She watched, resolved to watch scan until the last, to see everything until the station died or they reached jump-point, whichever might happen first.

*Damon,* she thought, and cursed Mazian, Mazian more than Union, who had brought this on them.

## v

## Green dock

A second time G surged out of balance. Damon made a startled grab for the wall and Josh for him, but it was a minor flux, for all the panicked screams outside the scarred door. Damon turned his back against the wall and rolled a weary shake of his head.

Josh asked no questions. None were necessary. Ships had peeled away on the rest of the rim. Even here they could hear the sirens . . . breach, it was possible. It was encouraging that they could *hear* sirens. There was still air out there on the dock.

"They're going," Damon said hoarsely. Elene was away, with those ships; he wanted to believe so. It was the sensible thing. Elene would have been sensible; had friends, people who knew her, who would help her, when he could not. She was gone . . . to come back, maybe, when things settled—if they settled. If he was alive. He did not think he was going to be alive. Maybe Downbelow was all right; maybe Elene—on those ships. His hope went with them. If he was wrong . . . he never wanted to know.

Gravity fluxed again. The screams and the hammering at the door had stopped. The wide dock was no place to be in a G crisis. Anyone sane had run for smaller spaces.

"If the merchanters have bolted," Josh said faintly, "they saw something . . . knew something. I think Mazian must have his hands full."

Damon looked at him, thinking of Union ships, of Josh . . . one of them. "What's going on out there? Can *you* reckon?"

Josh's face was drenched with sweat, glistening in the light from the scarred door. He leaned against the wall, lifted a glance at the overhead. "Mazian's liable to do anything; can't predict. No percentage for Union in destroying this station. It's the stray shot we have to worry about."

"We can absorb a lot of shots. We may lose sections,

but while we have motive power and the hub intact, we can handle damage."

"With Q loose?" Josh asked hoarsely.

Another flux hit them, stomach-wrenching. Damon swallowed, beginning to experience nausea. "While that goes on we don't have Q to worry about. We've got to chance it, try to get out of this pocket."

"Go where? Do what?"

He made a sound deep in his throat, numb, simply numb. He waited for the next G flux; it failed to strike with its former force. They had begun to get it in balance again. The abused pumps had held, the engines worked. He caught his breath. "One comfort. We're out of ships to do it to us again. I don't know how many of those we can take."

"They could be waiting out there," Josh said.

He reckoned that. He reached a hand up, pushed the switch. Nothing happened. Closed, the door had locked itself. He took his card from his pocket, hesitated, pushed it in the slot and the buttons stayed dead. If anyone in central had any desire to know where he was, he had just given the information to them. He knew that.

"Looks like we're staying," Josh said.

The sirens had stopped. Damon edged over, chanced a look out the scarred window, trying to see through the opaque slashes and the light diffraction. Something stirred, far across the docks, one furtive figure, another. The com overhead gave out a burst of static as if it were trying to come on and went silent again.

## vi
## Norway

Militia freighters scattered, stationary nightmare. One of them blew like a tiny sun, flared on vid and died while com pickup sputtered static. The hail of particles incandesced in *Norway*'s path and some of the bigger ones rang against the hull, a scream of passing matter.

No fancy turns: dead-on targets and armscomp lacing into them. A Union rider went out the way the merchanter had, and *Norway*'s four riders rolled, whipped out on a vector concerted with *Norway* and pulled fire, a steady barrage that pocked a Union carrier paralleling them for one visible instant.

"Get him!" Signy yelled at her armscomper when the fire paused; it erupted over her words and pasted into the spot the running carrier turned out to occupy. They forced Union to maneuver, to dump G to survive it. A howl of delight went up and sirens drowned it as helm jerked control away and sent their own mass into a sudden turn, comp reacting to comp faster than human brains could at such speeds . . . she hauled it back and paralleled the quarry. Armscomp ripped off another barrage right down the belly array and whatever came of it, scan started to show a field peppered with haze.

"Good!" the belly spotter shouted into com general. "Solid hit . . ."

There were wails as *Norway* half-rolled and swung into a new zig. Merchanters leaked past them, headed out as if they were a tableau frozen in space: *They* were doing the moving, whipped through the interstices of that still-standing race and went after the Union ships, keeping them zigging, keeping them from gathering room for a run.

Feint and strike: like their entry . . . a ship to draw them, attack from another vector. *Tibet* and *North Pole* were headed in to intercept, had been coming from the first moment scan image had reached them: longscan had just revised their position, set them as much closer, reckoning they would go at max.

Union moved. That scan had reached them in the same instant; shifted vector right into the fire they were laying down, *Norway, Atlantic, Australia* . . . Union lost riders, took damage, going rimward in spite of fire, going at *Tibet* and *North Pole*. There was a ringing oath over com, Mazian's voice pouring out a stream of obscenity. Twelve carriers left of the fourteen that had come in, a cloud of riderships and dartships, bore away from station and into their two outrunners, that were distance-blind and alone out there.

"Hit their heels!" Porey's deep voice came through.

"Negative, negative," Mazian snapped back. "Hold your positions." Comp still had them in synch; *Europe*'s command signal drew them unwillingly with Mazian. They watched the Union fleet pass their zone of fire, heading for *Tibet* and *North Pole*. Behind them, a flare of energy reached them: static that cleared . . . "Got him!" com echoed. *Pacific* must have taken out that crippled

Union carrier some minutes back. There were other things possible across the system, that they could lose track of. Could lose Pell. One strike could take it out, if that was Union's intent.

Signy flexed a hand, wiped her face, keyed to Graff, and he took up controls on the instant—they were dumping velocity again, pulling maneuvers in concert with Mazian. Protests garbled over com. "Negative," Mazian repeated. There was a hush throughout *Norway*.

"They haven't a chance," Graff muttered too audibly. "They should have come in sooner . . . should have come in—"

"Hindsight, Mr. Graff. Take it as it falls." Signy dialed up general com. "Can't move out of here. If it's a feint, one ship could come in and wipe Pell. We can't help them. . . . Can't risk any more of us than we're already about to lose. They've got an option . . . they've still got room to run."

Might, she was thinking, might, the instant their scan narrowed on them, and longscan started showing what they were into . . . veer off and jump. If scan techs on *Tibet* and *North Pole* fed the right data into longscan, if the picture on their scopes did not show Mazian and help coming right on Union's tail, misinterpreting their maneuver as one of following . . .

The Fleet slowed farther. Scan showed a fade-out among the merchanters, that slow-motion flight having reached jump limit. They bled away, Pell's life, drifting off into the deep.

She dead-reckoned time factors, Union's speed, proliferation of their image, *Tibet*'s and *North Pole*'s velocity incoming. About now, about now, *Tibet* should be figuring it out, realizing Union was on them. If their scan was telling them truth . . .

Their own scan kept showing history for a moment, then locked up, stationary, longscan having run out of speculations. Head to head, yellow haze, while red lines tracked through that haze, the real scan they were getting.

Closer. The red line reached decision-critical—kept going. Head on. Signy sat and watched, as all of them had to watch. Her fist was clenched and she restrained herself from hitting something, the board, the cushion, something.

It happened; they watched it happen, what *had* happened already, the futile defense, the overwhelming assault. Two carriers. Seven riders, to a man. In forty and more years the Fleet had never lost ships so wretchedly.

*Tibet* rammed . . . Kant hurled his carrier into jump near the mass of his enemies and took his own riders and a Union carrier into oblivion . . . there was a sudden gap in scan . . . a grim cheer at that; and again when *North Pole* and her riders hurtled through the midst of the Unioners . . .

They almost made it through Kant's hole. Then that image became a scatter of images. *North Pole*'s comp signal that had begun a sending . . . ceased abruptly.

Signy had not cheered, only nodded slowly each time to no one in particular, remembering the men and women aboard, names known . . . despising the situation they were handed. Longscan resolved itself, question answered. The surviving images that were Union kept on running, hit jump, vanished from the screens. The Unioners would be back, reinforced, eventually, simply calling in more ships. The Fleet had won, had held on, but now they were seven; seven ships.

And the next time and the next it would happen. Union could sacrifice ships. Union ships prowled the fringes of the system and they dared not go out hunting them. *We've lost,* she addressed Mazian silently. *Do you know that? We've lost.*

"Pell," Mazian's voice came quietly over com, "is under riot conditions. We do not know the situation there. We are faced with disorder. Hold pattern. We cannot rule out another strike."

But suddenly lights flashed on *Norway*'s boards; a whole sector sprang to renewed independence. *Norway* was loosed from comp synch. Orders flashed to the screen, comp-sent.

. . . SECURE BASE.

She was loosed. *Africa* was. Two ships, to go back and take a disordered station while the rest kept to their perimeter and room to maneuver.

She punched general com. "Di, arm and suit. We've got to take ourselves a berth, every trooper we've got on the line. Suit alterday crew to guard the docks. We're going in after the troops we had to leave."

A shout erupted from that link, many-voiced, angry, frustrated troops suddenly needed again, in something they were hot to do.

"Graff," she said.

They red-lighted despite the troops in prep below, pulled stress in coming about and headed deadon for the station. Porey's *Africa* pulled out of pattern in her wake.

## vii
## Pell Central

". . . Give us docking access," Mallory's voice came over com, "and open doors to central, or we start taking out sections of this station."

*Collision,* the screens flashed. White-faced techs sat at their posts, and Jon gripped the back of the chair at com, paralyzed in the realization of carriers hurtling dead at Pell's midline.

"Sir!" someone screamed.

Vid had them, shining massed filling all the screen, monsters bearing down on them, a wall of dark finally that split apart and passed the cameras above and below station. Boards erupted in static and sirens wailed as the carriers skimmed their surface. One vid went out, and a damage alarm went off, a wail of depressurization alert.

Jon spun about, sought Jessad, who had been near the door. There was only Kressich, mouth agape in the wail of sirens.

"We're waiting for an answer," another, deeper voice said out of com.

Jessad, gone. Jessad or someone had failed at Mariner and the station had died. "Find Jessad!" Jon shouted at one of Hale's men. "Get him! Take him out!"

"They're coming in again!" a tech cried.

Jon whirled, stared at the screens, tried to talk and gestured wildly. "Com link," he shouted, and the tech passed him a mike. He swallowed, staring at the oncoming behemoths on vid. "You have access," he shouted into the mike, as he tried to control his voice. "Repeat: this is Pell stationmaster Lukas. You have access."

"Say again," Mallory's voice returned to him. "Who are you?"

"Jon Lukas, acting stationmaster. Angelo Konstantin is dead. Please help us."

There was silence from the other side. Scan began to alter, the big ships diverting from near-collision course, dumping velocity perceptibly.

"Our riders will dock first," Mallory's voice declared. "Do you copy, Pell station? Riders will dock in advance to serve as carrier dock crews. You give them an assist in and then clear out of their way or face fire. For every trouble we meet, we blow a hole in you."

"We have riot conditions aboard," Jon pleaded. "Q has broken confinement."

"Do you copy my instructions, Mr. Lukas?"

"Pell copies clearly. Do you understand our problem? We can't guarantee there'll be no trouble. Some of our docks are sealed off. We accept your troops in assistance. We are devastated by riot. You will have our cooperation."

There was long hesitation. Other blips had come into scan, the riders which attended the carriers. "We copy," Mallory said. "We will board with troops. Get my number-one rider safely docked with your cooperation or we will blow ourselves an access for troops and blow section by section, no survivors. That is your clear choice."

"We copy." Jon wiped at his face. The sirens had died. There was a deathly hush in the command center. "Give me time to get what security I can muster to the most secure docks. Over."

"You have half an hour, Mr. Lukas."

He turned from com, waved a summons to one of his security guards, by the door. "Pell copies. Half an hour. We'll get you a dock clear."

"Blue and green, Mr. Lukas. You see to it."

"Blue and green docks," he repeated hoarsely. "We'll do our best."

Mallory signed off. He pushed past com to key in the main com center. "Hale," he exclaimed. "Hale."

Hale's face appeared.

"General broadcast. All security to docks. Get blue and green docks clear for operation."

"Got it," Hale said, and keyed out.

Jon strode across the room to the doorway where Kressich still stood. "Get back on com. Get on and tell those people you claim to control to stay quiet. Hear?"

Kressich nodded. There was a distractedness in his eyes, a not quite sanity. Jon seized him by the arm and dragged him to the com board, as the tech scrambled out of the way. He set Kressich down, gave him the mike, stood listening as Kressich addressed his lieutenants by name, calling on them to clear the affected docks. Panic persisted in the corridors where they still had cameras to see. Green nine showed milling throngs and smoke; and whatever they cleared panicked mobs would pour into like air into vacuum.

"General alert," Jon said to the chief at station one. "Sound the null G warning."

The woman turned, opened the security casing, punched the button beneath. A buzzer began to sound, different and more urgent than all other warnings which had wailed through Pell's corridors. "Seek a secure place," a voice interrupted it at intervals. "Avoid large open areas. Go to the nearest compartment and seek an emergency hold. Should extreme gravity loss occur, remember the orientation arrows and observe them as station stabilizes. . . . Seek a secure place. . . ."

Panic in the halls became headlong flight, battering at doors, screaming.

"Throw G off," Jon sent to the op coordinator. "Give us a variation they can feel out there."

Orders flashed. A third time the station destabilized. Green nine corridors began to show clear as people raced for smaller spaces, even smaller corridors. Jon punched through to Hale again. "Get forces out there. Get those docks clear; I've given you your chance, confound you."

"Sir," Hale said, and winked out again. Jon turned full circle, looked distractedly at the techs, at Lee Quale, who clung to a handhold by the door. He signaled Quale, caught his sleeve and hauled him close when he came. "The unfinished business," he said, "down on green dock. Get down there and finish it, understand? *Finish it.*"

"Yes, sir," Quale breathed, and fled . . . with sense enough to know, surely, that their lives rested on it.

Union might win. Until then they claimed station neutrality, held onto what they could. Jon paced the aisle, catching at chairs and counters in the occasional strong flux, trying to keep the whole center from panic. He had Pell. He had already what Union had promised him, and would have it under Mazian and under Union too, if he was careful; and he had been, far more than Jessad had ordered him to be. There were no witnesses left alive in Angelo's office, none in Legal Affairs, abortive as that raid had been. Only Alicia . . . who knew nothing, who harmed no one, who had no voice, and her sons. . . .

Damon was the danger. Damon and his wife. Over Quen he had no control . . . but if young Damon started making charges—

He cast a look over his shoulder, suddenly missed Kressich, Kressich *and* two who were supposed to be watching him. The desertion of his own enraged him, of Kressich—he was relieved. Kressich would vanish back into the hordes of Q, frightened and unreachable.

Only Jessad . . . if they had not gotten him, if *he* was loose, near something vital—

On scan the riders were moving closer. Pell had yet a little time, before Mazian's troops hit. A tech handed him positive ID on the ships that waited out there; Mallory and Porey, Mazian's two executioners. They had a name, the one for ruthlessness and the other for enjoying it. Porey was the other one, then. That was no good news.

He stood and sweated, waiting.

## viii
## Green dock

Something was going on outside. Damon walked over the littered floor of the dark shop and leaned there, trying again to see out the scarred window, jerked as the red explosion of a shot distorted in the scratches. There was screaming mingled with the grinding of machinery in operation.

"Whoever's out there now, they're moving this way and they've got guns." He edged back from the door, moving carefully in the lessened G. Josh stooped, gathered up one of the rods that had been part of a ruined display, offered it. Damon took it and Josh got another for himself. He moved up near the doorway, and Josh went to the other side of it, back to the wall. There was no sound near them outside, a lot of shouting far away. Damon risked a look, the light coming from the other way, jerked back again at the sight of human shadows near the scarred window.

The door whipped open, carded from outside, someone with priority. Two men dashed in, guns drawn. Damon slammed the steel rod down on a head, eyes unfocusing for horror of it, and Josh hit from the other side. The men fell strangely in the low G, and a gun skittered loose. Josh scooped it up, fired twice to be sure, and one jerked, dying. "Get the gun," Josh snapped, and Damon bent and pushed fastidiously at the body, found the unfamiliar plastic of the gun butt in a dead hand. Josh was on his knees rolled the other body, began to strip it. "Clothes," Josh said. "Cards. ID's that work."

Damon laid the gun aside and swallowed his distaste, stripped the limp body, took off his own suit, struggled into the bloody coveralls . . . there would be men aplenty in the corridors with bloodstains on them. He searched the pockets for a card, found the papers there, found the card lying where the body's left hand had dropped it. He canted the ID folder to the light. *Lee Anton Quale . . . Lukas Company . . .*

*Quale.* Quale, from the Downbelow mutiny . . . and Jon Lukas's employ; in Jon's employ, and Jon had comp in his control—when Q happened to get the doors open, when Konstantins happened to have been murdered in Pell's tightest security . . . when his card stopped working and murderers knew how to locate him—it *was* Jon up there.

A hand closed on his shoulder. "Come *on,* Damon."

He rose, flinched as Josh used his gun to burn Quale's face beyond recognition, the other corpse afterward. Josh's own face was sweat-slicked in the light from the door, rigid with horror, but the reactions were right, a man whose instincts knew what they were doing. He headed for the dock and Damon ran with him, out into the light, slowed at once, for the docks were virtually bare. White dock seal was in place; the seal of green dock was hidden up the horizon. They walked gingerly across the front of the huge seal of white, got in among the gantries across the dock, walked along within that cover, while the horizon unfolded downward, showing them a group of men working at the docking machinery, moving slowly and carefully in reduced G. Corpses and papers and debris lay scattered all across the docks, out in open spaces which would be difficult to reach without being seen. "Enough cards lying out there," Josh said, "to give us plenty of names."

"For any lock not voice-keyed," Damon muttered. He kept his eye to the men at work and those standing guard down by the green niner entry, visible at this range—walked out carefully to the nearest corpse, hoping it was a corpse, and not someone dazed or shamming. He knelt, still watching the workers, felt through the pockets and came up with a card and additional papers. He pocketed them and went to the next, while Josh plundered others. Then nerves sent him scurrying back to cover, and Josh joined him at once. They moved further up the dock.

"Blue seal is open," he said, as that arch came down off horizon. He entertained a wild, momentary hope of hiding, getting to blue sector when the traffic in the corridors returned to normal, getting up to blue one and asking questions at gunpoint. It was fantasy. They were not going to live that long. He did not reckon they would.

"Damon."

He looked, followed the direction Josh indicated, up through the gantry lines to the first berth in green: green light. A ship was in approach, whether Mazian's or Union's there was no telling. Com thundered out, echoing instructions in the emptiness. The ship was closing with the docking cone, coming in fast. "Come on," Josh hissed at him, pulling at his arm, insisting on a break for green nine.

"The G isn't going," he murmured, resisting Josh's urging. "Don't you see it's a trick? Central's got the corridors cleared for their own forces to move in them. Those ships wouldn't dock with G completely unstable; no way they'd risk that with a big ship. Just a little flux to quell the riot. And it won't stay cleared. If we run into those corridors we'll be in the middle of it. No. Stay put."

"ECS501," he heard over the loudspeaker then, and his heart lifted.

"One of Mallory's riders," Josh muttered at his side. "Mallory. Union's retreated."

He looked at Josh, at the hate which burned in the angel's haggard face . . . hope cancelled.

The minutes passed. The ship snugged in. The dock crew ran to secure the umbilicals, thrust the connections in. The access slammed into seal with a hiss audible across the empty distance. Machinery whined and slammed beyond it, the lock in function, and the dock-side crew started running.

A handful of men poured out of the obscuring periphery of the gantries, unarmored . . . two running across to the far side, to take up position with rifles leveled. There was the sound of others running, and com was on again, warning of *Norway* itself inbound.

"Get your head down," Josh hissed, and Damon moved slowly, knelt by the brace of one of the movable tanks where Josh had taken closer cover, tried to see what was happening farther up, but there was a skein of umbilicals in the way. Mallory was using her own men for dock crews; but Jon Lukas must still be in command up in central, cooperating with Mazian, and in the pressure of Union attack, Mazian would choose efficiency over justice. Go out there, approach armed and nervous Company troops, raise a charge of murder and conspiracy while Jon Lukas physically held central and station, and Mazian had Union on his mind?

"I could go out there," he said, unsure of his conclusions.

"They'd swallow you alive," Josh said. "You've *nothing* to offer them."

He looked at Josh's face. Of the gentle man Adjustment had turned out . . . there was nothing left, but perhaps the pain. Set him at a comp board, Josh had said once, and he might remember comp; set him into war and he had other instincts. Josh's thin hands clutched the gun between his knees, and his eyes were set on the arch of the dock, where *Norway* was moving in to dock. Hate. His face was pale and intense. He might do anything. Damon felt the butt of the pistol in his own right hand, shifted his grip on it, moved his forefinger onto the trigger. An Adjusted Unioner . . . whose Adjustment was coming undone, who hated, who might go on coming apart. It was a day for murders, when the dead out there were too many to count, when there were no rules left, no kinships, no friendships. War had come to Pell, and he had lived naïve all his life. Josh was dangerous—had been trained to be dangerous—and nothing they had done to his mind had changed that.

Com announced arrival; there was the boom of contact. Josh swallowed visibly, eyes fixed. Damon reached with his left hand, caught Josh's arm. "Don't. Don't do anything, hear me? You can't reach her."

"Don't intend to," Josh said without looking at him. "Only so you have as good sense."

He let the gun to his side, finger slowly removed from the trigger, the taste of bile in his mouth. *Norway* was in solidly now, a second crashing of locks and joinings, a seal hissing into union.

Troops boiled out onto the dock, formed up, with shouts of orders, took up positions relieving the rifle-bearing crewmen, armored figures, alike and implacable. And of a sudden there was another figure from high up the curve, a shout, and other troops came from the recess of the shops and offices along that stretch, from the bars and sleepovers, troops left behind, rejoining their comrades of the Fleet, carrying their wounded or dead with them. There was reunion, a wavering in the disciplined lines that took them in, embracings and cheers raised. Damon pressed as close to the concealing machinery as he could, and Josh shrank down beside him.

An officer bellowed orders and the troops started to move in order, from the docks toward the green nine entry, and while some held it with leveled rifles, some advanced within it.

Damon shifted back, farther and farther within the shadows, and Josh moved with him. Shouts reached them, the echoing bellow of a loudspeaker: *Clear the corridor.* Suddenly there were shouts and screams and firing. Damon leaned his head against the machinery and listened, eyes shut, once and twice felt Josh flinch at the now-familiar sounds and did not know whether he did also.

*It's dying,* he thought with exhausted calm, felt tears leak from his eyes. He shivered finally. Call it what they would, Mazian had *not* won; there was no possibility that the outnumbered Company ships had beaten off Union for good. It was only a skirmish, decision postponed. There would be more such, until there was no more Fleet and no more Company, and what became of Pell would be in other hands. Jump had outmoded the great star stations. There were worlds now, and the order and priority of things had changed. The military had seen it. Only the Konstantins had not. His father had not, who had believed in a way neither Company nor Union, but Pell's—that kept the world it circled in trust, that disdained precautions within itself, that valued trust above security, that tried to lie to itself and believe that Pell's values could survive in such times.

There were those who could shift from side to side, play any politics going. Jon Lukas could do so; evidently had. If Mazian had sense to judge men, he would surely see what Jon Lukas was and reward him as he deserved. But Mazian did not need honest men, only men who would obey him, and impose Mazian's kind of law.

And Jon would come out a survivor, on either side. It was his own mother's stubbornness, that refusal to die; his own, maybe, that did not seek approach to his uncle, whatever he had done. Maybe Pell needed a governor in these latter days who could shift and survive, trading what had to be traded.

Only he could not. If he and Jon in front of him now—hate . . . hate of this measure was a new experience. A helpless hate . . . like Josh's . . . but there was revenge, if he lived. Not to harm Pell. But to make Jon Lukas's sleep less than easy. While a single Konstantin was loose, any holder of Pell had to feel less secure. Mazian, Union, Jon Lukas—none of them would own Pell until they had gotten him; and that he could make difficult for them, for as long as possible.

## 3

### Downbelow main base; 1300 hrs.; local night

There was still no answer. Emilio pressed Miliko's hand against his shoulder and kept leaning over Ernst, at com, while other staff clustered about. No word out of station; no word from the Fleet; Porey and his entire force had gone hurtling offworld into a silence that persisted into yet another hour.

"Give it up," he told Ernst, and when there was a murmuring among other staff: "We don't even know who's in control up there. No panic, hear me? I don't want any of that nonsense. If you want to stand around main base and wait for Union to land, fine. I won't object. But we don't know. If Mazian loses he might take out this facility, you understand? Might just want to destroy it beyond use. Sit here if you like. I've other ideas."

"We can't run far enough," a woman said. "We can't live out there."

"Our chances aren't good here either," Miliko said.

The murmuring swelled into panic.

"Listen to me," Emilio said. "Listen. I don't think their landing in the bush is that easy, unless they've got equipment we haven't heard of. And maybe they'll try blowing up this place; but maybe they'd do that anyway, and I'd rather have cover. Miliko and I are taking a trip down the road. We're not going to work for Union, if that's what it comes to up there. Or stand here and deal with Porey when he comes back."

The murmuring was lower this time, more frightened than panicked. "Sir," said Jim Ernst, "you want me to stay by com?"

"You want to stay here?"

"No," Ernst said.

Emilio nodded slowly, looked about at all of them. "We can take the portable compressors, the field dome . . . dig in when we get somewhere secure. We can survive out there. Our new bases do it. We can."

Heads nodded dazedly. It was too hard to realize what they were facing. He himself did not, and knew it.

"Flash it down the road too," he said. "Roll up the operation or stay on as they choose. I'm not forcing anyone to head into the bush if he doesn't think he can make it. One thing we've already seen to, that Union won't get their hands on the Downers. So now we make sure they don't get their hands on us. We get food from the emergency stores we didn't mention to Porey; we take the portable com; take some essential units out of the machines we can't take with us . . . and we just take a walk down the road and into the trees, by truck as far as we can take the trucks, dump the heavy stuff in hiding, carry it to our new dig bit by bit. They might blast the road and the trucks, but any other answer is going to take them time to mount. If anyone wants to stay here and work for the new management . . . or Porey, if he shows up again, then do it. I can't fight you and I'm not interested in trying."

There was near silence. Then some pushed out of the group and started gathering up personal belongings. More and more did. His heart was beating very hard. He pushed Miliko toward their quarters, to gather up the few of their belongings they could take. It could go the other way. Something could start among them. They could deliver him and Miliko to the new owners, if that was what it came to, gain points with the opposition. They could do that. There were far and away enough of them . . . and Q, and the workers out there. . . .

Of his family . . . no word. His father would have sent some message if he could. If he could.

"Make it quick," he told Miliko. "Word of this is going every which way out there." He slipped one of the base's only handguns into his pocket as he snatched up his heaviest jacket; he gathered up a boxful of cylinders for the breathers, took up a canteen and the short-handled axe. Miliko took the knife and a couple of blankets rolled up, and they went out again, into the confusion of staff packing up blanketrolls in the middle of the floor. They stepped over it. "Get the pump shut down," he told a man. "Get the connector out of it." He gave other instructions, and men and women moved, some for the trucks and some for acts of sabotage. "Move it," he yelled after them. "We're moving in fifteen minutes."

"Q," Miliko said. "What do we do with them?"

"Give them the same choice. Get down the line, put it to the regular workers, if they haven't heard yet." They passed the lock door, through the second and up the wooden steps into night-bound chaos, with people moving as fast as the limited air would let them. There was the sound of a crawler starting up. "Be careful," he yelled at Miliko as their paths diverged. He headed down over the crushed rock path, down and up again onto the shoulder of Q's hill, where the patched, irregular dome showed wan yellow light through its plastic, where Q folk were outside, dressed, looking as if they had had no more sleep than others this night.

"Konstantin," one yelled, alerting the others, and word

went into the dome with the speed of a slammed door. He kept walking, went into the midst of them, his heart in his throat. "Come on, get everyone out here," he yelled, and they began to pour out with a swelling murmur of numbers, fastening jackets, adjusting masks. In a moment the dome began to collapse, and the lock sighed the air out, a gust of warmth and a flood of bodies that began to surround him. They were all but quiet, a murmur, nothing more; the silence did not comfort him. "We're pulling out of here," he said. "We don't get any word out of station and it's possible Union's in control up there; we don't know." There were outcries of distress, and some of their own number ordered silence. "We don't know, I say. We're luckier than station; we've got a world under us, food to eat; and if we're careful . . . air to breathe. Those of us who've lived here know how to manage that . . . even in the open. You have the same choice we do. Stay here and work for Union, or take a walk with us. It's not going to be easy out there, and I wouldn't recommend it for the older ones and the youngest, but I'm not so sure it's going to be safe here either. We've got a chance out there, that they'll think we're too much bother to come after. That's it. We're not sabotaging any machine you need for life. The base here is yours if you want it; but you're welcome with us. We're going . . . never mind where we're going; unless you're coming with us. And if you come, it's on equal terms. Now. Immediately."

There was dead silence. He was terrified. He was crazy to have come among them alone. The whole camp could not stop them if they panicked.

Someone at the back of the crowd opened the door to the dome, and of a sudden there was a murmur of voices, a backflow into the dome, someone shouting that they would need blankets, that they would need all the cylinders, a woman wailing that she could not walk. He stood there while all of Q deserted him into the dome, turned on the slope and looked across to the other domes, where men and women were coming from the residents' domes in businesslike haste, carrying blankets and other items, a general flow down to the trough of the hills, where motors whined and headlamps showed. They had the trucks ready. He started down there, faster and faster, walked into the chaos that swirled about the vehicles. They were putting on the field dome and some spare plastic; a staffer showed him a checklist as businesslike as if they were loading for a supply trip. Some people were trying to put their personal loads on the trucks and staff was arguing with them, and Q was arriving, some of them carrying more than they ought on Downbelow.

"Trucks are for essential materials," Emilio shouted. "All able-bodied walk; anyone too old or too sick can perch on the baggage, and any room left, you can put heavy items on . . . but you share loads, hear? No one walks light. Who can't walk?"

There were shouts from some of the Q folk who had caught up, and they put forward some of the frailer children, some of the old ones. They yelled that there were some still coming, shouts with a tone of panic.

"Easy! We'll get them all on. We'll not be going fast. A kilometer down the road, forest starts, and there're no armored troops likely to hike into it after us."

Miliko reached him. He felt her hand on his arm and put his arm about her, hugged her to him. He remained slightly numb; a man had a right to be when his world ended. They were prisoners up there on station. Or dead. He began to think of that possibility too, forcing himself to deal with it. He felt sick at the stomach, shaking with an anger which he kept in that numb place, away from his thinking process. He wanted to strike out at someone . . . and there was no one at hand.

They got the com unit on. Ernst supervised the loading of it onto the truckbed, and between emergency power and portable generator they had that for information . . . if any came.

Last of all, the people who would ride, and room enough for bedrolls and sacks, a protective nest. People moved at a run, panting, but there seemed less panic; two hours yet till dawn. The lights were still on, on stored power, the domes still glowing yellow. But there was a sound missing, in all the noise of the crawler engines. The compressors were silent. The pulse was gone.

"Move them out," he shouted when there seemed order, and the vehicles started up, began to grind their patient way along the road.

They fell in behind, a column shaping itself to the road as it began to parallel the river. They passed the mill and entered the forest, where hills and trees closed on the right hand of the night-bound landscape. The whole progress had a feeling of unreality, the trucks' headlamps shining on the reeds and the grass tops and the hillside and the trunks of trees, with the silhouettes of humans trudging along, the hiss and pop of breathers in curious unison, amid the grinding of the engines. There were no complaints, that was the thing most strange, no objections, as if a madness had seized them all and they agreed on this. They had had a taste of Mazian's governance.

The grass moved beside the road, a serpentine line in the waist-high reeds. Leaves moved among the bushes beside the road hillward. Miliko pointed to one such disturbance, and others had seen it, pointing and murmuring in apprehension.

Emilio's heart lifted. He reached for Miliko's hand and pressed it, left her and strode out into the weeds and under the trees while the trucks and the column kept on. "Hisa!" he called aloud. "Hisa, it's Emilio Konstantin! Do you see us?"

They came, a handful, shyly advancing into the lights. One came holding out his hands, and he did. The Downer came to him and embraced him energetically. "Love you," the young male said. "You go walk, Konstantin-man?"

"Bounder? Is it Bounder?"

"I Bounder, Konstantin-man." The shadowed face looked up at him, dim light from now-stopped trucks glinting off a sharp-edged grin. "I run, run, run come back again watch you. All we eyes to you, make you safe."

"Love you, Bounder, love you."

The hisa bobbed in pleasure, fairly danced with it. "You go walk?"

"We're running away. There's trouble in the Upabove, Bounder, men-with-guns. Maybe they come Downbelow. We run away like the hisa, old, young, some of us not strong, Bounder. We look for a safe place."

Bounder turned to his companions, called something which ran up and down scales and chattered from them back to the trees and into the branches above. And Bounder's strange, strong hand slipped about his as the hisa began to lead him back to the road, where all the column had stopped, those rearmost crowding forward to see.

"Mr. Konstantin," one of the staff called from the passenger seat of a truck, nervousness in his voice, "they all right coming in with us?"

"It's all right," he said. And to the others: "Be glad of them. The hisa are back. The Downers know who's welcome on Downbelow and who isn't, don't they? They've been watching us all this time, waiting to see if we were all right. You people," he called out louder still to the unseen masses beyond, "They've come back to us, you understand? The hisa know all the places we could run to, and they're willing to help us, you hear that?"

There was a murmuring of distress.

"No Downer ever hurt a man," he shouted into the dark, over the patient rumble of the engines. He closed his hand the more firmly on Bounder's, walked down among them, and Miliko slipped her hand within his elbow on the other side. The trucks started up again, and they walked, at the same slow pace. Hisa began to join the column, walking along in the weeds beside the road. Some humans shied from them. Others tolerated the shy touch of an offered hand, even Q folk, following the example of old staffers, who were less perturbed by it.

"They're all right," he heard one of his workers call out through the ranks. "Let them go where they like."

"Bounder," he said, "we want a safe place . . . find all the humans from all the camps, take them to many safe places."

"You want safe, want help; come, come."

The strong hand stayed within his, small, as if they were father and child; but for all of youth and size it was the other way about . . . that humans went as the children now, down a known human road to a known human place, but they were not coming back, might never—he acknowledged it—might never come back.

"Come we place," Bounder said. "You make we safe; we dream bad mans away and they go; and you come now, we go dream. No hisa dream, no human dream; together-dream. Come dream place."

He did not understand the babble. There were places beyond which humans had never gone among hisa. Dreamplaces . . . it was already a dream, this mingled flight of humans and hisa, in the dark, in the overturning of all that had been Downbelow.

They had saved the Downers; and in the long years of Union rule, when humans came who cared nothing for the hisa . . . there would be humans among the hisa who could warn them and protect them. There was that much left to do.

"They'll come someday," he said to Miliko, "and want to cut down the trees and build their factories and dam the river and all the rest of it. That's the way of it, isn't it? If we let them get away with it." He swung Bounder's hand, looked down at the small intense face on the other side. "We go warn other camps, want to bring all humans into the trees with us, go for a long, long walk. Need good water, good food."

"Hisa find," Bounder grinned, the suspicion of a great joke shared by hisa and humans. "Not hide good you food."

They could not hold an idea for long . . . so some insisted. Perhaps the game would pall when humans had no more gifts to give. Perhaps they would lose their awe of humans and drift their own ways. Perhaps not. The hisa were not the same as they had been when humans came.

Neither were humans, on Downbelow.

# 4

## Merchanter *Hammer:* deep space; 1900 hrs.

Vittorio poured a drink, his second since space around them had suddenly become filled with a battle-worn fleet. Things had not gone as they should. A silence had fallen over *Hammer,* the bitter silence of a crew who felt an enemy among them, a witness to their national humiliation. He met no eyes, offered no opinions . . . had only the desire to anesthetize himself with all due speed, so that he could not be blamed for any matters of policy. He did not want to give advice or opinions.

He was plainly a hostage; his father had set things up that way. And it occurred to him inevitably that his father might have double-crossed them all, that he might now be worse than a useless hostage . . . that he might be one whose card was due to be played.

*My father hates me,* he had tried to tell them; but they had shrugged it off as irrelevant. They did not make the decisions. The man Jessad had done that. And where was Jessad now?

There was supposed to be some visitor on his way to the ship, some person of importance.

Jessad himself, to report failure, and to dispose of a useless bit of human baggage?

He had time to finish the second drink before the activity of the crew and eventual nudge at the hull reported a contact. There was a great deal of machinery slamming and the noise of the lift going into function, a crash as the cage synched with the rotation cylinder. Someone was coming up. He sat still with the glass before him and wished that he were a degree drunker than he was. The upward curve of the deck curtained the lift exit, beyond the bridge. He could not see what happened, only noted the absence of some of *Hammer*'s crew from their posts. He looked up in sudden dismay as he heard them coming round the other way, from his back, into the main room through crew quarters.

Blass of *Hammer*. Two crew. A number of military strangers and some not in uniform, behind them. Vittorio gathered himself shakily to his feet and stared at them. A gray-haired officer in rejuv, resplendent with silver and rank. And *Dayin*. Dayin Jacoby.

"Vittorio Lukas," Blass identified him. "Captain Seb Azov, over the fleet; Mr. Jacoby of your own station; and Mr. Segust Ayres of Earth Company."

"Security council," that one corrected.

Azov sat down at the table, and the others found place on the benches round about. Vittorio settled again, his fingers numb on the table surface. He was surrounded by an alcoholic gulf that kept coming and going. He tried to sit naturally. They had come to see him . . . him . . . and there was no possible help he could be to them or to anyone.

"The operation has begun, Mr. Lukas," Azov said. "We've eliminated two of Mazian's ships. They won't be easy to get out; they're hanging close to station. We've sent for additional ships; but we've driven the merchanters out, all the long-haulers. The ones left are Pell short-haulers, serving as camouflage."

"What do you want with me?" Vittorio asked.

"Mr. Lukas, you're acquainted with the merchanters based out of station—you've *run* Lukas Company, at least to some extent—and you know the ships."

He nodded apprehensively.

"Your ship *Hammer,* Mr. Lukas, is going back within hail of Pell, and where it regards merchanters, you'll be *Hammer*'s com operator . . . not under your real name, no, you'll be given a file on the *Hammer* family, which you'll study very carefully. You'll answer as one of them. But should *Hammer* be challenged by merchanter militia, or by Mazian, your life will rely on your skill in invention. *Hammer* will suggest to the merchanters remaining that their best course for survival would be to get to the system fringe and have nothing to do with this matter, to get utterly out of the way and cease trade with Pell. We want those ships out of the way, Mr. Lukas; and it wouldn't at all be politic to have merchanters know we've tampered with *Hammer* and *Swan's Eye.* We don't intend to have that known, you understand me?"

The crews of those ships, he thought, would never be set free, not without Adjustment. It occurred to him that his own memory was hazardous to Union, that it would never be politic to have merchanters know Union had violated merchanter neutrality, which they claimed as a sin of Mazian's alone. That they had confiscated not just personnel by impressment, but whole ships, and names . . . most of all the names, the trust, the selves of those people. He fingered the empty glass before him, realized what he was doing and stopped at once, trying to seem sober and sensible. "My own interests lie in that direction," he said. "My future on Pell is far from assured."

"How so, Mr. Lukas?"

"I entertain some hopes of a Union career, captain Azov." He lifted his eyes to Azov's grim face, hoping that he sounded as calm as he tried to be. "Relations between myself and my father . . . are not warm, so he threw me to you quite willingly. I've had time to think. Plenty of time. I prefer to make my own understandings with Union."

"Pell is running out of friends," Azov observed softly, with a glance at the sad-faced Mr. Ayres. "Now the indifferent desert her. The will of the governed, Mr. Ambassador."

Ayres's eyes turned toward Azov, sidelong. "We have accepted the situation. It was never the intent of my mission to obstruct the will of the people resident in these areas. Only I am anxious for the safety of Pell Station. We are talking about thousands of lives, sir."

"Siege, Mr. Ayres. We cut them off from supplies and disrupt their operations until they grow uncomfortable." Azov turned his face toward Vittorio, stared at him a moment. "Mr. Lukas—we have to prevent their access to the resources of the mines, and of Downbelow itself. A strike there . . . possible, but militarily costly getting to it, and costly in its effect. So we proceed by disentanglement. Mazian has a death grip on Pell; he'll leave ruin if he loses, blow Downbelow and the station itself, fall back toward the Hinder Stars . . . toward Earth. Do you want your precious motherworld used for a Mazianni base, Mr. Ayres?"

Ayres shot him a troubled look.

"Ah, he *is* capable of it," Azov said, not ceasing to look at Vittorio, a cold, penetrating stare. "Mr. Lukas, that is as much as your duty involves. To gather information . . . to dissuade merchanters from trade. Do you understand? Do you think that's within your capacity?"

"Yes, sir."

Azov nodded. "You'll understand, Mr. Lukas, if we excuse you and Mr. Jacoby at this point."

He hesitated, a little dazed, realized it fuzzily as an order and that Azov's gray stare brooked no countersuggestions. He rose from the table. Dayin excused himself past Ayres, and that left Ayres, Blass, and Azov in council. *Hammer*'s captain prepared to receive orders the nature of which he much wished to know.

Ships had been lost. Azov had not told the truth as it was. He had heard the crew talking. There were whole carriers missing. They were to be sent into that.

He paused where the curve curtained the meeting area, looked back at Dayin, sank down on a bench at the table in this the crew quarters. "You all right?" he asked Dayin, for whom he had never had great affection; but a face from home was very welcome in this cold place, in these circumstances.

Dayin nodded. "And you?" It was more courtesy than he had generally had from uncle Dayin.

"Fine."

Dayin settled opposite.

"Truth," Vittorio asked him. "How many did they lose out there?"

"Took heavy damage," Dayin said. "I reckon that Mazian cost them some. I know there are ships missing . . . carriers *Victory* and *Endurance* gone, I think."

"But Union can build more. They're calling others in. How long is this going to go on?"

Dayin shook his head, rolled a meaningful glance at the overhead. The fans hummed, deadening conversation into local areas, but not shielding them from monitoring. "They've got him cornered," Dayin said then. "And they can get supplies indefinitely, but Mazian's bottled. What Azov said, that was the truth. He cost them, cost them badly, but they cost him worse."

"And what about us?"

"I'd rather be here than at Pell, frankly."

Vittorio gave a bitter laugh. His eyes blurred, a sudden pain in his throat, which was never really gone, and he shook his head. "I meant it," he said for those who might chance to be monitoring them. "I'll give Union the best I've got; it's the best thing I ever had going for me."

Dayin regarded him strangely, frowned and perhaps understood his meaning. For the first time in his twenty-five years he felt a kinship with someone. That it should be Dayin, who was three decades older and had a different experience . . . that surprised him. But a little time in the Deep might make comrades out of the most unlikely individuals, and perhaps, he thought, perhaps Dayin had already made such choices, and Pell was no longer home for either of them.

# 5

## i

## Pell: Green Dock; 2000 hrs. md.; 0800a.

Fire hit the wall. Damon flinched tighter into the corner they occupied, resisted half a heartbeat as Josh seized him and sprang up to run, followed them, dodged among the panicked and screaming crowds which back-washed out of green nine onto the docks. Someone did get shot, rolled on the decking at their feet, and they jumped that body and kept going, in the direction the troops meant to drive them.

Station residents, Q escapees . . . there was no difference made. They ran with fire peppering the supports and the storefronts, silent explosions in the chaos of screams, shots aimed at structures and not the vulnerable station shell itself. Shots went over their heads now that the crowd was moving, and they ran until the weakest faltered. Damon slowed as Josh did, found himself in white dock, the two of them weaving through the scattered number still running in panic, the last few who in their terror seemed to think the shots were still coming. He saw shelter among the shops by the inner wall, went that way and Josh followed him, to the recessed doorway of a bar which had been sealed against rioters, a place to sit quietly, out of the way of chance shots.

Several bodies lay out on the dock before them, new or old was not certain. It had become an ordinary sight in recent hours. There were occasional acts of violence while they sat there against the doorway . . . fights among stationers and what might be Q residents. Mostly people wandered, sometimes calling out names, parents hunting children, friends or mates hunting each other. Sometimes there were relieved meetings . . . and once, once, a man identified one of the dead, and screamed and sobbed.

Damon bowed his face against his arms. Eventually some men helped the relative away.

And eventually the military sent detachments of armored troops into the area, to round up work crews, ordering them to gather up the dead and vent them. Damon and Josh slunk deeper into the doorway and evaded that duty; it was the active and restless the troops picked.

Last of all Downers came out of hiding, timidly, with soft steps and fearful looks about. They took it on themselves to clean the docks, scrubbing away the signs of death, faithful to their ordinary duties of cleanliness and order. Damon looked at them with a slight stirring of hope, the first good thing he had seen in all these hours, that the gentle Downers returned to the service of Pell.

He slept a little, as others did who sat over in the docking areas, as Josh did beside him, curled up against the door frame. From time to time he roused to general com announcements of restored schedules, or the promise that food would be forthcoming in all areas.

Food. The thought began to obsess him. He said nothing of it, his knees tucked up within his arms and his limbs feeling weak with hunger; weakness, he thought it, regretting a neglected breakfast, no lunch, no supper . . . he was not accustomed to hunger. It was, as he had ever felt it, a missed meal on a day of heavy work. An inconvenience. A discomfort. It began to be something else. It put a whole new compexion on resistance to anything; played games with his mind; forecast whole new dimensions of misery. If they were to be caught and recognized it was likely to be in some food line; but they had to come out for that, or starve. Their very remaining still grew obvious as the aroma of food swept the docks and others moved, as carts trundled along, pushed by Downers. People mobbed the carts, started snatching and shouting; but the troops escorted each then, and it calmed down quickly. The food carts, stores diminished, came closer. They stood up, leaned there in the recess.

"I'm going out there," Josh said finally. "Stay back. I'll say you're hurt. I'll get enough for both of us."

Damon shook his head. It was perverse courage, to test his survival, sweaty, uncombed, in dirty, bloody coveralls. If he could not cross the dock for fear of an assassin's gun or a trooper recognizing him, he was going to go mad. At least they did not look to be asking for ID cards for the meals. He had three of them, and his own, which he dared not use; Josh had two and his own, but they did not match the pictures.

A simple act, to walk out with a guard watching, to take a cold sandwich and a carton of lukewarm fruit drink, and to retreat; but he retired to the sheltering storefront with a sense of triumph in his prize, crouched there to eat as Josh joined him . . . ate and drank, feeling in that mundane act as though a great deal of the nightmare were past, and he was caught in some strange new reality, where human feelings were not required, only an animal wariness.

And then a shrill ripple of Downer language, the one with the food cart speaking out across the dock to others of his kind. Damon was startled; Downers were generally shy when things were quiet around them; it startled the escorting trooper, who lowered his rifle and looked all about. But there was nothing, only quiet, frightened people and solemn round-eyed Downers, who had stopped and now went about their business. Damon finished his sandwich as the cart passed on along the upward curve of the dock toward green.

A Downer came near them, dragging a box into which he was collecting the plastic containers. Josh looked anxious as the Downer held out his hand, surrendered the wrappers; Damon tossed his in the box, looked up in fright as the Downer rested a gentle hand on his arm. "You Konstantin-man."

"Go away," he whispered hoarsely. "Downer, don't say my name. They'll kill me if they see me. Be quiet and go away quick."

"I *Bluetooth.* Bluetooth, Konstantin-man."

"Bluetooth." He remembered. The tunnels, the Downer who had been shot. The strong Downer fingers closed tighter.

"Downer name Lily send from Sun-she-friend, you name 'Licia. She send we, make Lukases quiet, not come in she place. Love you, Konstantin-man. 'Licia she safe, Downers all round she, keep she safe. We bring you, you want?"

He could not breathe for the moment. "Alive? She's alive?"

" 'Licia she safe. Send you come, make you safe with she."

He tried to think, clung to the furred hand and stared into the round brown eyes, wanting far more than Downer patois could say. He shook his head. "No. No. It's danger to her if I come there. Men-with-guns, you understand, Bluetooth? Men hunt me. Tell her—tell her I'm safe. Tell her I hide all right, tell her Elene got away with the ships. We're all right. Does she need me, Bluetooth? She needs?"

"Safe in she place. Downers sit with she, all Downers in Upabove. Lily with she. Satin with she. All. All."

"Tell her—tell her I love her. Tell her I'm all right and Elene is. Love you, Bluetooth."

Brown arms hugged him. He embraced the Downer fervently and the Downer left him and slipped away like a shadow, quickly occupied himself with picking up debris not far away, wandered off. Damon looked about him, fearful that they might have been observed, met nothing but Josh's curious gaze. He glanced away, wiped his eyes on the arm which rested across his knee. The numbness diminished; he began to be afraid again, had something to be afraid for, someone who could still be hurt.

"Your mother," Josh said. "Is that what he was talking about?"

He nodded, without comment.

"I'm glad," Josh offered earnestly.

He nodded a second time. Blinked, tried to think, feeling his brain subjected to jolt after jolt until there was no sense in it.

"Damon."

He looked up, followed the direction of Josh's stare. Squads of troops were coming off the horizon, out of green dock, formed up and meaning business. Quietly, nonchalantly, he rose, dusted his cothing, turned his back to the dock to give Josh cover while he got up. Very casually they began to move along in the other direction.

"Sounds like they're about to get organized out there," Josh said.

"We're all right," he insisted. They were not the only ones moving. The niner hall of white was not that far. They drifted with others who seemed to have the same motive, found a public restroom next to one of the bars that sat at the corner of white nine; Josh turned in there and he walked in after. They both made use of it and walked out again, taking a normal pace. Guards had been posted at the intersections of the corridor with the dock, but they were not doing anything, only watching. He walked further down nine, stopped at a public call unit.

"Screen me," he said, and Josh obligingly leaned against the wall between them and the opening of nine where the guards stood. "Going to see what cards we have, how many credits, where the original owners belonged. I don't need my own priority to do that, just a records number."

"I know one thing," Josh said in a low voice. "I don't look like a Pell citizen. And your face . . ."

"No one wants to be noticed; no one can turn us in without being noticed himself. That's the best hope we've got; no one wants to be conspicuous." He thrust in the first card and keyed the override. Altener, Leslie: 789.90 credits in comp; married, a child. Clerk, clothing concession. He put that one in his left pocket, not to use, not wanting to steal from the survivors. Lee Anton Quale, single man, staff card with Lukas Company, restricted clearance, 8967.89 credits . . . an amazing amount for such a man. William Teal, married man, no children, loading boss, 4567.67 credits, warehouse clearances.

"Let's see yours," he said to Josh. Josh handed his over together, and he shoved the first in, hastening feverishly, wondering whether so many inquiries in a row off a public terminal might not set comp central off. Cecil Sazony, single man, 456.78 credits, machinist and sometime loader, barracks privileges; Louis Diban, five-year marriage terminated, no dependents, 3421.56, dock crew foreman. He pocketed the cards and started walking as Josh followed and caught up with him, around the corner into a crosshall, and around the next corner to the right. There was a storeroom there; all the docks were mirror image one of the other when it came to the central corridors, and there was inevitably a storage room for maintenance hereabouts. He found the appropriate, unmarked door, used the foreman's card to open it, and turned on the lights. There was ventilation, a store of paper and cleaning supplies and tools. He stepped in with Josh behind him and punched the door closed. "A hole to hide in," he said, and pocketed the card he had used, reckoning it the best key they had. "We sit it out, go on alterday shift a day or so. Two of our cards were alterday people, single, with dock clearance. Sit down. Lights will go out in here in a moment. Can't keep them on . . . comp will find a storeroom light on and turn it out on us, very economical."

"Are we safe here?"

He laughed bitterly, sank down against the wall, legs tucked up in the cramped space to afford Josh room to sit down opposite him. He felt of the gun still in his pocket, to be sure it was there. Drew a breath. "Nowhere is safe." Tired, the angel's face, grease-smudged, hair stringy. Josh looked terrified, though it had been Josh's instincts that had saved them under fire. Between the two of them, one knowing the accesses and one with the right reflexes, they made a tough problem for Mazian. "You've been shot at before," he said. "Not just in a ship . . . close up. You know that?"

"I don't remember."

"Don't you?"

"I said I don't."

"I know the station. Every hole, every passage; and if shuttles start moving again, if any ships start going and coming from the mines, we just use the cards to get close enough to the docks, join a loading crew, walk onto a ship. . . ."

"Go where, then?"

"Downbelow. Or outworld mines. No questions asked in either place." It was a dream. He fabricated it to comfort them both. "Or maybe Mazian will decide he can't go on holding here. Maybe he'll just pull out."

"He'll blow it if he does. Blow the station, the installations on Downbelow with it. Would he want to leave Union a base to use against him when he falls back?"

Damon frowned at truth he already knew. "You have a better suggestion what we should do?"

"No."

"I could turn myself in, negotiate to get back in control, evacuate the station. . . ."

"You believe that?"

"No," he said. That account too he had already added up. "No."

The lights went out. Comp had shut them down. Only the ventilation continued.

## ii

## Pell: station central; 2130 hrs. md.; 0930 hrs. a.

"But there's no need," Porey said softly, his dark, scarred face implacable, "there's no further need for your presence, Mr. Lukas. You've done your civic duty. Now go back to your quarters. One of my people will be sure you get there safely."

Jon looked about at the control center, at the several troopers who stood there, with the safeties off the rifles, with eyes constantly on the fresh shift of techs who managed the controls, the others under guard for the night. He gathered himself to pass orders to the comp chief, stopped cold as a trooper made a precise move, a hollow scrape of armor, a lowered rifle. "Mr. Lukas," Porey said, "people are shot for ignoring orders."

"I'm tired," he said nervously. "I'm glad to go, sir. I don't need the escort."

Porey motioned. One of the troopers by the door stood smartly aside, waiting for him. Jon walked out, the trooper treading behind him at first and then beside him, an unwanted companion. They passed other troops back on guard in quiet, riot-scarred blue one.

More of the Fleet was docking. They had drawn in to a tighter perimeter, decided finally to dock, which seemed to him military insanity, a risk he did not understand. Mazian's risk. His now. Pell's, because Mazian was back.

Perhaps—he found it hard to think—Union *had* been beaten badly. Perhaps there were things kept secret. Perhaps there would be delay in the Union takeover. It worried him, the thought that Mazian's rule might be long.

Suddenly troops exited the lift ahead into blue one, troops bearing a different insigna. They intercepted him, presented his escort with a slip of paper.

"Come with us," one ordered.

"I was instructed by captain Porey—" he objected, but another nudged him with a gun barrel and moved him toward the lift. *Europe,* their badges said. *Europe* troops. Mazian had come in.

"Where are we going?" he asked in panic. They had left the *Africa* trooper behind. "Where are we going?"

There was no answer. It was deliberate bullying. He knew where they were going . . . had his suspicions confirmed when, after descent in the lift, he was walked down the blue niner corridor, out onto the docks, toward the glowing access tube of a docked ship.

He had never been aboard a warship. It was cramped as a freighter for all its exterior size. It made him claustrophobic. The rifles in the hands of the troopers at his back gave him no more comfort, and whenever he would hesitate, turning left, entering the lift, they would push him with the rifle barrels. He was sick with fear.

They knew, he kept thinking. He kept trying to persuade himself it was military courtesy, that Mazian wished to bluff or bully. But from this place they could do what they pleased. Could vent him out a waste chute and he would be indistinguishable from the hundreds of other bodies which now drifted, frozen, a nuisance in the station's vicinity for the skimmers to freeze together and boost off. No difference at all. He tried to pull his wits together, reckoning that he survived by them now or not at all.

They showed him off the lift into a corridor with troops standing guard in it, into a room wider than most, with a vacant round table. Made him sit down in one of the chairs there. Stood waiting with the rifles over their arms.

Mazian came in, in plain and somber blue, haggard of face. Jon rose to his feet in respect; Conrad Mazian gestured him to sit down again. Others filed in to take their places at the table, *Europe* officers, none of the captains. Jon darted glances from one to the next.

"Acting stationmaster," Mazian said quietly. "Mr. Lukas, what happened to Angelo Konstantin?"

"Dead," Jon said, trying to suppress all but innocent reactions. "Rioters broke into station offices. Killed him and all his staff."

Mazian only stared at him, utterly unmoved. He sweated.

"We think," Jon said further, guessing at the captain's thoughts, "that there may have been conspiracy—the strike at other offices, the opening of the door into Q, the timing of it all. We are investigating."

"What have you found?"

"Nothing as yet. We suspect the presence of Union agents passed somehow into station during the processing of refugees. Some were let through, may have had friends or relatives left back in Q. We're puzzled as yet how contacts were passed. We suspect connivance of the barrier guards . . . black market connections."

"But you haven't found anything."

"Not yet."

"And won't very quickly, will you, Mr. Lukas?"

His heart began beating very fast. He kept panic from his face; he hoped he succeeded at it. "I apologize for the situation, captain, but we've been kept rather busy, coping with riot, with the damage to station . . . lately working at the orders of your captains Mallory and . . ."

"Yes. Bright move, the means you used to clear the halls of riot; but then it had quieted a little by then, hadn't it? I understand there were Q residents let into central."

Jon found breathing difficult. There was a prolonged silence. He could not think of words. Mazian passed a signal to one of the guards at the door.

"We were in crisis," Jon said, anything to fill that terrible silence. "I may have acted high-handedly, but we were presented a chance to get control of a dangerous situation. Yes, I dealt with the councillor from that area, not, I think, involved in the situation, but a calming voice . . . there was no one else at the—"

"Where is your son, Mr. Lukas?"

He stared.

"Where is your son?"

"Out at the mines. I sent him out on a shorthauler on a tour of the mines. Is he all right? Have you had word of him?"

"Why did you send him, Mr. Lukas?"

"Frankly, to get him off the station."

"Why?"

"Because he had lately been in control over the station offices while I was stationed on Downbelow. After three years there was some question of loyalties and authorities and channels of communication within the company offices here. I thought a brief absence might straighten things out, and I wanted someone out there in the mine offices who could take over if communications were interrupted. A policy move. For internal reasons and for security."

"It wasn't to balance the presence on-station of a man named Jessad?"

His heart came close to stopping. He shook his head calmly. "I don't know what you're talking about, captain Mazian. If you'd be so good as to tell me the source of your information—"

Mazian gestured and someone entered the room. Jon looked and saw Bran Hale, who evaded his eyes.

"Do you know each other?" Mazian asked.

"This man," Jon said, "was discharged on Downbelow for mismanagement and mutiny. I considered a previous record and hired him. I'm afraid my confidence may have been misplaced."

"Mr. Hale approached *Africa* with some thought of enlistment . . . claimed to have certain information. But you flatly deny knowing a man named Jessad."

"Let Mr. Hale speak for his own acquaintances. This is a fabrication."

"And one Kressich, councillor of Q?"

"Mr. Kressich was, as I explained, in the control center."

"So was this Jessad."

"He might have been one of Kressich's guards. I didn't ask their names."

"Mr. Hale?"

Bran Hale put on a grim face. "I stand by my story, sir."

Mazian nodded slowly, carefully drew his pistol. Jon thrust back from the table, and the men behind him slammed him back into the chair. He stared at the pistol, paralyzed.

"Where is Jessad? How did you make contact with him? Where would he have gone?"

"This fiction of Hale's—"

The safety went off the pistol audibly.

"I was threatened," Jon breathed. "Threatened into cooperation. They've seized a member of my family."

"So you gave them your son."

"I had no choice."

"Hale," Mazian said, "you and your companions and Mr. Lukas may go into the next compartment. And we'll record the proceedings. We'll let you and Mr. Lukas settle your argument in private, and when you've resolved it, bring him back again."

"No," Jon said. "No. I'll give you the information, all that I know."

Mazian waved his hand in dismissal. Jon tried to hold to the table. The men behind him hauled him to his feet. He resisted, but they brought him along, out the door, into the corridor. Hale's whole crew was out there.

"They'll serve you as well," Jon shouted back into the room where the officers of *Europe* still sat. "Take him in and he'll serve you the same way. He's lying!"

Hale grasped his arm, propelled him into the room which waited for them. The others crowded after. The door closed.

"You're crazy," Jon said. "You're crazy, Hale."

"You've lost," Hale said.

## iii

## Merchanter Finity's End: deep space; 2200 hrs. md; 1000 hrs. a.

The wink of lights, the noise of ventilators, the sometime sputter of com from other ships—all of this had a dreamlike familiarity, as if Pell had never existed, as if it were *Estelle* again and the folk about her might turn and show familiar faces. known from childhood. Elene worked her way through the busy control center of *Finity's End* and pressed herself into the nook of an overhanging console to obtain a view of scan. Her senses were still muzzy with drugs. She pressed her hand to her belly, feeling unaccustomed nausea. Jump had not hurt the child . . . would not. Merchanters had proven that time and again, merchanter women with strong constitutions and lifelong habituation to the stresses; it was nine-tenths nerves, and the drugs were not that heavy. She would not lose it, would not even think of it. In time her pulse settled again from the short walk from main room, the waves of sickness receded. She watched scan acquire another blip. Merchanters were coming into the null point by drift, the way they had left Pell, frantically gathering all the realspace speed they could on entry to keep ahead of the incomers who were rolling in like a tide on a beach. All it needed was someone overshooting minimum, some over hasty ass coming into realspace too close to the point, and they and the newcomer would cease to exist in any rational sense, shredded here and there. She had always thought it a peculiarly nasty fate. They would ride for the next few minutes still with that end a very real possibility.

But they were coming in greater and greater numbers now, finding their way into this refuge in reasonable order. They might have lost a few passing through the battle zone; she could not tell.

Nausea hit again. It came and went. She swallowed several times in calm determination to ignore it, turned a jaundiced eye on Neihart, who had left the controls of the ship to his son and came to see to her.

"Got a proposition," she said between swallows. "You let me have com again. No running from here. Take a look at what's following us, captain. Most of the merchanters that ever ran freight for Company stations. That's a lot of us, isn't it? And if we want to, we can reach further than that."

"What do you have in mind?"

"That we stand up and safeguard our own interests. That we start asking ourselves hard questions before we scatter out of here. We've lost the stations we served. So do we let Union swallow us up, dictate to us . . . because we become outmoded next to their clean new state-run ships? And they could take that idea into their heads if we come to them begging license to serve their stations. But while things are uncertain, we've got a vote and a voice, and I'm betting some of the so-named Union merchanters can see what's ahead too, clear as we can. We can stop trade—all worlds, all stations—we can shut them down. Half a century of being pushed around, Neihart, half a century of being mark for any warship not in the mood to regard our neutrality. And what do we get when the military has it all? You want to give me com access?"

Neihart considered a long moment. "When it goes sour, Quen, word will spread far and wide what ship spoke out for it. It's trouble for us."

"I know that," Elene said hoarsely. "But I'm still asking it."

"You've got com if you want it."

## iv

## Pell: Blue Dock; aboard Norway; 2400 hrs. md.; 1200 hrs. a.

Signy turned restlessly and came up against a sleeping body, a shoulder, an inert arm. Who it was she did not remember for a moment, in her half-sleep confusion. Graff, she decided finally, Graff. She settled comfortably again, against him. They had come offshift together. She kept her eyes open on the dark wall for a moment, the row of lockers, in the starlight glow of the light overhead—not liking the images she saw against her lids, the remembered reek of dying in her nostrils, that she could not bathe away.

They held Pell. *Atlantic* and *Pacific* made their lonely patrol with all the riders in the Fleet, so that they dared sleep. She earnestly wished it were *Norway* on patrol. Poor Di Janz was in command over the docks, sleeping in the forward access when he got sleep at all. Her troops were scattered throughout the docks, in a dark mood. Seventeen wounded and nine killed in the Q outbreak did not improve their attitude. They would stand watch one shift on and the other off and keep on doing it. Beyond that, she made no plans. When the Union ships came in, they would come, and the Fleet would react as they had been doing in places of odds as bad as this . . . fire at the reachable targets and keep the remaining options open as long as possible. Mazian's decision, not hers.

She closed her eyes finally, drew a deliberately peaceful breath. Graff stirred against her, settled again, a friendly presence in the dark.

## v

## Pell: sector blue one, number 0475; 2400 hrs. md.; 1200 hrs. a.

"She sleep," Lily said. Satin drew in a breath and settled her arms about her knees. They had pleased Sun-her-friend; the Dreamer had wept for joy to hear the news that Bluetooth had brought, the Konstantin-man and his friend safe . . . so, so awesome the sight of tears on that tranquil face. All the hisa's hearts had hurt within them until they understood it was happiness . . . and a warmth had sat within the dark and lively eyes, that they had crowded close to see. *Love you,* the Dreamer had whispered, *love you every one.* And: *Keep him safe.*

Then at last she smiled, and closed her eyes.

"Sun-shining-through-clouds." Satin nudged Bluetooth and he who had been zealously grooming himself—trying vainly to bring order to his coat, for respect of this place—looked toward her. "You go back, go and set your own eyes on this young Konstantin-man. Upabove hisa are one thing; but you are very quick, very clever Downbelow hunter. You watch him, come and go."

Bluetooth cast an uncertain look at Old One and at Lily.

"Good," Lily agreed. "Good, strong hands. Go."

He preened diffidently, a young male, but others gave him place; Satin regarded him with pride, that even the old strange ones saw worth in him. And truth: there was keen good sense in her friend. He touched the Old Ones and touched her, quietly excused himself toward the outside of the gathering.

And the Dreamer slept, safe in their midst, although a second time humans had fought humans and the secure world of the Upabove had rocked like a leaf on the breast of river. Sun watched over her, and the stars still burned about them.

# 6

## Downbelow: 10/11/52; local day

The trucks moved at a lumbering pace through the clear area, forlorn, collapsed domes, the empty pens, and above all the silence of the compressors, telling a tale of abandonment. Base one. First of the camps after main base. Lock doors banged loosely, unfastened, in a slight wind. The weary column straggled now, all looking at the desolation, and Emilio looked on it with a pang in his own heart, this thing that he had helped to build. No sign of anyone staying here. He wondered how far down the road they were, and how they fared. "Hisa watch here too?" he asked of Bluetooth, who, almost alone of hisa, still remained with the column, beside him and Miliko. "We eyes see," Bluetooth answered, which told him less than he wanted.

"Mr. Konstantin." A man came up from the back, walked along with him, one of the Q workers. "Mr. Konstantin, we have to rest."

"Past the camp," he promised. "We don't stay in the open longer than we can help, all right? Past the camp."

The man stood still and let the column pass and his own group overtake him. Emilio gave Miliko's shoulder a weary pat, increased his own pace to overtake the two crawlers ahead of the column; he passed one in the clearing, overtook the other as they reached the farther road, got the driver's attention and signed him half a kilometer halt. He stopped then and let the column move until he was even with Miliko. He reckoned that some of the older workers and the children might be at the end of their strength. Even walking with the breathers was about the limit of exertion they could take over this number of hours. They kept stopping for rest and the requests grew more and more frequent.

They began to straggle as it was, some of them stringing further and further behind. He drew Miliko aside, and watched the line pass. "Rest ahead," he told each group as they passed. "Keep on till you get there." In time the back of the column came in sight, a draggled string of walkers. The older ones, patient and doggedly determined, and a couple of staffers who walked last of all. "Anyone left?" he asked, and they shook their heads.

And suddenly a staffer was coming down the winding road from the other end of the column, jogging, staggering into other walkers, as the line erupted with questions. Emilio broke into a run with Miliko in his wake, intercepting the man.

"Com got through," the runner gasped, and Emilio kept running, the slanted margins of the road, up the tree-curtained windings until he saw the trucks and people massed about them. He circled through the trees and worked his way through the crowd, which broke to let him, toward the lead truck, where Jim Ernst sat with the com and the generator. He scrambled up onto the bed, among the baggage and the bales and the older folk who had not walked, worked his way through to the place where Ernst sat, stood still as Ernst turned to him with one hand pressing the plug to his ear and a look in his eyes that promised nothing but pain.

"Dead," Ernst said. "Your father . . . riot on the station."

"My mother and brother?"

"No word. No word on any other casualties. Military's sending. Mazian's Fleet. Wants contact with us. Do I answer?"

Shaken, he drew in a breath, aware of silence in the nearest crowd, of people staring up at him, of a handful of old Q residents on the truck itself looking at him with eyes as solemn as the hisa images.

Someone else scrambled up onto the truckbed and waded through, flung an arm about him. Miliko. He was grateful . . . shivered slightly with exhaustion and delayed shock. He had anticipated it. It was only confirmation.

"No," he said. "*Don't* answer." A murmur started in the crowd; he turned on it. "No word on any other casualties," he shouted, drowning that in a hurry. "Ernst, tell them what you picked up."

Ernst stood up, told them. He hugged Miliko against him. Miliko's parents and sister were up there, cousins, uncles and aunts. The Dees might survive or, equally, they might die unnoted by the dispatches: there was more hope for the Dees. They were not targets like the Konstantins.

The Fleet had seized control, imposed martial law, Q—Ernst hesitated and doggedly continued, before all the uplifted faces below—Q had rioted and gotten across the line, with widespread destruction and loss of life, stationers and Q both.

One of the old Q residents was crying. Perhaps, Emilio acknowledged painfully, perhaps they too had people for whom to worry.

He looked down on row after row of solemn faces, his own staff, workers, Q, a scattering of hisa. No one moved now. No one said anything. There was only the wind in the leaves overhead and the rush of the river beyond the trees.

"So they're going to be here," he said, trying to keep his

voice steady, "they're going to be back here wanting us to grow crops for them and work the mills and the wells; and Company and Union are going to fight back and forth, but it's not Pell anymore, not in their hands, when what we grow can be taken to fill their holds. When our own Fleet comes down here and works us under guns . . . what when Union comes after them? What when they want more work, and more, and there's no more say any of us has in what happens to Downbelow? Go back if you like; work for Porey until Union gets here. But I'm going on."

"Where, sir?" That was the boy—he had forgotten the name—the one Hale had bullied the day of the mutiny. His mother was by him, in the circle of his arm. It was not defiance, but a plain question.

"I don't know," he admitted. "Wherever the hisa can show us that's safe, if there is any such place. To live there. To dig in and live. Grow our crops for ourselves."

A murmur ran among them. Fear . . . was always at the back of things for those who did not know Downbelow, fear of the land, of places where man was a minority. Men who were unconcerned by hisa on-station grew afraid of them in the open land, where men were dependent and hisa were not. A lost breather, a failure . . . they died of such things on Downbelow. The cemetery back at main base had grown as the camp did.

"No hisa," he said again, "ever harmed a human. And that despite things we've done, despite that we're the aliens here." He climbed down from the truck, hit the yielding ruts of the road, lifted his hands for Miliko, knowing she at least was with him. She jumped down, and questioned nothing. "We can set you up in the camp back there," he said. "Do that much for you at least, those of you that want to take your chances with Porey. Get the compressors running for you."

"Mr. Konstantin."

He looked up. It was one of the oldest women, from the truckbed.

"Mr. Konstantin, I'm too old to work like that back there. I don't want to stay behind."

"Lot of us going on," a male voice said.

"*Anyone* going back?" one of the Q foremen asked. "We need to send one of the trucks back with anyone?"

There was silence. Shaking of heads. Emilio stared at

the lot of them, simply tired. "Bounder," he said, looking to one of the hisa who waited by the forest edge. "Where is Bounder? I need him."

Bounder came, out from among the trees, on the slope of the hill. "You come," Bounder shouted down, beckoning up toward the hill and the trees. "All come now."

"Bounder, we're tired. And we need the things on the trucks. If we go that way we can't take the trucks and some of us aren't able to walk. Some are sick, Bounder."

"We carry sick, many, many hisa. We steal good things on trucks, teach we good, Konstantin-man. We steal for you. You come."

He looked back at the others, at dismayed and doubtful faces.

Hisa surrounded them. More and more came out of the woods, even some with young, which humans rarely saw. It was trust, that such came out among them. All of the company sensed it, perhaps, for there was no protest. They helped the old and the unwell down from the trucks. Strong young hisa made slings of their hands for them; others heaved down the supplies and the equipment.

"And what when they get scan after us?" Miliko murmured unhappily. "We've got to get deep cover, fast."

"Takes sensitive scan to tell human from hisa. Maybe they won't find it profitable to go after us . . . yet."

Bounder reached him, took his hand, wrinkled his nose at him in a hisa wink. "You come with."

They were not good for a long walk, however much the news had put the strength of fright into them. A little while climbing uphill and down through woods and bracken and they were all panting and some being carried who had started out walking. A little more and the hisa themselves began to slow the pace. And at length, when the number of humans they were having to carry grew more than they could manage, they called halt and themselves stretched out to sleep in the bracken.

"Find cover," Emilio urged Bounder. "Ships will see us, not good, Bounder."

"Sleep now," Bounder said, curling up, and nothing would stir him or the others. Emilio sat staring at him helplessly, looked out over all the hillside while humans and hisa lay down where they had dropped their bundles, curled up in their blankets some of them, others them too weary to spread them. He used his own for a pillow, lay down on Miliko's, gathered her against him there under the sun that slanted down through the leaves. Bounder snuggled up to them and put an arm about him. He let himself go, slept, a weary, healthy sleep.

And he waked with Bounder shaking him and Miliko squatting with her arms across her knees, with a light fog moistening the leaves, late, late day, and cloud, and threatening rainfall. "Emilio. I think you should wake up. I think it's some very important hisa."

He rolled onto the other arm, gathered himself to his knees, squinting in the cold mist as other humans were waking all about him. They were Old Ones who had come from among the trees, hisa with white abundantly salting their fur, three of them. He rose and bowed to them, which seemed right, in their land and in their woods.

Bounder bowed and bobbed and seemed more sober than he was wont. "No talk human talk, they," Bounder said. "They say come with."

"We're coming," he said. "Miliko, rouse them out."

She went, with quiet words spoke to the few still sleeping, and the word ran through all the number down the hill, weary, damp humans gathering up their baggage and their persons. There were even more hisa arriving. The woods seemed alive with them, every trunk in the woods likely to conceal a flitting brown body.

The Old Ones melted off through the woods. Bounder delayed until they were ready, and then started off, and Emilio took Miliko's blanket roll on his own shoulder and followed after.

At any hint of a human limping as they went, brushing through damp leaves and dripping branches, there were hisa to help, hisa to take them by the hand and chatter sympathetically, even those who could not understand human speech; after them came others, hisa thieves, bearing the inflatable dome and the compressors and the generators and their food and whatever else they could strip from the trucks, whether or not they themselves could possibly understand the use of it, like a brown horde of scavenger insects.

Night came on them, and much of it they walked, resting when they must, stringing through the wood, but hisa guided them so that none might stray, and snuggled close about them when they stopped so that the chill was not so bad.

And once there was a thunder in the heavens that had nothing to do with the rain.

"Landing," the word passed from one to the other. The hisa asked no questions. Their keen ears might have picked it up long ago.

Porey was back. It would probably be Porey. For a little time they would probe the stripped base and send angry messages up to Mazian. Would have to get scan information, decide what they were going to do about it and get Mazian's decision on it . . . all time consumed to their good.

Rest and walk, rest and walk, and whenever they would falter, the gentle Downers were there to touch, to urge, to cajole. It was cold when they stopped, and damp, though the rain never fell; and they were glad of morning, the first appearance of the light sifting through the trees, which the Downers greeted with trills and chattering and renewed enthusiasm.

And suddenly they were running out of trees, and the daylight broke clearer and clearer, on a hillside sloping down to a vast plain. The far distance spread before them as they came over the crest of a small rise, and the hisa were going farther, going from the trees, into that wide valley . . . that sanctuary, Emilio realized in sudden disturbance, that area the hisa had always asked remain theirs, free of men, a vast open range only theirs, forever.

"No," Emilio protested, looking about for Bounder. He made a gesture of appeal to him, who swung along with a cheerful step nearby. "No. Bounder, we mustn't go down into the open land. Mustn't. Can't, hear? The men-with-guns, they come in ships; their eyes will see."

"Old Ones say come," Bounder declared, never breaking stride, as if that settled it beyond argument. Already the descent began, all the hisa rolling like a brown tide from the trees, bearing humans and human baggage with them, followed by other humans and others, toward the beckoning sunlit pallor of the plain.

"Bounder!" Emilio stopped, with Miliko beside him. "The men-with-guns will find us here. You understand me, Bounder?"

"I understand. See we all, hisa, humans. We see they too."

"We can't go down there. They'll *kill* us, do you hear me?"

"*They* say come."

The Old Ones. Bounder turned away from him and continued downslope, turned again as he walked and beckoned him and Miliko.

He took a step and another, knowing it was mad, knowing that there was a hisa way of doing things and a human. Hisa had never lifted hands against the invaders of their world, had sat, had watched, and this was what they would do now. Humans had asked hisa for their help and hisa offered them their way. "I'll talk to them," he said to Miliko. "I'll talk to their Old Ones, explain to them. We can't offend them, but they'll listen—Bounder, Bounder, wait."

But Bounder walked on, ahead of them. The hisa kept moving, flowing down that vast grassy slope to the plain. At the center of it, where a stream seemed to flow, was something like an upthrust fist of rock and a trampled circle, a shadow, that he realized finally as a circle of living bodies gathered about that object.

"There must be every hisa on the river down there," Miliko said. "It's some sort of meeting place. Some kind of shrine."

"Mazian won't respect it; Union isn't likely to either." He foresaw massacre, disaster, hisa sitting helpless while attack came. It was the Downers, he thought, the Downers themselves whose gentle ways had made Pell what it was. Time was when humans back on Earth had been terrified at the report of alien life. There had been talk of disbanding colonies even then, for fear of other discoveries . . . but no terror on Downbelow, never here, where hisa walked empty-handed to meet humans, and infected men with trust.

"We've got to persuade them to get out of here," he said.

"I'm with you," Miliko said.

"Help you?" a hisa asked, touching Miliko's hand, for she was limping as she leaned on him. They both shook their heads and kept walking together, at the back of the flow now, for most of the others had gone ahead, caught up in the general madness, even the old, borne in the hands of the hisa.

They rested in their long descent, while the sun passed zenith, walked and rested and walked more, while the sun slid down the sky and shone beyond the low rounded hills. A cylinder gave out in his mask, ruined by the moisture and the forest molds, ill augury for the others. He gasped against the obstruction, fumbled after another, held his breath while he did the exchange and slipped the mask back on. They walked, slowly now, on the plain.

In the distance rose that indistinct fish-shaped mass, an irregular pillar, out of a sea of hisa bodies . . . and not alone hisa. Humans were there, who rose up from where they sat and walked out to meet them as they came through. Ito of base two was there, with her staff and workers, and Jones of base one, with his, who offered hands to shake, who looked as bewildered as they were. "They said come here," Ito said. "They said you would come."

"Station's fallen," he said; and the flow was going on, passing through toward the center, hisa urging at him, at him and Miliko most of all. "We've run out of options, Ito. Mazian's in control . . . this week. I can't speak for next."

Ito fell behind, and Jones, staying with their own people; and there were other humans, hundreds upon hundreds gathered there, who stood solemnly, as if numb. He met Deacon of the wells crew; and Macdonald of base three; Hebert and Tausch of four; but the hisa swept him on, and he held Miliko's hand so they should not be separated in the vast throng. Now there were hisa about them, only hisa. The pillar hove up nearer and nearer, and not a pillar, but a cluster of images, like those hisa had given to the station, squat, globular forms and taller ones, bodies with multiple hisa faces, surprised mouths and wide, graven eyes looking forever skyward.

Hisa had made the like, and it was old. Awe came over him. Miliko slowed at last and simply gazed up, and he did, with hisa all about them, feeling lost and small and alien before this towering, ancient stone.

"You come," a hisa voice bade him. It was Bounder who took his hand, who led them through to the very foot of the image.

Old Ones indeed sat there, the oldest hisa of all, those faces and shoulders were silvered, who sat surrounded by small sticks thrust into the earth, sticks carved with faces and hung with beads. Emilio hesitated, reluctant to intrude within that circle; but Bounder led them through, into the very presence of the Old Ones.

"Sit," Bounder urged. Emilio made his bow and Miliko hers, and settled cross-legged before the four elders. Bounder spoke in the chattering hisa tongue, was answered by the frailest of the four.

And carefully then that Old One reached, leaning on one hand, to touch first Miliko and then him, as if blessing them.

"You good come here," Bounder said, perhaps a translation. "You warm come here."

"Bounder, thank them. Thank them very many thanks. But tell them that there's danger from the Upabove. That the eyes of Upabove look down on this place and that men-with-guns may come here and do hurt."

Bounder spoke. Four pairs of aged eyes regarded them with no less tranquility. One answered.

"Ship come upabove we heads here," Bounder said. "Come, look, go away."

"You're in danger. Please make them understand that."

Bounder translated. The Eldest lifted a hand toward the images which towered above them and answered. "Hisa place. Night come. We sleep, dream they go, dream they go."

A second of the elders spoke. There was a human name amid it: Bennett; and another: Lukas. "Bennett," those nearest echoed. "Bennett. Bennett. Bennett."

The murmur passed the limits of the circle, moved like wind across the vast gathering.

"We steal food," Bounder said with a hisa grin. "We learn steal good. We steal you, make you safe."

"Guns," Miliko protested. "Guns, Bounder."

"You safe." Bounder paused to catch something one of the Old Ones said. "Make you names: call you He-come-again; call you She-hold-out-hands. To-he-me; Mihan-tisar. You spirit good. You safe come here. Love you. Bennett-man, he teach we dream human dreams; now you come we teach you hisa dreams. We love you, love you, To-he-me, Mihan-tisar."

He found nothing to say, only looked up at the vast images that stared round-eyed at the heavens, stared about him at the gathering which seemed to stretch to all the horizons, and for a moment he found himself believing that it was possible, that this overawing place might daunt any enemy who came to it.

A chant began from the Old Ones, spread to the nearest, and to the farther and farther ranks. Bodies began to sway, passing into the rhythm of it.

"Bennett . . ." it breathed again and again.

"He teach we dream human dreams . . . call you He-come-again."

Emilio shivered, reached and put his arm about Miliko, in the mind-numbing whisper which was like the brush of a hammer over bronze, the sighing of some vast instrument which filled all the twilit heavens.

The sun declined to the last. The passing of the light brought chill, and a sigh from uncounted throats, breaking off the song. Then the coming of the stars drew pointing gestures aloft, soft cries of joy.

"Name she She-come-first," Bounder told them, and called for them the stars in turn, as keen hisa eyes spied them and hailed them like returning friends. Walk-together; Come-in-spring; She-always-dance . . .

The chant whispered to life again, minor key, and bodies swayed.

Exhaustion told on them. Miliko grew glassy-eyed; he tried to hold her, to stay awake himself, but hisa were nodding too, and Bounder patted them, made them know it was accepted to rest.

He slept, wakened after a time, and food and drink were set beside them. He moved the mask to eat and drink, ate and breathed in alternation. Elsewhere the few awake stirred about among the sleeping multitudes, and for all the dreambound peace of the hour, attended normal needs. He felt his own, and slipped far away through the vast, vast crowd to the edges, where other humans slept and beyond, where hisa had made neat trenches for sanitation. He stood there a time on the edges of the camp, until others came and he regained his sense of time, staring back at the images and the starry sky and the sleeping throng.

Hisa answer. Being here, sitting here beneath the heavens, saying to the sky and their gods . . . see us . . . We have hope. He knew himself mad; and stopped being afraid for himself, even for Miliko. They waited for a dream, all of them; and if men would turn guns on the gentle dreamers of Downbelow, then there was no more hope at all. So the hisa had disarmed them at the beginning . . . with empty hands.

He walked back, toward Miliko, toward Bounder, and the Old Ones, believing in a curious way that they were safe, in ways that had nothing to do with life and death, that this place had been here for ages, and had waited long before men had come, looking to the heavens.

He settled beside Miliko, lay and looked at the stars, and thought of his choices.

And in the morning a ship came down.

There was no panic among the tens of thousands of hisa. There was none among humans, who sat among them. Emilio rose with Miliko's hand in his and watched the ship settle, landing probe, far across the valley, where it could find clear ground.

"I should go speak to them," he said through Bounder to the Old Ones.

"No talk," The Eldest answered through him. "Wait. Dream."

"I wonder," Miliko observed placidly, "if they really want to take on all Downbelow in their situation up on station."

Other humans had stood up. Emilio sat down with Miliko, and all across the gathering they began to settle back again, to sit, and to wait.

And after a long time there was the distant hail of a loudspeaker.

*"There are humans here,"* the metallic voice thundered across the plain. *"We are from the carrier* Africa. *Will the one in charge please come forward and identify himself."*

"Don't," Miliko begged him when he shifted to get up. "They could shoot."

"They could shoot if I don't go talk to them. Right into this crowd. They've got us."

*"Is Emilio Konstantin there? I have news for him."*

"We know your news," he muttered, and when Miliko started to get up he held her arms. "Miliko—I'm going to ask something of you."

"No."

"Stay here. I'm going to go; that's what they'll want—the base working again. I'm going to leave those that won't fare well under Porey; most of us. I need you here, in charge of them."

"An excuse."

"No. And yes. To run this. To fight a war if it comes to that. To stay with the hisa and warn them and keep foreigners off this world. Who else could I trust to do that? Who else will the hisa understand as they do you and me? The other staff?" He shook his head, stared into her dark eyes. "There's a way to fight. As the hisa do. And I'm going back, if that's what they ask. Do you think I want to leave you? But who else is there to do it? Do it for me."

"I understand you," she said hoarsely. He stood up. She did, and hugged and kissed him for such a long moment that he found it harder than it had been before to leave. But she let go then. He took his gun from his pocket, gave it to her. He could hear the noise of the loudspeaker again. They were being hailed, message repeated. *"Staff!"* he shouted out across the gathering. "Shout it across. I want some volunteers."

The cry went out. They came, wading through from the farthest edge of the gathering, from one base command and the next, and main base. It took time. The troops who had advanced within hail on the other side waited, for surely they could see the movement, and time and force were on their side.

He had his staffers turn their backs to that direction and crowd close, reckoning that they might have scopes on them. Hisa in the vicinity looked up, round-eyed and interested.

"They want bodies," he said softly. "And the sabotage fixed. That's all they can be here for. Strong backs. Supply list taken care of. Perhaps all that interests them is main base, because they can't use the others. I don't think we can ask Q to go back and take more of what we took from Porey before we walked out. It's a question of time, of holding out, of having men enough so we can stop some move against Downbelow—or maybe just of living. You understand me. It's my guess they want their ships provisioned and they want station supplied; and while they get that—we save something. We wait for things to sort themselves out on-station, and we save what we can. I want the biggest men from each unit, the strongest constitutions, those who can do most and take most and hold their tempers . . . field labor, not knowing what else. Maybe impressment. We don't know. Need about sixty men from each base, about all they can take with them, I'll reckon."

"You going?"

He nodded. There were reluctant nods in turn from Jones and other staffers. "I'll go," Ito said; all the other base officers had volunteered. He shook his head at her. "Not in this," he said. "Women all stay here under Miliko's command. All. No argument. Fan out and pass the word. About sixty volunteers from each base. Hurry about it. They won't wait forever out there."

They dispersed, running.

"*Konstantin,*" the metallic voice said again. He looked that way, made out the armored figures far across the seated gathering. Reckoned that they did have a scope and saw him plainly. "*We're running out of patience.*"

He delayed kissing Miliko yet again, heard Bounder nearby translating a steady flow to the Old Ones. He started through the camp in the direction of the troops. Others began to walk through the seated hisa, coming to join with him.

And not alone staffers and resident workers. Men from Q came, as many as the residents. He reached the edge of the gathering and found that Bounder was behind him, with a number of the biggest hisa males.

"You don't have to go," he told them.

"Friend," Bounder said. The men from Q said nothing, but they showed no inclination to turn back.

"Thanks," he said.

They were within clear sight of the troops now, at the very edge of the gathering. *Africa* troops indeed; he could make out the lettering. "*Konstantin,*" the officer said over the loudspeaker. "*Who sabotaged the base?*"

"I ordered it," he shouted back. "How was I to know we'd have Union down here? It's fixable. Got the parts. I take it you want us back."

"*What do you have going on here, Konstantin?*"

"Holy place. Sanctuary. You'll find it marked Restricted on the charts. I've got a crew together. We're ready to go back, repair the machinery. We leave our sick with the hisa. Open up main base only until we know the attack alert is firmly off up there. Those other bases are experimental and agricultural and produce nothing useful to you. This crew is sufficient to handle main base."

*"You making conditions again, Konstantin?"*

"You get us back to main base and have your supply lists ready; we'll see you get what you need, quickly and without fuss. That way both our interests are protected. Hisa workers will be cooperating with us. You'll get everything you want."

There was silence from the other side. No one moved for a moment.

*"You get those missing machine parts, Mr. Konstantin."*

He turned, made a move of his hand. One of his own staff, Haynes, went treading back, gathering up four of the men.

*"If you're missing anything, don't look for patience, Mr. Konstantin."*

He did not move. His staff had heard. It was enough. He stood facing the detail—ten of them, with rifles—and beyond them sat the landing probe, bristling with weapons, some aimed this way; with other troops standing by the open hatch. Silence persisted. Perhaps he was supposed now to ask news, to succumb to shock, learning of murder, of the death of his family. He ached to know, and would not ask. He made no move.

*"Mr. Konstantin, your father is dead; your brother presumed dead; your mother remains alive in a security-sealed area under protective custody. Captain Mazian sends his regrets."*

Anger heated his face, rage at the tormenting. He had asked for self-control from those who would go with him. He stood rock-still, waiting for the return of Haynes and the others.

*"Did you understand me, Mr. Konstantin?"*

"My compliments," he said, "to captain Mazian and to captain Porey."

There was silence then. They waited. Eventually Haynes and the others came back, carrying a great deal of equipment. "Bounder," he said quietly, looking at the hisa who stood near with his fellows. "Better you walk to the base if you come. Men go on the ship, hear. Men-with-guns are there. Hisa can walk."

"Go quick," Bounder agreed.

*"Come ahead, Mr. Konstantin."*

He walked forward, quietly, ahead of the others. The troops moved to one side, to guard their progress with lowered rifles. And softly, at first, like a breeze, a murmur, a chant rose from the multitude about the pillar.

It swelled until it shook the air. Emilio glanced back, fearful of the reaction of the troops. They stood by, unmoving, rifles in hand. They could not but feel suddenly very few, for all their armor and their weapons.

The chant kept up, a hysteria, an element in which they moved. Thousands of hisa bodies swayed to that song, as they had swayed beneath the night sky.

He-come-again. *He-come-again.*

They heard it as they approached the ship, with the hold gaping open and more troops to surround them. It was a sound to shake even the Upabove, when messages passed . . . something the new owners could not enjoy hearing. He was swept along in the power of it, thinking of Miliko, of his family murdered . . . What he had lost he had lost, and he went empty-handed, as the hisa went, to the invaders.

# BOOK FIVE

# 1

## Pell: Blue Dock: Aboard ECS 1 Europe; 11/29/52

Signy leaned back in her chair at *Europe*'s council table, shut her eyes a moment, propped her feet in the seat of the chair next to her. The peace was short-lived. Tom Edger showed up, with Edo Porey, and they took their places at the table. She opened one eye and then the other, arms still folded across her middle. Edger had sat down at her back, Porey in the seat one removed from her feet. She yielded wearily to courtesies, swung her feet to the floor and leaned against the table, staring dully at the far wall, out of sorts for conversation. Keu came in and sat down, and Mika Kreshov came at his heels, took the seat between her and Porey. Sung's *Pacific* was still out on patrol, with the unfortunate rider-captains of all the ships deployed under his command in perpetual duty, docking in shifts to change crews. They would not let down their guard, however long the siege became. There had been no word of the Union ships they knew were out there. There was one ship, a mote called *Hammer,* a merchanter they were sure was no merchanter at all, which hung at the edge of the system broadcasting propaganda . . . and long-hauler that it was, it could jump faster than they could get a ship within striking range of it. A spotter. They knew it. There might be another, a ship named *Swan's Eye,* a merchanter like *Hammer* which did no merchanting at all, and another whose name they did not know, a ghost that kept showing up on longscan and drifting out again, that might well be a Union warship—or more than one of them. The short-haulers who remained in the system kept the mines going, stayed far from Pell and far from what was going on about the rim, desperate merchanters pursuing their own concerns without acknowledging the whole grim business, the absence of the longhaulers, the fleet ghosting about the system rim, the spotter ships that kept an eye on them, the whole situation.

So did the station, attempting normalcy in some of its sections, with on-duty troopers and libertied troops moving among them. Fleet command had had to give the liberties. There was no keeping troops or crews pent up for months at dock, within arm's reach of the luxuries of Pell, when the living space on the carriers was spartan and crowded during prolonged dock.

And that had its peculiar difficulties.

Mazian came in, immaculate as usual. Sat down. Spread papers before him on the table . . . looked about him. Lingered last and longest on Signy. "Captain Mallory. I think your report had best come first."

She reached unhurriedly for the papers in front of her, stood up at her place, that being her option. "On 11/28/52 at 2314 hours I entered number 0878 blue of this station, a residential number in a restricted section, acting on a rumor which had reached my desk, having in company my troop commander, Maj. Dison Janz, and twenty armed troops from my command. I there discovered Trooper Lt. Benjamin Goforth, Trooper Sgt. Bila Mysos, both of *Europe,* and fourteen other individuals of the troops in occupancy of this four-room apartment. There were drugs in evidence, and liquor. The troops and officers in the apartment verbally protested our entry and our intervention, but privates Mila Erton and Tomas Centia were intoxicated to such an extent that they were incapable of recognizing authority. I ordered a search of the premises, during which were discovered four other individuals, male aged twenty-four; male aged thirty-one; male aged twenty-nine; female aged nineteen, civilians; in a state of undress and showing marks of burns and other abuses, locked in a room. In a second room were crates which contained liquor and medicines taken from the station pharmacy and so labeled; along with a box containing a hundred thirteen items of jewelry, and another containing one hundred fifty-eight sets of Pell civilian ID's and credit cards. There was also a written record which I have appended to the report listing items of value and fifty-two crew and troops of the Fleet other than those present on the premises with certain items of value by the names. I confronted Lt. Benjamin Goforth with these findings and asked for his explanation of the circumstances. His words were: If you want a cut, there's no need for this commotion. What share will it take to satisfy you? Myself: Mr. Goforth, you're under arrest; you and your associates will be turned over to your captains for punishment; a tape is being made and will be used in prosecution. Lt. Goforth: Bloody bitch. Bloody bastard bitch. Name your share. At this point I ceased argument with Lt. Goforth and shot him in the belly. The tape will show that complaint from his companions ceased at the same moment. My troops arrested them without further incident and returned them to the carrier *Europe*, where they remain in custody. Lt. Goforth died on the premises after giving a detailed confession, which is appended. I ordered items in the apartment delivered to *Europe*, which has been done. I ordered the Pell civilians released after intensive identification procedures, with a strong warning that they would be arrested if any details of this matter became public knowledge. I returned the apartment to station files after it was completely cleared. End of report. Appendices follow."

Mazian had not ceased to frown. "To your observation was Lt. Goforth intoxicated?"

"To my observation he had been drinking."

He waved his hand slightly, an indication for her to sit down. She did so, leaned back with a scowl on her face. "You neglect to account for your specific reason for this execution. I'd prefer it stated for clarity's sake."

"It was refusal to acknowledge an arrest not only by a troop major, but by a captain of the Fleet. His action was public. My answer was equally so."

Mazian nodded slowly, still grim. "I valued Lt. Goforth; and, in the normal practice of the Fleet, captain Mallory, there is a certain understanding that troops are not subject to the stricter disciplines of crew. This . . . execution, captain, places a severe burden on other captains now called upon to follow up this extreme penalty with decisions of their own. You force them to support your harshness against their own troops and crew . . . or to disagree openly by dismissing troops with the reprimand that such activities would normally merit; and thereby seem lax."

"The issue, sir, is refusal of an order."

"So noted and that will be the complaint lodged. Those troops determined in court-martial to have participated in that refusal will be dealt with by the severest penalties; bystanders will be faced with lesser charges and dismissed."

"Charges of willful and knowledgeable breach of security and contributing to a hazardous situation. I'm making progress with the new card system, sir, but the old ones are still valid in major areas of the station, and the personnel in that apartment were directly engaged in black-market traffic in ID's to the detriment of my operations."

The others murmured protests, and Mazian's frown grew darker. "You were faced with an immediate situation that may have had no other answer than the one you gave. But I would point out to you, Captain Mallory, that there are other interpretations that affect morale in this Fleet: the fact that there were no *Norway* personnel arrested, and none on the infamous list. It could be pointed out that this was a case of a rumor deliberately leaked to you by some rival interest among your own troops."

"There were no *Norway* personnel involved."

"You were operating outside the province of your own administration. Internal security is captain Keu's operation. Why was he not advised before this raid?"

"Because *India* troops were involved." She looked directly at Keu's frowning face, and at the others, and back at Mazian. "It did not look to be a major operation."

"Yet your own troops escaped the net."

"Were not involved, sir."

There was stark silence for a moment. "You're rather righteous, aren't you?"

She leaned forward, arms on the table, and gave Mazian stare for stare. "I don't permit my troops to sleepover on-station, and I keep strict account of their whereabouts. I knew where they were. And there are no *Norway* personnel involved in the market. While I'm being called to account, I'd also like to make a point: I disapproved of the general liberties when they were first proposed and I'd like to see the policy reviewed. Disciplined troops are overworked on the one hand and overlibertied on the other—stand them till they're falling down tired and liberty them till they're falling down drunk—that's the present policy, *which* I have not permitted among my own personnel. Watches are relieved at reasonable hours and liberties are confined to that narrow stretch of dock under direct observation of my own officers for the very brief time they're allowed at all. And *Norway* personnel were not involved in this situation."

Mazian glared. She watched the steady flare of his nostrils. "We go back a long way, Mallory. You've always been a bloody-handed tyrant. That's the name you've gotten. You know that."

"That's quite possible."

"Shot some of your own troops at Eridu. Ordered one unit to open fire on another."

"*Norway* has its standards."

Mazian sucked in a breath. "So do other ships, captain. Your policies may work on *Norway,* but our separate commands make different demands. Working independently is something we excel at; we've done it too long. Now *I* have the responsibility of welding the Fleet back together and making it work. I have the kind of independent bloody-mindedness that hung *Tibet* and *North Pole* out there instead of moving in as sense should have told them. Two ships *dead,* Mallory. Now you've handed me a situation where one ship holds itself distinct from others and then pulls an independent raid on an admittedly illicit activity involving every other crew in the Fleet. There's some talk that there was a second page to that List, do you know that? That it was destroyed. This is a morale problem. Do you appreciate that?"

"I perceive the problem; I regret it; I deny that there was a destroyed page and I resent the implication that my troops were motivated by jealousy in reporting this situation. It casts them in a light I refuse to accept."

"*Norway* troops will follow the same schedule hereafter as the rest of the Fleet."

She sat back. "I find a policy which gives us mutiny, and now I'm ordered to imitate it?"

"The destructive thing at work in this company, Mallory, is not the small amount of black marketing that's bound to go on, that realistically goes on every time we have troops offship, but the assumption of one officer and one ship that it can do as it pleases and act in rivalry to other ships. Divisiveness. We can't afford it, Mallory, and

I refuse to tolerate it, under any name. There's one commander over this Fleet . . . or are you setting yourself up as the opposition party?"

"I accept the order," she muttered. Mazian's pride, Mazian's ever-so-sensitive pride. They had come to the line that was not to be crossed, when his eyes took on that look. She felt sick at her stomach, boiling with the urge to break something. She settled quietly back into her chair.

"The morale problem does exist," Mazian went on, easier, himself settling back with one of those loose, theatrical gestures he used to dismiss what he had determined not to argue. "It's unfair to lay it to *Norway* alone. Forgive me. I realize you're a good deal right . . . but we're all laboring under a difficult situation. Union is out there. We know it. Pell knows it. Certainly the troops know it, and they don't know all that we know, and it eats at their nerves. They take their pleasures as they can. They see a less than optimum situation on the station: shortages, a rampant black market—civilian hostility, most of all. They're not in touch with operations we're taking to remedy the situation. And even if they were, there's still the Union fleet, sitting out there waiting its moment to attack; there's a known Union spotter out there we can't do anything about. Not even the normalcy of dock traffic on this station. We're beginning to go for each others' throats . . . and isn't that precisely what Union hopes for, that just by keeping us here without exit we'll rot away? They don't want to meet us in open conflict; that's expensive, even if they push us out. And they don't want to take the chance of us scattering and returning to a guerrilla operation . . . because there's Cyteen, isn't there; there's their capital, all too vulnerable if one of us decides to hit it at cost. They know what they've got on their hands if we slip out of here. So they sit. They keep us uncertain. They hope we'll stay here in false hope and they offer us just tranquility enough to make it worth our while not to budge. They gamble; probably they're gathering forces, now that they know where we are. And they're right . . . we need the rest and the refuge. It's the worst thing for the troops, but how else do we manage? We have a problem. And I propose to give our erring troops a taste of trouble, something to wake them up and persuade them there's still action at hand. We're going after some of the supplies Pell is short on. The short-haulers staying so carefully out of our way . . . can't run far or fast. And the mines have other items, the supplies supporting them. We're going to send a second carrier out on patrol."

"After what happened to *North Pole*—" Kreshov muttered.

"With due caution. We keep all the station-side carriers at ready and we don't stray too far from cover. There's a course which can put a carrier near the mines and not take it far out of shelter. Kreshov, with your admirable sense of caution, let that be your task. Get the supplies we need and teach a few lessons if necessary. A little aggressive action on our part will satisfy the troops and improve morale."

Signy bit her lip, gnawed at it, finally leaned forward. "I volunteer for that one. Let Kreshov sit it out."

"No," Mazian said, and quickly held up a pacifying hand. "Not with any disparagement, far from it. Your work here is vital and you're doing an excellent job at it. *Atlantic* makes the patrol. Herds a few haulers into line and restores station traffic. Blow one if you have to, Mika. You understand that. And pay them in Company scrip."

There was general laughter. Signy stayed sour. "Captain Mallory," Mazian said, "you seem discontent."

"Shootings depress me," she said cynically. "So does piracy."

"Another policy debate?"

"Before taking on any large-scale operations of that kind, I'd like to see some effort toward conscripting the short-haulers, not blowing them. They stood with us against Union."

"Couldn't get out of the way. There's a far difference, Mallory."

"That should be remembered . . . which of them were out there with us. Those ships should be approached differently."

Mazian was not in a mood for listening to her reasons, not today. He had a high flush in his cheeks and his eyes were dark. "Let me get through the orders, old friend. That's taken into consideration. Any merchanter in that category will obtain special privileges when docked at station; and we presume any merchanter in that category will not be among those out there refusing our orders to move in."

She nodded, carefully erased the resentment from her face. There was danger in upstaging Mazian. He had an enormous vanity. It overbalanced his better qualities on occasion. He would *do* what was sensible. He always had. But sometimes the anger lingered—long.

"I'd like to point out," Porey's deep voice interjected, "contrary to captain Mallory's expectations of local help, we have a problem case in the Downbelow operation. Emilio Konstantin snaps his fingers and gets what he wants out of his workers down there. It gets us the supplies we need and we put up with it. But he's waiting. He's just waiting; and he knows right now he's a necessity. If we get those short-haulers involved at station we've got other potential Konstantin types, only they'll be up here with us, berthed right beside our ships."

"They're not likely to jeopardize Pell," Keu said.

"And what if one of them is Unionist? We know well enough that they've infiltrated the merchanters."

"It's a point worth considering," Mazian said. "I've thought about it . . . which is one reason, captain Mallory, why I'm reluctant to take strong steps to recruit those haulers. There are potential problems. But we need the supplies, and some of them aren't available elsewhere. We put up with what we have to."

"So we make an example," Kreshov said. "Shoot the bastard. He's trouble waiting to happen."

"Right now," Porey said slowly, "Konstantin and his crew work eighteen hours a day . . . efficient work, quick, skilled and smooth. We don't get that by other methods. He gets dealt with when it's workable without him."

"Does he know that?"

Porey shrugged. "I'll tell you the hold we've got on Mr. Emilio Konstantin. Got ourselves a site with a lot of Downers and the rest of the human inhabitants, all in one place. All one target. And he knows it."

Mazian nodded. "Konstantin's a minimal problem. We have worse worries. And that's the second matter on the table. If we can forbear another raid on our own troops . . . I'd rather concentrate on the whereabouts of station-side subversives and fugitive staff."

Signy's face heated. She kept her voice calm. "The new system is moving into full use as quickly as possible. Mr. Lukas is cooperating. We've identified and carded 14,947 individuals as of this morning. That's with a completely new card system and new individual codes with voice locks on some facilities. I'd like better, but Pell units aren't designed for it. If they had been, we wouldn't have had this security problem in the first place."

"And the chances that you may have carded this Jessad person?"

"No. No reasonable likelihood. Most or all of our fugitives are moving into the uncarded areas, where their stolen cards still work . . . for the time being. We'll find them. We've got a sketch of Jessad and actual photos of the others. I estimate another week or two to begin the final push."

"But all the operations areas are secure?"

"The security arrangements for Pell central are laughable. I've made recommendations for construction there."

Mazian nodded. "When we get workers off damage repair. Personnel security?"

"The notable exception is the Downer presence in the sealed area of blue one four. Konstantin's widow. Lukas's sister. She's a hopeless invalid, and the Downers are cooperative in anything while it assures her welfare."

"That's a gap," Mazian said.

"I've got a com link to her. She cooperates fully in dispatching Downers to necessary areas. Right now she's of some use, as her brother is."

"While both are," Mazian said. "Same condition."

There were details, stats, tedious matters which could have been traded back and forth by comp. Signy endured it grimfaced, nursing a headache and a blood pressure that distended the veins in her hands, while she made meticulous notes and contributed stats of her own.

Food; water; machine parts . . . they were taking on a full load, every ship, fit to run again if it came to that. Repairing major damage and going ahead with minor repairs that had been long postponed in the operation leading up to the push. Total refitting, while keeping the Fleet as mobile as possible.

Supply was the overwhelming difficulty. Week by week the hope that the more daring of the long-haulers would come venturing in diminished. They were seven carriers, holding a station and a world, but with only short-haulers to supply them, with their only source of some machined items—the supplies those very haulers had aboard for their own use.

They were pent in, under siege, without merchanters to aid them, the long-haulers who had freely come and gone during the worst of the war. Could not now hope to reach to the Hinder Star stations . . . of which there was precious little remaining, mothballed, stripped, some probably gone unstable—a long, long time without regulation. Warships alone could not do the heavy cross-jump hauling major construction required. Without the long-haul merchanters, Pell was the only working station left them but Sol itself.

Unwelcome thoughts occurred to her as she sat there, as they had been occurring regularly since the Pell operations began to go sour. She looked up from time to time, at Mazian, at Tom Edger's thin, preoccupied face. Edger's *Australia* partnered with *Europe* more often than any other . . . an old, old team. Edger was second in seniority as she was third; but there was a vast gulf between second and third. Edger never spoke in council. Never had a thing to say. Edger did his talking with Mazian in private, sharing counsels, the power at the side of the throne, as it were; she had long suspected so. If there was any man in the room who really knew Mazian's mind, it was Edger.

The only station but Sol.

So they were three who knew, she reckoned glumly, and kept her mouth shut on it. They had come a long way . . . from Company Fleet to this. It was going to be a vast surprise to those Company bastards on Earth and Sol Station, having a war brought to their doorstep . . . having Earth taken as Pell had been. And seven carriers could do it, against a world which had given up starflight, which had, like Pell, only short-haulers and a few in-system fighters at its command . . . with Union coming in on their heels. It was a glass house, Earth. It could not fight . . . and win.

She lost no sleep over it. Did not plan to. More and more she was convinced that the whole Pell operation was busywork, that Mazian might be doing precisely what she had advised all along, keeping the troops busy, keeping even his crews and captains busy, while the real operation here was that on Downbelow and what he proposed with the mines and short-haulers, the gathering of supplies, the repairs, the sorting of station personnel for identification and capture of all those fugitives who might surface and make takeover easy and cheap for Union. Her job.

Only here there were no merchanters to be pressed into duty as transport, and no carrier was going to let itself become a refugee ship. Could not. Had no room. It was no wonder that Mazian was not talking, was refusing to say anything about contingency plans which were, under numerous pretexts, already swinging into operation. A scenario constructed itself: station comp blown, for they had all the new comp keys; Downbelow base thrown into chaos by the elimination of the one man who was holding it together and the execution of all those gathered multitudes of humans and Downers so that Downers would never work for humans again; the station itself thrown into descending orbit; and themselves running for a jump point with a screen of short-haulers that could only serve as navigation hazards. Jump for the Hinder Stars, and in quick succession, for Sol itself—

While Union had to decide whether to save itself a stationful of people and a base, and to battle the chaos on Downbelow which could starve the station out even *with* rescue . . . or to let Pell die and go for a strike unencumbered, having no base behind them closer than Viking . . . a vast, vast distance to Earth.

*Bastard,* she hailed Mazian privately, with a glance under her brows. It was typical of Mazian that he worked moves ahead of the opposition and thought the unthinkable. He was the best. He always had been. She smiled at him when he fed them dry, precise orders about cataloging, and had the satisfaction of seeing the great Mazian for a moment lose the thread of his thought. He recovered it, went on, looked at her from time to time with perplexity and then with greater warmth.

So now assuredly they were three who knew.

"I'll be frank with you," she said to the men and women who assembled kneeling and standing in the lower deck suiting room, the only place on *Norway* she could get most of the troops assembled with an unobstructed view, jammed shoulder to shoulder as they were. "They're not happy with us. Mazian himself isn't happy with the way I've run this ship. Seems none of you is on the List. Seems none of us is involved with the market. Seems other crews are upset with you and me, and there are rumors flying about tampering with the list, about a deliberate tipoff due to some black market rivalry between *Norway* and other ships . . . *Quiet!* So I'm given orders, from the top. You get *liberties,* on that same schedule and on the same terms as other troops; you get *duty* on their schedule too. I'm not going to comment, except to compliment you on doing an excellent job; and to tell you two more things: I felt complimented on behalf of this whole ship that there was not a *Norway* name involved in that blue section mess; second . . . I ask you to avoid argument with other units, whatever rumors are passed and however you're provoked. Apparently there is some hard feeling, for which I take personal responsibility. Apparently . . . well, leave that unsaid. Questions?"

There was deathly silence. No one moved.

"I'll trust you'll pass the news to the incoming watch before I get the chance to do it in person. My apologies, my personal apologies, for what is apparently construed by others as unfairness to the people under my command. Dismissed."

Still no one moved. She turned on her heel, walked away toward the lift, for the main level and her own quarters.

"Vent 'em," a voice muttered audibly in her wake. She stopped dead, with her back to them.

*"Norway!"* someone shouted; and another; "Signy!" In a moment the whole ship echoed.

She started walking again for the open lift, drew a deep breath of satisfaction for all the casual swing to her step. Vent him indeed, if even Conrad Mazian thought he could put his hand to *Norway.* She had started with the troops; Di Janz would have something to say to them too. What threatened *Norway*'s morale threatened lives, threatened the reflexes they had built up over years.

And her pride. That too. Her face was still burning as she strode into the lift and pushed the button. The shouts echoing in the corridors were salve for her pride, which was, she admitted to herself, as vast as Mazian's. Follow orders indeed; but she had calculated the effect on the troops and on her crew; and no one gave her orders regarding what happened within *Norway* itself. Not even Mazian.

# 2

## i

## Pell: sector green nine; 1/6/53

The Downer was with him again, a small brown shadow, not altogether unusual in the traffic in nine. Josh paused in the riot-scarred corridor, put his foot on a molding, pretended to adjust the top of his boot. The Downer touched his arm, wrinkled its nose in bending and peering up at his face. "Konstantin-man all right?"

"All right," he said. It was the one called Bluetooth, who was on their heels almost daily, managing to carry messages to and from Damon's mother. "We've got a good place to hide now. No more trouble. Damon's safe and the man's making no more trouble."

The furred powerful hand sought his, forced an object into it. "You take Konstantin-man? *She* give, say need."

The Downer slipped away in the traffic as quickly as he had come. Josh straightened, resisting the temptation to look about or to look at the metal object until he was some distance down the corridor. It turned out to be a brooch, metal that might be real gold. He pocketed it for the treasure it was to them, something salable on the market, something that needed no card, that would bribe someone unbribable by other means . . . like the owner of their current lodgings. Gold had uses other than jewelry: rare metals were worth lives—the going rate. And the day was coming when it would take greater and greater persuasion to keep Damon hidden. A woman of vast good sense, Damon's mother. She had ears and eyes, in every

Downer who flitted harmlessly through the corridors, and she knew their desperation—offered still a refuge that Damon would not take, because he above all did not want the Downer system subject to search.

The net was closing on them. The area of usable corridors grew less and less. A new system was being installed, new cards, and the sections the troops cleared stayed cleared. Those within a section when the troops sealed it were rounded up, checked against the wanted lists, and given new ID's . . . most of them. Some vanished, period. And the new card system hit the market harder and harder, the nearer it got. The value of cards and papers plummeted, for they would be valid only until the changeover was complete, and people were already getting shy of the old ones. Now and again an alarm went off, silent, somewhere in comp; and troops would come to some establishment and start trace procedure on someone they wanted . . . as if most of the people in unsecure sections were using their own cards. But the troops asked questions and checked ID's when they were roused—kept the areas open to their raids, kept the populace terrorized and suspicious each of the other, and that served Mazian's purpose.

It also gave them a livelihood. It was their stock-in-trade, his and Damon's, the purification of cards. It was their value within the system of the black market. A buyer wanted to check the worth of a stolen card, a new purchaser wanted to be sure that a card would not ring alarms in comp, someone wanted the bank code number to get at assets . . . the bars and sleepovers in the docks did not match up faces and ID's, not at all. And Damon had the access numbers to do it. *He* had learned them too, so that they worked a partnership and neither of them had to venture into the corridors on too regular a basis. They had it down to a science . . . using the Downer tunnels and even crossing through the section barriers—Bluetooth had shown them how—so that no single comp terminal would have a series of inquiries. They had never triggered an alarm, even though some of the cards had been dangerously hot. They were good; they had a trade—ironically of Mazian's creation—which fed and housed and hid them with all the protections the market could offer its valuable operators. He had at the moment a pocketful of cards, each of which he knew by value according to the level of clearance and how much was in the credit account. Nothing in the latter, in most instances. Families of missing persons had gotten wise very quickly, and station comp had taken to honoring family requests that an account be frozen from access by a particular number . . . so rumor ran, and it was probably true. Most cards now were trouble. He had a few useable ones in the lot and a collection of code numbers. Cards which had belonged to single persons or independent accounts were the only ones still good.

But there were omens of more rapid change. It was his imagination, perhaps, but the corridors on all levels of green seemed more crowded today. It might well be so. All those who dared not submit to ID and re-carding had crowded persistently into smaller and smaller spaces . . . green and white remained open sectors, but he personally had gotten nervous about white, not wanting to go into it longer than he must . . . had heard no rumors himself, but there was something in the air, something that reckoned another area was about to go under seal . . . and white was likeliest.

Green was the section with the big concourses, and the fewest troublesome bottlenecks where determined resistance could fight from room to room and hall to hall—if it came to fighting. He rather imagined another end for them, that when all the problems Mazian had on Pell were neatly herded into one last section, they would simply blow it, vent the section with doors wide open, and they would die without appeal and without a chance.

A few crazed souls had gotten pressure suits, the hottest item on the black market, and hovered near them, armed and wild-eyed, hoping to survive against all logic. Most of them simply expected to die. There was a desperate atmosphere in all of green, while those who had finally reconciled themselves to capture voluntarily moved into white. Green and white grew stranger and stranger, with walls graffiti'd with bizarre slogans, some obscene, some religious, some pathetic. *We lived here,* one said. That was all.

All but a very few lights in the corridors had been broken out, so that everything was twilight, and station no longer dimmed lights for mainday/alterday shifts; it would have become dangerously dark. There were some side corridors where all the lights were out, and no one went into those lairs unless he belonged there—or was dragged screaming into them. There were gangs, who fought each other for power. The weaker souls clung to them, paid them all their resources, not to be harmed, and perhaps to have the chance to harm others. Some of the gangs had started in Q. Some were Pell gangs which formed in defense and undertook other business ventures. He feared them indiscriminately, feared their unreasoning violence most of all. He had let his beard grow, let his hair grow, walked with a slouch and acquired as much dirt as possible, changed his face subtly with cosmetic . . . that commodity sold high on the market too. If there was any comedy in this grim place it was that most of these folk hereabouts were doing exactly the same thing, that the section was full of men and women who desperately did not want to be recognized, and who avoided each others' eyes in a perpetual flinching as they walked the halls . . . some who swaggered and tried to threaten, unless troops were at hand . . . more who flitted like downcast ghosts, scurrying along in evident hope no one would set a hue and cry after them.

Perhaps he had changed so much in appearance that no one did recognize him. No one had yet pointed a finger at him or at Damon in public. There was some loyalty left on Pell, perhaps—or their involvement with the market protected them, or others who knew them were just too frightened to start something. Some of the gangs were linked into the market.

Occasional troopers walked in the halls, some back in nine two, no less common than Downers about their business. Green dock was still open as far as the end of white dock; and *Africa* and occasionally *Atlantic* or *Pacific* occupied the first two berths of green, while the other ships berthed in blue dock, and troops came and went freely through the personnel access beside the section seals on that end of green. Troops entered green and white on liberty or on duty, mingling with the condemned . . . and the condemned knowing that all they had to do to escape was to go up to those troops or to the cleared-area access doors and turn themselves in. Some did not believe that the Mazianni would decompress the section, simply because of that close and almost friendly association. Troopers shed their armor on liberty, walked about laughing and human, hung out in the bars . . . staked out a couple of establishments for themselves, it was true . . . but mingled in other bars, turned an occasional benevolent smile on the market.

So much the easier to handle the victims until it came, Josh reckoned. They still had choices left, played the game with the troops, dodged and struggled . . . but all it took was a button pushed somewhere in central, no personal contact, no watching faces as they died. All clinical and distant.

He and Damon planned, wild and futile schemes. Damon's brother was rumored to be alive. They talked of stowing away on one of the shuttles, taking one over, getting to Downbelow and into the bush. They had as likely a chance of stealing a shuttle from armed troops as they did of walking to Downbelow, but the planning occupied their minds and gave them hope.

And more realistic . . . they could try to pass the seals into the cleared sections, and chance the alarm-rigged access doors, regimented security, checkpoints at every corner and card use at every move . . . that was the way of life over there. Mallory's doing. They had been checking it out. *Too many men-with-guns,* was Bluetooth's warning. *Cold they eyes.*

Cold indeed.

And meanwhile there was the market and there was Ngo's.

He approached the bar along green nine, not by the tunnel ways which led to the corridor outside Ngo's back door, for that was for emergencies and Ngo had no love for anyone using the back way without cause . . . wanted no one seen in the main room who had not come in by the front door and wanted no access alarms going off in comp. Ngo's was a place where the market flourished, and as such it tried to be cleaner than most, one of almost a score of bars and entertainment concessions along green dock and the niner access which had once thrived in the traffic of merchanters . . . a line of sleepovers and vid theaters and lounges and restaurants and one anomalous chapel completing the row. Most of the bars were open; the theaters and the chapel and some of the sleepovers were burned out shells, but the bars functioned, most like Ngo's, as restaurants as well, the channels through which station still fed the population, and black-market food augmented what the station was willing to supply.

He cast cautious glances one way and the other as he approached the front and ever-wide door of Ngo's, not obvious looks around, but a rhythm of walking and looking as a man might who was simply making up his mind which bar he wanted.

A face caught his eye, abruptly, heart-stoppingly. He delayed a half a beat and looked toward Mascari's, across the corridor at the emptying of nine onto the docks. A tall man who had been standing there suddenly moved and darted within Mascari's.

Dark obscured his vision, a flash of memory so vivid he staggered and forgot all his pattern. He was vulnerable for that instant, panicked . . . turned for Ngo's doorway blindly and went inside, into the dim light and pounding music and the smells of alcohol and food and the unwashed clientele.

The old man himself was tending bar. Josh went to the counter and leaned there, asked for a bottle. Ngo gave it to him, no asking for his card. That all came later, in the back room. But his hand shook in taking the bottle, and Ngo's quick hand caught his wrist. "Trouble?"

"Close one," he lied . . . and perhaps not a lie. "I got clear. Gang trouble. Don't worry. No one tracked me. Nothing official."

"You better be sure."

"No problem. Nerves. It's nerves." He clutched the bottle and walked away toward the back, stopped a moment against the back doorway that led into the kitchen and waited to be sure his exit was not observed.

One of the Mazianni, maybe. His heart still pounded from the encounter. Someone with Ngo's under surveillance. No. His imagination. The Mazianni did not to need to be so subtle. He unstopped the bottle and drank from it, Downer wine, cheap tranquilizer. He took a second long drink and began to feel better. He experienced such flashes . . . not often. They were always bad. Anything could trigger it, usually some small and silly thing, a smell, a sound, a momentary wrong way of looking at a familiar thing or ordinary person . . . That it should have happened in public—that most disturbed him. It could have attracted notice. Maybe it had. He resolved not to go out again today. Was not sure about tomorrow. He took a third drink and a last look over the patrons at the dozen tables, then slipped back into the kitchen, where Ngo's wife and son were cooking up the orders. He paid them a casual glance, received sullen stares in return, and walked on through to the storeroom.

He pushed the door open on manual. "Damon," he said, and the curtain at the rear of the cabinets opened. Damon came out and sat down among the canisters they used for furniture, in the light of the batteried lamp they used to escape comp's watchful economy and infallible memory. He came and sank down wearily, gave Damon the bottle and Damon took a drink. Unshaven, both of them, with the look of the unwashed, depressed crowds which collected down here.

"You're late," Damon said. "You trying to give me ulcers?"

He fished the cards out of his pocket, arranged them by memory, made quick notes with a grease pencil before he should forget. Damon gave him paper and he wrote the details for each one, and Damon did not talk to him the while.

Then it was done, his memory spilled, and he laid the batch on top of the next canister and reached for the wine bottle. He drank and set it down. "Met Bluetooth. Said your mother's fine. Give you this." He drew the brooch from his pocket and watched as Damon took it into his hands with that melancholy look that told him it might have some meaning beyond the gold itself. Damon nodded glumly and pocketed it; he did not much speak of his family, living or dead, not in reminiscence.

"She knows," Damon said, "she knows what it's coming to. She can see it from her vid screens, hear it from the Downers . . . Did Bluetooth say anything specific?"

"Only that your mother thought we needed it."

"No word of my brother?"

"It didn't come up. We weren't in a place we could talk, the Downer and I."

Damon nodded, drew a deep breath and leaned his elbows on his knees, head bowed. Damon lived for such news. When it failed him his spirits fell, and it hurt. Hurt both of them. He felt as if he had dealt the wound.

"It's getting tight out there," Josh said. "Lots of anxiety. I delayed a little along the way, listening, but no news; everyone's scared but no one knows anything."

Damon lifted his head, took the bottle, drank down half the remaining wine, hardly a swallow. "Whatever we're going to do, we've got to do soon. Either go into the secured sections . . . or try for the shuttle. We can't go on here."

"Or make ourselves a bubble in the tunnels," he said. In his reckoning, it was the only realistic idea. Most humans were pathologically frightened of the tunnels. What few humans who would try them . . . maybe they could fight them off. They had the guns. Might be able to live there. But they were about out of time . . . for any choices. It was not an existence to look forward to. *And maybe we'll be lucky,* he thought miserably, looking at Damon, who looked at the floor, lost in his own thoughts. *Maybe they'll just blow the area.*

The storeroom door opened. Ngo came in on them, walked up and gathered up the cards, read through the notation, pursed his wrinkled mouth and frowned. "You're sure?"

"No mistakes."

Ngo muttered unhappily at the quality of the merchandise, as if they were at fault, started to leave.

"Ngo," Damon said, "heard a rumor the market's going for the new paper. That so?"

"Where did you hear that?"

Damon shrugged. "Two men talking in front. That true, Ngo?"

"They're dreaming. You see a way to get your hands into the new system, you tell me."

"I'm thinking on it."

Ngo muttered to himself and left.

"That so?" Josh asked.

Damon shook his head. "Thought I might jar something loose. Ngo won't shake or there's no way anyone knows."

"I'd bet on the latter."

"So would I." Damon set his hands on his knees, sighed, looked up. "Why don't we go out and get something to eat? No one out there who's trouble, is there?"

The memory which had left him came back with dark force. He opened his mouth to say something, and of a sudden came a rumbling which shook the floor, a boom and crash which overrode screams from outside.

"The *seals,*" Damon exclaimed, on his feet. Cries continued, wild screams, chairs overturning in the front room. Damon rushed for the storeroom door and Josh ran with him, out as far as the back door, where Ngo and his wife and son had scrambled to get out, Ngo with his market records in hand.

"No," Josh exclaimed, "Wait . . . that would have been the doors to white . . . we're sealed—but there were troops up at nine two—they wouldn't have troops in here if they were going to push the button—"

"Com," Ngo's wife exclaimed. There was an announcement coming through the vid unit in the front room. They rushed in that direction, into the restaurant area, where a handful of people were clustered about the vid and a looter was busy gathering an armful of bottles from the bar. *"Hey!"* Ngo shouted in outrage, and the man snatched two more and ran.

It was Jon Lukas on the screen. It always was when Mazian had an official announcement to station. The man had become a skeleton, a pitiable shadow-eyed skeleton. ". . . been sealed off," Lukas was saying. "White-area residents and others who wish to leave will be permitted to leave. Go to the green dock access and you will be permitted to pass."

"They're herding all the undesirables in here," Ngo said. Sweat stood on his wrinkled face. "What about us who work here, Mr. Stationmaster Lukas? What about us honest people caught in here?"

Lukas repeated all the announcement. It was probably a recording; doubtful if they ever let the man on live.

"Come on," Damon said, hooking Josh's arm. They walked out the front door and around the corner onto green dock, walked far along the upward curve, where a great mass of people had gathered looking toward white. They were not the only ones. There were troops, moving out along the far-side wall, by the berths and gantries.

"Going to be shooting," Josh muttered. "Damon, let's get out of here."

"Look at the doors. Look at the doors."

He did look. The massive valves were tightly joined. The personnel access at the side was not open. It did not open.

"They're not going to let them through," Damon said. "It was a lie . . . to get the fugitives to the docks over there."

"Let's get back," Josh pleaded with him.

Someone fired; their side, the troops—a barrage came over their heads and into the shopfronts. People shrieked and shoved, and they fled with it, down the dock, into nine, into Ngo's doorway, while riot surged past and down the hall. A few others tried to follow them, but Ngo rushed up with a stick and fended them off, all the while shrieking curses at the two of them for running in with trouble after them.

They got the door closed, but the crowd outside was more interested in running, the path of least resistance. The room lights came on full, on a room full of tangled chairs and spilled dishes.

In silence Ngo and his family began cleaning up. "Here," Ngo said to Josh, and thrust a wet, stew-soiled rag at him. Ngo turned a second frowning look on Damon, although he did not order: a Konstantin still had some privilege. But Damon started picking up dishes and straightening chairs and mopping with the rest of them.

It grew quiet outside again, with an occasional pounding at the door. Faces stared at them through the plastic window, people simply wanting in, exhausted and frightened people, wanting the service of the place.

Ngo opened the doors, cursed and shouted, let them in, set himself behind the bar and started doling out drinks with no regard to credit for the moment. "You pay," he warned all and sundry. "Just sit down and we'll make out the tickets." Some left without paying; some did sit down. Damon took a bottle of wine and drew Josh to a table in the farthest corner, where there was a short ell. It was their usual place, which had a view of the front door and unobstructed access to the kitchen and their hiding places. The com music channel had come on again, playing something wistfully soothing and romantic.

Josh leaned his head against his hands and wished he dared be drunk. He could not be. There were the dreams. Damon drank. Eventually it seemed to be enough, for

Damon's shadowed eyes had an anesthetized haze which he envied.

"I'm going out tomorrow," Damon said. "I've sat in that hole enough . . . I'm going out, maybe talk to a few people, try to make some contacts. There's got to be someone who hasn't cleared out of green. Someone who still owes my family some favors."

He had tried before. "We'll talk about it," Josh said.

Ngo's son served them dinner, stew, stretched as far as possible. Josh sipped a spoonful of it, nudged Damon with his foot when he sat there. Damon gathered up his spoon and ate, but his mind still seemed elsewhere.

Elene, perhaps. Damon spoke her name sometimes in his sleep. Sometimes his brother's. Or maybe he was thinking of other things, lost friends. People probably dead. He was not going to talk; Josh knew that. They spent long hours in silences, in their separate pasts. He thought of his own happier dreams, pleasant places, a sunlit road, dusty grain fields on Cyteen, people who had loved him, faces that he had known, old friends, old comrades, far from this place. The hours were filled with it, the long, solitary hours each of them spent in hiding, the nights, with music from Ngo's front room jarring the walls most of the hours of mainday and alter-day, numbing, constant, or saccharine and pervasive. They stole sleep in the quiet times, lay listlessly in others. He did not intrude on Damon's fancies, nor Damon on his. Never denied the importance of them, which were the best comfort they had in this place.

One thing they no longer considered, and that was either of them turning himself in. They had Lukas's face before them, that death's-head forewarning of Mazian's dealing with his puppets. If Emilio Konstantin was still alive as rumor said . . . privately Josh wondered if it was good news or bad. And that too he did not say.

"I hear," Damon said finally, "that maybe some of the Mazianni crew are on the take. I wonder if they could be bribed for more than goods. If there are holes in their new system."

"That's crazy. It's not in their interests. It's not a sack of flour you're talking about. Ask *that* kind of question and we'll have them on us."

"Probably you're right."

Josh pushed the bowl back and stared at the rim of it. They were running out of time, that was all. In the sealing of white . . . they were sealed too. All it took now was a sweep starting from the dock or from green one, checking in those who were willing to surrender, shooting down those who were not.

When they had white in order . . . it came. And it was beginning over there. Was already underway.

"I'd have to make the approach to the Fleet," Josh said finally. "The troops would more likely recognize you than me. As long as I stay away from *Norway* troops . . ."

Damon was silent a moment, perhaps weighing odds. "Let me try another thing. Let me think about it. There's got to be a way onto the shuttles. I'm going to check out the dock crews, find out who's working there."

It was not going to work. It had always been a mad idea.

## ii

## Merchanter Finity's End: deep space; 1/6/53

Another merchanter in. Arrivals were not unusual. Elene heard the report and got up from her couch, walked *Finity's* narrow spaces to see what Wes Neihart had on scan.

"What's the deal here?" a thin voice asked in due time. The freighter had jumped in at a respectful distance, fully cautious; it would take her a while to work her way in out of the jump range. Elene sat down at the second seat at the scan, feeling after the cushion. Her thickening body vexed her subconsciously; it was a nuisance she had learned to live with. The baby was kicking, an internal and unpredictable companionship. *Quiet,* she thought at him, winced and concentrated on scan. Other Neiharts moved in to see.

"Someone going to answer me?" the newcomer asked, much closer now.

"Give me ID," said the voice of another ship. "This is *Little Bear,* merchanter. Who are you? Keep coming; just give us ID."

The answer time passed, still shorter now; and other merchanters had started to move. There was a gathering bunch of observers on *Finity*'s bridge.

"Don't like this one," someone muttered.

"This is *Genevieve* out of Unionside, from Fargone.

Rumor has it we've got something going on here. What's the situation?"

"Let me take it," another voice broke in. "*Genevieve,* this is *Pixie II.* Let me talk to the old man, all right, young fellow?"

There was a silence beyond what should have been. Elene's heart started pumping overtime, and she swung about with an awkward and frantic wave at Neihart, but the general alert was already on its way, Neihart passing the signal to his nephew at comp.

"This is Sam Denton on *Genevieve,*" the voice returned.

"Sam, what's my name?"

"Soldiers here," *Genevieve* sputtered, and the voice went off very quickly. Elene reached frantically after com as communications everywhere crackled orders to stand or be fired on.

"*Genevieve. Genevieve,* this is Quen of *Estelle.* Answer."

No one fired. On scan, ships, the hundreds of ships drifting within the null point range, sat reoriented to embrace the intruder.

"This is Union Lt. Marn Oborsk," a voice returned at last. "Aboard *Genevieve.* This ship will destruct before capture. The Dentons are aboard. Confirm your identity. The Quens are dead. *Estelle* is a dead ship. What ship are you?"

"*Genevieve,* you are not in a position to make demands. Put the Dentons off their ship."

Again a long pause. "I want to know who I'm talking to."

She let the silence ride for a moment. About her there was frantic activity on the bridge. Guns were being aimed, the relative positions calculated for speed, drift, and the probable sly use of docking jets to increase it. "This is Quen speaking. We demand you set the Dentons off that ship. We tell you this: that if Union sets its hands on another merchanter, there's going to be the devil let loose. That the port of origin of any ship attacking or appropriating a merchanter vessel will be subject to the full sanctions of our alliance. That's the name of what's going on out here. Look your fill, Lt. Oborsk. We're spreading. We outnumber your warships. If you want a kilo of commerce moved anywhere, from now on you deal with us."

"What ship is speaking?"

They might have started shooting instead of talking. Calm them down; keep them steady. She wiped her face and rolled a glance at Neihart, who nodded: they had them comped. "Quen is all you need to know, lieutenant. You're far outnumbered. How did you find this place? Did you get it out of the Dentons? Or did just the wrong ship contact you? I'll tell you this: the merchanter's alliance will deal as a unit. And if you want real trouble, sir, you go lay hands on another merchanter vessel. You and Mazian's Fleet can do what you like to each other. We're not Company and we're not Union. We're the third side in this triangle and from now on we negotiate in our own name."

"What is in progress here?"

"Are you able to negotiate or carry messages on your side?"

There was long delay.

"Lieutenant," she pursued, "when authorized negotiators are willing to approach us we are fully prepared to talk with you. In the meantime kindly put the Dentons off. If you are willing to talk reasonably you'll find us amiable; if on the other hand . . . harm comes to any merchanter, reprisals will be made for it. And that is a promise."

There was the requisite silence. "This is Sam Denton," another voice said finally. "I'm instructed to tell you that this ship is going to put about and that there is a destruct aboard. Got the whole family on here, Quen. That's truth too."

Of a sudden there was breakup. She flashed a look at vid and telemetry, saw the flare registered, suddenly grow, become a wash there was no mistaking even on vid. Her stomach tightened and the baby moved . . . she put her hand on the spot and stared at the screens in a moment of nausea, while static kept coming in.

A hand descended on her shoulder, Neihart's.

"Who fired?" she asked.

"This is *Pixy II,*" a voice came back, rough and thick. "I did. They were nosing zenith toward the gap; engines flared. They'd have carried out too much."

"We cope, *Pixy.*"

"Going in," another ship sent. "Going to search the area."

There was at least the possibility of a capsule . . . that Union might have allowed the Denton children to shelter there, for safety. There was not much chance that a capsule could have survived that.

Like *Estelle,* at Mariner. Like that. They were not going to find anything.

Other blips were showing up, ghostly presences in the sunless dark of the point, defined only as blips on scan, or by the sometime flick of runnings lights or a shadow on vid, occulting stars. They were friendly—hundreds of ships moving into the search area. "We're in it now," Neihart murmured; "Union won't rest." But they all knew that, from the time the word had gone out, from the time merchanters had begun to pass to merchanters the word where to come and the name that summoned them . . . a dead ship, and a dead name—from a disaster they all knew. Inevitable that Union get wind of it; by now Union was surely noticing the curious absence of ships from their stations, merchanters who did not come in on schedule. They were panicking perhaps, perceiving disappearances in zones where it could not be military action, with Mazian tied up at Pell. Union had appropriated ships—they had proven that—and before this ship came, it might have given its course to others. The next step was a warship sent in here . . . if Union could spare one from Pell.

And the word had not sped only to Union space. It had gone to Sol—for *Winifred* had recalled her Earthly ties, dumped her cargo, ridding herself of mass to jump as far as possible . . . had undertaken that long and uncertain journey to what welcome they did not know. *Tell them about Mariner.* Elene had asked of them. *And Russell's and Viking and Pell. Make them understand.* They did it dutifully, because they had once been Earth's. But it was gesture only. There was no answer coming.

They did not find a capsule, only debris and wreckage.

### iii

### Downbelow: hisa sanctuary 1/6/53; local night

The hisa had been coming and going from the beginning, quiet migration in and out of the gathering at the foot of the images, hushed and sober movement, by ones and twos and reverently, in respect to the dreamers who gathered there by the thousands. By day and by night they had come, carrying food and water, doing small and necessary things.

There were domes for humans now, diggings made by Downer labor, and compressors thumped away with the pulse of life, rude, patched domes unlovely . . . but they gave shelter to the old and to the children, and to all the rest of them as brief summer yielded to fall, as skies clouded and the days full of sun and the nights of stars grew fewer.

Ships overflew them, shuttles on their runs going and coming; they were accustomed to this, and it no longer frightened them.

*You must not gather even the woods,* Miliko had explained to the Old Ones through interpreters. *Their eyes see warm things, even through trees. Deep earth can hide hisa, oh, very deep. But they see even when Sun doesn't shine.*

Downer eyes had gotten very round at that. They had talked among themselves. *Lukases,* they had muttered. But they had seemed to understand.

She had talked day upon day to the Old Ones, talked until she was hoarse and she exhausted her interpreters, tried to make them understand what they faced, and when she would tire, alien hands would pat her arms and her face and round hisa eyes look at her with profound tenderness, all, sometimes, that they could do.

And humans . . . by night she came to them. There was Ito, and Ernst and others, who grew moodier and moodier—Ito because all the other officers had gone with Emilio; and Ernst, a small man, who had not been chosen; and one of the strongest men of all the camps, Ned Cox, who had not volunteered in the first place . . . and began to be ashamed. There was a kind of contagion that spread among them, shame perhaps, when they heard news from main base, that told of nothing but misery. About a hundred sat outside the domes, choosing the cold weather and the reliance on breathers as if by rejecting comfort they proved something to each other and to themselves. They had grown silent, and their eyes were, as the Downers said, bright and cold. Day and night . . . in this sanctuary, in the place of hisa images . . . they sat in front of the domes in which others lived, in which others were all too eager to take their turns—they could not all get in at once. They stayed because they must; any desertion would be noted from the sky. They had elected sanctuary, and there was nothing left to do but to sit and think of the others. Thinking. Measuring themselves.

Dreaming, the hisa called it. It was what hisa came to do.

*Use sense,* Miliko had told them in the first days, when they were most restless, talking wildly about action. *We're to wait.*

*Wait on what?* Cox had asked, and that began to haunt her own dreams.

This night, hisa were coming down the slope who had been sent for . . . days before. This night she sat with the others and watched them come, hands in her lap, watched small, distant bodies moving in the starless dark of the plain, sat with a curious tautness in her gut, and a tightness in her throat. Hisa . . . to fill up the number of humans, so that those who scanned the camp would find it undiminished. She carried the gun in a waterproof pocket; dressed warmly; still shivered in the uncertainty of things. Care for the hisa: that was what she was left to do; but *go,* the hisa themselves had told her. *You heart hurt. You eyes cold like they.*

Go or lose the people she commanded. She could no longer hold them otherwise.

*Are you afraid to be left?* she had asked the humans who would remain, the quiet, retiring ones, the old, the children, those men and women unlike those who sat outside—families and people with loved ones and those who were, perhaps, saner. She felt guilt for them. She was supposed to protect them and she could not; could not really even lead that band outside—she simply ran ahead of their madness. Many of these who would remain were Q, refugees, who had seen too much of horror, and were too tired, and had never asked to be down here at all. She imagined they must be afraid. The hisa elders could be perversely strange, and while Pell folk were used to hisa, they were still alien to these people. *No,* one old woman had said. *For the first time since Mariner I'm not afraid. We're safe here. Not from the guns, maybe, but from being afraid.* And other heads had nodded, and eyes stared at her with the patience of the hisa images.

Now hisa moved near them where they sat . . . a small

group of hisa, who came first to her and to Ito, and they stood up, looked back on the others who waited.

"See you," Miliko said, and heads nodded, in silence.

Several more were chosen, the hisa taking those they would, and slowly, in the dark, they walked that track across and up the slope, as others would come down, in small groups. One hundred twenty-three humans would go this night; and as many hisa come to join the camp in their place. She hoped that the hisa understood. They had seemed to, finally, eyes lighting with merriment at the joke on the humans who looked down to spy on them.

They went by the quickest route, passed other hisa on the way down, who called out cheerfully to them . . . and she walked at a human's best pace, panting, dizzy, resolved not to rest, for a hisa would not rest; and so they had all agreed to do it. She staggered as they made the final climb into the forest margin helped by the young hisa females who hovered about them . . . She-walks-far was one, and Wind-in-trees another, and more whose names she could not quite fathom nor the hisa say. Quick-foot, she had named the one and Whisper the other, for they set great store by human names. She had tried the names they called themselves, to please them as they walked, but her tongue could not master them and her attempts sent the hisa into nose-wrinkling gales of laughter.

They rested until the sun came up, in the trees and the bracken, and under a rocky ledge. By daylight they set out again, she and Ito and Ernst and the hisa who guided them, as other hisa had led others of them into the forest now, elsewhere. The hisa moved as if there were no enemies in all the world, with prank-playing, and once an ambush which stopped their hearts . . . Quickfoot's joke. Miliko frowned, and when the other humans did, the hisa caught the mood and grew quieter, seeming perplexed. Miliko caught Whisper by the hand and tried earnestly and once more to make sense to her, who knew less human speech than those hisa they were accustomed to deal with.

"Look." At last she grew desperate, seized a stick and crouched down, ripped up living and dead bracken to make a clear spot. She jabbed the stick at the ground. "Konstantin-man camp." She drew a line. "River." It was not likely, knowledgeable men said, that any drawn symbol was going to penetrate hisa imagination; it was not in their approach to things, lines and marks bearing no relationship to the real object. "We make circle, so, we eyes watch human camp. See Konstantin. See Bounder."

Whisper nodded, suddenly enthusiastic, a quick bob of her whole body on her haunches. She pointed back in the direction of the plain. "They . . . they . . . they," she said, and snatched the stick, waved it at the sky with the nearest thing to menace she had ever seen in a hisa. "Bad they," she said, and hurled the stick at the sky, bounced several times, clapped her hands and struck her breast with her palms. "I *friend* Bounder."

Bounder's mate. Miliko stared at the young female's intense expression, suddenly understanding, and Whisper seized her hand, patted it. Quickfoot patted her shoulder. There was a quick sputtering of conversation among all the hisa, and they suddenly seemed to take a decision, separated by pairs and each seized a human by the hand.

"Miliko," Ito protested.

"Trust them; let's go with it. Hisa won't get lost; they'll keep us in touch and get us back again when we have to. I'll send a message to you. Wait on it."

The hisa were anxiously urging them apart, each a separate way. "Take care," Ernst said, looking back; and trees came between. She, Ernst, and Ito had guns, half the guns there were on all of Downbelow, except the troops' and the other three were coming. Six guns and a little of the blasting materials for moving stumps—that was their whole arsenal. Go quietly, no more than three together, she had urged the hisa constantly, trying to keep their movements ordinary in human scan; and by threes the hisa had taken them, by their curious logic: she and Whisper and Quickfoot, three humans and six hisa, and now three units of three headed apart in haste.

No more pranks. Suddenly Quickfoot and Whisper were very serious indeed, slipping through the brush, turning this time to caution her when she made what their sensitive ears thought too much noise. The hiss of the breather she could not help, but she took care to break no branch, imitating the hisa's own gliding steps, their stop and start swiftness, as if—the thought reached her finally—as if they were teaching *her*.

She rested when she must, and only then; once fell, hard, from walking too long, and the hisa scrambled to pick her up and to pat her face and stroke her hair. They held her as they did each other, tucked her up with their warmth, for the sky was clouding and the wind was chill. It started to rain.

She rose as soon as she could, insisted on their pace. "Good, good," they said. "You good." And by afternoon more met them, more females and two males. There was no sign of them one moment and then they came from a little hill within the woods, and from out of the trees and leaves like brown shadows in the misting rain, the water beading like jewels on their pelts. Whisper and Quickfoot spoke to them, their arms about her, and had an answer.

"Say . . . far walk they place. Hear. Come. Many come. They eyes warm see you, Mihan-tisar."

There were twelve of them. One by one they came and touched Miliko's hands and hugged her, and bobbed and bowed in solemn courtesy. What Whisper said was long, and drew long answers from one and the other.

"They see," Quickfoot said, listening while Whisper talked. "They see human place. Hisa there hurt. Human hurt."

"We've got to go there," Miliko said, touching her heart. "All my humans, go there, sit on hills, watch. You understand? Hear good?"

"Hear," Quickfoot said, and seemed to translate.

The others started walking, leading the way; and what they should all do when they got there she did not know. Ito's madness and that of the others frightened her. Six pistols could not take a shuttle, nor the rest of them when they should come . . . unarmed and by no means able to go against armored, heavy-armed troops. They could only watch, and be there, and hope.

They walked throughout the day, with rain sifting cold through the leaves and the wind shaking drops down on them when it was not actually raining. Streams were up, bubbling freely; they passed into wilder and wilder thicket.

"Human place," she reminded them finally, despairing. "We have to go to the human camp."

"Go human place," Whisper confirmed, and in the next

moment she was gone, slipping through the brush with such speed she tricked the eyes.

"Run good," Quickfoot assured her. "Make Bounder walk far get she. Many he fall, she walk."

Miliko frowned, perplexed, as much of hisa chatter was perplexing. But Whisper was off about sober business, that much seemed likely, and she struggled to keep moving.

At long last she saw a break in the trees, staggered toward it with the last of her strength, for there was smoke, the smoke of the mills, and soon after that she could make out the twilit glimmer of a dome. She sank to her knees at the edge of the woods, took a moment to realize where she was. She had never seen the camp from this angle before, high in the hills. She leaned there with Quickfoot patting her shoulder, for she was gasping and her vision kept clouding. She felt after the three spare cylinders she had in her left pocket and hoped she had not ruined the one in the mask. She had reckoned they could live out here for weeks; they could not be using them up like that.

The sun was going. She saw the lights go on in the camp, and as she worked out on the edge of an eroded overhang, she could see figures moving out there under the lights, a burdened line toiling back and forth, back and forth between the mill and the road.

"She come," Quickfoot told her suddenly; Miliko looked back, suddenly missed the others, who had been behind them in the trees and now were nowhere in sight; blinked again as the brush parted and Whisper dropped to her haunches panting.

"Bounder," Whisper breathed, rocking with her breaths. "He hurt, he hurt work hard. Konstantin-man hurt. Give, give you."

She had a bit of paper clenched in her wet, furry fist. Miliko took it, smoothed out the sodden scrap very carefully, with the drizzle soaking it afresh and making it fragile as tissue. She had to bend very close and angle it to read it in the twilight . . . crabbed words and twisted.

"It's pretty . . . bad here. Won't pretend not. Stay out Stay away. Please. I told you what to do. Scatter and keep out of their hands . . . fear . . . they . . . maybe won't . . .

maybe want .. want more workers .. I'm all right. Please . . . go back . . . stay out of trouble."

The two hisa looked at her, dark eyes perplexed. Marks on paper—it was confusing to them. "Did anyone see you?" she asked. "Man see you?"

Whisper pursed her lips. "I *Downer,*" she said scornfully. "Many Downer come here. Carry sack, Downer. Bring mill, Downer. Bounder there, human see I, don't see. Who I? I *Downer.* Bounder say you friend hurt work hard; mans kill mans; he say love you."

"Love him too." She tucked the precious note within her jacket, crouched within the leaves with her hood pulled over her head and her hand within her pocket on the butt of the pistol.

There was no action they could take that might not make things worse . . . that might not mean the lives of everyone down there. Even if they could take one of the ships . . . it would only bring reprisals down on them. Massive strike. Here. Back at the shrine. Lives for lives. Emilio worked down there to save Downbelow . . . to save what of it they could. And the last thing he wanted was some quixotic move from them.

"Quickfoot," she said, "you run, find Downers, find all humans with me, understand. Tell them . . . Miliko talks with Konstantin-man; tell all wait, wait, make no trouble."

Quickfoot tried to repeat it, muddled, not knowing all the words. Quietly, patiently, Miliko tried again . . . and finally Quickfoot bobbed assent. "Tell they *sit,*" Quickfoot said excitedly. "You talk Konstantin-man."

"Yes," she said. "Yes." And Quickfoot fled.

The Downers could come and go. Mazian's men did not, as Whisper said, see any difference in them, could not tell them apart. And that was the only hope they had, to keep communication between them, to let the men down there know that they were not alone. Emilio knew she was there. Maybe, for all he wished her elsewhere, that was some comfort.

# 3

## i

## Pell: green sector nine; 1/8/53; 1800 hrs.

Rumors floated all of green, but there was no sign of a shutdown, no searches, no imminent crisis. Troops came and went to the usual places. The dock-front bars rocked to loud music and troops on liberty relaxed, drank, some even openly intoxicated. Josh took a cautious look out the doorway of Ngo's and ducked back in again as a squad of more businesslike troops headed up the hall, armored, sober, and with definite intentions. It made him somewhat nervous, as all such movements did when Damon was out of his sight. He endured the waiting under cover, his turn to sweat out the day in Ngo's storeroom, haunting the front room only at mealtimes . . . but it was suppertime, and late, and he was beginning to worry intensely. Damon had insisted on going yesterday and this day, following up leads, hunting a contract—talking to people and risking trouble.

Josh paced and fretted, realized he was pacing and that Ngo was frowning at him from the bar. He tried to quiet himself, finally walked casually back to the alcove, leaned his head into the kitchen and asked Ngo's son for dinner.

"How many?" the boy asked.

"One," he said. He needed the excuse to stay out in the front room. Reckoned when Damon got back he could order a refill and another helping. Their credit was good, the one comfort of their existence. Ngo's son waved a spoon at him, wishing him to get out.

He went to the accustomed table and sat down, looked toward the door again. Two men had come in, nothing unusual. But they were looking around too, and they started coming toward the back. He ducked his head and tried to camouflage himself in the shadow; market types, perhaps . . . some of Ngo's friends—but the move alarmed him. And they paused by his table, pulled a chair back. He looked up in apprehension as one of them sat down and the other kept standing.

"Talley," the seated man said, young, hard-faced with a burn scar across the jaw. "You're Talley, aren't you?"

"I don't know any Talley. You're mistaken."

"Want you to come outside for a moment. Just come to the door."

"Who are you?"

"There's a gun on you. I suggest you move."

It was the long expected nightmare. He thought of what he could do, which was to get himself shot. Men died in green every day, and there was no law except the troops, which he did not need either. These were not Mazianni. It was something else.

"Move."

He rose, walked clear of the table. The second man took his arm and guided him to the door, to the brighter light of the outside.

"Look over there," the man at his back said. "Look at the doorway directly across the corridor. Tell me if I've got the wrong man."

He looked. It was the man he had seen before, the one watching him. His vision blurred and nausea hit his gut, conditioned reflex.

He knew the man. The name would not come to him, but he knew him. His escort took him by the elbow and walked him in that direction, across the corridor and as the other went inside, took him into the dark interior of Mascari's, into the mingled effluvium of liquor and sweat and floor-jarring music. Heads turned, of those in the bar, who could see him better than his unadjusted eyes could see them for the moment, and he panicked, not alone at being recognized, but knowing that there was something in this place which *he* recognized, when he ought to know nothing on Pell, not after that fashion, not across the gulf he had crossed.

He was pushed to the leftmost corner of the room, to one of the closed booths. Two men stood there, one a hangdog middle-aged man who rang no alarms with him . . . and the other . . . the other . . .

Sickness hit him, conditioning assaulted. He groped for the back of a cheap plastic chair and leaned there.

"I knew it was you," the man said. "Josh? It is you, isn't it?"

"Gabriel." The name shot out of his blocked past, and whole structures tumbled. He swayed against the chair, seeing again his ship . . . his ship, and his companions . . . and this man . . . this man among them . . .

"Jessad," Gabriel corrected him, took his arm and looked at him strangely. "Josh, how did you get here?"

"Mazianni." He was being drawn into the curtained alcove, a place of privacy, a trap. He half turned, found the others barring the way out, and in the shadow when he looked back he could hardly make out Gabriel's face . . . as it had looked in the ship, when they had parted company—when he had transferred Gabriel to Blass, on *Hammer,* near Mariner. Gabriel's hand rested gently on his shoulder, pushing him into a chair at a small circular table. Gabriel sat down opposite him and leaned forward.

"My name here is Jessad. These gentlemen—Mr. Coledy and Mr. Kressich—Mr. Kressich was a councillor on this station, when there was a council. You'll excuse us, sirs. I want to talk to my friend. Wait outside. See we get privacy."

The others withdrew, and they were alone in the dim light of a fading bulb. He did not want to be alone with this man. But curiosity kept him seated, more than the fear of Coledy's gun outside, a curiosity with the foreknowledge of pain in it, like worrying at a wound.

"Josh?" Gabriel/Jessad said. "We're partners, aren't we?"

It might be a trick, might be truth. He shook his head helplessly. "Mindwipe. My memory—"

Gabriel's face contracted in seeming pain, and he reached out and caught him by the arm. "Josh . . . you came in, didn't you? You tried to make the pickup. *Hammer* got me out when it went wrong. But you didn't know that, did you? You took *Kite* in and they got you. Mindwipe . . . Josh, where are the others? Where are the rest of us, Kitha and—?"

He shook his head, cold inside, void. "Dead. I can't remember clearly. It's gone." He was close to being sick for a moment, freed his hand and rested his mouth against it, leaning on the table, trying to subdue the reactions.

"I saw you," Gabriel said, "in the corridor. I didn't believe it. But I started asking questions. Ngo won't tell whom you're with . . . but it's someone else they're after, isn't it? You've got friends here. A friend. Haven't you? It's not one of us . . . it's someone else. Isn't it?"

He could not think. Old friendships and new warred with each other. His belly was knotted up with contradictions. Fear for Pell . . . they had put that into him. And killing stations . . . was Gabriel's function. Gabriel was here, as he had been at Mariner—

Elene and *Estelle. Estelle* had died at Mariner.

"Isn't it?"

He jerked, blinked at Gabriel.

"I need you," Gabriel hissed. "Your help. Your skills . . ."

"I was nothing," he said. The suspicion that he was lied to grew stronger still. The man knew him and claimed things that were not so, were never so. "I don't know what you're talking about."

"We were a team, Josh."

"I was an armscomper, on the probe ship . . ."

"The undertapes." Gabriel seized his wrist, shook at him violently. "You're Joshua Talley, special services. Deep-taught for that. You came out of the labs on Cyteen. . . ."

"I had a mother, a father. I lived on Cyteen with my aunt. Her name was—"

"Out of the *labs,* Josh. They trained you on all levels. Gave you false tapes, a fiction, a fake . . . something to lie on the surface, lies you could tell and convince them if you had to. And it's surfaced, hasn't it? It's covered everything."

"I had a family. I *loved* them—"

"You're my partner, Josh. We came out of the same program. We were built for the same job. You're my backup. We've worked together, station after station, recon and operations."

He tore free of Gabriel's grip, blinked, blinded by a wash of tears. It began to shred, irretrievable, the farm, the sunny landscape, childhood—

"We're lab-born," Gabriel continued. "Both of us. Anything else . . . any other memory . . . they put it into us on tape and they can put something else in the next time. Cyteen was real; I'm real . . . until they change the tapes.

Until I become something else. They've messed with your mind, Josh. They've buried the only thing that's real. You gave them the lie and it washed right into your memory. But the truth's there. You know comp. You've survived here. And you know this station."

He sat still, his lips pressed against the back of his hand, tears rolling down his face, but he was not crying. He was numb, and the tears kept coming. "What do you want me to do?"

"What can you do? Who are your contacts? It's not among the Mazianni, is it?"

"No."

"Who?"

He sat unmoving for a moment. The tears stopped, the well of them dried up somewhere inside. All his memory seemed white, station detention and some far distant place confounded in his memory, white cells, and uniformed attendants, and he knew finally that he had been happy enough in detention because it was home, the universal institution, alike on either side of the lines of politics and war. Home. "Suppose I work it my way," he said. "Suppose I talk to my contact, all right? I might be able to get some help. It'll cost you."

"How, cost?"

He leaned back in the chair, nodded toward the outside of the booth, where Coledy and Kressich waited. "You have pull of your own, don't you? Suppose I contribute my share. What have you got? Suppose I could get you most anything on this station . . . and I don't have the muscle to handle it."

"I've got that," Gabriel said.

"I've got the other. Only there's one thing I want that I can't carry off without force. A shuttle. A run to Downbelow when it comes off."

Gabriel sat silent a moment. "You've got that kind of access?"

"I told you I had a friend. And I want off."

"You and I might take that option."

"And this friend of mine."

"The one you're working the market with?"

"Speculate what you want. I get you whatever accesses you need. You make plans to get us a way off this station."

Gabriel nodded slowly.

"I've got to get back," Josh said. "Start it moving. There's not much time."

"Shuttles dock in red sector now."

"I can get you there. I can get you anywhere you want. What we need is force enough to take it when we do get there."

"While the Mazianni are busy?"

"While they're busy. There are ways." He stared a moment at Gabriel. "You're going to blow this place. When?"

Gabriel seemed to weigh answering at all. "I'm not suicide-prone. I want a way off as badly as anyone here, and there's not a chance that *Hammer* can get to us this time. A shuttle, a capsule, anything that stands a chance of staying in orbit long enough. . . ."

"All right," Josh said. "You know where to find me."

"Is there a shuttle docked there now?"

"I'll check into it," he said, and rose, felt his way past the shadowy arch and out into the noise of the outside, where Coledy and his man and Kressich rose from a nearby table in some apprehension; but Gabriel had come out behind him. They let him pass. He wove his way among the tables, past heads which stayed bowed over drinks and dinners, shoulders which stayed turned.

Outside air hit him like a wall of cold and light. He drew a breath, tried to clear his head, while the floor kept developing lattices of shadow, flashes of here and there, truth and untruth.

Cyteen was a lie. He was. Part of him functioned like the automaton he reckoned himself bred to be . . . he acknowledged instincts he had never trusted, not knowing why he had them—drew another breath, trying to think, while his body navigated its way across the corridor and sought cover.

Only when he had gotten back to his cold dinner on the back table in Ngo's, when he sat in that familiar place with his back to the corner and the reality of Pell came and went at the bar in front of him, the numbness began to leave him. He thought of Damon, one life, one life he might have the power to save.

He killed. That was what he was created to do. That was why the like of himself and Gabriel existed at all.

Joshua and Gabriel. He understood the wry humor in their names, swallowed at a knot in his throat. Labs. That was the white void he had lived in, the whiteness in his dreams. Carefully insulated from humanity. Tape-taught . . . given skills; given lies to tell—about being human.

Only there was a flaw in the lies . . . that they were fed into human flesh, with human instincts, and he had loved the lies.

And lived them in his dreams.

He ate the dinner, which kept sticking in his throat, washed it down with cold coffee, poured another cup from the thermal pitcher.

He might get Damon off. The rest had to die. To get Damon out he had to keep quiet, and Gabriel had to mislead the others following him, promise them all life, promise them help which would never come. They would all die, except himself and Gabriel, and Damon. He wondered how he should persuade Damon to leave . . . or if he could. If he must use reason . . . what reason?

Alicia Lukas-Konstantin. He thought of her, who had helped him in the process of helping Damon. *She* could never leave. And the guards who had given him money in hospital; and the Downer who followed them about and watched over them; and the people who had survived the hell of the ships and of Q; and the men and the women and the children. . . .

He wept, leaning against his hands, while somewhere deep inside were instincts which functioned in cold intelligence, knowing how to kill a place like Pell, knowing that it was the only reason he existed.

The rest he no longer believed.

He wiped his eyes, drank the coffee, sat and waited.

## ii

## Union carrier Unity: deep space; 1/8/53

The dice rolled, came up two, and Ayres shrugged morosely, while Dayin Jacoby marked down another set of points and Azov set up for another round. The two guards always assigned here in the lower-deck main room sat watching from the benches against the wall, their young and flawless faces quite passionless. He and Jacoby, and rarely Azov, played for imaginary points, pledged against real credits when they reached some civilized point together; and that, Ayres thought, was an element as chancy as the dice rolls.

Tedium was the only present enemy. Azov grew sociable, sat black-clad and grim at the table, played with them, for he would not bend and gamble with his crew. Perhaps the mannequins amused themselves elsewhere. Ayres could not imagine it. Nothing touched them, nothing illumined those dull, hateful eyes. Only Azov . . . joined them from time to time as they sat in the main room, eight and nine hours a tedious day of sitting, for there was no work to do, no exercise to be had. Mostly they sat in the one room freely allowed them, and talked . . . finally talked.

Jacoby had no restraint in his conversation; the man poured out confidences of his life, his affairs, his attitudes. Ayres resisted Jacoby's and Azov's attempts to draw him out to talk about his homeworld. There was danger in that. But all the same he talked . . . about his impressions of the ship, about the present situation, about anything and everything he could feel was harmless; about abstracts of law and economic theory, in which he and Jacoby and Azov himself shared some expertise . . . joked lightly which currency they should pay their bets in; Azov laughed outright. It was inexpressible relief to have someone to talk to, and to exchange pleasantries with someone. He had a bond with Jacoby . . . like that of kinship, unchosen, but inescapable. They were each other's sanity. He began at last to conceive such an attachment to Azov, finding him sympathetic and possessed of humor. There was danger in this, and he knew it.

Jacoby won the next round. Azov patiently marked down the points, turned to the mannequins. "Jules. A bottle here, would you?"

One rose and left on the errand. "I rather thought they had numbers," Ayres said under his breath; they had already had one bottle. And then he repented the frankness.

"There's much in Union you don't see," Azov said. "But you may get the chance."

Ayres laughed, and suddenly cold hit his belly. *How?* stuck in his throat. They had drunk too much together. Azov had never admitted to his nation's ambitions, to any designs beyond Pell. He let his expression change ever so slightly, and in that moment Azov's did too . . . mutual dismay, a moment which lasted too long, slow-motion, alcohol-fumed, with Jacoby a third unwilling participant.

Ayres laughed again, an effort, tried not to show his guilt, leaned back in his chair and stared at Azov. "What, do they gamble too?" he asked, trying to mislead the meaning.

Azov pressed his lips to a thin line, looked at him from under one silvery brow, smiled as if he were dutifully amused.

*I am not going home,* Ayres thought despairingly. *There will be no warning. That was his meaning.*

## iii

## Pell: Downer tunnels: 1/8/53; 1830 hrs.

The dark place shifted with many bodies. Damon listened, started as he heard one moving near him, and again as a hand touched his arm in the blackness of the tunnel. He angled the lamp that way, shivering in the chill.

"I Bluetooth," the familiar voice whispered. "You come see she?"

Damon hesitated, long, looked toward the ladders which stretched like spiderweb out of the range of the lamp he carried. "No," he said sorrowfully. "No. I only walk through. I've been to white section. I only want to go through."

"She ask you come. Ask. Ask all time."

"No," he whispered hoarsely, thinking that there were fewer and fewer times, that soon there would be no chance at all. "No, Bluetooth. I love her and I won't. Don't you know, it would be danger to her if I came there? The men-with-guns would come in. I can't. I can't, much as I want to."

The Downer's warm hand patted his, lingered. "You say good thing."

He was surprised. A Downer reasoned, and though he knew that they reasoned, it surprised him to hear that train of thought follow human lines. He took the Downer's hand and squeezed it, grateful for Bluetooth's presence in an hour when there was little other comfort. He sank down on the metal steps, drew a quiet breath through the mask . . . drew comfort where it was to be had, to sit a moment safe from unfriendly eyes, with what had become, across all other differences, a friend. The hisa squatted on the platform before him, dark eyes glittering in the indirect light, patted his knee, simply companionable.

"You watch me," Damon said, "all the time."

Bluetooth bobbed slightly, agreement.

"The hisa are very kind," Damon said. "Very good."

Bluetooth tilted his head and wrinkled his brow. "You she baby." Families were a very difficult concept for hisa. "You 'Licia baby."

"I was, yes."

"She you mother."

"She is."

"Milio she baby."

"Yes."

"I love he."

Damon smiled painfully. "No halfway with you, is there, Bluetooth? All or nothing. You're a good fellow. How much do the hisa know? Know other humans . . . or only Konstantins? I think all my friends are dead, Bluetooth. I've tried to find them. And either they're hiding or they're dead."

"Make me eyes sad, Damon-man. Maybe hisa find, tell we they name."

"Any of the Dees. Or the Ushants. The Mullers."

"I ask. Some know maybe." Bluetooth laid a finger on his own flat nose. "Find they."

"By that?"

Bluetooth reached out a tentative hand and stroked the stubble on his face. "You face like hisa, you smell same human."

Damon grinned, amused in spite of his depression. "Wish I did look like a hisa. Then I could come and go. They nearly caught me this time."

"You come here 'fraid," Bluetooth said.

"You smell fear?"

"I see you eyes. Much pain. Smell blood, smell run hard."

Damon turned the back of his elbow to the light, a painful scrape that had torn through the cloth. It had bled. "Hit a door," he said.

Bluetooth edged forward. "I make stop hurt."

He recalled hisa treating their own hurts, shook his head. "No. But can you remember the names I asked?"

"Dee. Ushant. Mul-ler."

"You find them?"

"Try," Bluetooth said. "Bring they?"

"Come bring me to them. The men-with-guns are closing the tunnels into white, you know that?"

"Know so. We Downers, we walk in big tunnels outside. Who look at we?"

Damon drew a deep breath against the mask, stood up again on the dizzying steps, hugged the hisa with one arm as he picked up the lamp. "Love you," he murmured.

"Love you," Bluetooth said, and scampered away into the dark, a slight moving, a vibration on the metal stairs.

Damon felt his own way further, counting his turns and levels. No recklessness. He had come close enough, trying to enter white. He had rung an alarm over in white. He had a sickly fear it might bring investigation into the tunnels, trouble on the Downers, on his mother, on all of them. He still felt the tremor in his knees, although he had not hesitated to shoot when he had to; had fired on an unarmored guard; might have killed him; had meant to.

That sickened him.

And he still hoped he had, that the alarm had not involved his name. That the witness was dead.

He was still shaking when he reached the access to the corridor outside Ngo's. He entered the narrow lock, tugged down his mask, used the security-cleared card he reserved only for extreme emergency. It opened without alarms. He hurried down the narrow, deserted hall, used a manual key to open the back door itself.

Ngo's wife turned from the kitchen counter and stared at him, darted out into the main room. Damon let the door close behind him, opened the storeroom door to toss the breather mask in. He had forgotten it in his panic, brought it through with him. That was the measure of his wit. He went to the kitchen sink and washed his hands, his face, tried to wash the stink of blood and fear and memory off him.

"Damon."

"Josh." He turned a weary glance toward the door to the front room, dried his face on the towel hanging there. "Trouble." He went past Josh into the front room, walked to the bar and leaned against it. "Bottle?" he asked of Ngo.

"You come in that door again . . ." Ngo hissed unhappily.

"Emergency," Damon said. Josh caught his arm gently from the side.

"Never mind the drink for a moment," Josh said. "Damon. Come over here. I want to talk to you."

He came, back into the alcove which was their territory. Josh backed him into the corner, out of sight of the other patrons who ate in the place. There was the clink of plates in the kitchen, where Ngo's wife had retreated, with her son. The room smelled of Ngo's inevitable stew. "Listen," Josh said when they had sat down, "I want you to come with me across the corridor. I've found a contact I think can help us."

He heard it and still it took a moment to sink in. "Who have you been talking to? Who do *you* know?"

"Not me. Someone who recognized you. Who wants your help. I don't know the whole story. A friend of yours. There's an organization . . . stretches out among the Q folk and Pell. A number of people who know you might have the skill to help them."

He tried to absorb it. "You know what a candle's chance we have with a Q mob—against troops?—and why go to you? Why you, Josh? Maybe they're afraid I'd recognize faces and know something. I don't like this."

"Damon. How much time can we have? It's a chance. Everything's a risk at this point. Come with me. Please come with me."

"They're going to be checking all over white. I stumbled into an alarm over there . . . may have killed someone. They're going to be stirred up, searching for someone using accesses . . ."

"Then how much time can we have left to think it over? If we don't—" He stopped, looked sharply about at Ngo's wife, who brought them bowls of stew, setting them on the table. "We're going somewhere. Keep it hot for us."

Dark eyes stared at them both. Quietly, as everything about the woman was quiet, she gathered up the bowls and took them to another table.

"Won't take long to find out," Josh said. "Damon. Please."

"What are they talking of doing? Rushing central?"

"Causing trouble. Getting to the shuttle. Setting up resistance on Downbelow . . . a small number of us. Damon, it all relies on your knowledge. Your skills with comp, and your knowledge of the passages."

"They have a pilot?"

"I think there's someone who is, yes."

He tried to gather his wits. Shook his head. "No."

"What do you mean, no? *You* talked about a shuttle. *You* planned for it."

"Not to have another riot on the station. Not with more people killed, in a plan that's never going to work. . . ."

"Come and talk to them. Come with me. Or don't you trust me? Damon, how long can we wait on chances? You haven't even heard it out."

He let go his breath. "I'll come," he said. "They're going to start checking ID's in green soon enough, I'm afraid. I'll talk to them. Maybe I know better ways. Quieter ones. How far is this place?"

"Mascari's."

"Across the corridor."

"Yes. Come on."

He came, out amongst the tables, past the bar.

"You," Ngo said sharply as they passed. He stopped. "You don't come back here if you bring trouble. You hear me? I helped you. I don't want that kind of pay for it. You hear me?"

"I hear," Damon said. There was no time to smooth it over. Josh waited by the front door. He walked out to join him, looked left and right and crossed the corridor with him into the noisier and darker interior of Mascari's.

A man at the left of the entry rose and joined them. "This way," the man said, and because Josh went without question, Damon swallowed his protests and went with them, to the far side of the room, which was so dark it was hard to avoid chairs.

A dim light burned in a curtained alcove. They went inside, he and Josh, but their guide vanished.

And in another moment a second man came in at their backs, young and scar-faced. Damon did not know him. "They're coming," the young man said, and quickly the curtains moved again, admitted two more to the alcove.

"Kressich," Damon muttered. The other was not familiar to him.

"You know Mr. Kressich?" the newcomer asked.

"Only by sight. Who are you?"

"Name's Jessad . . . Mr. Konstantin, is it? The younger Konstantin?"

Recognition of any kind made him nervous. He looked at Josh, finding discrepancies, bewildered. They were supposed to know him. This man should not be surprised.

"Damon," Josh said, "this man is from Q. Let's talk details. Sit down."

He did so, at the small table, uncertain and apprehensive as the others settled with him. A second time he looked at Josh. He trusted Josh. Trusted him with his life. Would hand him his life at the asking, having no better use for it. And Josh had lied to him. Everything he knew of the man insisted Josh was lying.

*Are we under some threat?* he wondered wildly, seeking some cause for this charade. "What kind of proposal are we talking about?" he asked, wishing only that he could get himself out of here, and get Josh out, and get it all straight.

"When Josh said that he had contacts," Jessad said slowly, "I didn't suspect who. You're far better than I dared hope."

"Am I?" He resisted the temptation to look again in Josh's direction. "What precisely do you hope, Mr. Jessad from Q?"

"Josh didn't tell you?"

"Josh said I'd want to talk to you."

"About finding a way to get this station back into your hands?"

He did not change expression in the least. "You think you have the means to do that."

"I have men," Kressich interjected. "Coledy does. We can raise a thousand men in five minutes."

"You know what would happen then," Damon said. "We'd have ourselves neck deep in troopers. Bodies in the corridors, if they didn't vent us all."

"You know," Jessad said quietly, "that the whole station is theirs. To do with as they please. Except for you, there's no authority to speak for the old Pell. Lukas . . . is done. He says only what Mazian hands him to read. Has guards about him everywhere. One choice is bodies in the corridors, true. The other is what they've given Lukas, isn't it? They'd give you prepared speeches to read too. They'd let you alternate with Lukas, or outright dispose of you. After all, they do have Lukas, and he takes orders . . . doesn't he?"

"You put it neatly, Mr. Jessad." *And what about the shuttle?* he thought, leaning back in his chair. He looked at Josh, who met his eyes with a troubled stare. He glanced back again. "What's your proposal?"

"You get us access to central. We take care of the rest."

"It'll never work," Damon said. "We've got warships out there. You can't hold them off by holding central. They'd blow us; don't you count on that?"

"I have means to make sure it works."

"So let's have it. Make your proposal, flat, and let me have the night to think about it."

"Let you walk around knowing names and faces?"

"You know mine," he reminded Jessad, and obtained a slight flicker of the eyes.

"Trust him," Josh said. "It will work."

Something crashed outside, even over the music. The curtains came inward, with Coledy, who landed atop the table with a hole burned in his forehead. Kressich sprang up shrieking in terror. Damon hurled himself back, hit the wall with Josh beside him, and Jessad clawed for a pocket. Shrieks punctuated the music outside, and armored troops with leveled rifles filled the doorway of the alcove.

"Stand still!" one ordered.

Jessad whipped out the gun. A rifle fired, and there was a burned smell as Jessad hit the floor, twitching. Damon stared at the troopers and the leveled rifles in dazed horror. Josh, at his side, did not move.

A trooper hauled another man in by the collar—Ngo, who flinched from Damon's stare and looked apt to be sick.

"These the ones?" the trooper asked.

Ngo nodded. "Made me hide them out. Threatened me. Threatened my family. We want to go over to white. All of us."

"Who's this one?" The trooper nodded toward Kressich.

"Don't know," Ngo said. "Don't know him. Don't know these others."

"Take them out," the officer said. "Search them. Dead ones too."

It was over. A hundred thoughts poured through Damon's mind . . . going for the gun in his pocket—running for it, as far as he could get before they shot him down.

And Josh . . . and his mother and his brother . . .

They laid hands on him, turned him against the wall

and made him spread his limbs, him and Josh beside him, and Kressich. They searched his pockets and took the cards and the gun, which in itself was cause for a shooting on the spot.

They turned him about again, back to the wall, and looked at him more carefully.

"You're Konstantin?"

He gave no answer. One hit him in the belly and doubled him, and he flung himself at the man shoulder-on and low, carried him and a chair over under the table. A boot slammed into his back and he was trampled in a fight which broke above him. He tore free of the man he had stunned, tried to claw his way to his feet by the table rim, and a shot burned past his shoulder, hit Kressich in the stomach.

A rifle clubbed him. His knees loosened, refusing to drive him to his feet; a second blow, on the arm stretched on the table. He went out, doubled as a boot slammed into him, stayed doubled against the blows until they knocked him half senseless. Then they hauled him up between two of them. "Josh," he said dazedly. "Josh?"

They had Josh up too, slumped between two of them, trying to shake him into life, and he managed to get his feet under him. His head rolled drunkenly. He was bleeding from the temple. For Kressich there was no use in urging; he was still moving, gut-shot and bleeding fast. They were leaving him.

Damon looked about as they were taken out into the main room. Ngo had fled or they had taken him. The patrons had fled. There was only a scattering of corpses, and a few troops standing about with rifles.

The troops hauled him and Josh outside, into the corridor. A few at Ngo's stood outside to stare as they were marched along and Damon turned his face aside, shamed to be publicly paraded in his arrest.

He thought they would be taken to the ships across the docks. And then they turned the corner onto the docks and headed left, and he realized otherwise. There was a bar the troops had taken for themselves, a headquarters, a place civs avoided.

Music, drugs, liquor—anything the civ sector had to offer—Damon stared numbly as they were hauled inside, into a lowering smoke and a thunder of music. A desk was there, incredibly enough, a concession to something official. The troops brought them to it and a man carrying a drink sat down and looked them over. "Got ourselves something here," said the leader of the group which had brought them in. "Fleet's looking for these two. Konstantin, this one. And we've got ourselves a Unioner here. Adjusted man, the rumor says . . . but Pell did the Adjusting."

"Unioner." The sergeant at the desk looked past Damon, grinned unpleasantly at Josh. "And how did the likes of you get onto Pell? Got a good story, Union man?"

Josh said nothing.

"I do," a harsh voice said from the door, fit to shake the walls. "He's *Norway* property."

Laughter and conversation stopped, if not the music. The newcomers, armored as most in this place were not, came in with a brusqueness that startled the rest. "*Norway,*" someone muttered. "Get out of here, *Norway* bastards."

"What's your name?" the newcomer bellowed.

"Or you shoot all of us?" someone else said.

The short man with the loud voice punched the com button at his shoulder and spoke something the music drowned, turned and waved his hand at the dozen troopers with him, who fanned out. He looked then at the rest, a slow circuit of the room. "You're none of you in fit condition to handle anything. Straighten up this den. Any of our people in here I'll skin 'em. Is there?"

"Try down the row," someone shouted. "This is *Australia* territory. *Norway*'s got no call to be putting us on report."

"Hand the prisoners over," the short man said. No one moved. Rifles of the *Norway* troops leveled, and there were outcries of shock and rage from the *Australia* troopers. Damon stood with his vision hazing as two of the dozen moved in on him and Josh, as a rough grip seized his right arm and jerked him from the hand which held him, hauled him along toward the door. Josh came without struggling. He did. As long as they were together . . . it was the most they had left.

"Get them out," the little man bellowed at his troops. They were pushed and hastened outside; two troopers stayed with their officer, in the bar. It was not until they were passing the niner corridor that other troops intercepted them, other *Norway* troopers.

"Get to the *Australia* post," one yelled at the others, a woman's voice. "McCarthy's. Di's got them all at rifle point. He needs some numbers in there, fast."

The troopers headed past them at a run. Four of those escorting them kept on, taking them toward the blue dock access door, where guards stood.

"Pass us through," the officer of their escort demanded. "We've got a potential riot situation back there."

The guards were *Australia*. The lettering and emblem proclaimed it. Reluctantly the squad opened the emergency doors and let them through the passage.

Thereafter was blue dock, where *Norway* occupied a berth next *India, Australia,* and *Europe*. Damon walked, beginning to feel shock from his injuries, if not pain. There was only the military here, troops coming and going, supply bales being loaded by military crews in fatigues.

*Norway*'s access tube gaped before them. They walked the ramp, into the passage, passed through that chill into the airlock. Others met them, troops all with *Norway*'s emblem.

"Talley," one said with a surprised grin. "Welcome back, Talley."

Josh bolted. He made it as far as the middle of the access tube before they caught him.

## iv

## Pell: Norway; blue dock; 1/8/53; 1930 hrs.

Signy looked up from her desk, for a moment dialed down the com noise, the reports of her troops on the docks and elsewhere. She gave a quizzical smile at the guards and at Talley. He was considerably the worse for wear . . . unshaven, dirty, bloody. There was a swelling on his jaw.

"Come to see me?" she mocked him. "I hadn't thought you'd ask again."

"Damon Konstantin . . . they've got him aboard. The troops have got him. I thought you'd want to talk to him."

That perplexed her. "You're trying to turn him in, are you?"

"He's here. We both are. Get him out of there."

She leaned back, looked curiously at him. "So you do talk straight," she said. "You never talked."

And now he had nothing to say.

"They played games with your mind," she observed. "And now you're a friend of Konstantin's, are you?"

"I appeal to you," he said in a faint voice.

"On what grounds?"

"Reason. He's useful to you. And they'll kill him."

She regarded him from half-lidded eyes. "Glad to be back, are you?" There was a call blinking, which was something com evidently could not handle.

She dialed up the sound and punched it through. "There's a fight broken out," she heard, "at McCarthy's."

"Di out of there?" she asked. "Give me Di."

"Busy," she heard. She waved a hand at the guards, dismissing the business of Talley. Another light was flashing.

*"Mallory!"* Talley shouted at her, being forced out the door.

"*Europe's* wanting you," Com said. "Mazian's on."

She punched through. They had gotten Talley out, to lock him up somewhere, she hoped.

"Mallory here, *Europe*."

"What's going on over there?"

"I've got trouble on the dock, sir. Janz needs instruction, by your leave, sir." She punched out on him. "He's *down,*" she was hearing on another channel. "Captain, Di's *shot.*"

She clenched a fist and held it back from the unit. "Get him out, get him out, what officer am I talking to?"

"This is Uthup," a woman's voice came back. "One of *Australia*'s shot Di."

She punched another button. "Get me Edger. Quick!"

"We're through the door," she heard from Uthup. "We got Di."

"General alert *Norway* troops. We have dock trouble. Get out there!"

"Edger here," she heard. "Mallory, call your hounds in."

"Call yours in, Edger, or I'll shoot them on sight. They've shot Di Janz."

"I'll stop it," he said, and cut out. ALERT was sounding in *Norway*'s corridors, a raucous klaxon, blue lights flashing. Boards and screens in her office were coming to life as the ship turned out to emergency ready.

"We're coming in," Uthup's voice came back. "He's still with us, captain."

"Get him in, Uthup, get him in."

"Going down there, captain." That was Graff, heading to the dock. She started pushing buttons, hunting a visual and cursing at the techs; someone should have it on vid. She found it, the group coming in carrying more than one of their number, *Norway* troops pouring out onto the dock in haste and taking up positions around the umbilicals and access. "Get med on the com," she ordered.

"Med's ready," she heard, watched a familiar figure reach the troops and take charge. Graff was out there. She found leisure for a quieter breath.

"*Europe*'s still holding," com advised her. She punched that channel.

"Captain Mallory. What war are you fighting out there?"

"I don't know yet, sir. I'm going to find out as soon as I can get my troops aboard."

"You've got *Australia*'s prisoners. Why?"

"Damon Konstantin's one, sir. I'll be back in touch as soon as I can get a word out of Janz. Your leave, sir."

"*Mallory.*"

"Sir?"

"*Australia* has two casualties. I want a report."

"I'll get one to you when I can learn what happened, sir. In the meanwhile I'm dispatching troops to green dock before we have some sort of trouble with civs over there."

"*India* is moving forces in. Leave it at that, Mallory, and keep your troops out of there. Off the docks. Pull them all. I want to see you at soonest, hear?"

"With a report, sir. By your *leave,* sir."

The light and the contact winked out. She slammed her fist onto the console and shoved the chair back, headed for the cubbyhole of a surgery in the half corridor off from the main lift topside.

It was not as bad as she had feared. Di kept a steady pulse under the medic's ministrations, showing no signs of leaving them. Chest wound, a few burns. There was a great deal of blood, but she had seen far worse. A chance shot, in an armor joint. She stalked over to the door where Uthup stood, smeared with blood from head to foot of her armor. "Get your filthy selves out of here," she said, herding them out into the corridor. "It's going sterile in there. Who shot first?"

"*Australia* bitch, drunk and disorderly."

"Captain."

"Captain," Uthup said thinly.

"You hit, Uthup?"

"Burns, captain. I'll check in when they're done with the major and the others, by your leave."

"I tell you to stay out of that territory?"

"Heard over com they'd picked up Konstantin and Talley, captain. A sergeant was in charge and they were drunk as stationside merchanters in there. The major went in and they said it was off-limits to us."

"Enough said," she muttered. "I want a report, trooper Uthup; and I'll back you on it. I'd have skinned you if you'd backed away from Edger's bastards. Quote me on that where you like." She walked off, through the troops in the corridor. "It's all right, Di's in one piece. Get yourselves out of here and let the meds work. Get back to quarters. I'm going to have a word with Edger, but if you or any of the others take to the docks I'll shoot you with my own hand. That's my word on it. *Get below!*"

They scattered. She walked forward to the bridge, looked about her at the crew who had gotten to stations. Graff was there, himself liberally bloodstained.

"Clean yourself up," she said. "Mind your stations. Morio, get back there and interview trooper Uthup and anyone else in that detachment; I want names and ID's on those *Australia* troops. I want a formal complaint and I want it now."

"Captain," Morio acknowledged the order.

He left in haste; she stood on the bridge and looked about until heads turned to their work. Graff had left to put himself in order. She continued to pace the aisle until she realized she was doing it and stood still.

There was the matter of showing up on Mazian's deck. There was blood on her uniform, Di's blood. She decided finally to go and not to clean up.

"Graff's in command," she said brusquely. "McFarlane. I need an escort over to *Europe*. Move it."

She started for the lift, hearing the order echoing in the corridors. Troops met her in the exit corridor, fifteen of them in full rig. She walked out through the troops which guarded the access ramp on the docks. She had no armor. It was a secure dock and she was not supposed to need any, but at the moment she would have felt safer walking green dock naked.

## V

## Pell: Europe; blue dock; 1/8/53; 2015 hrs.

Mazian was not late showing up, not this time. It was an audience of two, herself and Tom Edger, and Edger had gotten there first. *That* was expected.

"Sit down," Mazian told her. She took a chair on the opposite side of the conference table from Edger. Mazian had his own, at the head, leaned on his folded arms, glared at her. "Well? Where's the report?"

"It's coming," she said. "I'm taking the time to interview and collect positive ID's. Di took names and numbers before they shot him."

"Your orders that sent him in there?"

"My standing orders to my troops that they don't back off from trouble if it sets itself in front of them. Sir, my people have been systematically harassed since the incident with Goforth. *I* shot the man, and my people are harassed, shouldered, subtle stuff, until someone got too drunk to know the difference between harassment and outright mutiny. A trooper was asked for her number and directly refused to give it. She was arrested and she drew her gun and opened fire on an officer."

Mazian looked at Edger and back again. "I hear another story. That your troops are encouraged to stick together. That they're still under your orders even on supposed liberty. That they go in squads and under officers and throw their weight around the dock. That the whole operation of *Norway* troops and personnel is insubordinate and provocative, direct defiance of my order."

"I have given my troops no duties during their liberties. If they're going in groups it's for self-protection. They're set upon in bars that are open to all but *Norway* personnel.

*That* kind of behavior is encouraged among other crews. You have my complaint of that matter on your desk as of last week."

Mazian sat and stared a moment, tapped the table in front of him, a slow, nervous gesture. Lastly he looked toward Edger.

"I've hesitated to file a protest," Edger said. "But there's a bad atmosphere building out there. Apparently there's some difference of opinion about how the Fleet as a whole is ordered. Ship loyalties—loyalties to certain captains—are encouraged in some quarters, for reasons I refuse to guess at, perhaps *by* certain captains."

Signy sucked air and slammed her hands down, all but out of her chair before colder sense asserted itself. Much colder. Edger and Mazian had always been close . . . were close, she had long suspected, in a way in which she could not intervene. She evened her breath, leaned back, looked only at Mazian. It was war; it was as narrow a chute as ever *Norway* had run, the straits of Mazian's ambition, and Edger's. "There is something vastly amiss," she said, "when we start shooting at each other. By your leave . . . we're the oldest in the Fleet, the longest survivors. And I'll tell you plainly I know what's afoot and I've played your charade, gone on with this station organization, which isn't going to have any importance whatsoever when the Fleet moves. I've done your make-work operations and done them well. I've said no word to my troops or my crew about what I know; and I get the drift of things, that the troops are allowed to do what they like on this station because in the long run it doesn't matter. Because Pell has stopped mattering, and the survival of it is now contrary to our interests. We're aiming at something different now. Or maybe we always were, and you've moved us to it by degrees, never to shock us too much, when you finally propose what it is you really have in mind, the only choice you've left us with. Sol, isn't it? *Earth.* And it's going to be a long run and dangerous, with plenty of trouble when we get there. The Fleet—takes over the Company. So maybe you're right. Maybe it's the only thing to do. Maybe it makes sense and it began to make sense a long time ago, when the Company quit backing us. But we don't get there if Pell destroys the disciplines on which this Fleet has functioned for decades. We don't get there if the units of it are homogenized into something that can't work apart. And that's what this harassment does. It tells me how to run *Norway.* If that starts, then it all breaks down. You take from the troops their badges and their designations, their identification and their spirit and it goes, it all goes . . . and whatever you call it, that's what's in progress out there, when a ship is made to conform to a standard against every rule they've ever known, when captains in this Fleet are subtly encouraging their troops to the harassment of mine, and they're taking to it, in the absence of another enemy. The Fleet as a whole hasn't existed in decades, but that was our strength . . . the latitude to do what had to be done, across all this vast distance. Homogenize us and we become predictable. And few as we are . . . then we're done."

"Amazing," Mazian said softly, "that somehow *you* end up arguing for separation of the crews, when you're the one complaining about lack of discipline. You're an amazing sophist."

"I'm being ordered to fall in line, to change every policy and order that exists on my ship. My troops perceive that as an insult to *Norway,* and they resent it. What else do you expect, sir?"

"The attitude of the troops rather reflects that of the officers in charge and of the captain, doesn't it? Maybe you've encouraged it."

"And maybe what happened in that bar was encouraged."

"Sir."

"With all respect—sir."

"Your men moved in and removed prisoners from the custody of the troops who performed the arrest. Credit-snatching, doesn't it seem so?"

"Removed prisoners from a drunken body of libertied troops in a bar."

"Dock headquarters," Edger muttered. "Tell it clear, Mallory."

"The troops were drunk and disorderly in your dock headquarters, and one of the prisoners involved was *Norway* property. There was no commissioned officer in this dock headquarters. And the other prisoner was valuable and one *my* make-work operation on the docks would find useful. The question is why the prisoners were taken to that so-named headquarters at all, instead of to the blue dock facilities or to the nearest ship, which was *Africa.*"

"The arresting troops were reporting to their sergeant. Who was present, when your troop major broke into the place."

"I suggest that that attitude is contributory to the atmosphere in which Maj. Janz was shot. If that *was* dock headquarters, Maj. Janz was fully entitled to walk in there and assume command of the situation. But he was told outright on entering that the so-named dock headquarters was staked out as *Australia* territory; the *Australia* sergeant present did not object to that insubordination. Now is a troop headquarters to be the private preserve of one ship, or what? Can it be that other captains are urging their crews to separatism?"

"Mallory," Mazian cautioned her.

"The point, sir: Maj. Janz gave a proper order for surrender of the prisoners to his custody and received no cooperation from the *Australia* sergeant, who contributed to the trouble."

"Two of my troopers were killed in that exchange," Edger said tautly, "and how it started is still under inquiry."

"From my side also, captain. I expect the information momentarily and I'll see that you get a copy when it goes in."

"Captain Mallory," Mazian said, "you make that report to me. At the soonest. As for the prisoners, I don't care what you do with them. Whether they're here or there is not the issue. Dissension is. *Ambition* . . . on the part of individual captains of the Fleet . . . is an issue. Whether you like it or not, Captain Mallory, you will walk in line. You're right, we've operated separately, and now we have to work as a body. And certain free spirits among us are having trouble with that. Don't like taking orders. You're valuable to me. You see through to the heart of a matter, don't you? Yes, it's Sol. And by telling me that, you hope to be on the inside of councils, don't you? You want to be consulted. Want to be in the line of succession, maybe. That's very well. But to get there, captain, you have to learn to walk in line."

She sat still, returned Mazian's stare. "And not know where I'm going?"

"You know where we're going. You said as much."

"All right," she said quietly. "I'm not adverse to taking orders." She looked pointedly at Tom Edger and back again to Mazian. "I take them as well as others. We may not have worked partners in the past; but I'm willing."

Mazian nodded, his handsome, actor's face quite, quite affectionate. "Good. Good. So it's settled." He rose, went to the sideboard, pulled a brandy flask from its clamps and glasses from the cabinet and poured. He brought the glasses back, set them before him, slid them in either hand to Edger and to her. "I hope it will be settled once for all," he said, sipping at his drink. "And I mean it should be. Any further complaints?"

There might be some from Tom Edger. She saw him sulk while she drank the liquid fire of the brandy. She smiled slightly. Edger did not respond.

"The other matter you brought up," Mazian said, "the disposition of the station—is the case. Yes. And I'll trust that information doesn't go beyond present company."

*Hence this show,* she thought. "Yes, sir," she said.

"No formalities. In time all the captains will be given their instructions. You're a strategist, in many ways the best. You would have been brought in early. You know that. Would have been already, but for the unfortunate incident with Goforth and the market operation."

Heat flushed her face. She set the glass down.

"Temper, old friend," Mazian said softly. "I have one too. I know my faults. But I can't have you split from me. Can't afford it. We're getting ready to move. Within the week. Loading's nearly finished. And we move before Union expects it . . . take the initiative, give them a problem."

"Pell."

"Just so." He finished his brandy. "You have Konstantin. He can't go back; we have to take out Lukas too. All those techs working and in detention. Anyone who could possibly manage comp and central and get Pell back into order. You rig it to collapse and you don't leave anyone alive who could correct it. And particularly Konstantin; he's dangerous in two regards, comp and publicity. Vent him."

She smiled tautly. "When?"

"He's already a liability. Nothing public. No display. Porey will see to the other one—to Emilio Konstantin. Clean wipe, Signy. Nothing left of help to Union. No refugees from this place."

"I understand you. I'll do the disposal."

"You and Tom, for all your bickering, have done a good job. I was very worried about having Konstantin unaccounted for. You've done an excellent job. I mean that."

"I knew what you were up to," she said levelly. "So the comp is already set up that way; a key signal can scramble it completely. A couple more of the comp operators are still missing. I'm fixing to shut down green tomorrow. They'll surrender or I vent the section and that fixes it anyway. I've got prints on the missing operators. I'll pull in the informer Ngo and his lot. Ask questions and pinpoint what I can before we move. If agents can pull the comp people out so we're absolutely sure, so much the better."

"My men will cooperate," Edger said.

She nodded.

"That's the way," Mazian said cheerfully. "That's the kind of thing I expect from you, Signy; no more of this quarreling over prerogatives. Now will the two of you get about it?"

Signy finished her glass, rose. Edger did. She smiled and nodded at Mazian, but not at Edger, and walked out with a deliberate lightness.

*Bastard,* she thought. She did not hear Edger's steps behind her. When she entered the lift and started down to meet her escort, Edger was not with her. He had stayed behind to talk to Mazian. *Whore.*

The lift whisked her down to exit level. Her troops were where she had left them, ramrod stiff and carefully avoiding any altercation with *Europe* troops who came and went in the suiting room. A trio of *Europers* were there with smiles which wiped themselves at once when she walked out among them.

She gathered up her escort and stalked out the lock, down the access to the dock, to the waiting lines of her own troops.

## vi

## Pell: Norway; blue dock; 1/8/53; 2300 hrs. md.; 1100 hrs. a.

It was better when she had had a chance to relax, to bathe, to get the dock mess straightened out and the reports written. She cherished no illusions that there would be anything done to the *Australia* trooper who had fired on Di and lived . . . not, at least, officially: but that woman would do well not to walk alone where *Norway* troops were docked, as long as she lived.

Di was all right, out of surgery and burning mad. That was healthy. He had a splice in a rib and a good deal of the blood in him was borrowed, but he was able to face vid and curse with coherency. It helped her spirits. Graff was with him, and there was a list of officers and crew willing to sit and keep Di quiet, a show of concern which would greatly disturb Di if he realized the extent of it.

Peace. A few hours' worth, until tomorrow, and operations in green. She propped her feet on her bed, sitting sideways at the desk in her own quarters, cross-handedly poured herself a second drink. She rarely had a second. When she did it went to thirds and fourths and fifths, and she wished Di or Graff were here, to sit and talk. She would go sit with them, but Di had a head of steam he was willing to let off, which would have his blood pressure up telling her the tale. No good for Di.

There were other diversions. She sat and thought a while, and, hesitating between the two, finally punched up the guard station. "Get Konstantin in here."

They acknowledged. She sat back and sipped the drink, keyed in on this station and that to be sure that operations were going as they should and that the anger below decks stayed smothered. The drink failed to tranquilize; she still felt the urge to pace the floor, and there was not, even here, much floor to pace. Tomorrow. . . .

She dragged her mind back from that. One hundred twenty-eight dead civs in stabilizing white sector. It was going to be far worse in green, where all who had real reason to fear identification had taken cover. They could vent it if the two comp-skilled techs could not be turned up in time; indeed they could. It was the sensible solution; a quick death, if indiscriminate; a means to be sure they had all the fugitives . . . and more merciful to those individuals than to be left on a deteriorating station. *Hansford* on a grand scale, that was the gift they would leave Union, rotting bodies and the stench, the incredible stench of it. . . .

The door opened. She looked up at three troopers and at Konstantin—cleaned up, wearing brown fatigues, bearing a few patches on his face the meds had done. Not bad, she thought remotely, leaned forward on one arm. "Want to talk?" she asked him. "Or otherwise?"

He did not answer, but he showed no disposition to quarrel. She waved the troopers out. The door closed and Konstatin still stood there staring at something other than her.

"Where's Josh Talley?" he asked finally.

"Somewhere aboard. There's a glass in the cabinet over there. Want a drink?"

"I want," he said, "to be set out of here. To have this station handed over to its own lawful government. To have an accounting of the citizens you've murdered."

"Oh," she said, laughed a breath and reassessed young Konstantin. Smiled sourly and pushed her foot against the bed, sending her chair back a bit. She gestured to the bed, a place for him to sit. "You want," she said. "Sit down. Sit *down,* Mr. Konstantin."

He did so. He stared at her with his father's mad dark stare.

"You don't really have any such illusions," she asked him, "Do you?"

"None."

She nodded, regretting him. Fine face. Young. Well-spoken; well-made. He and Josh were much alike. There were wastes in this war that sickened her. Young men like this turned into corpses. If he were anyone else . . . but his name happened to be Konstantin, and that doomed him. Pell would react to that name; and he had to go. "Want the drink?"

He did not refuse it. She passed him her own glass, kept the bottle for herself.

"Jon Lukas stays as your puppet," he said. "Does he?"

There was no need to torment him with the truth. She nodded. "He takes orders."

"You're moving against green next?"

She nodded.

"Let me talk to them on com. Let me try to reason with them."

"To save your life? Or to replace Lukas? It won't work."

"To save theirs."

She stared at him a long, bleak moment.

"You're not going to surface, Mr. Konstantin. You're to vanish very quietly. I think you know that." There was a gun at her hip; she rested her hand on it as she sat, reckoning that he would not, but in case. "Let's say if I can find two individuals, I won't vent the section. Names are James Muller and Judith Crowell. Where are they? If I could locate them right off . . . it would save lives."

"I don't know."

"Don't know them?"

"Don't know where they are. I don't think they're still alive, if they're supposed to be in green. I know the section too well; had means to have found them if they were there."

"I'm sorry for that," she said. "I'll do what I can as reasonably as I can. Promise you that. You're a civilized man, Mr. Konstantin. A vanished breed. If I could find a way to get you out of this I'd do it, but I'm hemmed in on all sides."

He said nothing. She kept an eye to him, sipped a mouthful from the bottle. He drank from the glass.

"What about the rest of my family?" he asked at last.

Her mouth twisted. "Quite safe. Quite safe, Mr. Konstantin. Your mother does everything we ask and your brother is harmless where he is. The supplies arrive on schedule and we have no reason to object to his presence down there. He's another civilized man, one—fortunately—without access to large crowds and sophisticated systems where our ships are docked."

His lips trembled. He drank the last remaining in the glass. She leaned forward and poured him more of the liquor. Took a deliberate chance in leaning close to him. It was gambling; it evened scales. It was time to call it quits. If he outlived tomorrow he would learn too much of what would happen and that was cruelty. There was a sour taste in her mouth the brandy would not cure. She pushed the bottle at him. "Take it with you," she said. "I'll let you go back to your quarters now. My regards to you, Mr. Konstantin."

Some men would have protested, cried and pleaded; some would have gone for her throat, a way of hastening matters. He rose and went to the door without the bottle, looked back when it would not open.

She keyed the duty officer. "Pick up the prisoner." The acknowledgment came back. And on a second thought: "Bring Josh Talley while you're at it."

That brought a flicker of panic to Konstantin's eyes. "I know," she said. "He's minded to kill me. But then he's undergone some changes, hasn't he?"

"He remembers you."

She pursed her lips, smiled then without smiling. "He's alive to remember. Isn't he?"

"Let me talk to Mazian."

"Hardly practical. And he won't agree to hear you. Don't you know, Damon Konstantin, he's the source of your troubles? My orders come from him."

"The Fleet belonged to the Company once. It was *ours*. We believed in you. The stations—all of us—believed in you, if not in the Company. What happened?"

She glanced down without intending to, found it difficult to look up again and meet his ignorant eyes.

"Someone's insane," Konstantin said.

*Quite possibly,* she thought. She leaned back in the chair and found nothing to say.

"There's more than the other stations involved at Pell," he said. "Pell was always different. Take my advice, at least. Leave my brother in permanent charge on Downbelow. You'll get more out of the Downers if you do things the slow way. Let him manage them. They're not easy to understand, but they don't understand us easily either. They'll work for him. Let them do things their own way and they'll do ten times the work. They don't fight. They'll give you anything you ask for, if you ask and don't take."

"Your brother will be left there," she said.

The light by the door flashed. She keyed it open. They had brought Josh Talley. She sat watching . . . a quiet exchange of glances, an attempt to question without asking questions . . . "Are you all right?" Josh asked. Konstantin nodded.

"Mr. Konstantin is leaving," she said. "Come in, Josh. Come on in."

He did so, with a backward anxious look at Konstantin. The door closed between them. Signy reached again for the bottle, added to the glass which Konstantin had left on the side of the desk.

Josh too was cleaner, and the better for it. Thin. His cheeks had gone very hollow. The eyes—were alive.

"Want to sit down?" she asked. From him she did not know what to expect. He had always been acquiescent, in everything. Now she watched, anticipating some act of craziness, remembering the time he had come to find her on the station, his shouting at her from the doorway. He sat down, quiet as he had ever been. "Old times," she said, and drank. "He's a decent man, is Damon Konstantin."

"Yes," Josh said.

"Still interested in killing me?"

"There's worse than you."

She smiled grimly and the smile faded. "Know a pair named Muller and Crowell? Know anyone by those names?"

"The names mean nothing to me."

"Have any contacts on Pell who could handle station comp?"

"No."

"That's the sole official question. I'm sorry you don't know." She sipped at the glass. "Considering Konstantin's welfare has you on good behavior. That it?"

No answer. But it was truth. She watched his eyes and reckoned well that it was.

"I wanted to ask you the question," she said. "That's all."

"Who are they . . . the people you want? Why? What have they done?"

Questions. Josh had never questioned. "Adjustment agreed with you," she said. "What were you up to when *Australia*'s men waded in on you?"

Silence.

"They're dead, Josh. Does it matter now?"

His eyes went unfocused, the old absent look . . . back

again. Beautiful, she thought of him, as she had thought a thousand times. And he was another one there was no sparing. She had thought she might, had reckoned without his sanity. When Konstantin went, he would become very dangerous. Tomorrow, she thought. It should be done tomorrow, at least.

"I'm Union," he said. "Not a regular . . . not what the records showed. Special services. You brought me here yourself. And there was another one of us who found his own way on . . . the way he did at Mariner. His name was Gabriel. And he ruined Pell. *He* acted against you, never the Konstantins. He and his operation assassinated Damon's family, lost him his wife . . . how it all went, I don't know. I didn't do it to him. But whatever the assumptions you've made, the power you've set in control of the station now . . . was bribed to murder by Gabriel. I know because I know the tactics. You've got the wrong man under arrest, Mallory. Your man Lukas was Gabriel's before he was yours."

The alcohol left her brain with cold suddenness. She sat with the glass in hand and stared into Josh's pale eyes and found her breath short. "This Gabriel . . . where is he?"

"Dead. You got the head of it. Him. A man named Coledy; another named Kressich; Gabriel. Station knew him as Jessad. They were killed by the troops that took us. Damon didn't know . . . didn't know a thing about it. You think he'd have been there meeting with them if he'd known they killed his father?"

"But you got him there."

"I got him there."

"He knew about you?"

"No."

She drew a deep breath, let it go. "You think it makes a difference to us, how Lukas got there? He's ours."

"I tell you so you know it's finished. That there's nothing more to go after. You've won. There's no need for any more killing."

"I should take a Unioner's word there's nothing more to hunt?"

No answer. He was not slipping off into nowhere. The eyes were very much alive, full of pain.

"It was quite an act, Josh, that you put on with me."

"No act. I'm born for what I do. My whole past is tapes. I had nothing when they got through with me on Russell's. I'm one of the hollow men, Mallory. Nothing real. Nothing inside. I belong to Union because my brain was programmed that way. I have no loyalties."

"But one, maybe."

"Damon," he said.

She considered the matter. Drained the glass until her eyes stung. "So why did you get him involved with this Gabriel?"

"I thought I saw a way to get us off Pell. To get a shuttle for Downbelow. I have a proposition for you."

"I think I know."

"You're in a position to get a man on a downbound shuttle . . . easily. Get him out of here if nothing else."

"What, not back in control of Pell?"

"You said it yourself. Lukas's mouth moves when you supply the words. "That's all you want. All you ever wanted. Get him out of here. Safe. What does it cost you?"

He knew what was ahead, at least where it regarded Konstantin's chances. She looked up at him and down at the glass again. "For your gratitude? You imply a certain soft-headedness on my part, don't you? Quite a trade. Does *any* deep-teach work with you?"

"Eventually, I imagine. What did you have in mind?"

She pushed the button. "Take him back."

"Mallory—" Josh said.

"I'll think on your deal," she said. "I'll think about it."

"Can I talk to him?"

She thought about that. Nodded finally. "That's cheap. You going to tell him how things were?"

"No," he said in a thin voice. "I don't want him to know any of it. In small things, Mallory, I trust you."

"And hate my guts."

He stood up, shook his head, looking down at her. The door light flashed.

"Out," she said. And to the trooper who appeared in the doorway: "Put him with his friend. Give them any reasonable comfort they ask for."

Josh left with the guard. The door closed and locked. She sat still, moved finally to prop her feet on the bed.

The thought had occurred to her that a Konstantin could be useful at a later stage of the war; if Union took the bait;

if Union seized Pell and restored it. Then it might be useful to produce a Konstantin, in their hands—if he were like Lukas; but he was not. There was no use for him. Mazian would never go for it. The shuttle was one way out of the dilemma. And the thing would not be known—if the Fleet moved out soon. A long time before Union could ferret young Konstantin out of the bush. Long enough for the rest of the plan to work, Pell to die, depriving Union of a base, or live, causing Union organizational trouble. Josh's idea might work. Might. She reached and poured yet another drink, sat with her hand white-knuckled round the glass.

Union operative. She was frankly embarrassed. Outraged. Wryly amused. She had some capacity for humility.

And that was what the Beyond came to be—a renegade Fleet and a world that bred creatures like Josh.

Who could do what Josh did. What Gabriel/Jessad had tried to do.

What they prepared to do.

She sat with arms folded, staring at the desktop. At last she sipped at the drink, reached and keyed the in-built comp. *Troop assignments?*

Locations and lists came back. They were all on the ship except the dozen guarding the access to the ship itself. She keyed the duty officer.

*Ben, take a walk outside and bring in those twelve we've got on the dock. Don't use the com. Report to me on comp when you've done that.*

New code. *Crew assignments?*

They flashed back to her. The alterday crew was on duty. Graff was still with Di.

She keyed into com and started with Graff. "Get to the bridge," she said. "Put a medic with Di. Di, stay quiet."

She started keying pager calls through comp for others; had gotten to armscomper Tiho when the duty officer keyed back mission accomplished. The armscomper keyed message received. She took a final sip and stood up, remarkably clear-headed. At least the deck did not pitch.

She shrugged on her jacket and walked out and down the corridor to the bridge, stood there and looked about her as bewildered mainday and alterday crew turned and stared back at her.

"Open intraship," she said. "All stations and quarters, every speaker."

The com tech pushed the main switch.

"They ran us off the docks," she said, clipping a button mike to her collar, as she did when they were on casual op. She reached her own station, the control post beside Graff's, central to the bowed aisles. "Everyone's aboard. Crew, troops, everyone's aboard. Mainday to stations, alterday to backup. Flash battle stations. I'm pulling us out of here."

There was stunned silence for a moment. No one moved. Suddenly everyone did, shifting seats, reached for controls and com, techs scrambling for the lateral posts shut down during dock. Boards hummed, tilting for use. Lights flashed red overhead and the siren went.

"No undock, rip her loose." She flung herself back into her own cushion, reached for straps. She would have taken helm herself, but she did not, at the moment, trust her reflexes. "Mr. Graff, skin her by Pell and take her out bearing . . ." She sucked air. "Bearing nowhere at all. I'll take her then."

"Instructions," Graff asked calmly. "If fired on do we fire?"

"No holds barred, Mr. Graff. Take her out."

There were questions coming in via ship's com, troop officers belowdecks wanting to know the emergency. The riders were on patrol. There was no bringing them in for consultation. There was no bringing them in at all. Graff was running his final check, setting up his sequence of orders, checking the positions of everything and making sure comp had it. Screens flashed a proposed course, a chute over Pell incredibly close to atmosphere, a whip behind the world and gone.

"Execute," Graff said.

There was a crash, the lock seal, the emergency disengage; and a jolt that wrenched them out of Pell's slow spin. They hammered into a zenith rise and mains cut in, slammed them over station. Something hit the hull and slid: trailing connection. They kept accelerating with Downbelow's dark side looming at them.

"*Mallory!*" a voice shouted over ship-to-ship.

It was alterday. Captains were abed. Crews and troops

were scattered on the dock and they had breached umbilicals . . .

She clenched her teeth as *Norway* hurtled over Pell's far rim and headed for a course closer to a planet than comfortable. Held her breath and listened to the curses that crackled over com.

*Pacific* and *Atlantic* were ordered to intercept. They had not a prayer of getting into line in time, the rest of the Fleet in the way; and *Norway* had Downbelow coming up for cover. *Australia* was breaking loose from station, with no obstructions between them, and that was the danger. "Armscomp," she ordered. "Aft screens. That's Edger. Get him."

No acknowledgment; Tiho reached for switches in rapid motion and lights flashed, screens shaping it up.

They had no riders for tail cover. *Australia* had none for bow. *Norway*'s combat seals went into place, segmenting them. G was increasing as cylinder synch calculated maneuver-possible. Over com came a frantic query from one of their own riders, asking instructions. She gave no answers.

Downbelow loomed in vid and they were still accelerating all out. Approach warnings were flashing. *Australia* was the bigger ship, the more at hazard.

Screens and lights flashed. They were fired on.

## vii

### Pell; blue dock; Europe; 2400 hrs. md; 1200 a.

"*No.*" Mazian hovered by his post, a hand pressed to the earplug while his bridge swirled in chaos. "Hold where you are, hold for troop pickup. Warn all troops blue dock is breached. Pick up any trooper on green no matter what ship. Over."

Acknowledgments crackled back. Pell was in chaos, a whole dock breached, air rushing out the umbilicals, pressure dropped. Debris floated between *Europe* and *India,* troopers who had been on the dock, dead and drifting, sucked out when an access two meters by two was ripped from its moorings without warning. The dock was void. Everything had gone. Ships' locks had closed automatically the instant the depressurization hit, cutting off even those closest to safety.

"Keu," he said, "report."

"I have given the necessary orders," the imperturbable voice came back. "All troops on Pell are moving for green."

"On the run . . . Porey, Porey are you still in link?"

"This is Porey. Over."

"Pass orders: destroy Downbelow base and execute all workers."

"Yes, sir," Porey said. Anger vibrated through his tone. "Done."

*Mallory,* Mazian thought, a word which had become a curse, an obscenity.

Orders were not yet disseminated, plans not firm. They had to assume the worst now and act on it. Disrupt the station's controls. Get the troops off and run for it . . . they had to have them. Ruin anything useful.

Sun. Earth. It had to be now.

And Mallory . . . if once they could get their hands on her . . .

## viii

## Pell central; 2400 hrs. md; 1200 a.

Jon Lukas turned from devastation on the screens to chaos on the boards, techs scrambling frantically to relay calls to damage control and security.

"Sir," one asked him, "sir, there're troops trapped in blue, a sealed compartment. They want to know when we can get to them. They want to know how long."

He froze. He had stopped having answers. The instructions did not come. There were only the guards, who were always about him, Hale and his comrades who were always with him, day and night, his personal and unshakable nightmare.

They had their rifles on the techs now. He turned, looked at Hale to appeal to him to use the helmet com to contact the Fleet, to ask information, whether it was attack or malfunction, or what had sent a Fleet carrier ripping over their heads and three others on its tail.

Of a sudden Hale and his men stopped, all at the same time, listening to something only they could hear. And all at once they turned, leveled rifles.

*"No!"* Jon screamed.

They fired.

## ix

## Downbelow main base; 2400 hrs. md.; 1200 a.; local night.

There was little chance for sleep. They took it when they could, man and hisa, crouched the one in Q dome and the other in the mud outside, sleeping as best they might, shift by shift in their clothes, in the same mud-caked, stinking blankets, what sleep they were allowed. The mills never stopped; and the work went on day and night.

The flimsy doors of the lock slammed, one after the other, and Emilio lay stiff and still, apprehension confirmed—a sound had wakened him. It was not time to wake, surely it was not time. It seemed only minutes ago that he had lain down to sleep. He heard the patter of rain overhead; heard a number of boots crunching the gravel outside. There was no shuttle down; they roused both shifts of them out only for loading.

"Up and out," a trooper shouted.

He moved. He heard moans about him, the other men wakened, winced in the strong light which swept over them. He rolled out of the cot, grimaced with the pain of strained muscles and blistered feet onto which he pulled water-stiffened boots. Fear worked in him, small things wrong, different from other nighttime rousings. He fastened his clothing, put on his jacket, groped at his throat for the breather mask which always hung there. Light hit his face again, drew groans of misery from others. He walked for the door among others who were going; outside, through the second door, up the wooden steps to the path. More lights in his face. He flung his arm up to shield his eyes.

"Konstantin. Round up the Downers."

He tried to see past the lights, eyes watering . . . on a second try made out shadows beyond, others of their number brought up from the mills. Shuttle had to be coming down. It must be. No need to panic.

"Get the Downers."

"All of you out," someone inside shouted; the doors

opened them straight through, deflating the dome crest as all others were herded out at gunpoint.

A hand found his, childlike. He looked down. It was Bounder. The Downers were up. All the other hisa had gathered, bewildered by the lights and the hard voices invoking their name.

"All of them out now?" a trooper asked another. "We got them all," the other said.

The tone of it was wrong. Ominous. Details became strangely clear, like the moment of a long fall, an accident, a time stretched thin . . . Rain and the lights, the glistening of water on armor . . . he saw them move . . . rifles lift . . .

"Hit them!" he yelled, and flung himself at the line. A shot popped into his leg and he hit the barrel, shoving it aside, following armored arms to armored body. He bore the man over, ripped for the mask while armored fists flailed, battered his head. Rifles went off; bodies hit the ground about him. He scooped up a handful of mud, Downbelow's own armament, slammed it into armor faceplate, into the breather intake, found a throat under the armor rings and kept after it while shouts and Downer shrieks rang through the rain.

A shot went overhead and the man under him stopped fighting. He scrabbled in the thick mud for the rifle, rolled with it and looked up into a gun leveling at his face; he squeezed the trigger and slagged it before it aimed, the trooper staggering under fire from another quarter, screaming in the pain of diffused burns. Fire from behind, near the dome. He fired at anything in armor, heard Downer shrieks.

Light hit him; they were spotted. He rolled again, fired for the light, no skill at aiming, but it went down.

"Run," a hisa voice shrieked at him. "All run. Quick, quick."

He tried to get to his feet. A hisa seized him up and dragged him until another could help, into cover by the dome, where his own men had taken cover. Fire was coming back at them from the hill, the path which led to the landing field, their ship.

"Stop them!" he yelled at whatever of his men could hear. "Cut them off!" He managed a limping run, a little distance; shots hissed into the puddles about him. He slowed as others of his men kept going, tried to keep going.

"You come," a hisa shrieked. "You come me."

He fired as he could, ignoring the hisa that wanted him to retreat to the woods. Fire came back and a man of his fell, and fire started coming from the flanking woods, hitting the troops, driving them to run again, and he limped after. The troops had reached the hillcrest, disappeared over the shoulder of the hill; had surely called for help, reinforcements, for the probe's big guns to be trained on that path to meet them the moment they charged over it. Emilio cursed tearfully, used the rifle for a crutch, and some of his men kept going still. "Keep low," he yelled, and struggled further, with visions of the ship lofting, of all the helpless thousands who waited by the images. The troops had distance on them, and armor that protected them, and once over that hill . . .

They came up over it. Fire lit the dark, and most of his men flung themselves down at once, squirming back to cover from a fire they could not face. He crouched, came as far as he could, lay on his belly to look down from the hill into the fire of the heavy guns. The ground itself began to steam downslope. He saw troops regrouping against the probe's lighted hatch, under an umbrella of fire that laced the slope, beams steaming through the rain and boiling earth as well as water. The troops could reach that safe haven; the ship would loft and hit them from overhead . . . nothing, *nothing* that they could do.

Shadow flooded toward the field, behind the lines of rallying troopers, like illusion, the pouring of a black tide toward that hatch. The troops silhouetted *in* the hatchway saw it, fired . . . must have called the others; they started turning and Emilio opened up fire on their backs, heart-chilled with the sudden realization what it was, what that other force *must* be. He scrambled to his knees, trying to get a shot at the troops in the open hatchway despite the beams slicing the hillside. The dark flood kept coming over their own fallen, carried the doorway, and suddenly gave way, retreating desperately.

Fire bloomed in the hatchway, spread and swept through the troops and the attackers; the sound came, and the shock hit his bones. He sprawled in the mud and lay there. Firing had stopped. There was silence . . . no more war, only the patter of rain in the puddles.

Downers babbled and chattered and scurried up behind him. He tried to gain his feet, meaning to get down there, where people of his own had fallen, blasting that hatchway.

Then the ship's lights came back on, and the engines rumbled, and it began to fire again, guns sweeping the slope.

Still alive. He raged at it, hardly felt the hands which crept about his arms and sides and tried to carry him . . . Downers, bent doggedly on helping him, chattering and pleading with him.

Then the ship shut down both the firing and the engines. Rested dormant, lights winking, but with the hatch gaping dark and fire-blackened.

Downers pulled him away, threw arms about him as he tried to stand, and dragged him when his leg went out from under him. A hisa's thin hand patted his cheek. "You all right, you all right," a voice pleaded. Bounder's. They crossed behind the hill, hisa gathering up more of the dead and wounded, and suddenly human figures were coming toward them out of the woods, humans and hisa together.

"Emilio!" he heard, Miliko's voice. Others were running toward him behind her . . . Men and women left behind . . . he struggled for a few running steps and reached her, hugged her insanely, with the taste of despair in his mouth.

"Ito," she said, "Ernst—they got them. The blast jammed their hatch."

"They'll get us," he said. "They'll call down the bigger stuff."

"No. Got a com station in the bush; one message . . . one fast message to base two com unit at the gathering . . . it'll get them out of there. We *got* them."

He let go, because he could, began to fade—looked back toward the ship, invisible behind the hill; there was another flare of engines, ominous thunder, a desperate ship trying only to save itself.

"Hurry," she said, trying to help him walk. He came, hisa hovering all about them. "Hurry," the hisa kept saying, over and over again, surrounding all of them, some walking, others silent, carried by the hisa, over the face of the hill and beyond, deep among the rain-dripping trees, up into the hills . . . they kept moving until sense grayed and blackened and he sank down into wet bracken, was hauled up again by a dozen strong hands and carried at the last almost running. There was a hole in the hillside, a place among the rocks.

"Miliko," he said, irrationally fearing the dark, close tunnel. They took him into it, and let him down, and in a moment arms gathered him up again and held him, rocking gently, Miliko's voice whispering into his ear. "We're all right," she kept saying. "The tunnels will hold us all . . . the deep winter burrows, deep in all the hills . . . we're all right."

# 4

## i

### Norway 0045 hrs. md.; 1245 hrs. a.

They were pulling back. *Australia* was veering off, *Pacific* and *Atlantic* gone off the track. Signy listened to the sigh of relief which ran the bridge as the channels gave good news instead of the disaster which had been heeling them. "Look sharp," she snapped. "Damage control, get to it." The bridge wavered in her vision. Alcohol, perhaps, though she doubted it. They had gone through maneuvers enough in recent minutes to sober her.

*Norway* was intact for the most part. Graff was still nominally at helm, but he had let it go to alterday's Terschad for a moment, and spared a look at telemetry, his face bathed in sweat and set in a long-held grimace of concentration. G went off combat synch and weight became definite, comfortingly stable.

Signy stood up, listening to the reports of longscan, testing her reflexes. Stood steadily enough. Looked about her. Eyes glanced furtively in her direction, darted back to business. She cleared her throat and punched in general address. "This is Mallory. Looks like *Australia* has decided to cash it in too for the moment. They'll all be pulling back to base and giving Mazian an assist. They'll be taking Pell apart. That was the plan. They'll be headed for Sol Station and Earth; and that was the plan. They'll carry the war there. But without me. That's the way it is. You've got your choice. You've *got* a choice. If you take my orders, we're headed out our own way, going back to what we've always done. If you want to follow Mazian, I'm sure turning me in would pay your way back to him in style. Right now there can't be anyone else he'd rather have his hands on. You go deal with Mazian, if enough of you want to. But for me . . . no. No one runs *Norway* but me so long as I'm in any condition to say so."

A murmur came back over com. Channels were wide open. The murmur took on distinction . . . rhythm. *Signy . . . Signy . . . Sig-ny . . . Sig-ny . . .* It spread to the bridge: "*Sig-ny!*" Crew rose out of their places. She looked about her, jaw set, and determined that her composure would hold. They were hers. *Norway* was.

"Sit *down!*" she shouted at them. "You think this is a holiday?"

They were in danger. *Australia* might have been diversion. They were moving too fast for reliable scan now, and *Atlantic*'s position and *Pacific*'s were conjecture: anything could turn up out of the hazed comp projections of longscan, and there were riders loose.

"Rig for jump," she said. "Lay for 58 deep. Keep us out of the way for a while." Her own riders were still at Pell. With luck they could dodge long enough. Mazian would be too busy to bother. With sense they would lay low, trusting her, believing in her, that she would come back for them if she possibly could. She meant to. Had to. They desperately needed the protective riders. With any sense at all the riders would have scattered to the far side of everywhere when they realized *Norway* was running. She had never yet failed them. And Mazian knew that.

She put her mind from it and punched the med station. "How's Di?"

"Di's fine," a familiar voice answered for himself. "Let me up there."

"Not on your life." She punched him out and pressed guard one. "Our prisoners break any bones in that?"

"All in one piece."

"Bring them up here."

She settled into her cushion, leaned back, watched the progress of events, mapped in her mind their position out of plane of the Pell System, moving out for safe jump, at half light speed. Damage control reported in, a compartment voided, a little portion of *Norway*'s gut spilled out into the cold, but not in a personnel section . . . nothing serious, nothing to impair jump capacity. No dead. No injured. She breathed easier.

Time to get out. For close to an hour the signals of what was going on at Pell had been flashing toward ships that would kick it on, until it ended up in Union scan. It was about to become an unhealthy region for bystanders.

A light went on her board. She powered her seat about, faced the prisoners who had come in the door aft, hands secured behind them, reasonable precaution in the tight aisles of the bridge. No one got on *Norway*'s bridge; no outsider . . . until these two. Special cases . . . Josh Talley and Konstantin.

"Reprieve," she said. "Thought you'd both want to know."

Perhaps they failed to understand. The looks they gave her were full of misgivings.

"We've quit the Fleet. We're bound for the Deep, for good. You're going to *live* Konstantin."

"Not for my sake."

She gave a breath of a laugh. "Hardly. But you get the benefit of it, you see."

"What's happened to Pell?"

"Your speakers were live. You heard me. *That's* what's happening to Pell, and now Union has a choice, doesn't it? Save Pell or chase after Mazian in hot pursuit. And we're getting out of here so we don't confuse the issue."

"Help them," Konstantin said. "For the love of God, wait. Wait and help them."

A second time she laughed, looked sourly on Konstantin's earnest face. "Konstantin, what could we do? *Norway*'s taking no refugees. Can't. Let *you* off? Not under Mazian's nose, or Union's. They'd dust us so fast . . ."

But it could be done . . . when they went back after their riders, a pass by Pell . . .

"Mallory," Josh said, coming closer to her, as close as the guards would let him. He shook at the restraint of their hands and she signed, so that they let him go. "Mallory . . . there is another choice. Go over. There's a ship, you hear me? Named *Hammer.* You could clear yourself. You could stop this . . . and get amnesty."

Something got through to Konstantin; the eyes went to Josh, to her, apprehensive.

"Does he know?" she asked Josh.

"No. Mallory—listen to me. Think, where does it go now? How far and how long?"

"Graff," she said slowly. "Graff, we're going back after our riders. Keep us set for jump. When Mazian clears the system, we'll move in crosswise, maybe shoot this Konstantin fellow out where he can take his chances with Union; freighter might pick him up."

Konstantin swallowed visibly, his lips bitten to a thin line.

"You know your friend's Union," she said. "Not was, you understand. Is. A Union agent. Special services. Probably knows a great deal that could be of use to us in our position. Places to avoid, what null points are known to the opposition . . ."

"Mallory," Josh pleaded.

She shut her eyes. "Graff," she said. "This Unioner is making sense to me. Am I drunk, or does it make sense?"

"They'll kill us," Graff said.

"So," she said, "will Mazian. It goes on from here. To Sol. To a place where Mazian can find new pickings, gather strength. It's not a fleet anymore. They're looking for loot, things to keep themselves going. For the same thing we are. And all the null points we know, they know. That's uncomfortable, Graff."

"It is," Graff acknowledged, "uncomfortable."

She looked at Josh, looked again at Konstantin, whose intense face hoped, desperately hoped. She snorted disgust and looked at Graff, at helm. "That Union spotter. Lay course that way. They'll jump out of scan when they get wind of us running. Get us contact. We're going to borrow ourselves a Union fleet."

"We're going to run dead on them stumbling about here

in the 'tween," Graff muttered; and that was true. Space was wide, but there was a hazard of collision, the nearer they ran to that particular vector out of Pell, two intersecting courses relying on longscan.

"We take our chance," she said. "Use the hail."

She looked then at Josh Talley, at Konstantin. Smiled with all the bitterness in her. "So I play your game," she said to Josh. "My way. Do you know their hailing codes?"

"My memory," Josh said, "is full of holes."

"Think of one."

"Use my name," Josh said. "And Gabriel's."

She ordered it, looked long and thoughtfully on the pair of them. "Let them go," she said finally to the troopers who guarded them. "Let them loose."

It was done. She half turned the cushion, averted her eyes momentarily to the screens and glanced back again, at the incredible presence of a Unioner and a stationer loose on her deck. "Find yourselves a secure spot," she said. "We're bending an arc in a moment . . . and maybe worse ahead."

## ii

## Pell: blue sector one, number 0475; 0100 hrs. md.; 1300 hrs. a.

The flying-feeling hit them from time to time. They huddled together, and some hisa outside in the corridor moaned in fear, but not those near Sun-her-friend. They held to her, so she should not fall, so that she at least should be safe. Even great Sun was shaken, and staggered in his course. The stars shook, in the darkness round about the white bed and the Dreamer.

"Be not 'fraid," old Lily whispered, stroking the Dreamer's brow. "Be not 'fraid. Dream we safe, safe."

"Turn up the sound, Lily," the Dreamer whispered, her eyes tranquil as ever. "Where's Satin?"

"I here," Satin said, easing her way through the others to Lily's place. The sound increased, the human voices which shrieked and wailed over the com and tried to call out instructions.

"It's central," the Dreamer said. "Satin, Satin, all of you—listen. They've killed Jon . . . harmed central.

They're coming . . . the Union men, more men-with-guns, you understand?"

"Not come here," Lily insisted, rejoining them.

"Satin," the Dreamer said, staring at the quaking stars. "I will tell you the way . . . each turn, each step; and you have to remember . . . can you remember so long a thing?"

"I *Storyteller,*" she declared. "I 'member good, Sun-she-friend."

The Dreamer told her, step by step; and the thing itself frightened her, but her mind was set on the remembering, each move, each turn, each small instruction.

"Go," the Dreamer bade her.

She rose and hurried, called Bluetooth, called others, every hisa within the sound of her voice.

## iii

## Norway; 0130 hrs. md.; 1330 hrs. a.

Com sputtered; vacant longscan suddenly erupted in solid blips. *Norway* veered tighter into her curve. Signy caught at the console and the cushion with the taste of blood in her mouth. They red-lighted, stress alarms ringing. Josh and Konstantin were clinging desperately to a hold halfway down the aisle, lost it, slid. "*Norway, Norway* speaking, Unioners. Hold fire. Hold fire. You want a way in, follow me."

There was the obligatory silence while com traveled and caught up to them.

"Say further."

Words, not shots.

"This is Mallory of *Norway.* I'm going over, you hear me? Run with me a space and I'll fill you in. Mazian's in the process of blowing Pell and running for Sol. It's already started. I've got your agent Joshua Talley and the younger Konstantin aboard. You're going to lose yourself a station if you hold off. You don't listen to me and you're going to have yourself an Earth-based war."

There was a moment of dead silence from the other side. The armscomp board was lit and tracking.

"This is Azov of *Unity.* What's your proposal, *Norway*? And how do we trust you?"

"We ran; you've got that signal. I'll lead back in. You

run tail guard, *Unity*, the whole lot of you. Mazian won't stand to fight here or anywhere in the neighborhood. He can't afford it, you understand me?"

The silence was longer this time. "They're tracking with us," scan advised her.

"Hard as we can, Mr. Graff."

*Norway* skimmed the edge of disaster, red-lighting in little flickers of stress that flesh protested, heart pounding, hands trembling in maintaining necessary control, experienced crew holding up together in sustained agony while combat synch and inertia warred. Calm and steady, hold it together on the long, long curve, keep the velocity they had gathered as much as possible, headed for Pell . . . They had a tail guard for certain, Union headed right at their backside all at max . . . to blow them as readily as they meant to blow Mazian.

"Come on," she muttered to Graff, "keep our way, hold onto it. We need all we've got."

"Scan caution," a calm voice advised her and Graff; long-scan flickered with hazed green and gold . . . obstacles in their path, still in comp's memory and shown to be right where comp remembered them, give or take a freighter's slow progress. Short-haul freighters. They were getting their chatter, as-received, a squeal of conversation and panic that deepened as they came in on it.

Graff threaded them. *Norway* shot through the interstices on a computer-aimed straight course and red-lighted to home again on Pell. The Unioners came after and all missed with a rush that would stop hearts on the dead-slow freighters. A deep howl of terror had reached them, vanished again.

*Norway* . . . *Norway* . . . *Norway* . . . their own comp was sending frantically, and if their riderships survived, they would rally to that summons.

Blips flashed red and solid ahead of them, too fast for freighters. Comp howled warnings. Mazian was loose. *Europe, India, Atlantic, Africa, Pacific.*

"Where's *Australia*?" she snapped at Graff. That recognition code had not come through with the others. " 'Ware of them!"

Graff must have heard. There was no time for chat. The Fleet was massed and collision-coursed for them. Their rider-ships were locked to, all home to mothers, readied for jump, that grace at least.

"*Mallory,*" she heard Mazian's voice over com. Graff heard too and dropped them in a sickening maneuver that comp transferred into armscomp's aim: they ripped a pattern of fire at *Europe* as fire came back at them and the hull sang. G slammed at them fighting contrary stresses, and of a sudden fire erupted aft. Union had plowed in, disregarding their safety, not savvy of their comp signals, and hungry for targets. "*Out!*" she ordered helm, and *Norway* maneuvered with all bearable angle, finding no precentage in this fight. Alarms rang. Pell and Downbelow lay ahead, minutes ahead at near-C.

They kept veering, comp calculating and recalculating that marginal curve.

A carrier blip exploded onto them, underside. *Norway* held to its necessary course, boards flaring red, alarms ringing, collision with a world imminent and too much speed to dump in time.

And of a sudden there were other blips, small and coming hard in a ring nose on to them.

*Norway* . . . *Norway* . . . *Norway* . . . their comp flashed.

Their own riders.

"Keep on!" she yelled at Graff over a cheer from the bridge. Comp took the maneuver as hard as the ship could bear, a move that tore at human bodies and made nightmare of half a dozen seconds. They started dumping speed hard, with *Australia* coming dead at them through the needle's eye of their riders, riderless itself or with none deployed.

"Barrage," she said, swallowing the taste of blood. The screens flashed terror: it was collision imminent fore and aft, a C-approximate ship bearing right down their tail and equally locked in escape curve from Pell. Fifty-fifty what maneuver would impact them, up, down, or straight on.

Graff dropped: topside fired and *Australia* whipped over as fields sent instruments into chaos. The hull moaned and the whole ship jolted.

Maneuver continued; suddenly there was breakup on scan, dust screaming over their hull. "Where are they?" Graff yelled at the scan tech. Signy bit through her lip and winced, sucked at the blood. *Australia* could have dumped chaff; could have blown; they kept dumping speed, her order unchanged.

"... cleared Pell," a rider voice came to them, what their own scan was beginning to show as they cleared the danger themselves. "And lost a vane ... think Edger's lost a vane."

There was no way they could see; *Australia* was on long-scan: it was the nature of the chaff they reckoned. "Form up," she ordered her riders, feeling more secure with them about *Norway* like four extra arms. Edger could not risk further damage now, not if a vane was gone; not for any revenge.

"They're going for jump," she heard. It was a Union voice, none that she knew—a foreign accent. Suddenly there was a vast coldness in her gut, a knowledge that it was all beyond recall.

*Be thorough,* Mazian had taught her, teaching her most that she knew. *No half-measures.*

She leaned back in the cushion. All over *Norway* there was silence.

## iv

## Pell: sector blue one, number 0475

Lily at least remained. Alicia Lukas-Konstantin let her eyes move about the walls, last of all to the small module, part of the molded white of the bed itself, two lights, one on, one off, one green, one red. Red now. They were on internal systems.

## 414

Power was threatened. Lily did not know, perhaps; she managed the machines, but what powered them was likely to be mysterious to her. And the Downer's eyes remained calm, her hand remained gentle, stroking her hair, a remaining contact with the living.

Angelo's gifts, the structures about her, had proven as stubborn as her own brain. The screens kept changing, the machines kept pumping life through her veins, and Lily stayed.

There was an off switch. If she asked Lily, Lily, ignorant, would push it. But that was cruel, to one who believed in her.

She did not.

v

## Norway

Carefully, Damon left his place, felt his way dizzily past the banks of instruments and the techs to reach Mallory. He hurt; an arm was torn, his neck ached in its joints. There could not be a soul on *Norway* spared such misery, the techs, Mallory herself. She turned bleak eyes on him from her place at the main boards, powered her cushion about to look at him, nodded slightly.

"So you've got your wish," she said. "Union's in. They don't need to track Mazian now. They know for certain where he's gone. I'm betting they'll find a base at Pell valuable; they'll save your station, Mr. Konstantin, no question now. And it's high time we got ourselves out of here."

"You said," he reminded her quietly, "you'd let me off."

Her eyes darkened. "Don't press your luck. So maybe I'll dump you and your Unioner friend on some merchanter when it suits me. If it suits me. Ever."

"My home," he said. He had gathered his arguments; but his voice shook, destroying logic. "My station . . . I belong back there."

"You belong nowhere now, Mr. Konstantin."

"Let me talk to them. If I can get a truce from Union to get close enough . . . I know the systems. I can handle the central systems; the techs . . . may be dead. They are dead, aren't they?"

She turned her face away, turned the cushion, returning to her own business. He reckoned his danger, leaned forward and set a hand on the arm of the cushion so that she could not ignore him; a trooper moved, but waited orders. "Captain. You've gone this far. I'm asking you . . . you're a Company officer. You *were*. One last time . . . one last time, captain. Get me back to Pell. I'll talk you out again, free. I swear I will."

She sat still a very long moment.

"You going to run from here beaten?" he asked her. "Or leave at your own pace?"

She turned, and it was not a good thing to look into her eyes. "You looking to take a walk?"

"Take me back," he said. "Now. While it matters. Or never. Because later won't matter. There'll be nothing I can do and I had as soon be dead."

Her lips tightened. For several moments she sat dead still, staring at him. "I'll do what I can. Up to a limit. If they make of your truce what I think I will . . ." She brought her hand down on the cushioned arm. "This is mine. This ship. You understand that. These people . . . I was Company. We all were. And Union doesn't want me loose. You're asking for what could turn into a firefight right next to your precious station. Union wants *Norway*. They want us badly . . . because they know what we'll do. There's no way I can live, stationer, because I've got no port I'll dare go to. I'll not come in. I never will. None of us will. Graff. Set us a quiet course for Pell."

Damon drew back, reckoned that the wisest move at the moment. He listened to the one-sided com he had accessible, *Norway* advising the Union fleet that they were moving in. There seemed to be some dispute. *Norway* argued back.

A hand touched his shoulder. He looked around, found Josh there. "I'm sorry," Josh said. He nodded, holding no grudge. Josh . . . had had few choices given him.

"They want you, all right," Mallory said. "Handed over to them."

"I'll go."

"Ignorant," Mallory spat. "They'll mindwipe you. You know that?"

He thought about it. Remembered Josh, sitting across from him at a desk and asking for the papers, end of a process Russell's had started. Men came out of it. Josh had. "I'll go," he said again.

Mallory frowned at him. "It's your mind," she said. "Till they get their hands on you, at least." And into com: "This is Mallory. We've got ourselves a standoff, captain. I don't like your terms."

There was a long delay. Silence from the other end.

On scan, Pell showed, with Union ships hovering about it like birds about carrion. One looked to have docked.

Longscan showed a scattering of red-dotted gold out by the mines, the short-haulers, and the lonely position of one other ship, indicated by a blinking light at the edge of the scope, offscan but in comp's memory. Nothing moved, save for four blips very near *Norway,* closing into tighter formation.

They had come to a relative halt, drifting in time with everything else in the system.

"This is Azov of *Unity,*" a voice came to them. "Captain Mallory, you have leave to dock with your passenger to let him off. Your approach to Pell is accepted, with thanks from the people of Union for your invaluable assistance. We're willing to accept you within the Union Fleet as you are, armed and with your present crew. Over."

"This is Mallory. What assurances has my passenger got?"

Graff leaned closer to her. Held up a finger. *Norway* resounded to the clang of something against her hull, a lock closing. Damon looked distractedly at scan.

"Fighter just docked," Josh said at his shoulder. "They're gathering the riders in. They can run for jump—"

"Captain Mallory," Azov's voice returned, "I have a Company representative aboard who will order you to take that action. . . ."

"Ayres can shove it," she said. "I'll tell you what I want for what I've got. Docking privileges at Union ports and clear paper. Or maybe I let my valuable passenger take a walk."

"These matters can be discussed later in detail. We have a crisis on Pell. Lives are in jeopardy."

"You have comp experts. Can it be you can't figure the system?"

There was another silence. "Captain. You'll get what you want. Kindly dock under our safeconduct if you want that paper. There's a situation on this station regarding native workers. They're asking for Konstantin."

"The Downers," Damon breathed. He had a sudden and terrible vision of Downers facing Union troops.

"You clear your ships back from that station, captain Azov. *Unity* can stay docked. I'll come in on the opposite side and you see to it your ships don't get out of synch with your position. Anything crosses my tail I'll fire with no questions asked."

"Granted," Azov answered.

"Insane," Graff said. "Now where's our profit? They won't come across with that paper."

Mallory said nothing.

# 5

## i

## Pell: White Dock; 1/9/53; 0400 hrs. md.; 1600 hrs. a.

The dockworkers were Union troops, fatigue-clad, but in green, a surreal sight on Pell. Damon walked down the ramp toward the armored backs of *Norway* troops who held the margin and guarded the access. Far across the deserted dock other troopers stood in armor . . . Unioners. He passed the safe perimeter, passed through the *Norway* troops, headed out that lonely crossing of the wide debris-littered decking. Heard disturbance behind him, heard someone coming, and looked back.

Josh.

"Mallory sent me," Josh said, overtaking him. "You mind?"

He shook his head, mortally glad of his company where he was going. Josh reached into his pocket and handed him a spool of tape. "Mallory sent it," Josh said. "*She* set up the comp keys. Says this might help."

He took it, stuffed it into the pocket of his brown Company fatigues. The Union escort waited for them with the troops, black-clad and silver-medaled. He started walking again, appalled as they came closer at the sameness, the beauty of them. Perfect humans, all of a size, all of a type.

"What are they?" he asked of Josh.

"My kind," Josh said. "Less specialized."

He swallowed heavily and kept going. The Union

troops fell in about them, wordlessly escorted them along the dock. Pell citizens stood, a handful here and there, stared at them as they walked. *Konstantin,* he heard murmured. *Konstantin.* He saw hope in some eyes, and flinched from it, knowing how little there was to be had. There was chaos in some areas they passed, whole sections with the lights out, with fans dead, with the stench of fire and bodies lying. G surged a marginal amount, minor instability. No knowing what had happened in the core, in life-support. There was a time beyond which the systems began to deteriorate beyond recovery, when balances were too far gone. Mindless, with central out, Pell had gone to its local ganglia, nerve centers which were not interconnected, automatic systems that fought for its life. Without regulation and balance they would pass out of phase . . . like a body dying.

They walked blue nine, where other Union forces stood, entered the emergency ramp . . . dead here too, bodies they and their escort filed past in their ascent; a long climb, from nine upward, to an area where armored troopers operated, where they stood facing upward, shoulder to shoulder. They could go no higher; the escort leader turned aside and took them through the door into two, into the hall lined with financial offices. Another knot of troops and officers stood there. One, silvered with rejuv and bearing a great deal of rank on his chest, turned toward them. With a dull shock Damon recognized those immediately behind him. Ayres, from Earth.

And Dayin Jacoby. If he had had a gun in his hands he would have shot the man. He did not. He stopped there staring dead at him, and Jacoby's face went a dull crimson.

"Mr. Konstantin," the officer said.

"Captain Azov?" he surmised by the signs of rank.

Azov offered his hand. He took it, in bitterness. "Maj. Talley," Azov said, and offered his hand to Josh. Josh accepted the greeting. "Glad to have you back."

"Sir," Josh murmured.

"Mallory's information is correct? Mazian's gone for Sol?"

Josh nodded. "No deception, sir. I think it's true."

"Gabriel?"

"Dead, sir. Shot by the Mazianni."

Azov nodded, frowning, looked at Damon directly again. "I'm giving you a chance," he said. "You think you can get this station back in order?"

"I'll try," Damon said, "if you let me up there."

"That's the immediate problem," Azov said. "We don't have access up there. Natives have the doors blocked. No knowing what damage they've done in there or what shooting could start with them."

Damon nodded slowly, looked back toward the door to the access ramp. "Josh comes with me," he said. "No one else. I'll get Pell settled for you. Your troops can follow . . . after it's quiet. If shooting starts, you may lose the station, and you wouldn't want that at this stage, would you?"

"No," Azov agreed. "We wouldn't want that."

Damon nodded and started for the doors. Josh walked beside him. A loudspeaker behind them began to recall troops, who came out the doors from the ramp in obedience to the summons, passing them as they entered and walked upward. The top was clear, doors to blue one closed. Damon pushed the button; it was dead. Manual opened it.

Downers sat beyond, huddled together, a mass that filled the main hall and the side corridors. "Konstantin-man," one exclaimed, scrambling up suddenly, hurt as many of them were hurt, and bleeding from burns. They surged to their feet, reached out hands as he walked in, to touch his hands, his body, bobbing in delight and calling, shrieking in their own tongue.

He walked through, Josh trailing in his wake through the hysterical press. There were more of them inside the control center, beyond the windows, on the floor, sitting on the counters, in every available niche. He reached the doors, rapped on the window. Hisa faces lifted, eyes stared, solemn and calm . . . and of a sudden brightened. Downers leaped up, danced, bounced, shrieked wild cries silenced by the glass.

"Open the door," he called to them. It was impossible that they could hear him, but he pointed to the switch, for they had it locked from inside.

One did. He walked in among them, touched and hugged, touched them in return, and in a sudden rush, found a hand locked viselike on his, clasping it to a furry breast. "I Satin," the hisa said to him, grinning. "Me eyes warm, warm, Konstantin-man."

And on the other side, Bluetooth. That broad grin and shaggy coat he knew, and hugged the Downer. "You mother send," Bluetooth said. "She all right, Konstantin-man. She say lock doors stand here not move, make they send find Konstantin-man, make all right the Upabove."

He caught his breath, touched furred bodies, went to the central console, with Josh behind him. Human bodies lay there on the floor. Jon Lukas was one, shot through the head. He sat down at the main board, began pushing keys, rebuilding . . . took out the spool of tape and hesitated.

Mallory's gift. To Pell. To Union. The tape might contain anything—traps for Union . . . a final destruct trigger. . . .

He wiped a hand across his face, finally made up his mind and fed the leader in. The machinery sucked it in, beyond recall.

Boards began to clear, lights flickering to greens. There was a stir among the hisa. He looked above him, at troops reflected in the glass, standing in the doorway with rifles leveled. At Josh, behind him, who had turned to face them.

"Hold it where you are," Josh snapped at them. They did, and rifles lowered. Maybe it was the face, the look that was Union's lab-born; or the voice, that expected no argument. Josh turned his back on them and stood with his hands on the back of Damon's chair.

Damon kept at work, spared a second glance to the reflecting glass. "Need a com tech," he said. "Someone to get on public channels and talk. Get me someone with a Pell accent. We're all right. They knocked some of the storage out, slagged some records . . . but we don't really need those, do we?"

"They won't know one name from the other," Josh said softly, "will they?"

"No," he said. The adrenalin that had gotten him this far was wearing off. He found his hands shaking; looked aside as a Unioner tech seated himself at com. "No," he said, rose and started over to object. Troops leveled guns. "Hold off," Josh said, and the officer in charge hesitated. Then Josh himself glanced aside and stepped back. There was another presence in the doorway. Azov and his entourage.

"Private message, Mr. Konstantin?"

"I need to get crews at their jobs," Damon said. "They'll move at a voice they know."

"I'm sure they would, Mr. Konstantin. But no. Stay away from com. Let our techs handle it."

"Sir," Josh said quietly. "May I intervene?"

"Not in this matter," Azov said. "Keep at non-public work, Mr. Konstantin."

Damon drew a quiet breath, walked back to the console he had left and carefully sat down. More and more troops had come in. The hisa crowded back against the walls and onto the counters, chattering soft alarm among themselves.

"Get these creatures out of here," Azov said. "Now."

"Citizens," Damon said, turning his chair to look at Azov. "Pell citizens."

"Whatever they are."

"*Pell,*" Mallory's voice came over com. "Stand by for undocking."

"Sir?" the Union com tech asked.

Azov signaled for silence.

Damon leaned and tried to hit an alarm. Rifles leveled and he thought better of it. Azov himself went to com. "Mallory," Azov said, "I'll advise you to stay put."

A moment's silence. "Azov," the voice returned softly, "somehow I thought there was no honor among thieves."

"Captain Mallory, you are attached to the Union fleet, under Union orders. Accept them or stand in mutiny."

Again a silence. And more silence. Azov gnawed at his lip. He reached past the com tech and keyed in his own numbers. "Captain Myes. *Norway* refuses orders. Move your ships out a little."

And on Mallory's channel: "You take our offer, Mallory, or there's no port. You can rip loose and you can run, but you'll be number-one priority for our ships in Union space. Or you can run join Mazian. Or you can go with us against him."

"Under your orders?"

"Your choice, Mallory. Free pardon . . . or be hunted down."

Dry laughter came back. "How long would I stay in command of *Norway* once I let Unioners on my deck? And how long would my officers or any of my troops live?"

"Pardon, Mallory. Take it or leave it."

"Like your other promises."

"Pell station," a new voice broke in, disturbed. "This is *Hammer*. We've got a contact. Pell station, do you read? We've got a contact."

And another: "Pell station: this is the merchanter fleet. This is Quen of *Estelle*. We're coming in."

Damon looked at longscan, that was rapidly compensating for new data, reckoning a signal two hours old. *Elene!* Alive and with the merchanters. He crossed the room to com, caught a rifle barrel in the stomach and staggered against the counter. He could get himself shot. Could do that, at this late hour. He looked at Josh. Elene would have been in reception of Pell transmissions that showed trouble four hours ago; two hours inbound. Elene would ask questions. If he gave wrong answers . . . if she got no response from known voices, . . . surely, surely she would stay out.

Eyes tuned to scan, one man at first, and at that expression, others. Not one blip now, but a dusting of them, sent in as other input reached them. A mass, a swarm, an incredible horde of merchanters moving in on them. Damon looked, and leaned against the counter watching it come, a smile spreading across his face.

"They're armed," he said to Azov. "Captain, they're long-haulers and they'll be armed."

Azov's face was rigid. He snatched up a mike and patched it in. "This is Azov of Union flagship *Unity,* fleet commander. Pell is now a Union military zone. For your own safety, stay out. Ships which intrude will be met with fire."

An alarm started blinking, a board flashing alarm across the center. Damon looked at the lights and his heart began to speed. White dock was warning of imminent undocking. *Norway.* He turned and hit that channel while the trooper stood paralyzed in the confusion. "*Norway.* Stay put. This is Konstantin. Stay put."

"Ah, we're just letting you know, Pell central. Warships might make quite a mess of those merchanters, armed or not. But they'll have professional help if they want it."

"Repeat," Elene's distance-delayed voice came over com. "We're coming in for dock. We've been monitoring your transmissions. The mechanter's alliance claims Pell, and we hold it to be neutral territory. We assume that you will respect this claim. We suggest immediate negotiation . . . or every merchanter in this fleet may well withdraw from Union territory entirely. Earthward. We don't believe this would be the first choice of any parties involved."

There was silence for a very long moment. Azov looked at the screens, on which blips spread like plague. The merchanter *Hammer* had ceased to be distinct, signal obscured by the reddening points.

"We have a basis for discussion," Azov said.

Damon drew a long, slow breath and let it go.

## ii

## Pell; Red Dock; 1/9/53; 0530 hrs. md.; 1730 hrs. a.

She came, with an escort of armed merchanters, onto the dock. She was pregnant, and walked slowly, and the merchanters about her took no chances exposing her to hazard on the wide dock. Damon stood by Josh, on the Union side, as long as he could bear, and finally risked himself and walked out, not certain whether either side would let him through to her. Rifles in merchanters' hands leveled at him, a nervous ring of threat; and he stopped, alone in that empty space.

But she saw him, and her face lit, and merchanters moved, ordered aside left and right until their ranks drank him in and he could reach her.

Merchanter, and back with her own, and long off the solid deck of Pell. In the back of his mind had been doubt, a preparation for changes . . . that vanished with a look at her face. He kissed her, held onto her as she did him, afraid of hurting her she held him so tightly. He stood there with the whole horde of armed merchanters about them in a glittering haze, and inhaled the scent and the reality of her, kissed her again and knew that they had no time for talking, for questions, for anything.

"Took me quite a roundabout to get home," she murmured.

He laughed madly, softly, looked about him and back at the Union forces, sober again. "You know what happened here?"

"Some. Most, maybe. We've been sitting out there . . .

a long time. Waiting a point of no choice." She shivered, tightened her arm about him. "Thought we'd lost it. Then Mazian did pull out, and we moved, from that moment. Union's got troubles, Damon. Union's got to move on to Sol and they've got to do it with all their ships intact."

"You can bet they do," he said. "But don't leave this dock. What's got to be said, whatever talking you do with them, insist on doing here, on the dock; don't walk into any small space where Azov can get troops between you and your ships. Don't trust him."

She nodded. "Understood. We're just the edge of it, Damon; I speak for the merchanter interest. They want a neutral port the way things are going, and Pell's it. I don't think Pell objects."

"No," he said. "Pell doesn't. Pell's got some house-cleaning to do." He drew his first whole breath in minutes and followed her glance across the dock at Azov, at Josh standing with Union troops, expecting approach. "Bring a dozen with you and keep the rest guarding that access. Let's see what Azov's idea of reason encompasses."

"The release," Elene said firmly and softly, leaning on the table with one arm, "—of the ship *Hammer* to the Olvig family; of *Swan's Eye* to its proper owners; of any other merchanter ship confiscated for use by Union military. The strongest possible condemnation of the seizure and use of *Genevieve*. You may protest you're not empowered to grant it; but you have the power of military decisions . . . on that level, sir, the release of the ships. Or embargo."

"We do not recognize your organization."

"That," Damon interrupted, rests with Union council. Pell recognizes their organization. And Pell is independent, captain, willing to afford you a port at the moment; but with means to deny it. I would hate to take that decision. We have a mutual enemy . . . but you would be tied up here, in long unpleasantness. And it might spread."

There were, from the other side of the table—set up on the open dock and ringed by opposing semicircles of merchanters and troops—frowns. "It's in our interest," Azov admitted, "to see that this station doesn't become a base for Mazianni operation; and that we cooperate in your protection . . . without which—you don't stand great chance, for all your threats, Mr. Konstantin."

"Mutual necessity," Damon said levely. "Rest assured that none of Mazian's ships will ever be welcome at Pell. They are outlaws."

"We have done you a service," Elene said. "Merchanter ships have already headed for Sun far in advance of Mazian. One early enough to get there ahead of him; not much, but a little. Sol Station will be warned before he arrives."

Azov's face relaxed in surprise. That of the man beside him, delegate Ayres, froze, took on a sudden smile, with the glistening of tears in his eyes. "My gratitude," Ayres said. "—Captain Azov, I'd propose . . . close consultation and quick moves."

"There seems reason for it," Azov said. He pushed back from the table. "The station is secure. Our business is finished. Hours are valuable. If Sol is going to prepare a reception for this outlaw, we should be there to follow it up from behind."

"Pell," Damon said quietly, "will gladly assist your undocking. But the merchanter ships you've appropriated . . . stay."

"We have crew aboard them. They come."

"Take your crew. Those ships are merchanter property and they remain. So does Josh Talley. He's a citizen of Pell."

"No," Azov said. "I don't leave one of my own at your asking."

"Josh," Damon said, looking to the side and behind him, where Josh stood with other Union troops, at last inconspicuous among others likewise perfect. "How do you feel about it?"

Josh's eyes slid past him, perhaps to Azov, returned to a forward stare. He said nothing.

"Take your troops and your ships," Damon said to Azov. "If Josh stays, that's his choice. Take Union presence off this station. You'll be received for docking hereafter by request and by permission of the stationmaster's office; it will be granted. But if time is of value to you, I'd suggest you take that offer and agree to it."

Azov scowled. He signaled his troop officer, who ordered the units to form up. They walked away, headed for the upcurving horizon, for blue dock, where *Unity* was berthed.

And Josh was still standing there, alone. Elene got up and hugged him awkwardly and Damon clapped him on the shoulder. "Stay put here," he said to Elene. "I've got a Union ship to get undocked. Josh, come on."

"Neiharts," Elene said to those nearest her. "See that they reach central in good order."

They went behind the Union forces; took the niner corridor as the Unioners headed for their ship, started to run. In the corridors there were doors open, the folk of Pell standing there to observe. Some began to shout, to wave, cheers for this last, merchanters' occupation. "They're *ours,*" someone yelled. "They're *ours!*"

They took the emergency ramp, came upward at a run; Downers met them in it, scampered along, bounced and bounded and chattered welcomes. The whole spiral echoed with Downer shrieks and squeals and human yells from the corridors outside as the word spread from level to level. A few Unioners passed on the way down, headed out at instructions over helmet com, likely feeling very conspicuous where they were.

They came out in blue one. Downers were back in occupation of central, and grinned welcome at them through the wide-open doors.

"You friends," Bluetooth said. "You friends, all?"

"It's all right," Damon assured him, and worked his way past a crowd of anxious brown bodies to settle himself at the main board. He looked back, at Josh, at the merchanters. "Anyone here who knows this kind of comp?"

Josh settled into place by him. One of the Neiharts took com, another one settled into another comp post. Damon keyed through to com. "*Norway,*" he said, "you've got first release. I trust you'll ease out without provocations. We don't need complications."

"Thank you, Pell," Mallory's dry voice came back. "I like your priorities."

"Hurry it down there. Have your own troops undock you. You can come in again when we're stable and pick them up. Agreed? They'll be safe."

"Pell station," another voice cut in: Azov's. "Agreements specified no welcome for Mazianni. This one is ours."

Damon smiled. "No, captain Azov. This ship is ours. We're a world and a station, a sovereign community, and apart from the merchanters who are not residents here, we maintain a militia. *Norway* constitutes the fleet of Downbelow. I'll thank you to respect our neutrality."

"Konstantin," Mallory's voice warned him, on the edge of anger.

"Undock and stand off, captain Mallory. You'll stay put until the Union fleet has vacated our space. You're in our traffic pattern and you take our orders."

"Orders received," she answered finally. "Stand by. We're going to pull back and deploy riders. *Unity,* see that you lay a straight course out of here. And give my regards to Mazian."

"Your own merchanters," Azov said, "are going to be the ones to suffer from this decision, Pell station. You're harboring a vessel that has to prey on shipping to live. Merchanter ships."

"Get your tail out of here, Union," Mallory shot back. "Trust at least that Mazian can't double back on you. He won't dock at Pell while I'm in the area. Go attend your own business."

"Quiet," Damon said. "Captain, move out."

There was a flurry of lights. *Norway* was loose.

## iii

## Pell System

"You too?" Blass asked wryly.

Vittorio adjusted his hold on his meager sackful of belongings, awkwardly hand-over-handed his way in the narrow access, null G, in line with the rest of the crew which had held *Hammer*. It was cold down here, and dimly lit. There was a vibration, the action of a shuttle tube grappling to their lock. "Don't see that I have much choice," he said. "I'm not staying to talk to the merchanters, Sir."

Blass gave a twisted smile, addressed himself to the lock, which opened to take them out a narrow tube and into the waiting warship. The dark gaped for them.

* * *

*Unity* moved, a steady acceleration. Ayres sat in the cushioned comfort of the *Unity*'s top-level main room, carpeted, severely modern, with Jacoby beside him. Screens apprised them of their course, a whole array of screens showing numbers and images. They made it clear through an avenue opened by merchanter vessels, a narrow tunnel through the surrounding horde, and finally Azov spared time to look in on them by vid link, occupying one of the screens. "All right?" Azov asked of them.

"Going home," Ayres said softly, self-satisfied. "I'll propose something to you, captain; that at this moment Sol and Union have more in common than not. That while you're sending that inevitable courier back to Cyteen, you include a proposal from my side: cooperation for the duration."

"Your side has no interest in the Beyond," Azov said.

"Captain, I suggest to you that that interest may be on the verge of awakening. And that it would be far from Union's advantage . . . for Union to be less forward in offering Earth its protection—than the merchanter's alliance is going to be. After all, the alliance has already sent Earth its messenger. So Sol can pick and choose, can't it? The merchanters' alliance. Union. Or—Mazian. I suggest a discussion of the matter. A renegotiation. It seems that neither of us has the authority to cede Pell. And I hope that I can give my government favorable recommendations toward yours."

Elene came, with a great crowd of merchanters, stood in the doorway of battle-scarred central, while Downers scampered aside in mild alarm. But Bluetooth and Satin knew her, and danced and touched her for joy. Damon rose from his place, took her hand, gave her a place to sit near him and Josh. "I don't feel much like long climbs," she said, breathing hard. "We've got to get the lift system working." He found time simply to look at her. Looked back to the screen by his own console, at a face lying sideways on white sheets, at tranquility and dark, lively eyes. Alicia Lukas smiled, the faintest of movements.

"Call just got through," he said to Elene. "Got word to and from Downbelow. A crippled probe appealing to Mallory for rescue out of main base . . . and an operator somewhere removed from base—saying Emilio and

Miliko are safe. Couldn't confirm it . . . things are badly torn up down there. The operator's base is somewhere in the hills; but evidently everyone was under cover and all right. I need to get a ship of our own down there, and probably some medics."

"Neihart," Elene said, looking up at her companions. A big merchanter nodded. "Anything you need," he said. "We'll get it down there."

# 6

## i

## Pell: green sector one; 1/29/53; 2200 hrs. md.; 1000 a.

It was a bizarre gathering, even for Pell, in the rearmost section of the concourse, in the area where separate, illusory screens afforded a little privacy to parties. Damon sat with Elene's hand locked firmly in his and amid the table, the red eye of a portable camera, a presence in itself, for he had wanted *her* to be among them tonight, as she had always been with this father and with all of them on family occasions. Emilio was by him; and Miliko; and Josh on his left, and next to Miliko and Emilio a small clutch of Downers, who obviously found chairs uncomfortable and yet delighted in the chance to try them, and to sample special delicacies, fruits out of season. At the far end of the table, the merchanter Neihart and Signy Mallory, the latter with an armed escort who relaxed sociably in the shadows.

About them was music, the slow dance of stars and ships across the walls. The concourse had settled somewhat back into routine . . . not quite the same, but nothing was.

"I'll be putting out again," Mallory said. "Tonight. Staying—was a courtesy."

"Where?" Neihart asked bluntly.

"Just do as I advise you, merchanter; designate your

ships Alliance. You're offlimits. Besides, I've got a full load of supplies for now."

"You'll not stray far," Damon wished her. "Frankly, I don't trust that Union won't try something yet. I'd just as soon know you're in the vicinity."

She laughed humorlessly. "Take a vote on that. I don't walk Pell corridors without a guard."

"All the same," he said. "We want you close."

"Don't ask me my course," she said. "That's my business. I've places. I've sat still long enough."

"We're going to try a run to Viking," Neihart said, "and see what kind of reception we'll get . . . in about another month."

"Might be interesting," Mallory conceded.

"Luck to us all," Damon said.

## ii

## Pell: Blue dock; 1/30/53; 0130 hrs. md.; 1330 hrs. a.

The hour was well into alterday, the docks nearly deserted in this non-commercial zone. Josh moved quickly, with the nervousness he always had outside someone's protective escort on Pell, with the vulnerable feeling that the few strollers on the dockside might know him. Hisa saw him, stared solemn-eyed. The Pell dock crew by berth four surely recognized him, and the troops on guard there did: rifles angled toward him.

"Need to talk to Mallory," he said. The officer was a man he knew: Di Janz. Janz gave an order and one of the troopers slung his rifle into carry and motioned him ahead up the access ramp, walked behind him through the tube and into the lock, past the quick traffic of troops this way and that in the noisy corridor and suiting room. They took the lift up, into the main central corridor, where crew hastened about last-minute business. Familiar noises. Familiar smells. All of it.

She was on the bridge. He started to go in and the guard inside stopped him, but Mallory looked his way from her place near the command post and curiously signaled both guards permission.

"Damon send you?" she asked when he stood before her.

He shook his head.

She frowned, set her hand consciously or unconsciously on the gun at her side. "So what brings you?"

"Thought you might need a comp tech. Someone who knows Unionside—inside and out."

She laughed outright. "Or a shot when I'm not looking?"

"I didn't go with Union," he said. "They'd have redone the tapes . . . given me a new past. Sent me out . . . maybe to Sol Station. I don't know. But to stay on Pell, right now—I can't do that. The stationers—know me. And I can't live on a station. Not comfortably."

"Nothing another mindwipe can't cure."

"I *want* to remember. I've got something. The only real thing. All that I value."

"So you go off and leave it?"

"For a while," he said.

"You talked to Damon about this?"

"Before coming down here. He knows. Elene does."

She leaned back against the counter, looked him up and down thoughtfully, arms folded. "Why *Norway*?"

He shrugged. "No station calls, are there? Except here."

"No." She smiled thinly. "Just here. Sometimes."

"Ship she go," Lily murmured, staring at the screens, and smoothed the Dreamer's hair. The ship pulled away from the Upabove, rolled, with a move quite unlike most ships which came and went, and shot away.

"*Norway,*" the Dreamer named her.

"Someday," said the Storyteller, who had come back full of tales from the big hall, "someday we go. Konstantins give we ships. We go, carry we Sun in we eyes, not 'fraid the dark, not we. We see many, many thing. Bennett, he give we come here. Konstantin, they give we walk far, far, far. Me spring come again, I want walk far, make me nest there . . . I find me star and go."

The Dreamer laughed, warm laughter.

And stared out at the wide dark, where Sun walked, and smiled.